The Good Shepherd

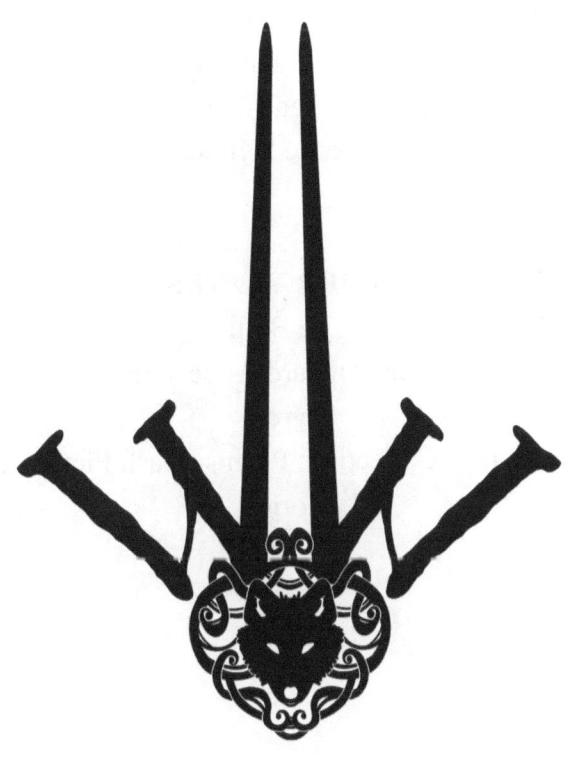

By D. Marie Prokop

WEREWOLF WARDEN SERIES
The Good Shepherd

DAYS OF THE GUARDIAN SERIES
The Red String
The Red Cloak
The Red Knot

OTHER WORKS
The Baiji
On the Outward Appearance
Tigress
The Shorter Things Collection: Poems, Flash Fiction, and Short
Stories

The Good Shepherd

by

D. Marie Prokop

Volume One
of the
Werewolf Warden Series

Copyright © 2018 D. Marie Prokop
All Rights Reserved.
Cover art and book design by Jock Hardesty and
Ethan A. Cooper for Zion Storm Studios
zionstormstudios@gmail.com
ISBN: 978-1-7328893-0-9

Dedication

For my father, Paul Eben Rode.

Acknowledgments

The people I would like to thank first are my family: my husband, Todd, my sons, Aiden and Bjorn, my father, Paul, and my brothers, Mike and David. My in-laws are pretty cool too. Thanks, Betty, Charlie, Aunt Betty, Myrtle, Bill, Becki, Collin, and Ashley. Thanks to Jamie, Charla, and Christina for sharing shenanigans and emotional support, often accompanied by music and/or delicious food.

Thanks to the participants of my local (and beloved) writing groups: Cypress Otherworldly Critique Group (Amanda, Amber, Brenda, Clancy, Clarence, Jessica, Michael, and Oleg), my Houston Writer's Guild Group in Spring, TX. (Ann, Alex, Graham, Kelly, Lara, Sabrina, and Thomas), and The Critique Group That Dare Not Speak Its Name (Shall I name them? Yes! Amber, Desiree, Emily, Jae, and Roger). In the same vein, thanks to the National Novel Writing Month organization for kickstarting my desire to write novels in 2011.

Jock Hardesty, thanks for devoting your time and talent to sketching out a fabulous cover. I think we both learned more than we'd bargained for about Edwardian fashion.

Russian translation by Sergei Javadoff—*spasibo!* German language assistance by Yvonne Thomas—*danke!*

Special thanks to my biggest literary supporter, my old friend and fellow author, Ethan A. Cooper. He's my own personal writing cheerleader, without the uniform and pigtails. Writing is hard. I quit every day. But my supporters, like Ethan, gather me up from the floor and plop me back in the chair. Usually, they're nice about it. It's awesome to have people around me that believe in the story and my ability to tell it. I'm extremely grateful.

Extra-special thanks to my beta-readers! I'm giving them their own space, in case they want to show off to their grandchildren someday…

Cheryl Biesterfeld
Isaac Chi
Kelly Lynn Colby
Ethan A. Cooper
Tobias Giesbrecht
Clarence Janelle
Audrey Javadoff
Hannah Snyder

Table of Contents

Chapter One

August 1903
Rural Massachusetts

Leona Schaeffer stared out the window at the waxing moon and watched the glowing orb grow ever closer to fullness.

Her parents sat across the table from a teenage boy with icy blue eyes. They schooled him on the established rules and planned to build him a sanctuary deep in the woods for the safety of everyone.

A deep pout formed on Leona's face. Papa still refused to let her assist them in their duties. He'd locked the Code book in the old oak chest with their weaponry, claiming fifteen was too young to train as a Warden. When her parents left to build the orphan boy's sanctuary, Leona stayed at the cabin with her grandparents. Again.

That summer had been extraordinarily hot. Leona awoke in the middle of the night, sweating profusely under her patchwork quilt. A strange rumbling captured her attention, preventing her from returning to her fitful slumber.

She smelled smoke.

Leona rose, calling out for her parents and grandparents as she left her bedroom. As she passed by a window, a bright light flashed, blinding her. She fell to the floor and crawled on her hands and knees through the cabin.

In the hallway, something on the floor blocked her path.

"*Babushka!*"

Her grandmother's beautiful blue eyes stared blankly at the ceiling. Racked with sorrow, Leona caressed her wrinkled cheek. Beside her lay her grandfather. His barrel chest was still. Leona's hopes fell. Her grandparents were dead.

Leona choked on her sobs. A glint of metal on the floor beside her grandmother's long gray locks glimmered through the smoky atmosphere and Leona's tears. It was the antique silver hairpin she always wore. Leona retrieved the pin. She kissed her grandparents' foreheads. Stumbling along the floor, she crawled toward her parents' room.

The door was a wall of flames. She screamed for her parents.

Papa's voice replied to her desperate calls, muffled by the door and the roaring fire.

"Run, Leona. Get out!"

Tears streamed from Leona's eyes. Hesitant to leave, she lingered, praying hard for a miracle.

A crossbeam crashed in the hallway behind her, near where her grandparents lay. Terrified, she stared at the fire climbing her parents' door. There was no way she could save them now. She obeyed her father and ran through the smoke. Wrapping her hand in her nightgown, she turned the doorknob and fell out the door.

The Good Shepherd

Sprinting away from the cabin, she finally collapsed under an evergreen. Curled up in a ball on the forest floor, Leona cried. Tears washed the bitter smoke from her eyes, but her heart was choking with despair. Leona grasped the hairpin tightly, watching her home turn into blackened timbers as the fire took everyone she loved away from her.

Two Years Later
Friday, September 15, 1905
Framingham, Massachusetts

"Thank you for lending me this beautiful hat, Mrs. Wickersham," Leona said. Her thin fingers caressed the black velvet. The elderly widow grabbed Leona's gray moth-eaten bonnet from the dresser and threw it in the bin.

Mrs. Wickersham pressed her lips taut. "Black is the appropriate color for a funeral. At least you have a decent bonnet now. It's a shame I never procured a black dress for you, just in case. Death delights in ambushing us yet again. Attending two funerals so close together is quite unusual, don't you agree?"

"Yes, ma'am."

"This is your darkest dress?" The dowager frowned at the gray plaid frock Leona was wearing for the second time that week. The wool dress suit was a hand-me-down from the dear girl whose funeral they had attended the day before.

"Yes, Mrs. Wickersham. It belonged to Justine. She outgrew it."

"Oh, poor Justine. The woods are a dangerous place these days. Lord have mercy."

"Yes, ma'am."

The old dowager tied the bonnet's ribbons into a bow under Leona's chin.

"Whatever creature is in those woods must be fierce indeed. Justine was a vulnerable young lady, but Luke Harris was quite a strapping young man. The magistrate is in a right bind trying to calm this town."

Mrs. Wickersham peered out the window to view some travelers on the road below. Everyone in town appeared to be on their way to the funeral.

"We must stay strong, Leona. It's the women folk who keep a community going, you hear me? When the men take off to fight another war or drink themselves into a damned grave and leave you a widow, it's women who carry on and rebuild. You may think you're just a poor little orphan girl, but you are more, much more, Leona. Being female is a privilege. By God's mercy, we are overcomers. Promise me you'll remember that."

"I promise, Mrs. Wickersham."

A little over a year ago, a frightful storm had forced Leona to seek refuge. She'd been wandering the Massachusetts countryside for months. Seeking salvation from the rain, Leona had searched for sanctuary. A streak of lightning had lit up the widow's massive white-framed house like a lighthouse.

Leona had collapsed on the porch swing right before the house maid came out to rescue the potted chrysanthemums. Mrs. Wickersham insisted on bringing her inside. The lonely, charitable widow had then spent the last year caring for Leona, a stranger, as if she were kin.

Yesterday they buried the house maid's eldest daughter, Justine. Today they would inter Luke Harris, the nephew of Mrs. Wickersham's groundskeeper.

"I haven't seen Mr. Harris since they found Luke's body. I wonder if he'll show up at the funeral. Chester claims he saw him lying in the cellar, cradling a bottle of whiskey. If I'd known he has a drinker, I'd have fired him years ago. But it explains his many absences each month, like clockwork," the widow said, her mouth downturned.

Leona stared at her old bonnet lying in the bin. She hadn't slept well all week, even though, as Mrs. Wickersham's ward, she was given the softest bed in the mansion—the one with the glorious feather mattress that once belonged to Mrs. Wickersham's mother. The rest of the household slept on muslin bladders stuffed with straw. All the luxury in the world couldn't bring Leona rest. She was especially burdened, feeling destined for a lifetime of nightmares, each one involving fire.

Horses whinnied outside the front door.

"That'll be Chester with the carriage," Mrs. Wickersham said, exiting the parlor.

Leona followed her, taking tentative steps. She stopped in front of a large stained-glass window on the north parlor wall, a portrayal of Jesus, the Good Shepherd. In his right hand, he held a crooked staff. In his left, he cradled a wooly lamb. A wolf lurked among the trees in the background.

"Leona, come," the widow said.

As the carriage rumbled along, Leona stared at the fading blue sky streaked with red and orange. A full moon awaited its turn to rise and shine. She sighed and rested her gloved hands in her lap.

Leona had met the deceased, Luke Harris, on a particularly cold winter day. She'd been exploring the grounds and found herself lost in the hedge maze, trapped like a foolish animal. Curled up in a ball on a snow-laden path, Leona had fought to keep warm. The next thing she knew, a strong, muscular arm had pulled her to her feet. A gruff young man had held her elbow and guided her back to the main house, his long dirty fingernails pressing through her sleeve. Justine had introduced him as the groundskeeper's nephew, Luke.

When Leona lifted her face to thank him, she was met by his icy blue eyes. She couldn't speak. For years, blue eyes like his had appeared in her dreams. She'd obsessed over them, though not in the romantic sense. It was an obsession much less pleasant.

Besides, Luke loved Justine, and it was obvious she welcomed his affections. Her fallow cheeks flushed every time he entered the room.

The two servants had soon become more than mere admirers. When Justine's waist had expanded, she passed on her few tailored outfits to Leona, including the dress suit she wore today.

They arrived at the cemetery behind St. John's Presbyterian

The Good Shepherd

Church at dusk. Leona hiked up her pleated plaid skirt and exited the carriage.

After the initial hymn, the preacher's low voice quoted the twenty-third Psalm.

"Yea, though I walk through the valley of the shadow of death, I will fear no evil, for Thou art with me. Thy rod and Thy staff, they comfort me."

Pallbearers lowered the casket into the freshly dug grave.

Leona scratched her collarbone. The garment she wore, like her, was *more*. The deep gray wool tartan with silver weft threads held a dual purpose. While pleasant to behold, it also resisted the cold and repelled stains.

Mrs. Wickersham's gift—the black bonnet—weighed on Leona's head, resting on the twisted bun of ebony hair gathered at the nape of her neck. Her coifed mass of dark curls was pierced through with her grandmother's silver hairpin.

A long howl from the nearby forest interrupted the preacher's Old Testament reading. The circle of mourners gasped. Mothers clutched their children, and the men's eyes scanned the woods for movement as they reached for their rifles.

"Everyone—remain calm!" the magistrate shouted. He gathered his deputies and they approached the tree line edging the cemetery.

The fearsome bellow of the mysterious predator, longer and louder this time, caused some of the men to step back. Mrs. Wickersham's eyes followed the men's progression into the forest.

The minister shepherded the rest of the townspeople into the church. But Leona slipped away unnoticed. Trained or untrained, she had a job to do. She flanked the men, sprinting along the edge of the forest before cutting in ahead of them.

From a distance, she heard the widow's frantic voice cry out, "Leona, where are you?"

The woods were littered with fallen leaves and dead branches, but Leona's footsteps were silent. She glided around the trees in search of the creature. As she tracked the beast, the pale blue eyes of the animal that had ripped out Justine's throat were clear in her mind.

Guilt filled her lungs, threatening to choke her. Leona had arrived on the scene too late to save Justine. She must do her best now to protect the crowd gathered at the church.

The impatient, fat moon pierced the trees and illuminated the frosty ground. At the sound of a cracking limb, Leona spun on her heels and faced the beast. Clouds of hot breath puffed into the chilly air from its snarling snout. It paced back and forth over the dead foliage.

She addressed the beast. "Mr. Harris, why didn't you tell Luke about his heritage? You promised to explain things to him before the next full moon. You could have helped him handle his condition. Now Justine is dead. And their baby."

But Mr. Harris was gone. The animal before her possessed no human reason or logic, only a predator's desire to attack. The groundskeeper, in the form of a large gray-and-brown wolf with silver-blue eyes, growled and leaned forward, snarling at Leona. Saliva dripped from its fangs onto the forest floor. Leona struggled to hold her trepidation at bay.

"I'm a Warden. This is what Wardens do," Leona reminded herself. She exhaled any remaining fear into the cool fall air with a huff.

Without warning, the beast lunged. Her senses heightened, Leona jumped instinctively to the right, out of the creature's path. In one swift move, she pulled out the antique pin nestled in her hair. When he lunged again, she thrust it into his throat. She wrapped her arms around his furry neck and cried as the life drained out of Mr. Harris's icy blue eyes. Blood dripped onto the skirt of her dress.

Mrs. Wickersham had been correct. Leona was indeed more than a poor little orphan girl. She possessed an ancient strength and an ancient burden, spurred on by instincts she'd never used before this full moon cycle began.

Anger and guilt swirled inside her as she walked back to the church, her heartbeat slowly returning to normal with each step. When she returned to Mrs. Wickersham's side, the widow squeezed her hand. The kind gesture tugged at Leona's tormented heart. Unable to hold back her emotions any longer, she released her tears onto the widow's shoulder.

The morning after the funeral, a messenger arrived with a telegraph for Leona.

D. Marie Prokop

Go to your uncle Ezra's residence at 22 Joy Street
Boston Stop Do not tell anyone your name Stop I
will meet you there ASAP Stop
> Warden Jacob Goldberg

When her parents died, Leona had hoped to seek refuge with her long-lost relative, Uncle Ezra, but the fire had destroyed everything, including addresses and money. Now Warden Goldberg had supplied her with both. It was time to leave.

Leona stuffed the telegram, along with a money order in her name, deep in her pocket. With a heavy heart, she packed her few belongings. There hadn't been time to wash the hand-me-down dress she'd worn to the funerals. Thankfully, the dark plaid of Justine's old frock hid bloodstains well and would serve as a satisfactory traveling frock.

Her parents had never mentioned a Warden Goldberg. In fact, they rarely discussed any of the Wardens. It was her impression they preferred to work independently of the Council. Maybe Warden Goldberg or her uncle would finally train her and teach her the Warden Code.

Fighting Werewolves was instinctual for Wardens. Yet, she'd failed Justine, arriving too late to battle Luke. The guilt of this pressured Leona to stop trying. *What if I fail again?* She dangled the telegram over the trashcan. Tears welled in her eyes.

She hadn't been officially trained. But she was born a Warden. Like it or not, her parents and her grandparents had passed on the gift to her. She felt it in her blood, her bones.

Leona sighed. Setting the pretty black bonnet on the feather

10

bed, Mrs. Wickersham's words echoed in her head.

By God's mercy, we are overcomers.

Chapter Two

Saturday, September 16
Boston, MA.

"Clementine Elizabeth Bell! Quit dawdling. We're going to miss her!"

The fourteen-year-old girl with golden braids reluctantly pulled her gaze away from a group of kittens in an alley along Joy Street. She scampered to catch up with her mother and their servants. As they walked along the cobblestone street, her wide, emerald eyes took a panoramic sweep of the prettiest part of Boston—of *her* Boston—Beacon Hill, near the Charles River.

Beacon Street bustled with pedestrians, trolleys, and buggies. Clementine and her mother were on their way to Boston Common to hear a lecture by Jane Addams, a *woman*. The street was filled with people, probably due to the fact that it was a lovely autumn morning, but Clementine guessed part of the crowd were also on their way to hear the lady reformer from Chicago speak.

The autumnal equinox was approaching, though the first frost wasn't expected for another month, according to the Farmer's Almanac. All the leaves in the Boston Public Garden would still be green.

Clementine always read the Almanac. She was fascinated by astronomy and had memorized the moon phases. Last night was the last full moon of September. It would start waning tonight.

Her boots clacked against the cobblestones. She hustled to catch up with her mother again, who was now yards ahead of her. A vendor's sign caught her eye.

"Oh, Mother, can I please have a sarsaparilla?" She imagined the sugary liquid gliding down her throat. The thought made her salivate.

There was no response. Mother must not have heard her, because she normally complied at once with Clementine's requests, with a few exceptions. The fancy dress she wore today had required minor begging before Mother had agreed to purchase it at the dressmaker's. It was mighty expensive.

As Clementine walked, the dress's blue-gray fabric rippled and swished, mimicking the winds blowing over the Harbor. The color matched her stepfather's favorite suit. When Mother bought it, she mumbled something about a *calming blue* and a *peaceful house*.

But the matching blues hadn't bonded Clementine and her stepfather. *Poor Mother.* She believed their family could become as happy and carefree as they pretended to be. But Ezra Schaeffer cared more about his status and his job than he did about them. Even in her matching dress, he ignored Clementine, not once looking up from the piles of papers on his desk to complement her beauty.

He worked long hours at his law office and usually ate supper with her and her mother in silence, sighing heavily, as if there were some great secret weighing him down.

Her mind ran wild during his bouts of silence. She invented stories to explain his sullenness. A secret affair. *How sinful!* Stealing money from a client's account. *How devious!* Spying for the Spanish. *How traitorous!* She smirked, picturing soldiers breaking down their door and carting him off to jail in his fine blue suit. Then Mother would have to find a new husband to fund her extravagant wardrobe and trendy humanitarian causes, as she'd done when Clementine's father died.

"Mother!"

"What, dear?"

"I want a sarsaparilla!"

Her mother reached into her black velvet coin purse and pulled out a nickel. She held it out in her petite hand, her eyes searching the crowd, probably looking for influential faces who would note her attendance at this auspicious event. Mother and Father took every chance they could to impress the Brahmin, the Boston elite.

Clementine rolled her eyes as she yanked the coin out of her mother's hand and ran toward the painted sign, *Sarsaparilla 5 cents!*

There was already a line. Frowning, she shuffled to a slower pace. She lowered the front of her skirt and took her time. Sauntering casually, Clementine's too-tight boots tripped over a large cobblestone.

Before she fell flat on her face, a hand reached out and grabbed her arm.

The Good Shepherd

"Are you all right, miss?" a husky voice said. The scent of Christmas trees entered her nostrils, which was odd, considering there were no evergreens near her, only oaks and maples, awaiting their cue to change from green to red, yellow, and orange.

"Yes, thank you," Clementine replied and smiled up at her rescuer. A young gentleman a head taller than herself, with coal black hair and twinkling eyes, blue as the autumn sky above, tipped the brim of his brown bowler hat and quickly departed.

She followed his path through the crowd, suddenly not thirsty anymore. Almost losing sight of him in the swarm of people, she breathed a sigh of relief as she spotted a familiar hat bobbing up and down amid the others. The brown hat crossed the street and came to a rest beside a long carriage. On the side of the carriage was painted in large letters, *The Home for Little Wanderers*.

Noting the location, Clementine rushed back to her mother and grabbed her hand.

"Let's go, Mother! Come *this* way. It's faster."

Her mother, notoriously bad at directions and always late for functions, allowed Clementine to drag her along. When they reached the carriage, Clementine searched the area for the brown bowler hat.

In her desperation to find the young man, she ran straight into something. Something soft. And wearing a brown bowler hat.

"Oi! Watch where yer going, lass! I'm walking here, too."

Twinkling blue eyes met hers. The eyes were surrounded by pale, freckled skin. A mop of curly red hair stuck out from under the brim of the same hat she'd followed—the one the strong, beautiful creature who'd saved her from a terrible fall had been wearing. But the boy donning it now was short, with spindly sticks for arms, much too weak for saving damsels in distress. He wore dingy brown tweed pants and smelled like vinegar.

Grimacing at the imposter, she curtsied a polite apology, then pinched her nose. He just stared at her, like he'd never seen a girl before.

A round lady with a knitted shawl draped over a cheap cotton blouse approached them. Her long skirt dragged on the muddy street as she walked, unlike Mother's, which was tailored and hemmed for travel.

"Fitz! Don't be rude, child. This handsome girl isn't one of your sisters. You mustn't speak to her in such an informal manner. Apologize."

The boy's freckled cheeks flushed pink and he removed the hat.

"I'm ever so sorry, lass."

"I accept your apology," Clementine replied, her eyes busy, searching for the other boy. But he was nowhere to be seen. Drooping with disappointment, her gaze returned to the ragamuffin in front of her. He placed the brown hat back on his mop of ruddy curls and winked shamelessly at her.

Disgusted, Clementine's eyes darted past the rogue. *I know he stopped here...*

"Excuse me—Mrs, er, Miss..." Mother interrupted, just now catching up to Clementine. She lowered her chin toward the petite woman who'd scolded the ruffian.

The woman addressed Mother, "Well, aren't I the rude one

now? I'm Mrs. Green. Please, call me Jane." She gestured to her left. "And over there is my handsome husband, Teddy Green, the one with the dark circles under his eyes. He's just returned from a trip to New York City. We run *The Home for Little Wanderers*. And this," she said, patting the red-haired boy's bony shoulder, "is Charles Fitzgerald. We call him Fitz. He's one of our charges. He came to us completely illiterate. Now he can read the primer without a bit of hesitation."

The boy grinned wide, his teeth all yellow.

The woman waved at a man with a full beard and wide mustache, "Teddy, come say hello."

Mother's eyes darted to and fro. Clementine didn't wonder why. She shared her mother's concern that someone important might see them conversing with the lower class, though Mother would spin the scene into an impressive tale of charitable concern.

"Hello, I'm Francine Schaeffer—everyone calls me Franny." Mother grasped the woman's outstretched hand. "And this is my daughter, Clementine."

The orphan, Fitz, tittered. "Clementine?"

She sneered at him. "What's wrong? Do you find my name humorous, *Fitz*?"

"No, lass. Only, I thought 'o that song." Then, with great exuberance, he sang, "Oh my darlin,' oh my darlin,' oh my—"

Clementine interrupted. "Yes, I've heard it, thank you."

Fitz grinned like a Cheshire cat. Clementine glared. Thankfully, the man approached and the conversation was redirected. Mother shook his outstretched hand. "Teddy? Like the President?"

He smiled weakly and replied, "Theodore's a family name. Could've been worse, I s'pose." He waved toward the Common, "We hold an art exhibit here every fourth Saturday—*next* Saturday—to raise money for the home. All the art is done by the orphans."

"Do many of the children in the asylum get adopted?" Mother asked.

"It's not an asylum. It's a Home, a sanctuary for orphans. We named it *The Home for Little Wanderers* because we desired to provide abandoned and orphaned children with a pleasant, clean, temporary home and a decent education," Mr. Green replied.

Clementine stared at the painted letters on the wagon. The sign was more complex than it had appeared from a distance. An intricate flourish decorated the first letter of each word. It was lovely. She wondered what it was like to grow up in an asylum, er, a Home.

Mrs. Green's soft voice found Clementine's distracted ear. She'd been addressing her mother, "…and matching them with a foster family."

"Did one of the children at the asylum, I mean, the *Home,* paint this?" Clementine interrupted, pointing at the sign.

"Yes, Bradlee did. He's a graduate of our onsite school. Now he teaches art and lives at the home. He's here today. Fitz, where's Bradlee?"

Fitz shrugged. "He made me hold his hat and ran off with his drawing book. I bet he's sketching over there," Fitz pointed up the street, where Boston Common began.

18

The Good Shepherd

Clementine spied a tall boy sitting cross-legged under an ash tree with a sketchbook in his lap.

It's him!

"Bradlee's an unusual name," Mother commented. Clementine thought it was lovely.

"He was found on Griffin's Wharf. Are you familiar with the story of Sarah Bradlee?"

"Certainly! She was the mother of the Boston Tea Party."

"Indeed." Mrs. Green turned to a confused Clementine and explained, "Sarah and her sister-in-law costumed the revolutionaries as Mohawks before they dumped all that tea into Boston Harbor."

Clementine nodded politely, her eyes fixed on the dark-haired boy.

"How old was the boy when he was found?" Mother asked.

"Four years old. Surprisingly, he remembered his birthday. Some of the orphans do not. He wouldn't tell us his name though, so we named him Bradlee Smith. He's a special young man, full of talent and intelligence," Mrs. Green said, sharing a knowing glance with the exhausted-looking Mr. Green.

Clementine listened intently to the boy's story, but only now dared to look away from the boy's figure on the grass. She turned to the couple who ran the orphanage. A dark shadow had darkened the man's blue eyes, a grayer version of the handsome Bradlee's crystal blue peepers.

Clementine decided right then and there that she would only marry a man with beautiful blue eyes. Then, even if he wasn't lovable, at least he would be lovely to look at.

Goose bumps rose on her arms where the young man had gripped her. He'd saved her life! Or, rather, saved her from serious injury. And, unlike this vinegar jar waif wearing his hat, he'd smelled like pine, like Christmas.

"... can't bear any more children. Giving birth to my darling Clementine almost killed me," Mother spoke, continuing a discussion with Mrs. Green that Clementine had missed while she'd been daydreaming about Bradlee. "It's so lonely in the house. It's usually just me and Clem—my husband works at the office so much. We should have adopted a boy years ago to carry on the family name and inherit the law business."

"Your Clementine's a beautiful girl," Mrs. Green remarked.

Mother grinned, showing off her perfect teeth, "Ah, yes. Thankfully she favors me, not her father."

Clementine whispered, "Nobody cares, Mother. Besides, my birth father is dead."

Mother wagged her finger at her. "Clementine! Don't be morbid. If Ezra hadn't come into our lives, you might've become an orphan, like the poor children at *The Home for Little Wanderers*. Be grateful, child!"

"Hmph! I want a sister, not a brother, anyway." She pouted and continued staring at Bradlee.

Her mother turned to Mr. and Mrs. Green and explained, "My first husband, Clementine's father, was a naval officer. He was on the *USS Maine* when it exploded and sunk into the ocean in Havana. It was in all the newspapers. Those evil Spaniards attacked their ship unprovoked and made me a widow. Did you know, only two officers died on that ship? Two out of eighteen!

I've had an unlucky, hard life." She hung her head. Mrs. Green patted her arm.

Clementine watched Bradlee drawing under the tree as her mother gossiped with the Greens. He tucked his gorgeous black hair behind one ear, but it fell back in his eyes. Clementine almost squealed with delight.

"… works on Beacon Hill in the law office of Lowell, Schaeffer, and Thornton. Where did you say your art exhibit will be?"

"Right here in Boston Common, providing the weather remains kind. Autumn is unpredictable."

"Yes, 'tis true. I do love the smell of the Common in the fall. The popcorn venders, smoking meats, autumn leaves, and salty ocean air. We should pick up some shellfish at Quincy Market on our way home, Clementine. Then Bridget can whip us up some chowder for supper tomorrow. Won't that be lovely?"

Clementine didn't respond. Her focus was on lovelier things than chowder and their silly new maid.

Fitz snapped his fingers in her face. "Lass, what're you staring at?" She ignored him. "Oh, I see. Yeah, all the lassies think Bradlee is a handsome bloke. He's bound to get hitched soon."

Clementine's heart felt as if it had been squeezed by a vice. She inhaled sharply and held her breath. She clutched her mother's puffy sleeve.

"Mother, can we adopt *that* orphan?"

Mrs. Green laughed. "Like I said earlier, Bradlee Smith is no longer a dependent at the Home. He turns eighteen soon and

21

teaches art and science. So, I suppose you could say, he's not for sale."

Mother giggled.

Mrs. Green continued, "His birthday is only a few months away. He has his heart set on going to college, but we are in desperate need for teachers and Bradlee forms a connection with the children that other teachers cannot. He's got a gift. We really want him to stay with us longer."

Mr. Green's ocean-blue eyes watered. He wiped the moisture away with his sleeve.

Clementine yearned to hear the young man's deep voice and drink in those twinkly eyes one more time. *Hey, Mr. Bradlee Smith! Stop drawing and come over here.*

"The speech is about to begin!" someone in the crowd yelled.

"Well, it was lovely to meet you, Mrs. Schaeffer, Clementine. Enjoy the speech. Jane Addams is my personal hero. *The Home for Little Wanderers* has benefitted greatly from her example and her desire for social reforms in the cities. Chicago is blessed to have her."

"She's sweet on a woman!" Fitz declared, a scandalous expression marring his childlike face.

"That's just a rumor," Clementine replied. She'd heard about the scathing article in the newspaper claiming the woman was a fornicator. Mother had gotten irritated over it and Father had called the reporter a yellow… something.

"No, it's true. I seen them holding hands! It's unnatural, it is."

"Love doesn't always follow popular beliefs, traditions, and laws, Fitz," Mrs. Green remarked. "It has a mind of its own. Ms.

Addams is an inspirational human being. I won't have you disparaging her, or her choice for companionship. This is a harsh world. We should all be so lucky to find someone to hold our hand in it."

Mrs. Green grasped her husband's large hand with her small one. He squeezed his wife's hand tight and kissed it. *Father never does that to Mother.*

They bid farewell to the Greens and Fitz and walked further into the Common. Attendance at the lecture was average, not as large as the crowd gathered to hear William McKinley during his Presidential campaign. He'd won the election, but only lasted six months before an assassin shot him. The famous Rough Rider, Theodore Roosevelt, "Teddy," took his place.

This was Clementine's first time attending a lecture in Boston Common. She'd read about Mrs. Addams and Hull House in the papers, but it was another thing altogether to hear the woman speak in person. The papers preferred to print sensational stories, not inspirational biographies.

Mrs. Addams had a surprisingly gentle voice for a rabble-rouser. Still, a lot of her statements confused Clementine. She thanked the stars she lived in Boston and not Chicago.

They stopped at Quincy Market to buy a bucket of clams for their Bridget to make into chowder.

"Oh, there's today's paper. I better buy one for Ezra. Can you grab one, dear?"

Clementine picked one up from a stack as high as the young boy selling them and put some pennies in the bucket he held.

"Thank you, miss!" he said, his face smudged with

newspaper ink.

All the way at the bottom of *The Boston Globe* on September 16, 1905 was a byline that declared, *"A Rash of Animal Attacks Worry South Boston Shepherds."*

Again, Clementine was thankful they lived in Boston. She loved the sea air, the changing leaves on the trees lining the streets, the hustle and bustle. She imagined she would grow quite bored caring for sheep or tending to a field. Nothing could change her mind.

What if *Bradlee* wanted to become a farmer? Would she leave the city for him? She panicked.

She felt quite strongly about him already. *Is this love? Is this what it feels like?* Wonderful, light, as if she were floating on air. Just the thought of his pretty eyes made her stomach flutter. If he asked her to, she would live on a *pig* farm.

Laughing at herself until reality rested its weight back on her, she folded the paper in half and tucked it under one arm. *I might not even get to choose who I marry. After all, Mother married Ezra Schaeffer for his money, not for love.*

Clementine's eyes narrowed as she peered at her reflection in a glass window. She smoothed her braids and took a deep breath, tasting salt from the harbor on her tongue.

"Mother, we're going to *The Home for Little Wanderers* art exhibit next Saturday, aren't we?"

"Of course, dear. Remind me to tell all the ladies at Bridge club."

"Yes, Mother," Clementine replied.

Bradlee Smith's crystal blue eyes had already started to fade.

The Good Shepherd

One week is an eternity.

Chapter Three

Leona walked through the quiet Massachusetts countryside until she reached the Worcester Turnpike, where she spotted a farmer with a herd of sheep. Her feet were sore, and she'd grown thirsty.

The wooly animals grazed peacefully in the field by the road. Leona passed them as she approached the shepherd. He introduced himself as Farmer Thompson. He was on his way to Boston. She asked him for a drink.

"Sure, miss. But all I have is water. You know, it's been over one hundred years since the Boston Tea Party. After paying my taxes, I can't afford tea! Independence surely has its price, miss." He shook his head and handed her a cup.

"I'm grateful, sir," she replied, chuckling, and drank some of the water. "If it's not too much trouble, may I ride in the back of your wagon with the sheep until you reach the city?"

"Yes, young lady. But don't get attached. These little fellas are on their way to the slaughterhouse." He whistled and ran in a circle around the small flock. Waving his crook, he herded them back into the wagon.

Leona swallowed the last of the tepid water. She hiked up the skirt of her gray plaid dress and climbed into the wagon. Sitting on one of the bales of hay, she greeted her new animal companions, noting they each wore a rope collar with a numbered cloth tag.

It's hard to get attached to a number.

Soon the sheep settled down on the hay. When Farmer Thompson started the horses, the wagon lurched. The wooly beasts bleated loudly, protesting the sudden move, and possibly their fate.

The dusty turnpike paralleled the railway. A sign declared it was eleven miles to Boston. Farmer Thompson promised they would reach the city before suppertime.

The sun shone high above the horizon, warming Leona's face as she journeyed, the wagon jostling her and her wooly companions. She admired nature's display as they traveled along the turnpike. The leaves in the trees flittered, on the cusp of change. Soon the sugar maples would turn fire red, the oaks pumpkin orange, and the ashes golden yellow.

Surely Mrs. Wickersham had noticed by now that Leona hadn't come down for breakfast or lunch.

Has she read my note yet? In her mind, Leona reviewed the message she left for the widow.

Dear Mrs. Wickersham,
I've just been made aware of my uncle's address in Boston.

Due to your tender care, I'm strong enough to travel and finally inform my uncle of his brother's death.

Thank you for your hospitality in allowing me to live in your home. I will never forget your Christian service or your words of wisdom.

I hope to return to Framingham to visit you. Please pray for me. And do not fret, I will overcome.

By God's mercy,
Leona Schaeffer

They traveled past the road marker for Newtonville and Farmer Thompson parked the wagon at a lush green spot by a wooded area. The sheep bleated and grunted as they trudged down the wooden planks and out into the field.

Leona took this opportunity to stretch her legs and look for a solitary place to relieve her bladder.

Hiking back through the thick woods, she heard a loud noise. *A gunshot.* The sheep bellowed in fear. One of them bolted like a shot of lightning into the woods, running past Leona like a fleecy miniature racehorse. She called after the spooked animal, but it was useless. She would have to chase it down.

Her blistered feet had healed already. Her Warden parents had always recovered quickly from physical injury—so it must be hereditary. But her heart still ached from the disastrous incident involving Luke, Justine, and Mr. Harris. *Are there some kinds of pain that never heal—the sting of death, the bristling rash of guilt?*

Leona caught up with the foolish, frightened sheep. She moved in slow motion and grasped its collar. Holding tight to the rope around its neck, she read its tag— *#29.*

"You deserve a proper name. How about Gunshot?"

The animal bleated. Leona chuckled and guided Gunshot back to the fold.

"Ah, miss! Thank you! You'd make a good shepherd, you know."

Leona returned Farmer Thompson's compliment with a melancholy smile. Poor Gunshot. Saved for the slaughter. *Maybe I shouldn't have rescued him.*

"Thank—"

Another shot rang out.

Farmer Thompson attempted to herd the startled sheep back onto the wagon. It took four tries. As he closed the wagon's gate, a fox burst through the trees, followed by a boisterous hound dog, its long brown ears flapping up and down. Two men, rifles in hand, chased after them.

One of the men tripped over a tree root. His whole body twisted, and he landed hard on the ground. He rolled on his back and grabbed his leg, moaning in pain. The other man kept running.

"Help me, Professor!" cried the fallen man.

The other man puffed out a frustrated breath and turned back to assist him, then whistled for the dog. It abandoned the chase and jogged back to the men, its floppy ears lifted by the cool breeze.

"Let me see it, Hartman."

Pulling off his blood-stained sock, the other man examined his ankle. The hound whimpered beside the man on the ground, resting its head on its paws.

"Damn, it's broken, for sure. Your boots aren't fit for orphans, Hartman. If your feet weren't so much larger than mine, you could've borrowed my old ones. They're in better condition than yours." The man frowned at his injured companion. He rifled through his pack and pulled out a flask.

"I'm gonna pour some whiskey on your foot." His hand searched the ground around him. "Here—bite down on this twig—this is gonna hurt."

The two hunters were so preoccupied with the injury they didn't pay any heed to Leona or Farmer Thompson, who watched them as they continued comforting the sheep.

The injured man tried to stand, bolstered by his companion. Intense pain registered on his face. It made Leona wince. Though his broken foot was tightly wrapped in the other man's handkerchief, she spotted a small dot of bright crimson peeking through.

Farmer Thompson approached the men. "Looks like you could use a ride. We're heading into the city. You two can join this young lady in the wagon. Your dog can sit up front with me. The sheep can't handle being around a strange dog." He offered his hand to the hound, who proceeded to sniff it, then lick it.

"Thank you," the older man said. His companion grunted his thanks. They climbed into the back of the wagon. Leona waited until they were settled and joined them.

The uninjured man pushed the flask of whiskey he'd used to sterilize the wound into his companion's hand. "Drink this, George, it'll ease the pain until we get to town and see the doc."

The younger man took a large gulp and coughed uncontrollably.

"I forgot—your parents are temperance folks. Have you ever had whiskey before?"

The other man shook his head. Leona sympathized. After the preventable tragedy with Luke and Mr. Harris, Leona supported temperance wholeheartedly. Admittedly, she felt a small twinge of sympathy for Mr. Harris. He'd probably taken to the bottle because of his condition. The rogue Werewolf had never had a Warden's guidance or support until Leona arrived at the mansion.

Compassion aside, his drunkenness was a sin. It caused him to break his promise to warn Luke that he would turn into a monster that night.

Leona glared at the silver flask.

"You disapprove, miss?" the older man asked.

Leona turned away. "It's none of my business."

"That's mature of you. How old are you, if you don't mind my asking?"

Leona hesitated. "I'll be eighteen next month."

"Hmm... and you live in Boston?"

The man made a gesture, encouraging her to keep talking, to distract his companion from his pain until the alcohol numbed it.

She answered, "Um, no. I'm—just visiting. Unfortunately, I'm on my way there to deliver bad news."

"Oh, that's awful. I'm sorry to hear that. Allow me to introduce myself. I'm William Taylor. I'm a professor of sociology at Harvard. And this is my assistant, Mr. George Hartman."

"My name is... Leona." She winced as she broke Warden Goldberg's command not to give out her name. It was an odd thing to ask of her anyway. These men probably wouldn't even remember her name. They were simply making conversation.

She smiled empathetically at Mr. Hartman. He returned her smile with a quick, painful grimace. Sweat dripped down his face. He couldn't have been older than twenty-five.

His companion, the professor, appeared old enough to be his father, but their obvious physical differences eliminated that likelihood. The professor was muscular, with rounded shoulders, a rugged jaw, and blue eyes. His assistant was quite skinny, with emerald eyes.

After taking another sip, Mr. Hartman's green eyes fluttered shut.

The professor commented, "Leona is an unusual name. Are you a lioness?" He laughed and didn't wait for her answer before explaining, "I also study the origin of names. It's an intriguing facet of sociology."

"What is sociology, Mr. Taylor?"

"It's a fairly new subject, an increasingly popular and important field of study. Sociology examines the development, structure, and function of human society. Of course, it goes much deeper than that. I could talk your ear off about it, sweetheart, but—" He shrugged.

The Good Shepherd

"But I'm a girl and wouldn't understand?" Leona retorted.

Professor Taylor chuckled. "You *are* a lioness! Are you also a proponent of women's suffrage?"

"Women are the backbone of the community. They deserve a voice in its government."

"Ah, you would make an excellent scholar of the social sciences, Leona. Have you considered applying to Boston College? They accept women students."

"I'm afraid I have other priorities."

"Like message bearing?" He smirked.

This man's smile carries a double meaning. I wish I hadn't told him my name. She changed the subject. "Your rifle looks old, sir. Were you a soldier?"

"Yes, it is old, but it was never used in war. It was my father's hunting rifle. This is real silver inlay on the handle."

"It's beautiful. He was a hunter, too?"

"Yes. Quite a reluctant one. If he had been named Leon, not Howard, maybe he would have lived up to the moniker. Alas, most of us are not named for our gifts. My name, William, means *determined protector.*"

"Hmm… I suppose hunters can be protectors, if they're hunting for predators who attack the innocent."

Professor Taylor smiled a sincere grin. "Indeed. Even shepherds like Farmer Thompson use guns to protect their flocks."

Hunters. Protectors. Shepherds. They all reminded Leona of her family, of Wardens. And their inherited responsibility. She wished that Papa hadn't kept the Warden Codebook under lock and key and refused to train her until she was "older." If she had been trained, she wouldn't have failed Justine and Luke.

She stared at the silver inlay on the rifle. "Is your father still alive?" Leona asked the professor.

"No. Even the greatest hunters can be taken down by the wrong predator in the wrong situation. My father went hunting one day and never returned."

At this, Leona had to choke back her sorrow.

Remembering the quick fox bolting out of the trees, she cleared her throat and asked, "Do you only hunt foxes?"

A hearty chuckle rose from deep inside his broad chest. "No, I hunt whatever I can to keep my skills sharp, as my father taught me. Today it was a fox."

I wish Papa had trained me like that. "You hunt often, then?"

"At least once a month."

Mr. Hartman leaned precariously against the wooden slat behind his back. The wagon jostled, and he jiggled with it, snoring loudly. Professor Taylor whispered to his inebriated companion, "We're almost there."

Leona peeked over the side of the wagon. Her jaw dropped, and her eyebrows rose sharply. Professor Taylor addressed her strange expression, "What's wrong, miss?"

"I've never seen the ocean. It's terrifying."

He chuckled. "That's the Charles River. We're entering from the west. The Atlantic's on the east side. Boston is a city cradled by water."

Cool air floated like a specter from its source, chilling Leona's skin. She shivered as she stared at the waves below.

The Good Shepherd

The road into Boston was cluttered with wagons, pedestrians, trolley cars, and bicycles. She even saw a few automobiles. The bleating sheep joined the raucous symphony of the city. A new pungent smell caused Leona to wrinkle her nose.

Professor Taylor chuckled again. "That's the ocean," he said, pointing behind him, away from the late-afternoon sun. Leona glimpsed clusters of buildings back-dropped by a blanket of steel blue. She couldn't believe its immensity. Sky and ocean were morphed into one. The scene overwhelmed her.

Mr. Hartman stirred and attempted to sit up. Professor Taylor knocked on the back of the wagon's front seat and Farmer Thompson turned around.

"You can let us out here. I'll take a taxi to get my assistant to a doctor before he empties the contents of his stomach all over your fine wagon."

The cart came to a stop. The professor handed Leona a piece of paper, an advertisement.

"I'm giving a free lecture in Boston Common on Saturday. Come and hear more about the social sciences, if you're interested, that is." He winked and jumped down onto the cobblestone street. Leona helped his wobbly assistant down the ramp. When Mr. Hartman's feet landed on the uneven street surface, Professor Taylor took over.

They thanked Farmer Thompson for the ride and whistled for their dog. The floppy-eared canine ran to Professor Taylor's side immediately. Leona re-boarded the farmer's vehicle.

Latching the back of the wagon, the professor smiled. "It was a pleasure meeting you, Miss Leona. May I ask what your last name is—for sociological purposes?" he quipped.

She answered loudly as the wagon pulled away, its wheels laboring against the cobblestones. "Schaeffer."

Leona winced. Now she'd given out her full name, against Warden Goldberg's instructions.

Surely it doesn't really matter.

Farmer Thompson stopped at the intersection of Beacon Street and Joy Street and let Leona out. She thanked him for the ride and bid farewell to Gunshot.

Leona walked down Joy Street, reading the house numbers displayed on each identical home.

22 Joy Street. This is it.

Her hand shook. Ezra Schaeffer was her last remaining relative. Would he look like her father, with impossibly wavy dark hair and confident blue eyes? Would he prove to be as kind and strong?

She yearned to be welcomed here at 22 Joy Street, despite the cloud of sad news she carried. Leona dreamed of being with family again. Surely her uncle would be as thrilled to meet her as she was to meet him. A determined burst of hope filled her heart.

I won't be alone anymore.

Chapter Four

Clementine heard a loud knock issue from the front door.

"Coming," exclaimed Bridget.

All their maids had been called Bridget, though Clementine had no idea why. But she liked this Bridget the best out of all the ones who'd worked for them over the years. Mother hired her two months ago, after the last one had destroyed her favorite gown—a lavender chiffon and violet silk Victorian monstrosity.

Bridget opened the door slightly and addressed the visitor. Clementine peeked around the top of the staircase, watching intently as the maid closed the door and sprinted to the parlor.

Mother shadowed Bridget back to the door, chattering like a sparrow about the rare occurrence of visitors to their home. Bridget's white hat tipped up and down, like a boat on stormy waves, acknowledging her comments politely.

Suspense held Clementine captive as Mother spoke to the unseen visitor behind the door. The conversation didn't carry. Mother did a lot of gasping.

All of a sudden, she squealed gleefully and pulled the guest inside, embracing her. Clementine was surprised to discover that the mysterious evening visitor was a tall, thin young lady with dark, wild curls cascading over her shoulders, past the middle of her back. Clementine tucked an errant, stick-straight blond hair behind her ear and frowned.

"Clementine! Ezra! Come here right now. I have a surprise for you!"

Clementine descended the stairs two at a time.

The girl's face brightened as Clementine approached her. *Golly, she's almost too pretty. Her eyes are blue as a summer sky, and her eyelashes extend for miles.*

She flashed the girl a pearly grin. Mother once proclaimed Clementine's smile was her best feature. In fact, many people had remarked on the impressive health of her teeth.

The dark-haired beauty smiled back.

"Hello. I'm Leona Schaeffer, your cousin."

"I have a cousin?" *What a surprise.* "Hello! I'm Clementine."

She'd never had a cousin before today—or many friends, for that matter.

Father entered the foyer, walking tentatively forward. He stared at the girl as if she were a ghost. He grasped the edge of the writing desk and took a deep breath.

"Where are Eben and Katarina?"

Before she could answer, the girl's knees buckled. Clementine grabbed her arm to support her.

Mother rushed to Leona's other side. "Oh, your poor cousin has traveled all day, Clementine. You must be exhausted, dear. Have you eaten supper?" she asked.

"No," Leona replied.

"Come sit at the dining table. Bridget, warm up some soup."
Bridget scampered away, her black boots clacking against the
hardwood floor.

"Do you like clams?" Mother asked Leona.

"I don't know," she replied.

Father just stood there, still staring, chewing his lip.

Clementine helped her tired cousin into the dining room and
lowered her into a cushioned high-back dining chair. She sat
beside her, prepared to catch her if she fainted.

"Leona, where are Eben and Katarina? Why aren't they with
you?" Father asked. The sharp annunciation of his usual droning
tenor voice made Clementine raise her eyebrows. *He's angry.*
Why?

Leona's dark lashes closed over her glittering blue eyes. She
took a long breath and replied,

"There was a fire. I escaped, but my grandparents and my
parents didn't. They're gone, Uncle Ezra. I've been on my own
for two years now."

Mother gasped and went to Father's side, taking his hand in
hers.

"Two years ago, you say?" he asked, ignoring Mother's
caresses.

"Yes."

"Why didn't you come to see me right away?" he demanded,
his tone harsh.

"I couldn't. I lost everything in the fire. I wandered the
countryside for months, staying with families from local

churches and cleaning for them in return for their hospitality. About a year ago, I saved enough money to come to the city, but there was a storm and I got lost. A kind widow took me in and made me her ward. I lived with her until—" the girl stopped.

Clementine couldn't stand the suspense. "Until what?"

The girl sighed. "I think it's best if I speak to Uncle Ezra alone."

Bridget returned, placing a bowl of chowder and a hunk of golden bread in front of the weary traveler. The girl sniffed the soup and wrinkled her nose.

"It's a Boston favorite," Mother commented.

"It smells odd," Leona remarked.

"It smells like the *ocean*," Clementine corrected her. "It's clam chowder."

"The ocean?" Her cousin paled, frowning. "I don't think I like the ocean."

"Well, you've come to the wrong city then," Mother guffawed, attempting humor, as she often did, and again failing. Father flashed her a look of disapproval. She asked Bridget to bring Leona some dried meats and fruit from the cellar.

Leona chewed on the bread. Color slowly returned to her face. Clementine stared. Her cousin grew lovelier and lovelier as her cheeks pinked.

"You're so pretty!" Clementine blurted.

Leona's eyebrows rose and she answered, "Thank you. So are you, cousin. Your hair reminds me of corn silk." This made Clementine grin. "Tell me about yourself. Then we'll be strangers no longer."

The Good Shepherd

Clementine began, "Well, I'm fourteen. My birthday is January 1—that's right—New Year's Day! I like to read and sing. And I absolutely adore cats. I have the most beautiful kitty cat in the world. You'll just love him. Mother, have you seen Mr. Flufferbutter?"

Mr. Flufferbutter was a white Persian. She'd received the kitten last year, after a little begging. He loved the smell of clams. Surely, he was prowling the dining room.

Maybe he's under the table. Clementine grinned when her hypothesis proved correct and two green cat eyes blinked at her in the shadows under the lengthy dining table.

She called to him. He ignored her. Instead, he growled, low and fierce, entranced by Leona's presence. Then, without provocation, Mr. Flufferbutter jumped on the table and swiped his paw across Leona's arm, drawing blood. He hissed at her viciously.

"Get that blasted cat out of here, Clementine!" Father yelled.

Clementine scooped up Mr. Flufferbutter and took him upstairs. When she returned, Leona wasn't in the dining room anymore. Clementine pouted.

"Where's my cousin?" she asked Mother.

"Father is speaking with her in his study. Help Bridget prepare the guest room for her."

She's staying overnight! Like a bosom friend. Or, well, like a cousin! Clementine's pout dissipated.

What's it like to have a cousin?

Clementine couldn't wait to find out.

"Tell me what you know," Uncle Ezra demanded, his face devoid of compassion.

"What do you mean?" Leona didn't understand why he sounded so gruff.

"Do you know about your family inheritance?"

Ah, he was worried she'd been raised ignorant of her Warden heritage. But that still didn't explain his harsh attitude.

Leona reassured him, "I know that Schaeffers are Wardens. My parents were going to start my training when I got older. But they died, along with my grandparents. I had no one to train me."

Hope bubbled inside her. Maybe he would volunteer. She went on, "Papa was amazing. He could sense rogues before their first transformation. Can you do that?" She leaned forward in her chair, excited to finally have someone to discuss these matters with.

Her uncle squirmed in his chair. "It doesn't matter because I don't want to."

"But—"

He avoided her eyes as he smoothed his mustache and replied, "I'm not a Warden. I gave up that life when I moved to the city. Now I'm a lawyer, and the Brahmin—the Boston aristocracy— have accepted me into their circle. I have a good, respectable life here. I'm not going to train you, child."

The Good Shepherd

Leona's hope fizzled in an instant. She couldn't believe her only living relative had refused to help her train as a Warden. She straightened her back, refusing to look weak or sad in front of this callous man.

"I have no desire to disturb your life," she said. "I can find employment and provide for myself. I only came here to inform you of the fate of your kin. I shall leave you to grieve alone, as I have these past two years."

A shadow fell over Uncle Ezra's face upon hearing her words. "I do grieve for Eben and Katarina. My brother and I were once very close, but—" He paused. "The past is best left behind. Alas, since you are an orphan and my kin, allow me to make inquiries and assist you in procuring employment. You're seventeen, correct?"

"Yes, sir."

His eyes wandered over the pictures facing him on the desk. Their backs displayed nothing to Leona but hinges and wood. She waited for him to speak, but he seemed distracted by the pictures.

He cleared his throat. "You're cursed, child. You must not pass the curse on to another generation. The Wardens are an endangered species. Soon they will disappear. The sooner, the better." He shifted in his seat and loosened his ascot.

"I'm proud of my heritage. It's not a curse. Mama and Papa are gone. I must continue their good work."

"Good work?" he scoffed, adjusting a crooked frame on his desk. He inched the picture forward until it fell in line with the others. "You'll only get hurt. Stop before it's too late. Become a happy spinster and spare yourself some heartache."

Leona's mouth twisted. Her hands tightened into fists. "The rogues need help and the world needs protection. Have you forgotten—"

He slammed one of the frames face down on the desk. The sudden noise made Leona flinch. He scowled at her. "I have forgotten nothing! *You're* forgetting that Werewolves are beasts. If they kill a human, their bloodlust in unquenchable. They'll never stop hunting for human prey when they transform. That's why the Wardens call the execution of murderous Werewolves *exacting mercy*. It's a mercy killing, like shooting a rabid dog."

Leona's nails dug into her palms. "Yes, for three nights a month, Werewolves are beasts. But for the rest of their lives, they're people—with families, friends, and souls."

Her uncle's moustache curled into a crescent shape over his pointed chin as he frowned at her. His cold blue eyes pierced hers as he asked, "Have you ever exacted mercy?"

A shadow fell over Leona. She released her fists. Blood reached the cold digits of her hand, causing prickles to travel up her arm. "Yes, I have. Twice. And I failed to protect an innocent. I'll bear the guilt of it the rest of my life."

Her uncle stared at her, a strange look played in his pale eyes. Pity? Revulsion?

He exhaled slowly, rubbing his temples. "Give it up. Normalize. Guilt and death cling to Wardens like a shadow. Eben and Katarina should have warned you how destructive exacting mercy is. Failure is worse. You said it yourself, the guilt is unbearable."

The Good Shepherd

Anger bubbled inside her. "No, what I said was, I *bear* it. I was *destined* to bear it. Even if my parents didn't train me, I understood that." Thrusting her chin out, she added, "They were good Wardens. Everyone loved them."

"You don't know that for certain, do you? What if someone didn't? What if someone wanted them to stop protecting the rogues?"

"Like who?" Leona asked, appalled by the idea.

Uncle Ezra's moustache twitched. "I guess you haven't heard. The Wardens have split. There are now two branches, Shepherds and Hunters. Shepherds still help rogues. They follow the Code, establish sanctuaries, and only execute those who kill humans. Hunters have no such pity. They ignore the Code and eliminate all rogues—and their protectors, if they get in their way. Eventually, they intend to eliminate the entire species."

Leona collapsed back onto her chair. *Eliminate the species?*

"Did my father know about these Hunters?" she asked.

"I don't know. But he wouldn't have been surprised. The Warden Code is vague about many things. It was bound to lead to division. Your father and I have—had—our own issues with the Warden Council. We both chose to live our lives without their interference."

Leona gathered her hair into a bun. She pierced it with her grandmother's silver hairpin. She'd killed two Werewolves with this hairpin. *Does that make me a Hunter? No, they broke the Code. They were guilty—and the bloodlust would take over.* She'd been protecting the world, not eliminating a species.

Her uncle cleared his throat. His expression was stern.

"Leona, if you become a Normalizer like me, you may stay and live here, with me, Franny, and Clementine."

"But if I want to be a Warden? A Shepherd?"

He frowned. "Then you must leave."

Leona was shocked. How could this man really be her kind father's kin, his only living relative, his *brother?* They were so different. Papa would never turn away someone in need. It went against everything he believed in. A hot tear fell down her cheek. *What should I do?*

Her uncle was right. Exacting mercy on Luke and Mr. Harris had left her floundering. Her parents had been good Wardens, but she had failed. Still, she couldn't abandon everything they stood for and Normalize. She couldn't adopt her uncle's attitude, pretending he had no responsibilities, no inherited duties. Especially now that she'd discovered rogues were being hunted down—rogues who'd never violated the Code.

"I need to ask you something. What's your issue with the Warden Council?" Leona asked.

"That's *my* business," he replied, his blue eyes dark and stormy. He arranged the pictures on his desk in a neat row, ignoring her. "No matter what you decide about Normalizing, at least promise me you'll stay away from other Wardens. You don't know where their loyalties lie."

Leona was shocked by the revelation that there were untrustworthy Wardens. But she gathered her strength and replied, "I'm afraid I cannot abide by your wish to Normalize. I'll find somewhere else to live, as you've commanded. You can explain to Warden Goldberg why I left." She rose to leave. "I'll be gone by morning."

"Don't be hasty. You're just like your father, independent and stubborn. Stay here for one week. Fully consider your future. When the week is over, if you decide to be a Warden, then you must leave and never return. I'll speak with Warden Goldberg." He waved a finger at her. "Oh—do not mention the Wardens to Clementine or Franny. They are blissfully unaware of our family's heritage. I would like to keep it that way. Kindly allow them to remain living in ignorance, like happy sheep."

Leona nodded her agreement, managing to bite her tongue, holding back from voicing a severe attack on his character, which she found cowardly.

She walked to the door. As she placed her hand on the doorknob, her uncle cleared his throat and stuttered, "W-were you... happy with Eben and Katarina?"

Without turning around, she replied, "Yes," then exited the room.

Leona waited until she'd exited the office before wiping away a fat tear from her cheek. The heavy oak door closed with a thud behind her. Exhausted from the exchange, she leaned against the wall and sighed.

She was alone again.

Her uncle's belligerence toward her was disappointing, to say the least. But the schism in the Warden world scared her. Her parents hadn't spoken of the Warden Council often, but when they did, she'd detected fear in their voices. Had they expected this division?

What if the fire *hadn't* been an accident? Were these Hunters responsible for her family's deaths? Her heart ached. The memory of the fire, the loss of her parents and grandparents, her years of mourning, the disappointing reunion—it was too much.

A hand squeezed hers. Leona lifted her head. Through the thick fog of heavy thoughts shone the wide, glittering, toothy smile of her young cousin, Clementine.

"Hey, cousin! I'm sorry about Mr. Flufferbutter. I locked him in my room, so you don't have to be afraid of that little rascal attacking you in the middle of the night. Come on. I'll show you where you'll be sleeping."

Clementine's porcelain hand tightened around hers and pulled her away down the hallway. Leona let the girl escort her up the stairs. Her cousin's enthusiasm, like the radiance of the sun, was inescapable and warming. As they climbed up and up, Leona's burdens felt further and further away. When they reached the landing, she desired only sleep.

"Thanks," she said. "I'll see you in the morning."

She turned to go in the room. Clementine hugged her from behind. "I'm so glad you're here. I have a *cousin*—how exciting! It's like an instant friend. Oh, Leona, I just know we're going to have loads and loads of fun together."

Leona was relieved Clementine couldn't see her tear-streaked face. "Yes, loads of fun. Well, goodnight."

"Goodnight—*cousin!*"

Chapter Five

Tuesday, September 19
22 Joy Street

When Leona entered the dining room, Clementine's chair screeched. The finely dressed girl bolted from her chair and escorted Leona to the table, holding her firmly by the elbow.

Leona donned a blue cotton dress that the maid, a tiny woman in a black and white uniform, had delivered to her room upon informing her breakfast was being served downstairs.

Clementine shot her with questions. "You're awake! How did you sleep? Do you like bacon, or boiled eggs, or ham, or apples, or brown bread? Is that dress too short?"

Leona wasn't sure which question to answer first.

"I—it—" she began. Clementine set a plate in front of her.

Leona sat in awe of the vast amount of food spread across the long table. A platter of bacon was within arm's length, so Leona put a few pieces on her large plate.

"I like bacon, too." Clementine giggled.

Clementine stood and moved the other dishes, placing them in a semi-circle around Leona as if she were a castle requiring a wall of food for protection. Clementine took on the task of filling Leona's plate with fruits, breads, and meats.

Leona wasn't sure she had ever eaten this much for breakfast before, even at Ms. Wickersham's. The tiny widow ate like a bird and was quite frugal. They often repeated the same meal for days, but Leona had never complained. She was grateful not to be scavenging the woods for berries, roots, and tubers to eat. The third day of eating leftover pot roast would always be better than the first day of eating roasted squirrel.

Her uncle lived well indeed. *Surely not all city folk eat like this.* Leona had never been to Boston before yesterday. Mama and Papa rarely ventured into small towns, let alone a big city like Boston. Rogue Werewolves usually kept away from populated areas.

Aunt Franny entered the room. Thick ringlets hung from both sides of her round face like bouncy bookends.

Clementine whispered in Leona's ear, "Mother adored Queen Victoria. She's been mourning her death by imitating her hairstyle."

"Queen Victoria?"

"The queen of England, silly. Well, she *was*. She died. There's a king now—King Edward. No one wants to copy *his* hair. He doesn't have much."

Aunt Franny sat across from the girls. Her voluminous skirt flared. The chairs on both sides tipped slightly.

"Would you like some tea, Leona? I must say, it's quite chilly this morning."

Leona nodded. "Aunt Franny, what day is it?"

The Good Shepherd

Her aunt cocked her head slightly, one golden spiral resting against her cheek, and answered, "You must have a very hard journey. You've been sleeping for days. Poor thing. It's Tuesday, September nineteenth."

Clementine waved a thin book in the air. "Every morning, I read the Farmer's Almanac, so I always know what day it is. Leona, do you like astronomy? I know everything about astronomy. Go ahead. Ask me anything you want to about the moon."

The mouthful of yeast roll Leona was chewing stuck in her throat. She coughed.

"The moon?" she whispered before swallowing hard.

"Yes, the Almanac lists the lunar phases for each month. Tonight is a third-quarter moon. Do you know what the next phase is?" Clementine sounded like a Sunday School teacher Leona had in Framingham. Of course, Leona hadn't gained her knowledge of lunar phases from church, nor from the Almanac.

"A third-quarter moon, also called a half-moon, is followed by a waning crescent moon," Leona replied.

Clementine gasped. "Mother, Leona is not only pretty, she's smart, too."

Franny smiled wide at Leona. "Is that dress too short? I can have Bridget alter it for you."

"No, that's not necessary," Leona replied.

"Nonsense, it's the least I can do for my niece." Aunt Franny leaned forward and winked at Leona, her curls bouncing dangerously near the ceramic syrup pitcher.

It was a nice feeling, to be cared for by family. But a twinge of sadness crept over Leona. She'd been isolated from others most of her life. Her grandparents had educated her, teaching her the usual school subjects of reading and writing, at home. After much begging, they taught her some basic tenements of the Warden Code, which involved memorizing the lunar phases.

Her grandparents expressed such pride in her. Leona frowned. She'd failed them. And now her uncle wanted to keep her from his family, the only family she had left. She must enjoy the time that remained with Aunt Franny and her cousin Clementine.

When they finished breakfast, Leona's stomach felt solid as a rock, the blue dress taut around her waist. The maid, donning a white apron edged in delicate tatted lace over her black dress, cleared the dishes.

"Thank you, Bridget," Aunt Franny said to the maid.

When the woman had finished her task, Leona turned to Clementine and commented, "I've never met anyone named Bridget."

"It's an Irish name," Aunt Franny said.

Clementine leaned toward Leona and whispered, *"She's Catholic."*

"Why are you whispering?"

"I don't know," she shrugged. "It's just that—well— Catholics aren't like us. We're Episcopalians. We're members of Christ Church, the oldest church in Boston. Paul Revere was a bell ringer there. Surely you've heard of him! He lit the lanterns at the church during the Revolutionary War to warn the colonists that the British were coming. Paul Revere was a patriot. And he certainly wasn't Catholic. Catholics aren't true Yankees."

The Good Shepherd

"Yankees?"

Aunt Franny answered, "Descendants of the first colonists. Most Catholics are foreigners. Irish or Italian immigrants. Ezra isn't a true Yankee either—he's quite German—but at least he acts American. He's well-respected by the Brahmin. Clementine and I are very proud of him."

Leona twisted the linen napkin in her hand. So much bigotry existed in the world. It was near impossible to comprehend the intolerance of the Hunters, but Clementine and Franny's debasement of Catholics and immigrants was disturbing as well.

She smoothed her wrinkled napkin. "But the original colonists were immigrants too. My mother's parents came here from Russia. My parents were gone a lot, um, helping people in need, so I spent a lot of time with my grandparents. Grandfather could always make me laugh. I really miss him." Leona sighed, recalling her grandfather's sparkly eyes, snowy hair, and round tummy. "I used to call him *Ded Moroz*."

"Dead what?" Clementine asked.

"*Ded Moroz. Grandfather Frost.* He's like Santa Claus."

Aunt Franny and Clementine shared awkward smiles. Clementine wrinkled her brow. "I don't remember my grandparents. I've never met any of my extended family—except you." Sadness darkened her face.

Aunt Franny rose. "Yes, we were all alone before you came along, Leona. If you'll excuse me, girls, I'll be going. I need to speak to Allen about cleaning the fireplace."

The second her mother left the room, Clementine jumped up from her chair. Sadness had evaporated from her countenance, and, with a twinkle in her eyes, she grasped Leona's hands in hers.

"Dear cousin! I have a secret I want to share with you."

Leona was weary of secrets, but replied, "Go on."

Clementine leaned over and whispered in Leona's ear, "I'm in love!"

Leona was unsure how to respond to this. "That's... wonderful?"

Clementine's smile grew as her eyes glassed over. Leona suspected she was being swept away by a dashing knight in her imagination. She waited for Clementine to return to the Schaeffer's dining room.

"He has the most beautiful blue eyes. And he's an artist. He has an art exhibit on Saturday in the Common. Mother and I are going. Please say you'll come with us. It's for charity—for the poor unfortunate orphans. Besides, if you're with me, I won't be so nervous. I made a total fool of myself when I first met him. I tripped over a tree root. But he caught me. Isn't that romantic?"

"Um—"

"It's settled, then. Mother will buy you a dress to wear—one that fits. We could match—like sisters!"

Leona's stomach gurgled.

"Do you need to visit the water closet?"

Leona's face flushed.

"Don't be embarrassed. I'll show you where it is."

When Leona had finished up in the water closet, she reached out to turn the doorknob, but heard a threatening sound from the other side of the door. *The cat.*

Leona growled like an animal, fierce and territorial. Mr. Flufferbutter uttered a short retort of *Rrreowll!* and bolted away. Leona sighed in relief.

Mr. Flufferbutter is a fluffy coward, Leona thought, snickering to herself.

On her journey back to the dining room, Leona passed an open door in the kitchen. She peered inside and glimpsed a figure ascending the stairs. It was Bridget.

"Excuse me, miss," Bridget said, passing Leona. She set quart jars of preserved food gently on the table and turned to go back down the stairs.

"Can I help you?" Leona asked.

Bridget froze. After a few seconds, she shrugged. "Aye, miss. If you like."

Leona followed her down the dark staircase. A gas lamp hanging from a hook on the ceiling cast an eerie glow over the cool dirt cellar.

Wooden shelves stored canned vegetables, fruits, and juice. Baskets lined the floor, displaying onions, potatoes, squash, and tomatoes. Another rack held dark glass bottles. Wine or beer, Leona guessed.

In the corner, there was a large cedar chest, like a young woman's hope chest. Leona had never possessed a hope chest. In her home, wooden chests were places to store Warden items—weapons and books—not gifts for a future husband and children. Maybe this was Clementine's hope chest. But the chest was padlocked, and a layer of dust covered the lid.

Bridget gathered jars. Leona relieved her of two filled with floating pickles and then gestured with her chin at the cedar chest.

"What's in there?"

"I don't know," Bridget said, shrugging her shoulders. "Mr. Schaeffer keeps the key for it. Excuse me, I need to take the lantern back upstairs." She reached behind Leona and retrieved the lantern from the hook.

They climbed the stairs and set the jars down on the center table.

"Thank ye, Miss Leona," she said with a grin. Leona adored Bridget's slight Irish brogue. Light as it was, Leona guessed Bridget had resided in America for many years. Her smooth skin gave her a young glow, but her stylish pinned hair indicated she was a few years older than Leona.

"You're welcome, Bridget. Thank you for breakfast this morning. And supper last night."

Bridget giggled, but covered her mouth conspicuously.

"What?" Leona asked.

"Tis nothing bad. It's just that—you and I have something in common."

"Oh? What's that?"

"We both hate clams!"

Leona enjoyed Bridget's hearty laughter just as much as her Irish accent. Chuckling in the kitchen with the maid, Leona realized she had little desire to return to the dining room, to her cousin. But she determined to show Clementine some grace. They'd lived different lives, so they were bound to have differences in worldview.

Maybe there was a way to help widen her younger cousin's

view in the short time Leona was allowed to stay with her uncle's family, before she gained employment and housing of her own. Soon Leona would be forced to move out and Clementine's uppity opinions wouldn't bother her anymore.

Chapter Six

"Leona, have you ever been on a trolley?"

"No."

"Do you like adventures?"

"Um…"

"I have an idea!"

A mischievous expression slid onto Clementine's face. Leona worried about where this conversation would lead.

"I was thinking of taking a little trip after school. If you meet me at the trolley stop a few blocks away at around three o'clock, we could go together. Come on. It'll be fun!"

Leona tilted her head. "Would your mother approve?"

"You sound like a rotten, mean older sister, not a fun country cousin," Clementine joked. She leaned in closer and whispered, "Remember that boy I told you about? The artist?"

"Yes."

"He teaches art at an orphanage on the south side of town. Father mentioned you needed a job. I know the lady who runs the place. What kinds of things are you good at?"

"Oh, well," Leona began. "I'm, uh… a good runner?"

"Running? That's all you can do? You can read and write,

can't you?"

"Yes."

"Then you can teach."

"But—"

"I need to leave for school, now, Leona. I'll see you at the trolley stop later, okay? Okay?"

Clementine's eyes burned with hope. Leona sighed.

"Okay."

Leona stood alone in a crowd of strangers waiting for one familiar face to appear. The people around her at the trolley stop were a variety of ages and backgrounds. Some were dressed like Bridget, servants running errands. On both sides of the street, men in dark suits marched like soldiers toward their destinations, mothers dragged their children by the hand, teens on bicycles dodged pedestrians, and vendors sold various foods in exchange for pennies, nickels, and dimes. Horse-drawn wagons and carriages rumbled over the dusty streets.

Leona breathed Boston in. Her mind sifted the odors into three categories—industrial, street, and ocean smells. Factory chimneys puffed gray smoke into the sky. Sewage seeped up from the street. These stenches were awful, but the odors floating in from the harbor and seafood markets really turned her stomach.

A hand tapped her back. Leona prepared to throw the person attached to the hand over her shoulder. Before she took action, a familiar voice sung, "Yay! You're here. Have you been waiting long?"

Clementine's melodic voice relaxed Leona. She began to feel a kinship with the younger girl.

Leona missed family; her parents and grandparents, plus those who had become family, like Mrs. Wickersham. The lonely widow had welcomed Leona into her home even though she was a stranger, offering her shelter, respect, comfort, and time to recuperate.

Now that she was in Boston, and instead of feeling supported by her relatives, her uncle had insisted she keep her Warden powers a secret from Franny and Clementine. Would she ever be able to share what she was with someone who understood? *I can't wait for Warden Goldberg to arrive.*

"Hello? Leona, did you hear me? I asked if you've been waiting long."

Leona shook her head and focused her eyes on Clementine. "I guess it's been a little while. I've been watching the city."

"Is it different from the country? It is, isn't it? Oh, I just love Boston," Clementine said. Her face glowed and she stood taller.

Leona asked, "Have you lived here all your life?"

"Yes. It was hard to move houses when Mother married Father, but the house on Joy Street is so cozy and quaint," Clementine commented.

Leona was confused.

"When your mother married your father?"

"Oh, I thought you knew! Ezra is my stepfather. My birth father was a naval officer, Admiral George W. Bell, a true

Yankee. The Bells came to America on the Mayflower a long time ago. He died fighting in the Spanish-American War seven years ago." Clementine's expression conveyed pride, edged with a tinge of sorrow. "I was just a little girl. I don't really remember him all that well."

Leona was surprised; yet sympathized with Clementine. Without Mrs. Wickersham around, who reminded her of her grandmother, her face had begun to fade from Leona's memory.

"I see. So, we're not related by blood?"

Clementine cocked her head. "Hmm... I suppose we aren't. Do you hate me now?"

"What? No, I could never hate you." Leona said, though she felt a touch of disappointment that they didn't share the Warden heritage. She'd hoped to change Uncle Ezra's mind about many things, like telling Clementine about the Wardens. Now that wasn't an issue. Clementine was a full-blooded human.

Clementine's apple-shaped face brightened. She beamed at Leona, her dimples deepening. "Good. I could never hate you either—though I am exceptionally jealous of your beautiful curly hair. But I'll forgive you for outshining me if you allow me to play with it, cousin."

Leona nodded her agreement.

The girls boarded the next streetcar. Leona held the seat rails with both hands, the cushion squeaking under her skirt as the trolley jostled along Boston's streets.

Clementine giggled. "You're such a country girl, Leona. The trolley is safe. Don't be afraid."

Leona didn't feel reassured, especially when the buildings

outside began passing by unnaturally fast. The wagon she rode into Boston had been much slower. The streetcar was smoother, but the acceleration spooked her. She closed her eyes. *It'll be over soon.*

"Excuse me, ladies, do you know if this trolley stops at *The Home for Little Wanderers*?"

Leona opened her eyes. In front of them stood a scruffy-faced, thin man in a tattered coat, smelling strongly of tobacco. Clementine's green eyes flitted, jumping everywhere except to the raggedy stranger.

The man held a large, leather-bound Bible in one hand. Leona nudged Clementine to answer him.

Clementine was holding her breath. Leona nudged her harder.

"Yes, sir," her cousin finally replied, exhaling sharply. She turned her golden head away from the man and gulped some air.

The man sighed in relief. "Thank the Lord. I'm scheduled to lead a study there for the teachers, to encourage their Christian service."

"That's nice," Clementine said, exhaling. Leona returned his grin.

The man bowed his head toward Leona. "My name is Reverend Holland Busch."

"I'm Leona Schaeffer, and this is my cousin, Clementine Bell," she replied. *Oh no, I gave out my name again.*

Clementine grinned quickly at the man, then pulled her scarf tight over her nose.

The trolley rumbled along. The wheels screamed and then quieted. Leona's back thumped against the chair.

The Good Shepherd

"What is your study about today?" Leona said, initiating conversation to distract her from the discomfort of the trolley ride.

"The social crisis," Reverend Busch replied.

"Isn't that nice?" Clementine remarked with a sardonic tone. Turning to Leona, she thrust her chin at some empty seats at the front of the trolley. Leona ignored her.

The reverend continued, "Many are in need of mercy and grace but there are so few workers in the field. The teachers and volunteers at the Home are doing God's work. I hope to encourage them not to grow faint and give up their good deeds."

Leona agreed—there were too few workers of good in this dark world. Some *were* giving up. The rebellion of the Hunters proved this. Though Leona's responsibility as a Warden wasn't exactly what the preacher meant, the rhetoric was familiar. Leona couldn't give up on her belief that it was a Warden's duty to help rogue Werewolves. They were often orphans, too.

A lycanthrope without a reliable pack needed someone to teach him or her how to live with their condition. That's what her parents had done. If no one helped the rogues, they endangered society and themselves. Seen as outcasts to the packs, rogues were sometimes attacked and killed by them.

Leona respected the reverend's good intentions and took his encouragement to heart. Would the right words change her uncle's mind about shirking his inherited responsibilities? She doubted they would. The sacrificial life of a Warden—a Shepherd—would never harmonize with his goals. He wanted to be accepted by the elite. *What had he called them?* Brahmin.

Anyway, he had made his choice.

She might not be able to change her uncle, but the Hunters were a problem she could not ignore.

The trolley driver pulled a cord and a bell rang. Clementine's eyelids fluttered. Her face was beet red. Leona suspected she'd been holding her breath for a while. When the streetcar slowed and came to a stop, Clementine was the first to exit.

Leona hurried to keep up with the petite girl, who was fueled by either the hope for fresh air or for romance, possibly both. Clementine had claimed she wanted to help Leona find employment. But the look on Clementine's face as they arrived made it clear to Leona that infatuation was what guided them here today.

Leona stepped out of the trolley car. Reverend Busch remained a good distance behind them.

Clementine ran to the front door of the orphanage and rang the doorbell. A dark-skinned girl in braids greeted them. Clementine's eyes widened. She stuttered, "Is-is Mrs. Green available?"

"Yes, miss. Come in and wait inside. I'll let her know you're here. What's your name?"

"Clementine Elizabeth Bell. Th-thank you."

They sat on a sofa in the lobby. Reverend Busch, carrying only a Bible, entered and walked down the hall. When his raggedy figure disappeared. Clementine took a deep breath of fresh air.

Within minutes, a woman approached. She wore a gray blouse tucked into a pleated blue skirt and carried a sleeping baby wrapped in a patchwork quilt.

Clementine brightened. "Mrs. Green, do you remember me?"

"Of course, Miss Bell. How is your mother?"

Mrs. Green patted the baby's back lightly with her palm. The fragile infant's fingers poked out of the wrappings.

"She's fine. Mrs. Green, this is my cousin, Leona Schaeffer. She's looking for a job and I thought maybe, well… that you could give her one?"

Mrs. Green turned to Leona. Her cautious eyes examined her from head to toe. A sudden wave of nerves struck Leona. Maybe Mrs. Green held strange prejudices also. Maybe she only wanted Yankees to work here.

"What kind of work are you seeking?" asked Mrs. Green.

Leona hadn't given this much thought. She was willing to do almost anything.

"Are there any jobs that would also provide lodging?"

Clementine exclaimed, "What?"

Leona shushed her. Mrs. Green answered, "A position for a female dorm monitor is open. This person is charged with watching over the children overnight as well as during the day. It's not a difficult job, but I expect my monitors to be responsible adults and abide by my rules. These children need consistency."

"Mrs. Green, I am also an orphan. And I would be grateful for the opportunity to prove myself."

"Ah, you understand more than many, then. I'll have the old monitor's room cleaned out by Monday morning. Can you come at noon?"

"Yes." Leona raised her hand to shake Mrs. Green's. The

baby in the woman's arms stirred. Mrs. Green caressed the baby's sleeping face. The child gurgled and opened its eyes. Beautiful, deep brown irises peered back at her.

Clementine stood on her toes, looking beyond Mrs. Green and the adorable baby, straining her neck. Her eyes narrowed as she searched the hall, obviously looking for the artist she'd told Leona about—her handsome hero.

"Is Mr. Smith here?" she asked Mrs. Green, completely ignoring the adorable child in the woman's arms.

"He's in the garden," she replied, tipping her chin in the direction of the side yard. "He spends most of his free time outside, drawing. Oh, that reminds me. Leona, I'd like to invite you to our art exhibit on Saturday in the Common. Clementine, are you and your mother coming?"

"Yes, of course," Clementine replied in a rush. She walked toward the garden, the heels on her boots clacking like an overzealous telegraph operator.

Leona scampered to catch up to her cousin. Clementine burst through an arbor covered with rusty Virginia Creeper vines. The morning had blossomed into a lovely fall afternoon. The foliage in the garden showcased leaves in various stages of beautiful demise.

"There he is!" Clementine pointed to a hunchbacked figure sitting on a rock, feverishly sketching in a notepad. Sticks of colored chalk lay scattered beside him. A knife rested on the ground with freshly whittled pencils. Leona inhaled the refreshing aroma of pine trees.

She groaned inwardly as Clementine sprinted toward the

young man.

"What are you drawing?" she asked him, her voice high-pitched and louder than usual, which startled even Leona. But the man's head remained bowed over his notebook. He didn't seem to hear Clementine. He selected a different color chalk and continued scribbling.

"I said—"

He raised his hand, holding his palm toward her face. Clementine reluctantly stopped speaking. She rocked back and forth on her heels as she waited for his permission to speak again.

He set the chalk down and blew on the paper. A miniature cloud of yellow dust burst from the page and dissipated into the air.

When he looked up, he met Leona's eyes. She inhaled sharply. His eyes were the same icy blue as Luke's. He stopped staring at Leona and turned to address Clementine.

"Who are you?" he asked.

"Don't you remember, Mr. Smith? You saved me at the Common on Saturday when I tripped on that awful cobblestone. You're my hero."

His forehead wrinkled as he thought. "I'm sorry, I don't remember."

"Oh," Clementine said, fidgeting with the fringe on her scarf. Leona wanted to reach out and pat her back, like Mrs. Green had done with the baby in her arms.

But Clementine rallied, cocking her chin up and smiling bright. The girl cleared her throat and said sweetly, "That's an interesting drawing."

"Thanks," was his vague response. He stood, then wiped his chalky hands on a rag from his pocket, then extended a slender, muscular hand to Leona.

"My name is Bradlee. And who are you?"

Leona shook his hand. "I'm Clementine's cousin, Leona."

"Leona's from the country. She was homeless," Clementine blurted.

Bradlee raised one eyebrow. "Homeless?"

Leona grimaced at Clementine, then answered, "Well, not for long. Mrs. Green hired me as monitor for the female dorm."

"That's wonderful. I live here, too. I teach art. Sometimes I substitute for the science teacher as well."

"Really?" Clementine stepped between them. "I love science. I know all about astronomy, you know, constellations and moon phases, and—"

Bradlee ignored Clementine. He asked Leona, "You're not from Boston?"

Clementine pouted. Leona tried to detour the man's attention.

"No. But Clementine has been teaching me about city life. Today she introduced me to the trolley. We should probably go wait for the next one now. Right, Clementine?"

Bradlee chuckled. "The trolley is fun, especially for kids. Did Mrs. Green invite you to the exhibit?"

"Yes, Clementine also invited me to go with her, but I'm not sure I can make it."

"Oh—please come! The art exhibition raises money for the orphanage. The children drew animals this time. I always assign them a theme. To be honest, I only enjoy drawing one animal.

The Good Shepherd

Some art teacher I am."

He revealed his sketch. "Do you like it?"

Leona gasped. The chalk drawing of a gray and white wolf below a full yellow moon took her breath away.

Leona stepped off the trolley first, followed by a sulking Clementine. Leona couldn't sympathize with her cousin. She didn't understand her obsessive infatuation with the rude young art teacher. He seemed oblivious to Clementine, at best.

Papa had forbidden Leona to court anyone outside the fold without his approval. Though he was gone, she still planned to abide by his rules. She had no desire to Normalize, like her uncle. Therefore, she would only marry a Warden. How could a non-Warden understand her responsibilities?

Clementine pushed past Leona, walking at a brisk pace toward the house on Joy Street. Leona sighed. The girl was young and immature, only fourteen. At this rate, she was bound to have her heart broken multiple times before she married. Though she considered her cousin a silly girl, deep inside she felt a twinge of jealousy at her freedom. Clementine lived without a Warden's burdens and restrictions, able to love whomever she desired.

Pedestrians bumped into Leona as she stood still in front of the house on Joy Street, staring at her cousin's slumped shoulders as her figure disappeared into the crowd.

"Clem—" Leona began. A sharp pain in her side made her

stop. She placed her hand over the painful spot and felt wetness. Blood seeped between her fingers. People continued passing and jostling her, unaware and unconcerned that she had just been attacked.

Leona groaned and scanned the dark, crowded sidewalk. The streetlamps weren't lit yet. All the faces bustling past her were anonymous suspects. Clementine was far beyond shouting range. Finally, a familiar face came into view.

"Miss Leona, are you ill?"

"Yes, Bridget, my stomach hurts. Could you help me to the door?" Bridget nodded and held out an arm. Leona grabbed it and leaned on the maid until they reached the stairs, hiding the stab wound from her.

No need to scare her. It will heal soon.

Indeed, by the time they entered the foyer, the pain had subsided, and the bleeding soon stopped. She felt her separated skin and muscles knit back together as her body healed itself. It was amazing.

"Thank you, Bridget," Leona said, still holding her hand over her stomach.

"Are you all right, miss? Shall I bring you a hot water bottle?"

Leona took a slow breath and shook her head. "No, thank you. I just need to lie down."

Bridget curtsied and excused herself. She carried a small brown bag in her left arm and exited the foyer, heading toward the kitchen. Leona climbed the stairs slowly. *Clementine must already be in her room.*

Alone in the guest room, Leona removed her frock and

examined the wound. A fading scar, the short line a half-inch wide, indicated it had been a thin knife. She wished she had worn the gray plaid dress instead of this light blue one. The stain was obvious. She threw on an ivory nightgown and laid the stained garment on the bed.

Clementine. Did the attacker hurt her too?

She ran to her cousin's door and knocked hard.

After a few long minutes, Clementine opened her door, both hands on her hips.

"What do you want?" she asked Leona with a pout.

Leona examined her visually. Satisfied her cousin was physically unharmed, she said, "Oh, I just wanted to thank you."

Clementine's eyebrows shot up.

"I've been without a family for so long, I forgot how wonderful it is to have their support and love. I'm thankful you're my cousin, Clementine, even if we aren't related by blood."

Clementine beamed at Leona. "That's so sweet, Leona. Family is more important than anything else in the world, right? I've been foolish today. Thank you for reminding me what's important. You are much wiser than I, cousin."

"I don't blame you for acting a bit foolish. He's quite handsome." Leona winked. "But, Clementine, don't chase him. Be his friend. I know that I consider your friendship a blessing. I'm sure he will as well."

Clementine leaned against the doorframe, looking contemplative. "I guess my prayer will be for God to bless Bradlee too."

Leona returned to her room and examined the torn, stained dress. Why had someone stabbed her? Was this something that happened often in cities? Or... was it just her? She gasped.

If someone had indeed targeted her, the culprit must know she was staying with the Schaeffers. The only person who knew she was here was Warden Goldberg. *Is he a Hunter?* But that didn't make sense. If he wanted to, he could have attacked her in Framingham instead of sending her all the way to Boston and attacking her here.

Whoever had assailed her, for whatever reason, Leona worried her presence endangered her remaining family.

Maybe I should leave before Monday.

No, she had promised Clementine she would accompany them to *The Home for Little Wanderers* art exhibit in the Common on Saturday.

There was only one solution. On Saturday, she would pack her travel bag, take her belongings with her to the exhibit, and beg Mrs. Green to allow her to return with them to the orphanage after the art show.

Leona felt a wave of sadness. She had found her family. But it was a family that only partially wanted her. Aunt Franny doted on her, but Uncle Ezra would be relieved she was leaving. Clementine usually acted loving toward her, but Leona feared the girl's fickleness. What would happen if she fell out of Clementine's favor?

It didn't matter. Soon, Leona would be alone again.

Chapter Seven

Saturday, September 23
22 Joy Street

Clementine unfolded the crinkled pamphlet Leona had removed from her pack and set on the table. "What's this?" she asked Leona.

"Oh, I met a professor on my travels. He invited me to attend a lecture. It's about a new study called sociology."

"Sociology? Never heard of it. *Saturday, September 23—* that's today! In Boston Common? How convenient. You can attend the lecture while *I* go to the art show."

"But I planned on attending the art show with you, cousin." Leona stared at Father's study door, looking forlorn. "Um, Clementine, I'm going to ask Mrs. Green if I can accompany them back to the Home and start my job early."

Clementine clutched her collar. "Start early? You're leaving us *today*?"

"Yes, if possible. I don't want to be a burden to Uncle Ezra and your mother," Leona replied.

"Could I visit you at the Home?" Clementine's skin tickled. *And see the beautiful Bradlee?*

Leona shrugged. "I don't know if that's a good idea. I have responsibilities, you know."

Clementine didn't allow her cousin's reply to dash her hopes. Contrary to Leona's disapproving look, Clementine kept her chin up and forced a wide grin. Leona's serious expression showcased her ridiculously pretty eyelashes. Her dark hair, like curled ribbon on a birthday present, cascaded down her back.

God, Leona was gorgeous. *Ugh. What if Bradlee thinks Leona is prettier than me?*

She couldn't believe he didn't remember saving her life at the Common last week. *Maybe he saves lots of girls. Or maybe he's not very smart. Have I fallen for a simpleton? What's taking Mother so long?*

"Mo-ther! It's time to leave!"

"Stop yelling, Clementine. It's not very ladylike," her mother scolded from the top of the stairs.

Mother wore a black crinoline petticoat under her brown brocade dress. An ebony velvet ribbon adorned her constricted waist. She raised her skirts above her shoelaces with one hand and grasped the banister with the other. Clementine rocked on her heels as Mother slowly descended the carpeted stairs. One misstep and she could fall. *Then I'll never get to see Bradlee.*

Finally, Mother's shoes clacked steady beats on the hardwood floor in the foyer. Clementine stretched her fingers, cracking her knuckles impatiently. "Let's *go!*"

"Yes, dear. Ezra has work to do at the office, so he'll meet us there later." She turned to the maid. "Bridget, do you have the picnic basket? Allen is waiting for us outside with the cart. We

74

have folding chairs and—"

"—you packed my—what's that thing called again?"

"An easel," Mother replied.

"Right!"

"Yes, dear. I gave Allen your list. Leona, your travel bag is also in the cart. If Mrs. Green agrees, you may leave with her, though I must plead with you to stay with us a few days longer. We've just been reunited. Truly, I'm not ready to say goodbye."

Mother wiped a tear from her eye. Clementine hoped she was not in another one of her moods. If she cried in public today, it would mortify her. Mother's drama strained Clementine's nerves. Leona wasn't really Mother's family. She was Ezra's niece. And, for some unknown reason, he didn't want her around.

Clementine had been excited when Leona first arrived, but now—now she was competition. I *should've applied for the job at the Home.* An image of Leona working alongside Bradlee entered her mind: the sharing pencils evolving to deep conversations, leading to pronouncements of mutual affection. Clementine couldn't breathe.

A loud knock distracted Clementine from her imaginings. Bridget, with the picnic basket slung on one elbow, scampered off to answer the door. Clementine was shocked when she saw the visitor's uniform. *A policeman?*

"Is there a Le-o-na here?" the man asked. His handlebar mustache was so thick, it barely moved when he exaggerated the syllables of Leona's name.

Bridget set the basket down and fetched Leona. Mother stared at the policeman's badge. Her wide eyes indicated disbelief at this intrusion to her prim and proper world. She stepped aside when Leona approached.

The cop handed Leona an envelope. Clementine pretended to adjust the level of a gold-framed portrait on the wall.

"This envelope, with the name Leona Schaeffer and this address written on it, was found on the body of a dead man. A Mister, uh, Goldberg. Did you know him, miss?"

Mother gasped. Leona, her face quite pale, reviewed the note and shook her head. "W-we never met. He was supposed to visit me here. He was a friend of my parents."

The policeman appeared satisfied with her answer. "I'm sorry to be the bearer of bad news, miss."

"How did he die?" Mother asked. Clementine paused in her alignment project and leaned an ear toward the door.

"Stabbed through the heart sometime last night, poor chap. He bled out in an alley two blocks away. Miss, if there's anything you remember that can help solve this case, stop by the station and ask for me. I'm Officer Buchanan."

"May I keep this, officer?" Leona asked, her breaths uneven. She appeared on the verge of a breakdown.

"No, miss. This is evidence now. Besides, it's empty."

The policeman tipped his hat to Mother and Leona and left the house. The interruption frazzled Clementine's nerves. Her patience faded.

"Can we go *now*?" Clementine asked.

"Yes, dear. Bridget! Allen! We're leaving! Come along, Leona," Mother replied, her eyes darting to Leona's skirt.

Father's longtime servant, Allen, a Negro, pushed the cart

behind them as they walked to Boston Common. The air was chilly. The sun remained behind the clouds, threatening to stay there.

"Oh, Mother, if it rains, will the art exhibit be cancelled?"

"I don't know, dear. Hike up your skirt, girls, the horses have been this way."

They traveled without conversation, though Clementine could tell Mother was dying to ask Leona about the dead man. Soon their tributary street emptied into the bay of people gathering in the Common. Women rode on bicycles, and men in casual attire were running around the park for exercise. *Probably training for the Patriots' Day marathon in April.* Footraces were all the rage now.

Clementine and her cousin walked ahead of Mother and the servants. Clementine held onto Leona's arm, pulling her along sometimes. They scanned the area for *The Home for Little Wanderers* wagon. Goose pimples formed on Clementine's arms. *Where's Bradlee?*

"'Ello, my darlin'," a voice chimed behind them.

She turned. It was the little Irish orphan she met last week. She opened her mouth to scold him when Bradlee approached.

The imp slapped Bradlee's back. "Hey, come meet my future wife!" The ridiculous leprechaun winked at Clementine and smiled a wide, gray-toothed grin.

She readied herself to give him a proper lashing, but Bradlee's smile beamed bright as the North Star and froze her boots to the ground, as if he possessed some powerful supernatural force. She stood still as a statue, dumbfounded by his eyes, the crystalline blue reminding her of the bay when the sun sparkled on its waves.

He turned his gaze to Leona. "Did you hear the happy news? My best chum is planning to wed your cousin!"

Leona smiled lightly at his remark, demurely beautiful.

"I'm quite certain Clementine is way too young to be pondering marriage," Leona said.

"She's above marrying an orphan, you mean. Like me. Is that what you mean, lass?" The leprechaun's grin faded, his expression sour.

Leona's face darkened. "That is certainly not what I meant."

"Oh, I'm a just having a bit of fun, lass," the imp said, his moronic grin returning.

Mother caught up to them. Clementine cleared her throat. "Where's the wagon?"

She practically swooned when Bradlee met her eyes and addressed her, "We were heading that way now. Fitz and I would be honored to escort you three fine ladies." His teeth were as white as oyster shells.

Clementine blinked hard. Mother replied in her stead, "Thank you, young man," she said to Bradlee, completely ignoring the red-haired leprechaun beside him, whose name Clementine had forgotten until now.

Fitz, the Stinky Elf.

Clementine, Leona, Mother, and the two servants followed Bradlee to the wagon. They were greeted by a jovial Mrs. Green.

She thanked them all for coming and then pulled Bradlee aside. Clementine overheard her say, "Don't get too friendly.

Remember, you're a teacher."

Clementine's spirits lifted. *That explained everything!* Bradlee was only pretending not to remember Clementine or act interested in her because he was a teacher. His job meant their love was forbidden. Her heart filled with renewed admiration for him. *He must be struggling inside.*

"Leona, Bradlee said you enjoyed his sketches. Would you like to see what he's drawn for the exhibit today?" Mrs. Green asked. Leona nodded and blinked her pretty eyes at Bradlee.

Clementine spoke, her voice louder than she'd intended, "We'd like to see them, too. I brought my art supplies in case I get inspired to paint today, Bradlee. The Common is so beautiful in the fall." She gestured to Allen standing on the outer edges of the circle of people, guarding the cart, which was filled with baskets, chairs, and Clementine's brand-new drawing easel.

The three ladies followed Mrs. Green to the front of the *Little Wanderers* wagon. Framed drawings hung from a cord, pinned like laundry on a clothesline. Bradlee pointed out his sketches. Clementine admired each one, commenting in detail how wonderful they were.

Leona's face adopted a sour expression as she stared at one of Bradlee's sketches of a dog—no—a wolf.

Clementine slid past her and raved about the next one to Mother.

"Do you like nature pictures?" Bradlee asked Leona.

"Sometimes," Leona replied.

Clementine interrupted, "Leona's not familiar with art and culture. She's from the country."

"Yes, I remember," Bradlee replied. "You said that Leona had been homeless." He turned his shoulder toward Leona, blocking Clementine out of their conversation. "So, were you homeless like a gypsy? Or were you the traditional kind of homeless, without parents, like me? Were you a little wanderer, too?"

"If those are my options, I suppose I'd have to say I was a traditional orphan. Like you," Leona replied, her pitiful expression transforming her into a tragic beauty.

Clementine imagined a line being drawn, dividing her from Leona and Bradlee. Clementine wanted to shove her mother and stepfather off a cliff so she could be a traditional orphan too.

"What happened to your parents?" Bradlee asked Leona.

Clementine interrupted, "They died in a fire. Leona escaped and left them behind to burn!" As soon as the words left her mouth, she felt sick.

"Clementine!" Mother chided.

Leona paled. Her long eyelashes drooped, and her eyes reddened. It was too painful to look at her face. Clementine's gaze flew to Bradlee. He looked at her with such disgust. It pierced through Clementine's heart like an arrow. She grasped her cousin's hands and bowed her head. "I'm so sorry! Forgive me, cousin."

Leona didn't speak. The humiliation was too much for Clementine to bear. She ran, flying past Allen and Bridget and into the heart of the Common.

She collapsed on an empty bench at the edge of the frog pond. She'd never impress Bradlee now, no matter how many prayers she prayed or how much she complimented his artwork. Hiding her face in her hands, she convulsed into tears. Sensibility couldn't fight the overpowering emotions that accompanied her affections for Bradlee. She had spoken without thinking of the consequences.

It's all Leona's fault. He'll never see me with her around.

"Aye, you've got an untamed tongue, lass," a familiar voice teased her.

"Go away, you leprechaun," she grumbled between sobs.

"Leprechaun? There you go again, lass. Speakin' yer mind and feck anyone else."

Clementine gasped. "You—are so—uncouth!"

When the boy finished hee-hawing like a donkey, he sat down beside her. His vinegary stench almost choked her.

"You and I are a lot alike."

"We are not!"

"Aye, we are. Before I came to the Home, I was much like you. In Ireland, me mam and pap were rich. I know ya don't believe it, but 'tis the truth. I thought I was king of the mountain and treated everyone like shite. Everyone in the village hated me. Everyone probably hates you, too."

"Go away!"

"No, lass. I aim to help ya. If yer smart, you'll listen."

"Ugh. Then talk fast and then leave me alone."

"A'right, I'll be quick, darlin'. Aye, you're gorgeous and dress mighty fine. But, darlin,' yer tongue needs a right taming."

Clementine stood up and slapped Fitz across his freckled face. Fitz rubbed his cheek and chuckled.

"This may take more time then I thought," he muttered.

Clementine marched away from the vile boy. She wandered around the Common, trying to shove Fitz's words out of her mind; except, the more she tried to exterminate them, the more they thrived. *Her* tongue needed taming? She couldn't believe his audacity. He didn't know her at all. Whatever he said was trash, just like him—worthless, immigrant, low-class, pauper trash.

Clementine found herself among a crowd gathered around an empty stage. A stern young lady in a pleated brown frock met her gaze. Clementine asked, "What are you waiting here for?"

"A professor from Harvard is about to give a lecture on inherited traits and the social order. It should prove quite fascinating."

"Oh, yes. Indeed. I was invited personally," Clementine pulled out Leona's pamphlet. "I was here last week for a lecture, too."

"You came to hear Jane Addams?" The woman's eyebrows rose.

A man in wire-framed glasses standing beside the woman scoffed. He interjected, "She thinks she can change things in Chicago. What a fool. What can one woman do?"

Clementine felt slighted for a second, but let the derogatory remark slide. She didn't want to anger anyone here. "My mother dragged me along with her. I didn't understand what the woman was talking about most of the time."

The man grimaced, then continued pontificating. "Jane Addams is a bleeding-heart reformer. What America should follow are the ideals set forth by Karl Marx. The Socialists have a viable plan to solve America's socio-economic problems," the man declared, his volume rising with each word.

The woman's sour expression made her disagreement quite obvious.

Clementine was confused but felt determined to contribute to the discussion. "Marx? That sounds like a German name," she said with a frown.

The man had no answer at first. His jaw tightened, and his eyebrows arched toward the center of his pince-nez. He peered down at Clementine, making her feel more petite than usual.

"You must be one of Edward Bellamy's followers. Look, girl, the bourgeois control everything. America will be destroyed by pandering to capitalists. They're too busy fighting over silver and gold standards to pay attention to the rest of us. We need a social revolution."

"A revolution? Like, a war?" the woman in the brown dress said, shaking her head.

Clementine interjected, "War is bad. My father died in a war."

The two impassioned debaters allowed a moment of silence to pass before continuing their argument. But a military officer's death wasn't enough to completely sober their passion.

The woman addressed the spectacled man, "War is always about money. Do you really believe a redistribution of wealth is the answer? People who work hard should reap the benefits of their hard work and be allowed to decide what to do with their own wealth, not have it dictated to them by the government. 'The plan of plundering each other produces nothing.' That's what

Professor Sumner of Yale says."

She turned to Clementine and explained, "He was the very first professor of sociology in America."

"Oh," Clementine responded.

This conversation befuddled her. But it pushed out Fitz's stupid voice. Clementine decided to stick around for the lecture and procrastinate returning to the *Little Wanderers'* wagon.

The Harvard sociology professor took the stage and introduced himself. He delivered a speech about the recent trends in sociology and listed the multitude of studies that were currently taking place. He threw names, words, and statistics at the crowd.

Clementine didn't comprehend much; but the crowd nodded and cheered, so Clementine did too. It was a lot like attending a sermon, except the congregation gathered here in the Common was louder and more animated in their responses, sometimes even booing.

To her surprise, the professor's lecture on the social order made Clementine feel better. It bolstered her self-esteem and pushed away the dark clouds Leona, Bradlee, and Fitz had brought into her day.

By applying current social theories expounded upon by the professor, Clementine concluded that she was misunderstood. Due to her higher social standing and superior inherited traits, Leona, Bradlee, and Fitz were not her equals. Her jealousy melted away.

The professor and his assistant sat in wooden folding chairs behind a card table. A line of people formed. The attendees shook the speaker's hand and asked questions or offered compliments. Clementine followed the lady in the drab brown dress with the high cheekbones and serious demeanor. She learned the lady had gone to college. She was a teacher with an education degree from Boston College.

"You're not from Harvard, where the professor teaches?" Clementine asked.

"Very funny," the lady replied.

Another attendee pulled on Clementine's sleeve and whispered, "Harvard doesn't take female students, you silly goose."

"Oh, yes. I forgot," Clementine replied, feeling foolish.

When it was her turn to greet the professor, Clementine extended her arm to shake his hand, as she had witnessed everyone else doing. He shook it briefly.

"Hello, young lady. Thank you for coming out on this fine fall day. What's your name?"

"I'm Clementine Elizabeth Bell."

"Are you here alone, Claudia?"

"It's Clementine, sir. Well, I was supposed to accompany my cousin, Leona."

"Leona Schaeffer?" asked the professor, to Clementine's surprise. Then she remembered the pamphlet in her pocket and pulled it out.

"Yes, Leona changed her mind about coming, even though she said you invited her personally. I hope you're not offended by her rudeness. She's an unreliable girl."

"Oh? She seemed quite reliable and mature when we met. A

spirited gal, if I recall, like her name implies, a lioness. Hartman, this girl's cousin is the one who helped me take care of your injured foot when I took you fox hunting. You don't remember, I suppose, since you were in such delirious pain."

The assistant nodded politely while he perused Clementine. She felt uncomfortable under his scrutiny and avoided meeting his eyes.

"I'm curious—what are your views on the social order, Miss Bell?" the assistant asked.

Clementine had no views on any movement, really, but she replied, "Oh, I certainly can understand why it's an important issue. You're right—Boston is overpopulated. There are too many undesirables." She'd reassembled some of the terms and phrases he'd used in his speech, hoping to sound intellectual.

The professor and the assistant exchanged glances. "Thankfully, recent studies are being conducted on the over-population and lack of regulated immigration in growing urban areas so solutions can be found. How would you suggest we address the overflow of undesirables in the city, Cordelia?"

"My name is Clementine, Professor. Couldn't they live in asylums outside the city? Boston isn't the only place for immigrants, deviants, and the mentally handicapped can live, right?"

The men nodded in approval. She'd impressed them. Clementine sighed in relief, grateful she'd paid enough attention to the lecture for her to reiterate the things she'd heard. Though she'd never given much thought to overpopulation or immigration, it seemed many others had. She couldn't remember what Miss Addams had said about the subject. Surely she'd said something...

"Well, Christina, give my regards to your cousin. Tell her I was earnestly looking forward to meeting her again. I'm giving another lecture next month. If you're free, bring her along with you."

Why does everyone prefer Leona? He can't even remember my name.

"I don't think she'll be able to come. She's starting a new job at an asylum for orphans."

"A lioness to guard orphan cubs? How apropos. Well, thank you again for coming, Caroline. Next, please!"

Clementine didn't want to return to the *Little Wanderers* art exhibit, but she had no choice. She hung her head and tried to appear as apologetic as possible.

Leona was the first person she encountered. She feigned a humble expression. "Cousin, I'm so ashamed of my untamed tongue. Please forgive me."

Leona lent her a modest smile. "I forgive you. Oh, your mother was worried sick, so she sent Allen and Bridget to search for you. She almost contracted a policeman."

"Speaking of policemen, what did that copper want to talk with you about earlier?"

Leona chewed her lip. "He was just doing his job. There's no need for you to worry, cousin. Everything is fine. Go check in with Aunt Franny."

Clementine didn't believe everything was fine, but she nodded politely. She saw her mother chatting with Mrs. Green like they were old friends.

"Oh, she's busy. Where's Bradlee? Did he sell any drawings yet?"

"Yes. The artwork is selling very well. As you can see, there are only five left."

Clementine was surprised. She thought the drawings were decent, but simple. Who really cared about boring old sketches of animals and nature scenes?

I can draw a stupid bird, and no one has ever asked me to hold an exhibition.

Bradlee's appeal had lessened after attending the professor's lecture. When Clementine considered their social order, she realized he wasn't worthy of her. He was an orphan—like that vulgar boy—a burden on the city and a drain on the economy. She was part of the social elite, the Brahmin, helping Boston progress into a strong future.

"I met your professor friend," Clementine informed Leona with a sly grimace.

"Professor Taylor? How was the lecture?"

"It was... educational. The professor thanked me personally for coming."

Fitz sauntered around the corner, whistling. "Oh ma darlin,' oh ma darlin," he murmured. Clementine scoffed at him and continued her conversation with Leona.

"He invited me to come back next Saturday and hear the other half of his speech. He said you should come, too, but I told him you were busy," Clementine said.

Mrs. Green leaned forward and smiled at Leona. "Oh, since

The Good Shepherd

Miss Leona is coming to help out early, I think I can let her have next Saturday off. Mr. Green will be back in town and I can stay with the girls. Education is a worthy endeavor. Just remember, the truth isn't as plain as some teachers profess. You must think for yourself, girls, and form your own opinions. This is a new era for American women, I can feel it."

Leona smiled at Mrs. Green, but Clementine felt burdened. All this thinking gave her a headache.

"Thief!" Mother howled, pointing at a pimple-faced boy in grungy clothes bolting into the Common. He clutched the cigar box holding the exhibit money in his spindly arms.

Bradlee and Leona ran after the thief. Clementine couldn't believe her cousin's immodesty. Fitz strained his neck to gawk at the chase, leaning unreasonably close to Clementine.

"Why do you smell like vinegar all the time?" Clementine asked him.

"It's me job at the Home—I work in the kitchen. We make our own vinegar, mostly from apples. Nothing kills fleas on an urchin like a good soak in vinegar," he said with pride. "I keep tryin' to convince 'em to make some wine, too, but Mr. Green keeps 'a sayin' nay." He chuckled. "We get visits from the clergy from time to time, so I swore to abide by the rules. Ever been stricken by a man of the cloth? Righteous anger's a powerful thing, it 'tis!"

Golly, could he talk nonsense.

"C'mon, they almost have him," Clementine exclaimed, walking at a brisk pace. Fitz flew by her in a vinegary breeze.

Leona and Bradlee caught the robber faster than Clementine

expected. They both held an arm each. The thief struggled to get free but couldn't. Fitz retrieved the box. Leona held the robber's dirty chin in her hand and demanded, "Why did you steal that money? It's for orphans."

Tears washed over the boy's pockmarked face.

"My sisters and I are gonna be orphans soon. Without that money, we won't eat tonight. The factory my pa worked in had a fire. He's dead. Ma went to see Jesus when little Cassie was born," he explained.

Bradlee patted the thief's back. He took the money box from Fitz, pulled out some coins, and gave them to the boy. By now, everyone had gathered around. Mrs. Green approached the skinny teenager. "Come to *The Home for Little Wanderers*. We can provide some temporary assistance until you get back on your feet."

"You won't take my sisters away?"

"No, we won't. Say, Fitz here could use some help in the kitchen, if you'd like a job, young man. What's your name?"

"Calvin."

"Nice ta meet ya," Fitz said, holding out his hand to shake Calvin's. Clementine wrinkled her nose. *Whoa! I thought Fitz smelled awful.*

Mother waved at someone behind them.

"Ezra!" she exclaimed.

Father walked toward the group. Allen followed him with the wagon. Father's sharp eyes examined the scene.

"What's going on here, Franny?"

Mother flashed Mrs. Green a look of desperation. The

woman stepped forward. "Hello, I'm Mrs. Green. My husband and I run the orphanage. We were just helping this young man out. How are you, sir?"

Father's scowl deepened. He ignored Mrs. Green's extended hand. Instead, he put his hand on Mother's back and led her away. When he passed Clementine, he lowered his voice and said, "Clementine, come with us. Now." She bowed her head and obeyed.

Leona jogged over to them. "Uncle Ezra, can I at least say good bye?"

Father frowned at her.

At least there's one person in the world who doesn't worship Leona.

"Do it quickly. Why are you sweating, girl?"

"There was a—nevermind." Leona wiped her forehead with her sleeve.

So unladylike.

Father grimaced at her. Clementine had never seen him look so aggravated. He was always stern and serious, but Leona brought out a side of him Clementine feared.

"Everything is settled? You have a job and a place to stay?"

"Yes, sir. Though I hope to visit."

"N—"

Mother interrupted, "Oh, yes, dear. After the lecture next week, please come to the house and I'll have Bridget prepare a meal for you. No clam chowder, I promise. By the way, where's Bridget?"

"I sent her home to start supper. What lecture?" Father asked.

Clementine jumped in, "I met a professor. From Harvard! Oh, there he is." She pointed at a man walking toward them. "Hello, Professor Taylor. It's me, Miss Bell," she shouted, waving her arm high in the air.

The professor, accompanied by his assistant, who stumbled along on his crutches, waved back and approached them.

Professor Taylor shook Father's hand. "It's good to see you again, Ezra."

"You know each other?" Clementine, Leona, and Mother asked at the same time.

"Yes, we were friends as children," the professor said. The remark caused Father's firm frown to quiver. "Leona, your cousin, Camille—"

"Clementine," Leona corrected.

"Right. *Clementine* told me you weren't interested in coming to my lecture today."

Clementine avoided Leona's eyes.

Leona replied, "It wasn't that I wasn't interested. I had a promise to keep." She turned to the assistant. "How's your leg, Mr. Hartman?"

"It's much better. Thank you. I'm afraid I don't remember much after the fall," the man said.

"How did you get hurt?" Father interrupted.

Professor Taylor spoke for Mr. Hartman. "Fox hunting is a dangerous hobby."

"Still hunting, then, William? You're getting old, like me. Maybe you should stop. Find a new hobby. Something not quite so… risky. Leave the hunting to younger men."

The Good Shepherd

Professor Taylor grinned. "I find it exhilarating and quite worthwhile. Anyway, it was wonderful to see you all. Have a lovely evening."

As the two men left, Clementine felt the tension in the air fizzle. She and Leona locked eyes.

"Cousin, I want to wish you well. I will miss you," Clementine said, with as big a smile as she could muster, hiding her real feelings.

Her cousin returned her smile and embraced her and Mother.

Father leaned over and whispered something in Leona's ear. Her pale face turned beet red.

What did he tell her?

Chapter Eight

Saturday Evening, September 23
The Home for Little Wanderers

Leona spent the journey staring out the window, obsessing over her uncle's whispered words.

The Hunters killed Goldberg.

How did he know? Maybe the man had been knifed by a hoodlum. But Leona had to consider, as her uncle implied; the Hunters had murdered him. Because of her.

How many times did I give out my name against Goldberg's instructions?

The Hunters could have found her through the farmer who brought her to Boston, Professor Taylor, Uncle Ezra, *The Home for Little Wanderers*, or even Reverend Busch. Maybe the same person who'd killed Goldberg had stabbed her in the street. She hoped could live anonymously at the orphanage. No one would think to look for a Warden there.

The late afternoon sun hung low in the sky, a fading yellow backdrop for the city's silhouette. The wagon wheels rumbled along the street, slowing in front of a large building. Two rows of identical windows reflected the lingering sunlight.

Leona had never lived in such a large place. The orphanage was three times the size of the Wickersham mansion and composed of the muddy red brick everyone in Boston called brownstone. Uncle Ezra's federal-style, three-story row house also had a ruddy face, its windows edged with black wooden shutters like all the buildings in the upscale Beacon Hill neighborhood.

Bradlee insisted on carrying Leona's travel bag. She let him, but she felt awkward. She'd been silent during the whole trip. They probably assumed she was sad to part with the Schaeffers, or anxious about starting a new job and a new life. They didn't know the truth. She was angry—at Uncle Ezra, the Hunters, and herself.

"Supper will be served in thirty minutes," Mrs. Green told them. "Don't be late. Leona, please line up the girls and escort them to the cafeteria."

Fitz ran up to Bradlee and handed him the box of remaining artwork.

"Only five pictures left?"

"Yep. I shoulda bought one. Might be worth a fortune someday," Fitz teased.

Bradlee's mouth pulled up in one corner. He pulled up his sleeves before reaching out to take the box. Suddenly Fitz grabbed his wrist.

"Yer skin is all blotchy! Looks like ya got poison ivy."

Bradlee examined his hand and shrugged.

"It can't be poison ivy. I'm not allergic."

"I thought everyone was allergic to poison ivy," Fitz replied.

"I'm not," Leona interjected. *But I've never met anyone else who isn't.*

"That's not the only thing you two have in common. You're both mighty quick runners. Ya oughta train for the marathon—both of ya. I can't believe you chased down that thief so fast." He elbowed Bradlee, "Aye, lots of chasing goin' on lately." Bradlee's cheeks turned pink.

Leona redirected the conversation. "Um… hey, Fitz, do you fancy Clementine?"

Instead of blushing from embarrassment like Bradlee, Fitz's face lit up like a lamp and he inhaled deeply.

"Aye, but the lass is an outright mess," he said, shaking his head and exhaling.

Leona smirked and said, "She lives in a different world. Some of the things she says and does aren't all her fault."

"I know, miss. I told her she's a pretty picture, but some humility would do 'er good."

Bradlee scoffed. "What did she say to that?"

"Oh, she clobbered me good," he said, with a sideways grin.

Leona and Bradlee laughed. She liked Fitz. The ragamuffin was a kind, sensitive soul. She suspected a huge, tender heart hid behind his lackadaisical exterior—a heart Clementine wouldn't think twice about stepping on.

Inside, Bradlee gestured to the right. "Your room is in the female dormitories. I can't take you to it without breaking the rules. Do you think you can find it on your own?" he asked her, rubbing his hands together.

The Good Shepherd

She couldn't believe how pale his blue eyes were. And how fast he could run. And how he wasn't allergic to poison ivy. Lost in her thoughts, she asked him a random question, "Bradlee, when is your birthday?"

"Next month—October 31," he replied.

"All Hallow's Eve? That's the same day as mine," Leona said.

"Another thing we have in common, hmm?" he said with a wink. "Strange."

Leona managed a small smile. "Yes, strange." She didn't think before asking her next question. "Do you remember your parents?"

He frowned. "So, because we have so much in common, you think you can ask me personal questions now, do you?"

"Oh, um…"

"I'm just kidding, Leona. I remember my mother a little. She was pretty. She had blue eyes and dark hair like me."

"You don't remember anything else?"

"I don't. When I think about my childhood, I remember Mr. and Mrs. Green. They're my family. I owe them everything."

Leona stopped questioning him, despite her concern. With eyes like his, she couldn't help but wonder if he had inherited a special problem, a problem *she* was destined to help him with.

And, if Bradlee *were* a lycanthrope, as a Warden, it was her responsibility to help him.

I'm jumping to conclusions. Not everyone with blue eyes had an intimate relationship with the moon. If that were the case, Leona herself would be a possible candidate.

Something fell out of her pocket. Bradlee picked it up and

handed it to her. It was the telegram Warden Goldberg had sent her in Framingham.

"Hope this isn't too important. If it wasn't for my keen eyesight, you might have lost it," he teased. She tried to return his carefree grin but failed.

"What's wrong?" He raised an eyebrow. "Is it from a beau?"

"Um, it's hard to explain. I—"

His smile faded. "It's none of my business. Everyone has secrets. Feel free to keep yours."

Leona stuffed the paper into her pocket. The telegram was all she had that linked her to Goldberg, the dead Warden. She'd never know what Warden Goldberg was. Hunter or Shepherd? Friend or foe? Mentor or attacker?

She wished her father had trained her. He'd never trusted her with his secret—how to tell if someone was a lycanthrope before their first transformation. After a Werewolf transformed, Wardens could smell them, even from long distances. But a young, unturned lycanthrope smelled human because, essentially, they still were. The first full moon after their eighteenth birthday changed everything. She'd learned this much from observation and a healthy amount of snooping.

Now that Warden Goldberg was dead, Leona's only chance of discovering Papa's big secret was to interrogate Uncle Ezra. But she wasn't allowed to visit Joy Street. Besides, he claimed he didn't use his Warden powers anymore. Maybe he didn't know, or had forgotten.

Her father had been a renowned Warden, greatly admired for his diligence and compassion. Together, her parents helped dozens of lycanthropes build sanctuaries and live safely outside the pack's communities. Some of the rogues were completely unaware of the monster lurking under their eighteen-year-old skin, waiting to be revealed by the unmerciful light of the moon. But her father had known. *How?*

The orphanage might be housing lycanthropes oblivious of their condition. Leona needed to discover what it was her father did to detect immature Werewolves, especially in light of the division in the protectorate. What if Hunters possessed this secret? She needed to know, and *soon*.

Alone with her thoughts, Leona walked down the dim hallway of the girls' dormitory. Butterflies fluttered in her stomach. Her gnawing hunger didn't help her nerves.

She stood in front of a door labeled with a brass number twelve and took a deep breath. When she opened the door, her eardrums almost burst.

Two squealing girls sprinted at her. "Are you Miss Leona?" "Why is your hair so curly?" "You're so tall!" "Do you have a beau?" "Do you snore?"

The girls continued questioning her, giggling and shrieking. Leona couldn't help enjoying the youngsters' enthusiasm.

Mrs. Green had informed her that the children were housed by age. Twenty twelve-year-old girls were in Leona's charge. Since she was younger than most dorm mothers, Mrs. Green thought placing Leona with the smallest group would be best. Twenty sounded like a lot to Leona, especially after being an only child. She worried she wouldn't be able to care for each of them sufficiently.

But as she scanned the menagerie of young, round faces surrounding her, she memorized each one. Leona couldn't wait to get to know them all.

That afternoon at the Common, Mrs. Green had briefed Leona on her girls: one was in the process of being adopted, three were entering foster homes next week, six had siblings, and two of them had been there since they were babies.

And one was brand new. "Which one of you is Regina?" she asked.

Most of the girls donned side braids and wore muslin dresses. But the girl who raised her hand wore a bright blue headscarf over a mess of dark curls.

Leona stepped toward her. "I heard that you're new here too. Is that correct?"

The girl stared at her, silent.

"Regina's dumb. She can't talk right," a girl behind Leona remarked. The rest of the room roared in laughter.

Leona fell to one knee and met the girl's eyes. She addressed her in the girl's native language. "*Ti Regina?*"

The girl's eyes brightened. "*Da! Vui govorite po Russki?*"

She held out her hand. "*Ya Leona Schaeffer, tvoya vospitatelnitsa.*"

Leona rose and addressed the rest of the children in English. "It's almost time for supper. Form a straight line, please!"

The girls scrambled and formed a semi-straight line. Regina took her hand. Leona winked at the girl. Regina giggled and winked back.

Leona felt hopeful. Though this job wouldn't be easy, it was one she could be proud of. Mrs. Wickersham would approve—and probably lecture her on setting a good example for the female sex. Caring for orphans was a heavy responsibility in the best of circumstances; and, unfortunately, she lacked the skill to identify girls who needed her help as a Warden.

Uncle Ezra wouldn't like her asking questions, but she had no choice. He was the only one who might know the answer.

Mrs. Green visited the girls' dorms every evening to say goodnight and meet with the dorm mothers to discuss concerns with their charges and review the next day's schedule.

"Any problems, Leona?"

Leona scanned the room. The girls were all in their beds, feigning sleep.

"No, ma'am."

"Good. If you have any issues, let me know. I'll tell Mr. Green. The children have a healthy fear, or rather, respect, for him."

"Yes, ma'am."

"How's Regina doing?"

Leona sighed. "The other girls tease her."

"They'll tire of that soon enough. The newest addition always gets the most attention. It will fade when the next girl arrives. They like fresh blood."

"You make them sound like predatory animals, Mrs. Green."

The kindly matron grimaced. "I believe there's both a beast

and a lamb inside all of us. Whichever receives nourishment and attention grows stronger. Remember that, Leona. The beast of hatred lurks, desiring to starve the lamb of love inside us. Reverend Busch spoke on this recently. He would be pleased that I remembered his words," the woman laughed.

"Are you a religious woman, Mrs. Green?"

Leona waited as she contemplated the question.

"I believe in love. I cannot claim to understand everything about God or the Bible. Everyone interprets it differently. But I believe the word inside the Word is love. These orphans have taught me that's one thing we can't live without. Leona, one reason I hired you is because you're an orphan too. Tell me, were you loved?"

Tears crept out of Leona's eyes. The memory of her mama's off-key voice singing Russian lullabies to her as a child rose to the surface. She could feel her papa's warm embrace, the scratch of his stubbly cheek.

"Yes."

"Then you were blessed. Follow their example. Their love has equipped you to care for these girls and guard their hearts. You're their shepherd now."

Leona's heart skipped a beat. "Excuse me?"

"You're a shepherd, dear. These are your lambs."

"Yes, ma'am."

After Mrs. Green left, Leona prayed, thanking God for her safe arrival and asking for the strength to be a responsible guardian over these children. She added one more supplication, a plea to discover her father's secret.

The Good Shepherd

Lord, make me a good Shepherd. Amen.

One of Leona's duties was to escort her group of girls to their classes. They whined and dawdled on the way to arithmetic and spelling. But no one ever complained when they walked to art class.

"Mr. Smith is my favorite teacher," a girl named Mary announced.

"Why?" Leona asked. The girls all giggled.

"He's beautiful," Regina answered slowly. The girls ignored her heavy accent, instead of teasing her like they usually did. Instead, they all nodded in agreement.

"Is he a good teacher?" Leona asked.

They shrugged, then leaned against the wall, waiting for the eleven-year-old boys to be dismissed. Before the door opened, the girls pinched their cheeks and smoothed their dresses.

Mr. Smith addressed the girls, "As always, take an apron from the bin, and put it on. Today we're going to use oil paint. It is very difficult to remove from fabric, so roll up your sleeves. Leona, could you assist the girls?"

Leona nodded and helped shorten their long sleeves while they stole glances at Mr. Smith, who appeared oblivious to their adoration.

Mary shivered slightly as Leona tightened her cuff. She rubbed the girl's hands in hers. The afternoon sun was hours away from warming the facility. The large building was drafty and cool in the mornings.

"Canvases await you on the easels at the windows. Please gather palettes and fill them with five basic colors—black, white, and the three primaries."

Leona helped Regina squeeze yellow, red, and blue onto her palette.

"What are we painting today, Mr. Smith?" Mary asked.

"A landscape. I want you to look outside the window and paint what you see."

Bradlee sat down at a chair without a canvas in front of it.

"Why aren't you painting, too, Mr. Smith?" Leona asked him, with undisguised disappointment.

He rubbed his palms together.

Leona studied his hands. "You still have a rash?"

"It's getting worse. I can't even hold a brush now."

The door opened. The girls, who had been dawdling and listening in to their conversation, suddenly began painting.

Something odd mixed in with the usual smell of the art room. Leona turned to see a man holding a bucket.

He held it up and explained, "I brought linseed oil for cleaning the paintbrushes."

Bradlee threw a cloth over the top of the bucket. "Thanks, Mr.

Green. It's awfully strong-smelling." He turned to Leona, "The girls will get a headache if it doesn't stay covered, Miss Schaeffer."

"I imagine so," Leona replied.

This was the first time she'd seen Mr. Green in person. *I should introduce myself.* She coughed. Another smell floated in the air, mixing with the linseed. She couldn't decipher it.

"How's your rash, Bradlee?" Mr. Green inquired.

"I was just telling Leona—I mean, Miss Schaeffer—that it's gotten worse."

"Have you applied the balm I gave you?"

"Sorry, sir, I didn't. It smells worse than that linseed oil."

Mr. Green's mouth lifted at the side as he chuckled. "That's because it works. Trust me, young man. I've had rashes like yours. That balm is like a miracle cure."

"Yes, sir," Bradlee replied. He opened his desk and pulled out a small tin.

"Let me open it for you," Leona offered.

She wrenched the top off. He was right. It smelled horrible. Leona pinched her nose.

Bradlee dipped his finger in the tin and smeared the balm onto his other hand. He rubbed his hands together. With a surprised expression on his face, he held out both hands and stared.

"The rash is gone! Wow—you were right, Mr. Green—it's a miracle."

Mr. Green's light eyes twinkled as he smiled. "Glad I could help. Is there anything else you need, Mr. Smith?"

Bradlee shook his head, still entranced by his healed palms.

"Then I'll be on my way. Oh—you're still able to substitute for me in the dorms on those days we talked about, correct?"

Bradlee murmured, "Mmm-hmm."

"Thanks again. Usually Mr. Martin takes my place when I travel, but he's going into town to help his siblings pack up their deceased mother's home, so he can't be here."

"What were the dates again? I should mark them on my calendar."

"October thirteenth, fourteenth, and fifteenth. It's a few weeks away. I wanted to alleviate my worried mind. And, to be honest, Mrs. Green has been insistent, if you understand me."

"It's not a problem, Mr. Green. I'm scheduling it in now." Bradlee grasped the pencil and wrote in his planner, a relieved expression dressing his face. Leona was amazed at how quickly the balm had healed his skin.

"Thanks for easing my mind, Mr. Smith," Mr. Green said, patting him on the back.

From across the room, Mary, her hands smeared with paint, called out in a panic, "Miss Schaeffer, can you scratch my nose?"

Leona stifled her laughter.

"Of course, Mary. If you'll excuse me, gentlemen. I am needed."

"Yes, Miss Schaeffer," Bradlee replied with a wink.

Leona's mind wandered as the girls painted.

October thirteenth, fourteenth, and fifteenth. The dates seemed important. Why?

Leona examined the girls' paintings. While the rest had almost completed their landscapes, Regina was only half finished. Her sky included a white crescent. The moon. Leona peered out the window. Indeed, there was a sliver of moon clinging to the azure sky.

The dates Mr. Green asked Bradlee to sub for him were the three nights of October's full moon cycle.

Leona inhaled deeply. The strange odor she smelled when Mr. Green entered the room was stronger now. She faced Mr. Green and Bradlee, conversing happily in the back of the art room as the girls painted, and inhaled again.

She had no doubts now. Mr. Green... was a Werewolf.

Chapter Nine

Clementine scratched Mr. Flufferbutter's chin. He purred with pleasure, a steady rumble possessing his furry body.

"What do you think about Leona, sweet kitty?"

To her surprise—and delight—Mr. Flufferbutter hissed.

"I agree," Clementine replied.

"Miss? You have a visitor," Bridget announced through the door.

Clementine glanced in the mirror on her armoire and tucked straw-colored hair behind her ear. Wondering who it could be, she answered, "I'll be right down!"

She descended the stairs slowly, cradling Mr. Flufferbutter in her arms. When she entered the foyer, Bridget stood there with a dapper, finely-dressed young man on crutches. He looked slightly familiar.

"Miss Clementine Bell? I'm George Hartman. I'm Professor Taylor's assistant."

"Oh! Yes, I remember. His lecture changed my life. Er—at least—it changed my mind about a lot of things. Or rather—it confirmed many ideas I'd been considering."

Mr. Hartman chuckled.

Does he find me delightful or a laughingstock?

Clementine's nerves calmed when he replied, "I understand. Sociological topics aren't discussed in most schools, not even in most colleges. In fact, Professor Taylor is one of the first professors of sociology in the whole country. Professor William Sumner of Yale was the first."

"Father says Harvard and Yale are fierce competitors," Clementine said, stroking Mr. Flufferbutter's soft head.

"That's a fact. But a little competition is healthy, wouldn't you agree?"

She twisted a strand of stick-straight blonde hair around her fingers and thought of Leona's magnificent curls.

"What brings you all the way to Joy Street from Cambridge on a weeknight, Mr. Hartman? Father and Mother are both out. I can have our servant, Allen, fetch them for you, if you like."

"Where are they?"

"Father is still at his office. It's Wednesday, so Mother is at the Lowell's playing bridge."

"Well, firstly, I would like to make a request of you, Miss Clementine. Depending on your answer, I'll assess whether it will be necessary to gain your parents' approval."

"Oh?" *Is this a marriage proposal?* Mr. Hartman was not attractive to Clementine. And he was an underling, an assistant. Did this man believe himself worthy of her? Surely not. Besides, Mother would not allow her to marry until she was at least eighteen.

"As you can see," Mr. Hartman began, "I have an injury. I could use an assistant of my own and Professor Taylor suggested you."

"Assist you?" Clementine released a breath, relieved. "But I have to attend school. It's a very prestigious school for girls. Mother wouldn't approve."

"I will speak to your parents about it, of course, but you are welcome to complete your studies in the professor's office on campus. You would be in an institute of higher learning. A tutor can be acquired for you. There are any number of intelligent people there who would relish helping you with your schoolwork. Have you taken algebra yet?"

What's algebra? But Clementine kept her expression pleasant, hoping it hid her confusion.

She replied, "N-no. I'm learning lots of other things, though. I'm quite skilled with a compass."

"I will pass that on to your tutor," he replied. His eyes twinkled, making him appear momentarily younger.

"How would I assist you at the college?"

"Simple things like carrying books and papers, pushing me along in a wheelchair—I get tired on these crutches—and fetching things for the Professor. I can't really fetch things anymore. It takes me forever to walk across campus now."

"I can do all those things."

"So, is that a yes? If your parents agree, that is?"

"Yes!"

Mr. Hartman's thin mustache curled on his face as he grinned. "I can tell already that I'm going to find it amusing to work with you, Clementine. Well, I'll visit your father and discuss the details. I need you to start as soon as possible. I'll be taking over one of the professor's classes to allow him time to prepare for his next lecture at the Common. I'll certainly need your help."

"I can't wait! I learned so much last Saturday. It was truly enlightening, and, uh, liberating. Thank you ever so much for thinking of me."

And not Leona.

"Certainly. You're a hard person to forget, Miss Bell. Good night," Mr. Hartman said. Clementine blushed at the scholarly gentleman's compliment.

"Good night," she replied. He stumbled on the rug with his crutches, but Bridget held the door for him as he exited. A cool breeze blew inside, and she closed the door quickly after him. The bang of the door echoed in Clementine's ears.

Bridget shivered. "It feels like winter out there, not autumn, Miss Clementine."

"Is Ireland cold in September?" Clementine asked.

Bridget shrugged. "I don't recall. I was a tiny lass, just three years old, when my brothers and I left Ireland with my parents. All I know are Boston Septembers."

"Oh," Clementine replied and ascended the stairs. Mr. Flufferbutter scurried along behind, racing her to the top.

D. Marie Prokop

Friday, September 29
22 Joy Street

"I received a visitor from Harvard today," Father said at supper. He wore his favorite suit coat again, the dusty blue one. Mother cocked her head and raised an eyebrow.

"Yes?"

"Professor Taylor has requested Clementine's assistance. It seems Mr. Hartman's injury prevents him from doing his job to Taylor's satisfaction."

"Assisting a professor? Clementine is no scholar," Mother replied. She patted Clementine's hand and offered her an apologetic grin.

Clementine worried they weren't going to consent. She prepared to throw a royal fit.

"I'm a good worker," she blurted out. Her argument sounded weak, even to her own ears.

"I think it's a good idea," Father said.

Clementine and her mother exclaimed in unison, "What?"

"Yes, it will be good for Clementine to see the academic world. Harvard is a beacon of intellectual fervor. Maybe she'll realize that fancy dresses and art are a waste of her energy. There're more important things, like befriending those with bright futures. You start Monday."

Giddy from the shock, Clementine replied, "Thank you, Father. Be sure to mention to your colleagues that your daughter works at Harvard."

"Clementine!" her mother scolded.

But Father chuckled. "Oh, I will. This is a prime opportunity for both of us to better our family's standing. Keep your head down and obey your superiors. Then someday, you may marry a superior, and everyone will bow to you. That's the American dream, my girl."

Her stepfather's statement prickled at her. "I'm not *your* girl," Clementine mumbled.

"What was that?" Father asked.

Clementine washed away her irritation with an agreeable smile and said, "How wise you are, Father. I promise to make you proud."

Mother sighed. "My little girl is almost a woman. I feel so old."

"You're a spring chicken, Franny. Your childlike spirit keeps us all young," Father said. Mother beamed with joy at his comment and snapped her fingers in the air.

"Bridget, bring us a bottle of Champagne. We need to celebrate."

Bridget lowered her chin sharply and spun on her heels.

Father stood, his chair scraping the floor, making a loud screech that hurt Clementine's ears.

"No, Bridget. Allow me. I want to choose the bottle myself."

"Yes, sir," she replied, curtsying as he strode past her.

When Father returned, he carried a glistening green bottle in one hand and a black velvet bag in the other. The bag was embroidered with shiny white thread.

He set the items on the table and proceeded to remove the cork from the bottle. The loud *pop* made Clementine and her

Mother gasp.

Mother held up a fluted glass for Father to fill. She handed the gold bubbly liquid to Clementine. She'd never drunk a libation, so she sipped it slowly. The bubbles tickled her lips and tongue. The cool liquid meandered down her throat, reminding her of apple cider.

"I want to give you a gift to celebrate this new endeavor of yours, Clementine. I know you're not my child by blood, but you have been my responsibility for a year now and I have grown fond of your smile. I hope I have not failed to provide for your needs and wants."

At his magnanimous words, Clementine felt sentimental. She had assumed her stepfather considered her a burden. Maybe he cared for her after all. She tried not to show her shock.

"You have done well, Father. I have never been in need. After meeting real live orphans, I have grown even more grateful of your generosity to Mother and me."

"We were lost before you came into our lives, Ezra."

By lost, she means bankrupt.

Father set the velvet bag in front of Clementine. She petted the fuzzy exterior, her fingers lingering over the silky embroidery.

"Is this a wolf?"

"Yes. The name Schaeffer is German. My grandfather came to New York from a little village outside Hamburg. This is our family crest."

"Ezra, you've never spoken about your family history. You gave me the impression there was some deep, dark secret in your past." Mother touched the velvet bag. "This is beautiful," she commented.

"Are you going to tell us a family secret?" Clementine asked. Excitement bubbled up in her like the air effervescing in her champagne glass.

Father grimaced. "There are no secrets you need to know about. As I was saying, this wolf symbol is the Schaeffer family crest. In German, Schaeffer means *shepherd*."

"Shepherd? Then shouldn't it have sheep?" Mother asked, her voice dippy. She'd practically sung the question. Her fluted glass sat empty in front of her.

"The symbol is not a simple representation. The wolf is a reminder of a shepherd's challenge—to guard his sheep from predators. It was an important symbol for my ancestors. As I have not followed their legacy of shepherding, this symbol is merely that—a symbol. It means something different to me, as I'm a lawyer. I guard assets and property rights. But you are my heir now, Clementine. It is my duty to pass on what's inside this pouch to you. And someday, you may pass it onto your heir."

Clementine couldn't imagine having an heir, a child. She hadn't even kissed a boy yet. Motherhood was a distant dream. She basked in the attention her stepfather lavished on her, longing to see what the bag held inside.

A distracting thought crossed her mind and she voiced it before considering the ramifications. "Isn't Leona your heir, Father? I mean, scientifically, she is your flesh and blood."

Father's face turned dark.

"Leona is no longer my family. She chose to leave us. My

brother possessed a similar family heirloom. It was his responsibility to pass it on to her. Unfortunately, he died before doing so. The blame rests, along with him, in his grave."

"Ezra, don't speak ill of the dead." Mother shook her head at the ceiling apologetically, her side curls bouncing against her flushed cheeks.

Clementine bowed her head, pleased to own something Leona did not.

"I'm honored, Father."

He opened the pouch, pulled out a silver pendant, and placed it in her palm. A wolf head set on an oval plate of silver.

"I can almost feel the fur," she noted. "It's so detailed. Look, Mother."

Mother agreed with her assessment. She flipped the pendant over and squinted her eyes.

"What does this say on the back, Ezra?"

"*Siehe, ich sende euch aus wie Schafe inmitten Wölfe.*"

"What does that mean?" Clementine asked.

"Behold, I send you out as sheep in the midst of wolves," Father replied with a severe expression.

"Well, it's lovely, dear," Mother said. "Is it real silver?"

"Yes. If you'd prefer, I can have it melted down and invest its monetary worth for your dowry, Clementine, though it might be wise to wait for the government to stop quibbling over the value of silver. This could be worth a few dollars today but a hundred dollars tomorrow. Or the other way around."

Clementine clutched the pendant close to her chest.

"I would never melt down such a priceless gift!" *Probably*

not.

"Keep it in a secure place. Someday you'll marry and have children of your own. Then you can tell them about your embarrassing stepfather and his awkward speech at supper, when you drank champagne and became a young woman with an occupation, a New Woman, as the newspapers describe."

Clementine dared to embrace her stepfather. She had never done this before and did it quickly. Returning to her place at the table, she gulped down the remaining champagne, maybe a little faster than she should have.

"Thank you for your permission to work, and for the gift, Father. This pendant will be my good luck charm. I'll wear it every day."

Father stared at the pendant and sighed, seemingly pleased. Then he patted her back and excused himself to the smoking room, pipe in hand.

Monday, October 2
22 Joy Street

Clementine tossed and turned all night. As the sun rose, its light peeked through her curtains and she gave up trying to sleep. Approaching her wardrobe on tiptoe, she searched through her closet to find something for a fashionable young woman to wear. She wasn't a child anymore, now that she was working.

Wait—should I dress as a Gibson Girl or a New Woman?

What would be expected at Harvard? She imagined the campus, crowded with smart young men. Her pulse raced.

What if I say something stupid? Will they laugh at me?

Suddenly she wanted to back out, to run away and hide, to stay safely in her home on Joy Street, away from the students, the professor, and Mr. Hartman forever.

According to the papers, New Women desired to gain the right to vote. Clementine didn't understand the urgency of the suffragettes. What was so horrible about being a traditional female, a classic Gibson Girl? The women's rights advocates clanged their bells so loudly. Clementine admired their fervor, though she was undecided on her views about the matter. She would find out for herself whether an occupation or domestic life suited her. This opportunity would help her discover who she was: a New Woman or a Gibson Girl.

Clementine settled on a navy-blue pleated skirt and matching peplum jacket over a baby blue linen blouse with no less than six ruffles down the center. She pinned the Schaeffer family crest to her blouse's collar. In the mirror, the silver shimmered against the light blue fabric.

Clementine, accompanied by Mr. Flufferbutter, descended the stairs and approached the dining room.

"What a smart young lady you look!"

Allen's voice echoed from the fireplace in the living room. He wiped the soot from his hands with a rag before picking up a suede cloth, dipping it in polish, and rubbing the brass fireguard.

"Thank you for the compliment."

His tight curly hair was peppered gray, but when Clementine

came to live at the house on Joy Street, his hair was raven black.

"Mr. Allen, do we have polish for silver?"

"Of course, Miss Clementine. Bridget polishes the cutlery every Monday."

"Good. I have a new piece of silver jewelry that I will need polished from time-to-time," she said, touching the pendant on her blouse lightly.

"If you just tell Bridget, she'll polish it for you, miss."

"Oh, I'd like to do it myself. I'm not a little girl anymore. I start working today!"

"Yes, Miss Clementine. Miss Franny set the trolley schedule on the breakfast table for you so you can find your way there. Best of luck to you," Allen said with a grin. His teeth were a light yellow, but his smile shone.

"Were you nervous when you first started working here?" Clementine asked.

"Well, it weren't my first job. I've been employed since I was ten. I was past nervous then, for sure."

"What kind of job was it?"

"Chimney sweep." Allen pointed to the fireplace. "I guess I haven't come very far in my illustrious career." He chuckled.

"Oh, Allen, you've done well, considering you're a... a... "

"A Negro?"

"Well..." Clementine avoided his eyes, which were equal in brightness to his smile.

"Ah, the Lord's been good to me, Miss Clementine. My pappy didn't live to see his twenty-fifth birthday."

"I'm sorry. My father died young too. He drowned on a ship,

fighting Spaniards. How did your father die?"

"I guess you might say it was a misunderstanding." Allen's eyes went to the floor and he cleared his throat. "I don't think a young person like yourself is ready to be a' hearing the details of my pappy's demise, miss. Forgive me for mentioning it."

"Oh, I…"

Clementine was flabbergasted. *Why do I converse with the servants?* The conversations always left her feeling awkward, rotten, or plain embarrassed, as if she had stumbled into a room full of naked people.

"Well, I am sorry for your loss, Allen."

"Thank you, miss." He shook his gray head. "Ah, hatred and fear. Them's evil twins, Miss Clementine. Best not to feed them."

"Right." *Could this get any more awkward?* "Excuse me, I-I better get that schedule."

"Yes, miss."

She exited the room and bumped her hip on the breakfast table in her haste. Tucking the schedule in her leather satchel, she bolted out the front door before she ran into another servant.

The street bustled with people. The trolley bell rang out a sweet tinkling noise. Clementine's heart flew into her throat. She hadn't eaten a thing, knowing her stomach would reject it. Her fingers tapped a repetitive rhythm on the seat all the way to Harvard Square.

She followed the instructions Mr. Hartman had given Father on how to find the sociology department office. She passed students in pairs, trios and quads, all male, some with full beards. They examined her as she passed, as if they were uncertain whether she was real or a ghost. Her self-consciousness heightened.

Her long blonde hair was no longer styled in two braids, like a childish pupil. Bridget had curled, fluffed, and twisted her stubborn straight hair into a fashionable pompadour. Unlike Leona's low, messy chignon, Clementine's hair was belle époque. Unfortunately, the style required twenty hairpins to secure.

She checked if her heirloom pendant was still firmly attached to her collar as she waltzed down the hall and examined the names on each door. Finally, she found a brass placard that read, "Professor William Taylor, Sociology Chair." She knocked on a wooden door, more solid and scholarly-looking than Clementine imagined she would ever be.

Professor Taylor greeted her and invited her inside.

"I'm grateful you're willing to help us out temporarily, Miss Bell. Mr. Hartman is in the library. I'm leaving to meet him there. We can walk together. I just need to grab something first." He pulled out a wheelchair. Its large wheels, like a bicycle's, squeaked as it rolled past.

"Is this for Mr. Hartman?"

"Yes. Crutches are a burden to the poor fellow. Now that you're here, you can push him around and help him recover quicker."

"Yes, sir."

They strolled down the hall. Portraits of previous academic laureates and distinguished alumni decorated the walls, including the current President of the United States, Theodore

Roosevelt, which was the most prominent. The hall resembled a proper art gallery, unlike the paltry exhibit *The Home for Little Wanderers* held in the Common.

Clementine attempted casual conversation. "I was told Mr. Hartman's injury occurred while you were hunting, sir?"

"Yes, we were assisting a friend of mine, a chicken farmer. A fox had been attacking his chickens and stealing eggs. We hunted down the pesky critter and almost caught him."

"Almost?"

"Well, the rascal escaped our grasp when Mr. Hartman was bested by a tree root. He broke his foot tripping over the devilish fiend. The shattered fibula bone pierced straight through the skin of his ankle, poor gent. Sorry, miss, I shouldn't have offered up the gory details. I hope you aren't too horrified. Anyway, we hitched a ride with a shepherd, along with your cousin, Leona— interesting girl—and delivered Mr. Hartman to a doctor as soon as possible. The cast will be on for another four weeks. Are you able to commit to helping us out that long?"

"Oh, yes. My father approved. He's quite proud of me." She adjusted her pendant.

"Jolly good. May I be blunt again, Miss Bell?"

"Yes."

"Well, I was just thinking how different you are from your cousin, Leona."

"How so?" Clementine clutched the silver pin, caressing the miniature wolf under her grasp.

They stopped at a stairwell. The professor turned the chair around. Facing backwards, he pulled it up the three steps leading to the library. The doors were massive. Clementine held one open for him, hoping her strength wouldn't give out.

"Thank you. Well, Leona was quiet and—this is just my opinion—stubborn."

"Stubborn?"

"Yes. She seems quite set in her ways."

"Well, Leona isn't related to me by blood. I'm nothing like her. I'm not stubborn at all!"

The professor grinned at her. "Is that right? I thought as much. Your mind seems more open to fresh ideas than Leona's. Hartman mentioned that you enjoyed my lecture."

"Yes, I've never heard anyone speak about sociology before."

"It's a fascinating subject. One I hope will take root and grow. Americans don't often think for themselves. They parrot what they read in the newspapers instead of researching and observing their environment. They're like sheep."

Clementine nodded, again touching her pendant, making sure it was still there.

"What an interesting decoration," the professor said, leaning close. Clementine could smell his breath. The herbal aroma of tobacco reminded her of the smelly reverend on the trolley the day she and Leona traveled to the orphanage.

"It's an heirloom. Father gifted it to me last night, in honor of my procuring employment."

"I was relieved to hear he approved of sending you to work with me. We grew up in the same town, you know. Once upon a time, I wanted to be a Schaeffer boy, too. They were renowned as the best hunters in all of New York."

"That's funny. I don't think Father even owns a rifle. Did you know Leona's father also?"

"Eben? Of course. I revered him. How is Eben?"

"He's…um… I guess you don't know…"

He stopped at the entrance to the Peabody Museum Library, backing up the chair to allow some students to enter.

"Just a minute—Miss Bell, would you wait here with the wheelchair? I need to peek around the corner and see if Mr. Hartman is still at the research desk. I'd rather not take the wheelchair in yet."

"Yes, sir."

He left her standing with the wheelchair for a minute. He returned and gestured for her to follow. She pushed the chair and glided it along the shiny wood floor.

"Now tell me, what don't I know?"

Clementine hesitated. She didn't want to shock her new employer on her first day, but it couldn't be helped.

"I'm sorry to be the bearer of sad news. Leona's parents died in a fire two years ago. Eben Schaeffer is deceased."

The professor's mouth scrunched up painfully, as if he had been stung by a wasp.

"Oh my. That *is* sad news, sad news indeed."

Chapter Ten

Thursday, October 5
The Home for Little Wanderers

Late Thursday afternoon, Leona stood on the playground behind the school, monitoring the girls during their play hour. Her eyes lazily followed their movements. Her mind was fixated on Mr. Green, the master of the orphanage—and a rogue Werewolf.

A whistle blew, signaling the end of the girls' turn. The boys would be rushing out to the playground soon. Leona herded her group of rambunctious twelve-year-old girls. "Line up! In a *straight* line. This looks like a dog's hind leg!"

She counted heads. One girl was missing.

"Where's Regina?" she asked her charges.

They pointed toward the forest. One replied, "She's collecting leaves. Like always."

Bradlee approached, leading a group of boys. He greeted Leona with a polite head bob.

"Mr. Smith, Regina is out in the woods. I need to fetch her," she informed him.

His mouth turned down as he glanced at the forest behind her. "I'll help you."

He addressed the teachers nearest him, "Mr. Fredericks and Mr. Carson, can you watch the boys? Miss Leona has a little lost lamb in the forest that needs rescuing. I think I should accompany her." The two men nodded.

Bradlee turned his sky-blue eyes to Leona. "Ready?"

Leona flashed a stern look at her most mature girl, Mary Fitzgerald. "You're in charge until I get back. Escort the others to the dorm and wash up for supper. I will return with Regina before mealtime."

"Yes, ma'am," Mary said. To Leona's surprise, Mary then approached Bradlee. Her solemn expression turned sorrowful. she asked him, "Is Fitz still mad at me?"

The question puzzled Leona. A look of compassion dawned in Bradlee's eyes, complementing his already handsome face.

"Oh, Mary, he's your brother. It's no wonder he's upset. He doesn't want to be parted from you," he told the somber, red-haired girl.

"What are you two talking about?" Leona asked.

"Didn't Mrs. Green tell you?" Mary said. "I'm leaving on the orphan train on Sunday, Miss Schaeffer. Grace and I are going to a place called Omaha. Fitz doesn't want us to go. He says we'll never see each other again." Tears escaped Mary's eyes.

Leona's heart fell. She had grown to admire Fitz's little sisters. Grace was only five, a bold, tiny female version of her brash sibling.

She leaned over and embraced Mary. "Oh, I see. Well, it's

normal for Fitz to be worried. I'm so sorry we can't talk more now, but I need to fetch Regina before it gets dark. Sit beside me at supper so we can continue this conversation. For now, I'm depending on you to be a responsible monitor in my place."

"Yes, Miss Schaeffer."

Bradlee and Leona jogged toward the tree line. They slowed as they entered the shadowy forest. Leona could understand how Regina lost track of time while exploring this beautiful world. The trees around them showcased their deep autumn garb, displaying a kaleidoscope of hues from a rich, golden-brown to a luminous yellow. Accents of bright red maple and rich amber beech trees offered finishing touches to the exquisite array.

Bradlee appeared even more mesmerized by the beauty around him than Leona was. He was the artist between them, so it was no wonder. With a devout expression, he inhaled slowly, then exhaled the cool fall air. His cheeks and nose turned rosy.

"New England in the autumn is exquisite," Leona said.

"Have you seen a lot of New England?" Bradlee asked, trudging over the variegated carpet of crunchy leaves.

"I was once a little wanderer too." Leona reminded him. "Before that, my parents traveled often, but I always stayed home with my grandparents."

"I've never been outside Boston," he replied. His sparkly eyes filled with wanderlust.

Leona cleared her throat. "Clementine told me that you were found at the harbor when you were very young."

"Yes, Mr. and Mrs. Green took me in before they came to the orphanage. When I entered *The Home for Little Wanderers* for the first time, I didn't feel like an orphan. I was already loved and cherished, unlike many of the children who have crossed that same threshold over the years."

"The Greens are certainly a unique couple. I always thought of orphanages as sad, awful places. But this place is the opposite. Can you tell me more about the orphan train?"

Bradlee kicked a broken branch out of their path and answered, "For some, the orphan train offers a brighter future. Reverend Busch sings its praises, that's for certain. I hope he's right."

"Why isn't Fitz going to Omaha with Mary and Grace?"

"He wasn't chosen. He loves it here, so I think he was partially relieved."

Leona swatted a fly away from her head. "He also fancies Clementine. A bit too much, I fear. I don't know my cousin that well, but I fear she'll never see Fitz as anything but a poor orphan. A sweet, sincere boy like him deserves someone less selfish than Clementine."

"Sweet? Sincere? I think you're confusing Fitz with *me*, Miss Schaeffer." He chuckled. "What kind of gal do you think *I* deserve?" Bradlee's playful smile brightened the shadowy autumn landscape.

Her face warmed. She cleared her throat and, instead of answering his question, pointed north toward a smattering of fiery maples and said, "I bet Regina went that way. Those leaves are too beautiful for her to resist. She's wearing a blue headscarf, by the way."

Leona walked toward the maples, fully aware of his

handsome eyes staring at her back. Over her shoulder, she asked him, "Does Mrs. Green know where Fitz's sisters are going? I mean, to which family?"

Bradlee caught up with her and walked at her right side. He shaded his eyes from the sudden bursts of sunlight breaking through the trees. His blue eyes flitted left and right, searching for Leona's lost charge.

"No—it's all set up by Reverend Busch. He visits the orphan train children a year after their departure, but refuses to discuss their situations with the Greens. He says it's confidential. I'm not completely comfortable with the orphan train. Townspeople line the children up at the train station and check their teeth, as if they were horses—I've seen that for myself. And I've heard rumors—some good, some bad—of children forced to work in the fields, requested because of their strength and gender, claimed months in advance. A lucky few live pampered lives."

Leona felt a sting of nostalgia. "I was pampered once. For a year, I was the ward of a rich widow—until I had to leave."

"Why did you have to leave? Did she die?"

Leona avoided glimpsing Bradlee's pale blue eyes, so akin to Luke's.

"No, I bet Mrs. Wickersham will outlive us all," she said with a laugh. "I was finally able to seek out my only remaining family member, my father's brother."

Bradlee pushed a low hanging branch out of Leona's way. She ducked under his arm, her eyes and ears scouting the dense forest for signs of Regina. They turned east, toward the steady cadence of crunching leaves.

"That must have been difficult," Bradlee remarked, his voice muted.

"It was. I had no memory of my Uncle Ezra, so I didn't know what to expect. My father always said they were *estranged*. I didn't know what *estranged* meant until I was older. I had hoped to find a home with my uncle, but he refused to take me in. He's nothing like my papa. He's selfish, arrogant, and—"

She stopped. She couldn't explain her disappointment in her uncle, the Normalizer, who was a coward and demanded she be a coward too. Leona was confident in her decision to part with him, especially in light of the Hunters' rebellion. She could never stand by and allow rogues to be exterminated indiscriminately. Her parents would never approve of such things.

"Did something happen that made you start your work here early?" he asked. "That day in the Common, I recall Clementine acting strangely. Your uncle was standoffish, but your aunt appeared sincerely crestfallen about your departure."

Leona frowned.

"Clementine's impulsive and I've forgiven her. Aunt Franny is almost too nice. But my uncle? Well, like I said, he isn't anything like my father."

"What was your father like? Unless talking about him depresses you—"

"Talking about him makes me stronger, though it also makes my heart ache. He taught me that love requires sacrifice. My parents were good people—compassionate, strong, brave, and humble. They weren't rich, but they had many gifts."

Like the ability to detect immature lycanthropes.

"He sounds like Mr. Green—good, kind, strong, sacrificial. I've caught him staring at the sky sometimes, especially at night, looking as if he were about to weep. Running an orphanage is a tough job."

Her head bowed. Her eyes focused on the leafy ground as she asked Bradlee, "Do you trust Mr. Green?"

Bradlee was taken aback by her question. "Y-yes. With my life."

Leona smiled, half-relieved. She couldn't be certain yet, but she expected Mr. Green was a responsible rogue, unlike Mr. Harris.

After all, Mr. Green had a regular substitute for his inevitable absence on those days each month, so it was likely he had long ago established a sanctuary. His wife must be aware of his condition, though she was not a lycanthrope herself, which was rare, and forbidden by the Council. Leona suspected Bradlee had no knowledge of the man's condition, since he didn't act secretive or nervous when she asked him about Mr. Green.

Soon she would have to confront the man and introduce herself as a Warden, as she'd seen her parents do time and time again. Waiting any longer was foolish.

Her ears perked at the sound of whistling in the distance. They walked toward it.

The whistling grew louder. Bradlee and Leona exchanged smiles and pushed through a copse of junipers. Their smooth evergreen fronds parted like a curtain, revealing the object of their search.

Leona greeted her, "*Privet, Regina. Mui tebya iskali.*"

The girl's eyes were focused on the smattering of leaves in her pinafore. She smiled up at Leona, then tossed the leaves into the air and caught a large yellow one as it floated down.

"*Pora muit ruki pered uzhinom,*" Leona told her, explaining it was time to wash up for supper.

"You speak two languages, Miss Schaeffer? I'm impressed," Bradlee remarked.

"My mother's parents were Russian immigrants."

"I like discovering new things about you," he said. His comment caused Leona's heart to skip a beat. Her foot slid on some wet leaves. Bradlee caught her before she landed flat on her back onto the moist ground.

"T-thanks," she said.

Regina waved the yellow leaf over Leona's face, fanning her.

"You swoon?" she asked, giggling.

Leona stood up, backed away from Bradlee, and grabbed the runaway orphan's hand.

"*Poshli,*" she said cheerfully in Russian. She turned to Bradlee and said the same thing, but in English, "Let's go."

"*Poshli,*" Bradlee copied. Regina giggled some more. He grinned at her and then at Leona, his crystalline eyes sparkling.

The three returned to the playground. Regina waved her golden leaf at Bradlee as they parted ways.

Leona sensed Bradlee's eyes staring at the back of her head again. His gaze remained fixed on her until she entered the building. Undeniably pleased, yet bewildered by this, her heart fluttered.

The Good Shepherd

Leaving Mary in charge once again, Leona left the dormitory. Mrs. Green passed her in the hall, on her way to check in with the laundry staff downstairs. When asked, she informed Leona that Mr. Green was doing paperwork in the main office.

Leona knocked on the door. Mr. Green opened it a crack.

"May I speak with you—in private?" she asked him.

"Sure, Miss Schaeffer."

She entered the office and closed the door behind her.

Clearing her throat, Leona said, "I know what you are."

The pale blue of Mr. Green's eyes flashed silver. "What I am?" he replied. His full beard hid his facial expression.

"Mr. Green, I'm a Warden."

His eyes darted back and forth, as if looking for the quickest exit, then narrowed at her. "I've heard the Wardens are now a divided house. Which side are you on, Miss Schaeffer?"

Beads of sweat appeared on his forehead. His Werewolf scent became more pronounced.

"Calm yourself; I'm a Shepherd," she replied quickly, hoping to subdue his fright.

He sighed. "I'm a responsible man. I've never—um—Jane and I have taken every precaution imaginable. You can trust me."

"Unfortunately, I've heard that before. And people died. My *friends* died. I can never let that happen again. May I inspect your safeguards? I assume you have a hidden sanctuary."

"I do," he replied.

Leona struggled inwardly. But she had a job to do. An

interrogation was necessary to determine the next course of action. It's what her parents would've done. This man ran an orphanage, one that sincerely cared for the children residing within its walls. Bradlee trusted him completely. Could she?

"How long have you been without a pack?" she continued.

Mr. Green sat down. "Since I met Jane. They made me choose—them or her. I chose Jane."

Leona was shocked. Leaving the pack was a rare occurrence; leaving for love was unheard of. Her faith in Mr. Green's discipline wavered. Papa used to say that love was a more powerful intoxicant than whiskey. And more dangerous.

She replied, "Lycanthropes aren't allowed to marry humans, right?" If only Papa had taught her the Warden Code, then she wouldn't have to ask this question. She would know. *What else am I ignorant about?*

Mr. Green's eyebrow rose. But he answered. "Correct. This is one area both the Wardens and the packs agreed on. Intermixing with humans has always been discouraged, often punished."

"That's a very risky choice you made," she commented.

"Nevertheless, it was the best choice. Jane knows what I am and understands what I need to do to keep everyone safe. We work together to ensure this. By the way, Jane will never leave my side, so if you report us to the Council, you'll be hurting her as well."

Report to the Council? She'd never considered this. Her parents had always avoided involving the Council. Besides, she had no idea how to contact them even if she wanted to.

The Good Shepherd

She wanted to trust Mr. Green. But the memory of Luke and Justine—and the baby left her unable to fully trust another Werewolf. Yes, Mr. Harris had been a haphazard, drunk groundskeeper and Mr. Green was an upright, philanthropic community leader. Still, mistakes happen. And there were children at risk. She groaned.

"I want to trust you. Mr. Smith trusts you. But the children—"

"Can I show you my sanctuary? Would that help?"

"Yes, it would."

They made plans to meet at midnight. Leona turned to go.

She pushed the door of the office open fast, but it stopped suddenly.

"Ow!"

Leona leaned her head out the door. A freckled hand rubbed a familiar mop of reddish-brown curls."Fitz?"

Fitz rubbed his freckled forehead and grimaced at her. "Miss Leona? 'Ello."

"What were you doing there? Everyone else is getting ready for bed." She worried he had overheard their conversation. Though, if he had, there was no way he could've understood it.

"Aye, Miss Leona. I was delivering this jug of apple cider vinegar to the office. I was about to set it down outside the door when ya clobbered me in the head. Why are you here?"

Leona tried to think up a believable reason.

"I—uh—had an issue with one of the girls I needed to discuss with the Greens."

"It wasn't my sister, was it?"

"No, it wasn't Mary." She tilted her chin, taking a moment to examine him. What was his story? "Fitz—if you don't mind telling me—when did you come to live here?"

They walked together down the hall toward the kitchen.

"Da ran off when I was ten and Mary was seven. Mum went to work at a factory. Grace was barely weaned, but Mum had run out of money to feed us. Then she got the consumption. When she passed, we were brought here. *Little Wanderers* is my home, my sanctuary. That's why I could never go with my sisters on the train, even if someone out there wanted me. I can't leave the best home I ever had. No strangers could ever replace the Greens. That skinny, rambling preacher man picked my sisters to leave on that damned orphan train. They act like they won some bloody prize."

"Fitz!"

"Excuse my language, Miss Leona. I'm not proper, like Bradlee. Come to think of it, I've *never* heard him swear—not a word—even when he stubbed his toe."

Leona grinned, but then turned serious. "Fitz, you're scaring your sisters by telling them the orphan train is bad."

"I'm only speakin' the truth. I've heard stories about orphans, both lads and lasses, leaving on that train with high hopes only to end up working like slaves in the corn fields of Iowa or the factories of Chicago. Some get beaten by them who's meant to care for 'em. The orphan train is a gamble, not a guarantee."

"But Mary and Grace could be placed with families who will love and cherish them."

"Not everythin' goes as planned in this world. You knows that, Miss Leona. I know ya do."

Leona grimaced, feeling the pain in the truth of this. "Let's hold on to hope, Fitz. God will provide."

"Aye, but the Lord must be one busy bloke, seeing as he ain't rescuing everyone every single time they cry his name, is he?"

Leona couldn't refute his statement. "My grandfather always said the Lord does as he pleases, and what pleases him most is for us to be lights in this dark, dark world."

Fitz sighed. "Sometimes the dark just seems so bleedin' dark, lass, pardon my language."

"I know, Fitz. Trust me, I know."

It seemed like every time Leona had found rest, she'd entered a new fight. She was constantly kicking against the darkness. First her family died, then Justine. Exacting mercy on Luke and Mr. Harris still weighed heavily on her heart. She'd been abandoned by Uncle Ezra, and Warden Goldberg was murdered before she'd had a chance to meet him. She might never be properly trained as a Warden. She was truly alone.

During their conversation, Fitz kept rubbing his forehead. Now it was redder than a ripe tomato. Leona pulled his hand away. "Stop. You're making it worse. Is there still ice in the icebox? Go wrap some in a cloth and hold it against the bump." She sighed. "I'm so sorry I hit you with the door, Fitz. Can you forgive me?"

"Aye, Miss Leona. I suppose I should follow the sweet Lamb o' God's example. Don't mention it to the reverend, though. I'm not ready to be nice ta him yet. Anyways, I forgive ya for clobbering me in the noggin, Miss Leona." He made the sign of the cross sloppily and bowed his head. When his chin rose, his bright face, though sincere, held a hint of mischievousness.

"Well, I better go get tha' ice. G'night!"

"Good night, Fitz."

At midnight, Leona followed the Greens down the dusty road on the south side of the orphanage. She rode a dappled palomino with a beautiful gold mane, introduced to her as Hugo. Mrs. Green rode side saddle behind Mr. Green on a fat gray mare named Myrtle.

Mr. Green patted Myrtle's side. "This old lady and I have been friends for a long time, though she didn't trust me much at the beginning, either, Miss Schaeffer."

Leona grasped the reins of the pretty palomino. The muscular steed strode confidently along the road but maintained a comfortable distance behind the Greens.

The sky was dark and bedazzled. A dozen twinkling stars and a thin crescent moon became silent witnesses to the odd party journeying below.

Mr. Green guided Myrtle off the wide road. They traveled along a thin dirt trail through the forest for a few miles. The salty aroma of the sea became stronger.

Leona's stomach wrenched. *I'll never get used to that repulsive smell.*

Mr. Green commanded Myrtle to halt. "We'll tie the horses up here and continue the rest of the way on foot."

The women followed him up a rocky path. Everyone carried

a lantern. Eventually, Mr. Green announced, "Here's the cabin."

He placed a key into the large metal lock hanging on the door and turned it. The women entered first.

Mrs. Green hoisted her lantern up and to the left, illuminating a door at the back of the room. Five padlocks adorned it. "That door leads to the cellar where Teddy stays during his... transformations. I'm the only one with spare keys." She proceeded to unlatch each lock.

They descended the stairs. Leona raised her lantern and examined the shadowy cellar. A large cage sat in the center of the room. Four thick metal rings were bolted to the stone floor outside it, attached to chunky iron chains. Mr. Green marched over to the cage and sat on the floor. Mrs. Green clasped restraints over his arms and legs. She fettered his neck with a thick metal collar.

Mr. Green squirmed uncomfortably in his manacles. The hairs on the back of his hands rose. He jerked on the chains. The clanging of metal reverberated throughout the confined space. The harsh echo hurt Leona's ears.

"Is this safe and secure enough to satisfy you, Miss Schaeffer?"

Leona nodded. Surely this setup was able to hold even the strongest, angriest Werewolf in place.

Mrs. Green freed her husband and kissed his hairy cheek. He rubbed his wrists and took purposeful, slow breaths. His icy eyes met Leona's.

"I know the rule."

"The rule?" she asked.

"No second chances."

"Right. No second chances," she copied.

"If I take a human life, you must exact mercy."

Mrs. Green broke into sobs. "You mean you'll kill him, right? Just say it, Leona. You'll kill him," she cried, choking on her words. She clasped her hand over her mouth, attempting to hold in her fierce sobs.

Leona remained stern, mimicking her Papa. "Only if he kills first. His desire to taste human blood will be unstoppable."

"We understand, Miss Schaeffer," Mr. Green replied, grasping his wife's hand firmly.

The conversation with the Greens and the trip to the sanctuary helped to settle Leona's anxiety. She felt assured they had done everything they could to keep Mr. Green and those around him safe. As long as he found shelter in the sanctuary before the light of the full moon shone in the night sky, Leona was confident his iron locks were strong enough to hold him.

But Leona's confidence in herself was shaky. After all, she'd failed to protect Justine. She barely knew what she was doing, so she'd copied her parents' confidence when they'd confronted rogues. Her mother had been a skilled fighter. All Wardens possessed the ability to fight a Werewolf. It came instinctively. Leona wished confidence did too.

By God's mercy, she'd never have fight Mr. Green. But if she had to, she would. The safety of everyone depended on her being a good Shepherd. She touched the silver pin in her hair, always there, waiting.

Leaving the protection and comfort of a pack was uncommon. Mr. Green had rejected his lycanthrope community for a human woman. Someone from the pack might be watching Mr. Green, ready to attack him if he exposed them. For their own safety, Werewolves preferred to remain a myth. The packs would do whatever it took to keep their existence a secret. They had their own system of justice. Leona knew less about that than she did about the Warden Code.

Mr. Green lived without a pack to be with the woman he loved. It was romantic, albeit dangerous, Leona admitted.

A tug on her foot interrupted her thoughts. It was past midnight.

"Yes, who is it?"

"Regina."

Leona sat up. The outcast had changed over the last week. Her greasy, tangled hair, along with her Prussian blue headscarf, had been washed with lye soap and rinsed with vinegar to kill any possibility of lice. It had taken an hour to comb out the tangles, even after applying a good amount of lanolin to her long tresses. Standing by Leona's bed in her bleached white dressing gown, she resembled an angel.

Regina held up a piece of paper. An image of an oak leaf resided in the center, made by placing a sheet of paper on top of a fresh leaf and rubbing it lightly with a stick of colored wax.

Leona took the paper, holding it at the edges so she wouldn't smudge it. "*Spasibo*, Regina. It's beautiful."

"I am happy you are here," Regina spoke slowly.

Leona's heart filled with warmth. Like so many others, *Little Wanderers* had become her new home, her sanctuary.

Still, she knew better than to get too attached to the children, as Mrs. Green had recommended, because they could leave at any time. They were not her children, just her sheep to guard.

"I'm glad to be here, too. Now, go to bed, *moya malenkaya hudoznitsa!*"

Regina's smile reached her ears. She was clearly pleased to be called an artiste. Skipping away, she hummed a happy tune as she left Leona's bedside.

Leona stared at the sketch. *Life isn't always all dark and burdensome. Some days the light wins.*

Instead of her usual nightmare featuring growling beasts with ice blue eyes, that evening Leona's dreams were filled with a mixture of images—iron chains, golden leaves, a tilted smile, and a whistling train.

Chapter Eleven

"Professor Taylor is continuing his series on natural selection in the Common. In his next lecture, he's going to report on a controversial new topic. He'll need to bring Charles Darwin's renowned book as a visual prop for the audience. Clementine, could you locate *On the Origin of Species* on the bookshelf for me please?"

"Sure, Mr. Hartman," Clementine said, retrieving the leather-bound volume and handing it to him.

"Please, call me George. You make me feel old when you address me so formally in private. I'm only eight years your senior. We could be siblings."

Clementine smiled politely at Mr. Hartman. Based on their appearance alone, it was believable they could be related. They resembled each other—dark blonde hair, green eyes, round faces, though Mr. Hartman's circular face was obscured by his slight mustache and brief beard. His dark brown bowler was much more fashionable than the old Victorian top hat Father wore.

"But I hardly know you."

"Ask me questions, then. Anything you like!"

"All right. Where are you from, Mr. Hart—um—George?" Clementine asked.

Mr. Hartman flipped through the book, found what he was searching for and put a piece of scrap paper in the crease before closing it.

"Ah, you noticed I don't possess a Brahmin accent, hmm? That's because I'm from New York."

"New York City?" Clementine asked with sincere excitement.

Mr. Hartman's mustache rose on one side. "Nowhere near as exciting as that. I'm from Rochester, in the western part of the state. But I've been to New York City many times. I saw a play there recently."

"Really? I've never seen a play. Father isn't fond of the theatre. Mother and I dream of going someday. What did you see?"

"*The Wonderful Wizard of Oz*. It was more of a musical. Vaudeville, perhaps? Have you read the book by L. Frank Baum? The newspapers claim it's the first American fairytale. As a sociologist, I find that idea fascinating. It begs the question—does entertainment reflect culture or does culture reflect entertainment?"

"I don't know. I haven't read it, and I don't know much about sociology. I'm learning, though."

Mr. Hartman strained his neck as he scanned the shelves behind Clementine. He pointed to the left, on the opposite end from where *On the Origin of Species* had been resting.

"Take my copy. It's a fun read, with witches, munchkins, and a twister. It takes place in Kansas—and in the fictious land of Oz. There's some speculation about Mr. Baum's fairytale being allegorical, though he denies it. Proponents of the silver standard claim Oz represents ounces, a reference to silver. Do you know what allegorical means, Clementine?"

"Of course," she replied, though she had no idea what the word meant. She often fell asleep during writing class.

Mr. Hartman continued, "Then, as you must already know, such stories include symbolic representations. For example, the Wizard in the story represents the bankers of today and Dorothy's silver slippers represent the concept of silver as a precious, standard commodity. This idea irritates the gold standard proponents, like our president—and Harvard alumni— Mr. Roosevelt."

"Then entertainment reflects society."

"Ah, you *are* learning! But you could also make an argument that this is a case of entertainment attempting to *influence* society. It's food for thought, indeed. Something a person of influence, like yourself, should ponder."

Ooo… a person of influence… I like that.

Clementine blushed. She pulled *The Wonderful Wizard of Oz* off the shelf and examined it.

This better not be one of those books that teachers claim to be interesting but turn out to be an awful bore. There were witches in Shakespeare's plays too, and Clementine didn't enjoy them at all.

Stopping at an illustration of a scarecrow, Clementine's brain manufactured an image of Fitz. She guffawed. That little leprechaun was just as frumpy and stupid-looking. Stifling her amusement, she attempted to look studious. After all, she was at Harvard.

"Would you do me a favor?" Mr. Hartman asked. "I left my notes for tomorrow's class over on Professor Taylor's desk. Could you fetch them for me?"

Clementine nodded, *The Wonderful Wizard of Oz* held tight in her hand. She walked through the door connecting the two men's offices. Mr. Hartman's office was a transformed closet with a modest-sized desk taking up most of the space. Professor Taylor's large desk was ironically more cluttered. She searched the professor's massive messy desk for the class notes. She'd come to recognize their handwriting and spied Mr. Hartman's distinctive curly longhand script.

Ah- ha!

As she snatched the assistant's notepad, something underneath caught her attention—a scrap of unlined paper with a list of names. What grabbed her attention was the first name on the list—Eben Schaeffer. Holding the paper closer, she read the other names listed under it: Katarina Schaeffer, Leona Schaeffer, and finally, Ezra Schaeffer. The names Eben, Katarina, and Ezra were crossed out. Leona's name was circled. The chicken scratches of Professor Taylor's handwriting were undeniable.

Why did the professor write this?

Mr. Hartman called to her, lifting his whiskered nose above the book he'd been reading.

"Clementine? Did you find it?"

The Good Shepherd

"Yes! I'm coming!" she replied, the notepad in her hand, on top of the borrowed book.

Clementine made a speedy decision. She picked up the odd list, folded it up, and stuffed it into *The Wonderful Wizard of Oz*.

Sunday, October 8
The Home for Little Wanderers

"Welcome, Reverend Busch!" Mrs. Green said, waving the pastor into the orphanage foyer. "Please make yourself at home. The children are excited to hear your message."

"It's my privilege to commission the blessed children of the orphan train. How grateful they must be to find asylum and shelter in homes where they are needed and welcomed. To God be the glory."

"To God be the glory," Mrs. Green repeated. She ushered him into the waiting room usually reserved for visitors interested in adoption. Framed art lined the walls. Rev. Busch stood staring at the artwork instead of taking a seat.

"This is an interesting drawing," he commented, pointing to a charcoal sketch of *Little Wanderers*.

"Yes, one of our teachers, a former resident, drew that. He's now an art teacher for the intermediate age students."

"I would love to meet the lad. His skills are impressive."

"His favorite medium is charcoal. Sometimes he even whittles pine branches and burns them to use for drawing."

"What a devoted artiste—using the most rudimentary resources of the earth! The Creator himself formed Adam from dust. How long has this young man been at the Home?"

"Teddy found him when he was four years old. His parents never came to claim him. We adopted him right before we came to *Little Wanderers*. He's the reason we become caretakers."

The reverend sighed. "God is most pleased with you, I am sure, for giving these city urchins a home. If only they were as gifted as your son. Some people have difficulty finding a way to contribute to society. Art is, sadly, an overlooked blessing. The church was once the largest patron of the arts, but, alas, our renaissance is at an end."

"I don't know about that, Reverend. Have you seen the new cathedral in town? The beauty of the stained-glass windows there brought me to tears. I praise the Lord for such delightful artistry."

"Are you referring to the series of stained-glass renderings of the so-called 'stations of the cross?' That's a papist display. As Protestants, our faith and understanding of God's word is not subjugated to or regulated by Rome. We cannot bestow value to the mystical practices of the Catholics. That new Irish Catholic mayor of ours had something to do with that frivolous waste, I assure you. They could have spent the money on charity instead."

Mrs. Green wrung her hands together. She stared at Bradlee's simple, yet impressive rendition of the Home in black and white

148

and took a slow breath.

"God will provide, Reverend," she responded.

"Yes, of course He will." He cleared his throat and turned a knob on his pocket watch. "What time is it?" he asked her. "I forgot to wind this last night. I didn't realize how dependent I've become on knowing the exact hour and minute. I'm quite a legalist on the matter of punctuality."

Mrs. Green gestured to the clock on the wall with large scripted Roman numerals. The preacher frowned at it.

She cleared her throat. "The children are washing up. The dorm monitors will escort them to the chapel soon."

"Good. I pray the farewell ceremony can begin promptly at nine. I have to perform a wedding at noon."

"We'll do our best, Reverend Busch."

"May that be sufficient," he replied.

Leona hadn't intended to overhear their conversation, but she didn't want to interrupt, so she had waited outside the room for a chance to enter and ask Mrs. Green for advice.

When she came in, the sweet stench of tobacco emanating from Reverend Busch overwhelmed her.

"What is it, Leona?" asked Mrs. Green.

"Well, Mary and her sister are crying uncontrollably. It seems that on the playground yesterday, one of the girls regaled them with horror stories about orphan train children who met terrible ends, ma'am. They fear the train will take them to their doom."

"What superstitious nonsense, young lady," Reverend Busch replied. "The orphan train isn't a horror tale. It's a blessing. A blessing, I say!"

His ears turned red with fervor.

"Excuse me, sir, I was addressing Mrs. Green," Leona said. Today it was more than his tobacco stench that repulsed Leona. Her recent conversation with Fitz about darkness in the world prodded her to defend the girls' understandable anxiety.

"Well!" He scowled at her.

Clearly, he had never been an orphan. Leona endeavored to explain their state of mind, "The children's fears are not unfounded, Reverend. Can you promise they will all grow up in loving homes?"

"They will live in God-fearing homes. Is that not enough?"

"No," Leona stated. He stared at her, silent.

Mrs. Green stepped between them. "Are the girls dressed and packed yet?" she asked.

"Yes, but they refuse to leave the dorm. Would you come speak to them? Please?"

Mrs. Green grasped Leona's arm gently. "Of course."

The reverend clucked his disappointment. "It appears I need to revise my devotional and impress upon the children the importance of humility," he said.

The honorable statements he once made to her and Clementine on the trolley were muddied by this side of him. Submission and gratitude were Christian traits, but so were empathy and kindness. Jesus, the Good Shepherd gathered children into his arms. *For the kingdom of heaven belongs to such as these.*

Leona stepped back to avoid breathing his repulsive air, inhaled deeply, and then addressed the man, "Sir, these children are orphans. Their lives have been turned upside down by death, sickness, or poverty. Can you guarantee they will be delivered to people who will cherish them? Can you assure them that they will not be abused and neglected? Can you promise them this?"

The reverend's eyes fell. He inhaled deeply and replied, "Young lady, you are over-reacting. Children are a gift from God."

"God isn't adopting these children, Reverend—human beings are. Human beings with both a good and a bad nature."

The reverend was dumbstruck. Leona wiped her eyes. She hadn't realized she'd been crying as she spoke to the man. She turned away from the reverend and said to Mrs. Green, "I apologize, ma'am. It seems I am quite emotional today."

"I understand, Leona. You bear an especially large burden on your shoulders. I know you've grown fond of your wards, but this is a temporary sanctuary for most. Over the years, I've watched many children leave *Little Wanderers* on the orphan train and my heart aches for days afterwards. We must trust in the Lord's provision."

Her words reminded Leona of dear Mrs. Wickersham.

"By His grace, I will try," Leona replied.

Mrs. Green squeezed her hand. Despite the authority Leona possessed over Mrs. Green's husband as a Warden, the two women were united in their concern for the children's welfare.

"Dear Leona, trying is all any of us can do."

Reverend Busch's devotional was a deep theological treatise on chapter four of Ephesians. After the children were severely cautioned not to grieve the Spirit, those children taking the orphan train were loaded onto a wagon. They would leave Boston on a train at the brand-new South Central Station.

Mr. Green started the horses, with Fitz sitting between him and Mrs. Green. They departed *Little Wanderers,* leaving whispers of dust circling behind them on the road.

Bradlee stood beside Leona. "It's hard to say goodbye," he commented.

She took a deep breath and nodded, afraid that if she spoke, her sorrow might overcome her. Bradlee slid his arm across her shoulders. She felt stronger with him there, holding her. But she couldn't allow him to be so kind to her.

Reluctantly, she slipped under his arm and excused herself.

"I'm sorry if I offended you," he said, walking briskly to keep up with her.

"I'm not offended. I just—"

"Just what?"

"I prefer to be alone. I'm used to it."

Bradlee's eyes twinkled jauntily as he replied, "Everyone needs a friend, Leona. May I be your friend?"

Leona smiled a little and tipped her chin, though she wasn't sure she wanted Bradlee to be just a friend. She couldn't deny feeling a deeper attraction. But it was for naught. She could only marry another Warden.

"How long have you and Fitz been friends?" she asked him, staring at the wagon in the distance.

"For about six years, I suppose." He gasped. "Oh, no!"

She was confused by his outburst. "What?"

"I forgot—I promised to take Fitz's shift in the kitchen. If you're free, I could use some company."

She sighed in relief. Kitchen duty wasn't a disaster, after all. "You're a good friend, aren't you?"

He threw her a beguiling look. "I'm a *great* friend." Sincerity and hope gleamed from those lovely eyes of his.

Leona's heart raced. She had secrets. Dangerous, unbelievable secrets. She and Bradlee could never be anything more than friends. But what if she couldn't settle for mere friendship with this beautiful, sincere, intelligent, and talented young man?

They entered the kitchen, bustling with helpers washing dishes, cutting vegetables, and organizing the pantry. Some of them stood on stools to reach the top shelves. Fitz loved this kitchen. The place seemed dull without him dancing around it, checking on the progress of the soup for dinner, or snatching a roll from the hot oven "to inspect its doneness."

"What job do you have for me, Calvin?" Bradlee asked. The reformed thief from Boston Common smirked at Bradlee. He was Fitz's protege now.

Calvin shoved a wooden box into Bradlee's arms. "Polishing silverware. Have a blast," he said, grinning from ear to ear.

"At least we don't have to bottle the vinegar," Leona whispered under her breath. She didn't desire to smell like rotten apples or to spend her time swatting at gnats.

Bradlee's neck muscles bulged as he carried the heavy box to a table. He set it down with a thud. Leona tried not to laugh as he wavered on his feet after relinquishing the load.

He pulled out a chair for her to sit in. She obliged.

"Where's the polish?" she asked.

Calvin set a jar of paste and two white rags on the table. "Here ya go."

"Thanks again," Bradlee said. "Maybe we *should* have taken you to jail instead of putting you to work in the kitchen."

"Ha-ha, Mr. Smith. Afraid of getting your hands dirty?"

Bradlee shrugged.

"His hands are always dirty," Leona commented. "He's an artist."

She examined his dark cuticles and his smudged forefinger and thumb, holding his wrist in the air as she displayed it to Calvin. Looking up, she found Bradlee grinning at her holding his hand. She released her grip and cleared her throat, looking away.

They polished the knives, forks, spoons, and serving utensils until they could see their reflections in them. The muscles in Leona's hands ached. She glanced at Bradlee's hands.

"Bradlee! Your skin's all red and blotchy. Go wash off the silver polish. You must be sensitive to it."

He stared down at his hands in shock. "Good grief. Not again." He rose and washed his hands thoroughly.

"I'll put these away," Calvin said, dismissing them from the kitchen.

"Let me see your hands now," Leona demanded when they reached the common area, hoping a good wash had helped. He sat down on a sofa and held them out to her.

Leona shook her head. The horrible state of his skin was undeniable.

"Do you have more of the balm Mr. Green gave you?"

He nodded, then sighed. "I'll put it on later. I was hoping to spend some time with my friend." That hopeful smile of his returned.

Leona smirked. "I'm sorry, but I need to go to the dorm now. Some of the girls are especially upset about Mary leaving. And they still pick on Regina. I'll have to defend her until they get weary of it."

A look of disappointment washed over his countenance, but his eyes twinkled. "Did Regina give you her leaf rubbing?"

"How did you know about that?"

"She carried that leaf around for days. Before it dried up, I showed her how to make an impression of it. I thought she wanted to keep it for herself, but she wanted to give it to you. She really likes you."

Leona grinned. "She's a sweet girl. I'm glad I can be here for her."

"I don't blame her for liking you. You're an amazing person, Leona," Bradlee said. He leaned closer. She forgot how to breathe. Her eyelids fell as she slowly leaned toward him, pulled by an invisible force, like a magnet to iron.

"Miss Schaeffer? Hurry! Regina's bleeding!" one of Leona's girls shouted, running down the hall toward them.

Bradlee stood up quickly. "I guess this is goodbye for now," he said. "I can't go down the girls' dorm hallway with you. I do hope everything's all right."

"Me too. Well… goodbye," Leona said. She felt like a page being torn from a book as she walked away from him but considered poor Regina and sobered.

When she arrived in the dormitory, Regina's thumb was wrapped up and the bleeding had stopped.

"Who bandaged this?"

A large girl named Meredith raised her hand. She was one of the girls who teased Regina the most.

"What did you use?"

Meredith lifted her skirt. The hem was ripped.

"Smart thinking, Meredith. You did good. I'm proud of you." The girl's chest puffed and she tipped her head, then returned to playing with the others.

Leona led Regina to the water basin in the back of the dorm and washed the wound with soap and water, replacing the emergency wrap with a clean cotton cloth. As she tucked in the end of the bandage, Regina broke into sobs.

"What's wrong? Does it hurt?" Leona sked.

She spoke in English. "No. I am sad."

"Sad? Why?"

"I miss Mama."

Leona held Regina tight and let her cry. She missed her mama, too.

The dorm was unusually silent Sunday evening. Leona stared

at the blank page in her journal. She couldn't seem to express her feelings in writing. They were too muddy. She was afraid, excited, hopeful, and worried all at the same time. The image of Fitz returning without Mary and Grace, tears washing down his ruddy face, weighed on her heart. The girls promised to write, but if their foster families didn't mail their letters, Fitz may never know how they were faring in Nebraska.

Her thoughts wandered to Bradlee—his pretty eyes, his offer of friendship, and the odd rash on his hands. The more she thought about it, the wilder her imagination grew. Was Bradlee's rash a result of a reaction to silver, or an ingredient in the polish?

Her hand touched the pin in her hair. Silver was poison to mature lycanthropes. The purer the source, the more powerful a weapon it was against them. Her grandmother's hairpin was extremely potent, as it was pure silver. The heirloom had passed through many generations of Wardens.

The first time Bradlee's rash occurred, he had been handling money. Though there was much turmoil over the declining value of silver, U. S. coins still contained significant amounts of the precious metal. But silverware definitely contained more pure silver than the coins.

Leona bit her lip. Bradlee's birthday was approaching. They both turned eighteen on the same day—October 31. Hypothetically, if Bradlee was a lycanthrope, he would experience his first turning in mid-November.

It wasn't impossible. He showed some of the signs—blue eyes, a reaction to silver—but nothing definitive. Many humans shared these characteristics. Theoretically, any orphan could be a lycanthrope. They wouldn't even know it themselves, which was the most dangerous scenario. How could she help them without the ability to discern them?

Leona grew frustrated. *I must convince Uncle Ezra to divulge Papa's secret to me.*

Did other Wardens have this ability? If a Hunter located an immature, unturned lycanthrope before a Shepherd did, would they destroy them? According to what Uncle Ezra told her, she was certain they would be killed, robbed of the chance to live a peaceful life.

The lycanthrope curse was inherited. Some of the children at *Little Wanderers* had never known their parents. Most of them did, however. Fitz, for example, remembered his mother's death. She had no suspicions about him. He would know if his parents had been werewolves. If his mother had been one, her pack would have taken care of him and his sisters.

Leona shook the anxious thoughts about Bradlee being a Werewolf from her mind. There wasn't enough proof.

Mr. Green was an exceptional lycanthrope. He'd established his sanctuary without a Warden looking over his shoulder. He'd made a good life with Jane and cared for orphans. His secret remained well hidden, allowing him to become a highly respected Bostonian. Her papa would be proud of Theodore Green, as was she.

Leona was his Shepherd, but she felt unworthy of her authority. After all, she hadn't been properly trained, and she didn't possess her father's unique knowledge.

Maybe her family wasn't alone in this knowledge. Surely

others knew how to detect immature lycanthropes. Wardens…
and…

Leona inhaled sharply.

Could Mr. Green detect immature lycanthropes?

Chapter Twelve

Monday, October 9
Harvard College

Clementine stoked the fire in the professor's office. He and Mr. Hartman were teaching a class. She poked at the glowing red coals, sending sparks in the air. They fizzled quickly. She poked the coals again. Soon she bored of the game.

Voices in the hall announced the teachers' return. She rose and hung the poker back on the rack. She brushed the ashes off her skirt and stood, ready to apologize for arriving after class had already started and forcing the professor to push Mr. Hartman around in the rickety wheelchair.

The two men's voices grew louder and louder as they neared the office.

Clementine heard them clearly now. They must have stopped in front of the thick door. The professor's husky voice sounded angry.

"Then where is it?"

"Professor, I'm telling you the truth. I don't know!"

They're talking about the list I stole.

"Fine. By the way, don't pretend you don't have an attraction to Ezra Schaeffer's step-daughter. I see the way you look at her. You're like a hungry wolf ready to pounce."

"Sir, that's not fair. I have no designs on the girl. I'm only interested in learning how a girl of her social status thinks."

Whew. Wait—what does that mean?

"Isn't it obvious? She's a doll. I see you gave her a children's book to entertain her."

A doll?

Clementine thought of the dolls in the Sears catalog. Pretty, with eyes that closed when you laid them down. Then she thought of the corncob dolls the street children played with. *Which kind of doll were* they *thinking of?*

"Yes, well, at least she can read."

"Of course she can. Anyway, we should discuss my next public lecture, not our little assistant."

"Professor, this girl is a Brahmin from bourgeois origin. They seem eager to believe whatever anyone from Harvard tells them. Giving lectures in the Common is all fine and good, but don't you think it's time to act?"

"Sociology is in its adolescence. The theories we possess remain experimental, Hartman. We're scientists, observers. Besides, I *am* taking action, but my recent experiment isn't ready to share with anyone yet."

"Keeping secrets, are you? Well, I hope you don't keep it to yourself for long. This country is ripe for new ideas, Professor. Change occurs from those unafraid to act on their words. All your talking makes you appear timid."

"Look, Hartman, words have power. My lecture on Saturday

will cause more than a few activists to curse my name, especially those social gospel proponents. Appealing to the guilty consciences of the upper class works for them. 'Alms are a Christian's duty,' they claim. We do not owe anything to the poor! The sooner we educate the masses on the consequences of such charity, the better."

"Your lectures are surely educating Boston."

"What's good for the rich is good for society as a whole."

Clementine smiled smugly at this.

Professor Taylor continued, "Conscience wringers like Jane Addams will starve from lack of support and funding. Prosperity trumps charity." The wheelchair creaked. Clementine backed away from the door. A hand rested on the doorknob, but it didn't turn.

"I wish you could join me on the hunt Sunday. You must heal soon, Hartman."

"Sorry to let you down, Professor. It won't be long before I'm back at your side. Besides, there's a full moon this weekend."

"You don't seem the superstitious type. Are you afraid of the moon?" the Professor teased.

Mr. Hartman chuckled. "Of course not. I'm afraid of the hunters! Many believe that animals are fiercer this time of the month. It makes them jumpy. Be careful out there, Will. You could get shot by a fellow hunter."

"Oh, I'll be fine. Thanks for your concern." Professor Taylor paused. "You really don't know what happened to that list?"

"No, sir."

The list was now a bookmark, holding her place in *The*

The Good Shepherd

Wonderful Wizard of Oz.

Should I have put it back? No, she'd folded it, making it obvious it had been examined. She could only hope that the Professor would forget about the missing list and focus on his speech.

The doorknob turned. The heavy door crawled open. Clementine held it back for them. Mr. Hartman smiled pleasantly up at her as Professor Taylor pushed him inside.

She was confused by the conversation she'd just heard. She feared she'd been insulted but chose not to believe it. *They like me. Everyone likes me.*

"We were beginning to worry about you! Did you miss the trolley this morning?"

"Yes, well, it was all Mr. Flufferbutter's fault," she began. "That silly cat got into the pantry. Father was furious. I had to rescue him. The poor thing was so frightened he ripped my dress, so I had to change. And that's why I was late."

Professor Taylor chuckled. "Cats. You know, when I knew the Schaeffer family as a child, they owned a dozen cats. Ezra's favorite feline was a black and white rascal named Boots, if I recall."

"Really?" Clementine's eyes widened. She couldn't picture her stern stepfather as a child, definitely not as a child with a pet cat named Boots. He could barely tolerate Mr. Flufferbutter.

"We all change as we get older. Some for the better and some for the worse."

Clementine agreed, tipping her chin at him politely.

Minutes after they entered, a knock sounded from the other

side of the door.

"Yes? Who is it?" she spoke without opening it.

"Is that you, my darlin' Clementine?" a familiar brogue voice replied. Clementine gasped.

What is that leprechaun doing at Harvard College?

She panicked. Her voice sounded an octave higher as she addressed her employer, "Excuse me, Professor, Mr. Hartman. It's one of my mother's servants. May I be excused momentarily?"

The two men exchanged looks and Professor Taylor shrugged.

"Take no more than ten minutes. We have work for you to do."

"Yes, sir."

She exited in a hurry. She turned her angry face on the visiting rascal, ready to tear Fitz to pieces with insults. But, standing a few feet behind him was the beautiful Bradlee. She didn't intend to feel anything for the blue-eyed boy, since he was beneath her socially, and sadly, obviously attracted to her lowly country cousin, a sign of his complete lack of sophistication and bad taste. Still, at the sight of him, her heart fluttered without her permission.

He joined Fitz.

"Fitz, Bradlee," she began. "What brings you here? Is Leona ill? Did she die?"

"Nay, all is well with Miss Leona."

"Fitz missed you," Bradlee stated, his periwinkle eyes twinkling as he winked at his friend. Clementine felt a bit weak in the knees standing before Bradlee's magical eyes. She clutched at her shawl, her hand grasping her new pin.

"Ow!" She pulled her hand away. A red mark appeared on her finger. Looking down at her wolf pendant, she tapped it lightly with another finger.

"My pendant is burning hot. I guess I stood too close to the fireplace. How annoying!"

Fitz stepped toward her. His eyebrows dipped in concern, his leprechaun green eyes studying her hand.

"Are ya all right, ma darlin'?"

"Stop calling me that!" She glared at him.

Fitz's smile increased in size. She frowned and shoved her injured hand in her pocket, out of view from his concerned, freckled face.

"Why are you here?" she asked again.

Bradlee stepped back. "I'd like to study this artwork on the walls. If you'll excuse me, I'll just be over there, Fitz."

Fitz didn't even tip his chin to acknowledge Bradlee's comment. His bright, wide eyes were fixed on Clementine. He took a deep breath but didn't speak.

The ticking of the grandfather clock down the hall grated on Clementine's nerves.

"Well?" she said after waiting in silence for what seemed like centuries.

"M-my sisters. They, uh, they left the orphanage."

"That's nice. Why didn't you go with them? The family didn't want a stinky idiot like you?"

"Nay, lass. I chose ta stay. Little Wanderers is me home."

"I see," Clementine replied.

"They went to live with a family in someplace called Omaha. I may ne'er see them again."

Clementine tapped her foot. "What does this have to do with me?"

"Aye, I'm comin' ta the point, lass. I, well, I wondered if ya thought 'bout what I said at the Common last month."

"Your rude remarks about how I have an ugly heart? No, I forgot about that completely. Utterly. Allegorically."

Fitz's mouth turned up at the corner and a mischievous leprechaun look dawned on his freckled face. "Allegorically? Why, you've been a learning some mighty big words here at 'Arvard, haven't ya?"

His teasing tested her tolerance. "Why are you *here*, Fitz?" She sighed with exasperation over the ridiculous boy. He stared at her as if he'd never seen a lady before, in awe. Intimidated, maybe? *He* should *be intimidated. I'm rich and pretty while he's poor and ridiculous.*

"I been thinkin', lass. Life is too short not to be telling folks how ya feel. So I came to tell ya that I love ya. I don't know why. You're mean and sassy and dumb as a doornail, but I love you."

Clementine stuck her chin out and pouted. This was too much. "And my ugly heart? What about that?"

"I figured out the remedy for that."

She guffawed. "Which is?"

"Love. Ya need love. And, as I said, I love you. Warts 'an all."

Clementine sighed. This had been a bad day from the start, thanks to Mr. Flufferbutter. Now this idiot had come and made it worse.

"I do *not* have warts. And I certainly don't love you back!"

"Aye, but ya could."

She turned away from Fitz and opened the office door. She did her best to slam the heavy door behind her, but it took forever for the stupid door to erase the leprechaun from her sight.

As it closed, Fitz waved vigorously and yelled, "Bye, darlin'!"

Wednesday, October 11
The Home for Little Wanderers

"How did it go?" Leona asked Bradlee. He had confessed Fitz's plan to profess his love to Clementine after being interrogated at supper Monday night by Mr. Green, who demanded to know where the two had been during chapel that morning.

"About as well as you'd expect."

"She laughed at him, didn't she?"

Bradlee grimaced. "Oh, I don't think Fitz even noticed that. He's still grinning from ear to ear." Leona followed his pointing chin to Fitz's gleeful face. She couldn't believe it. "Is Fitz, well, touched?"

"You mean, is he slow?" Bradlee chuckled. "I can see why you'd ask that, but he's quite intelligent. He's in love, though. I suppose an argument could be made over whether love makes a person dumb—or brave."

Leona tilted her head.

"What are you thinking about?" Bradlee asked her.

"Mr. and Mrs. Green," she replied.

"Well, I wasn't expecting you to say that. What about them?"

She remembered her visit to the sanctuary; how Mrs. Green's trembling hand grasped her husband's, the man she loved despite the monster lurking inside. She loved him enough to chain him up every full moon.

"Their love for each other is inspiring, that's all."

"As opposed to nonsensical, like Fitz's feelings for Clementine?"

Leona smiled lightly. "I don't have the knowledge required to judge anyone's feelings, I guess. There are some things only the Lord can know fully."

"We feel what we feel. There's not much one can do to stop feelings. Actions, on the other hand…"

Leona thought again of Mr. Green. He could have stayed with his pack. How powerful love must be, to cause a man to abandon his safe community.

Bradlee's piercing blue eyes stared at Leona. All of a sudden, he turned away and picked up a box, setting it on the table between them.

"What's in there?" Leona asked, relieved to change the topic. The subject of love made her head hurt and her heart pound.

"The art exhibit is this Saturday. These are the submissions the students have made. Our theme this month is leaves." He showed her some of the artwork. She recognized the leaf rubbings, like Regina's. There were also lovely watercolors and charcoal sketches.

"Why do you like to draw?" she asked him.

He scrunched up his mouth in thought.

"To be honest, it's a thrill."

"A thrill? What do you mean?"

Bradlee ripped a piece of white paper out of his notepad and set it on the table in front of them.

"Look at the paper. What do you see?"

"Nothing. It's blank."

"Look harder."

She stared at the white page. Then, she gasped.

"Ah, you saw something, didn't you?"

She did. An image had suddenly appeared in her head. She knew it wasn't really on the paper, but it was as clear in her mind as if it were actually there.

"Now draw what was in your mind."

Leona frowned. "I'm no artist. Maybe if I describe it, you could draw it for me?"

They worked together to recreate Leona's vision. After a while, Leona was surprised at how accurate the picture was.

"Why did you see this?" Bradlee asked, scratching his nose.

Leona picked up the paper and grimaced. It was a painful sight.

"It's the Schaeffer family crest. The only thing missing is the inscription at the bottom."

Bradlee picked up a pencil. "Here, you do it."

Leona wrote the words on the crest.

"What language is that? Russian?"

"No. In German, Schaeffer means *shepherd.*"

"Shouldn't your family crest have a sheep on it, not a wolf?"

"It's complicated. The wolf is a reminder of a shepherd's hardest responsibility—to protect sheep from predators."

"Interesting. Do you know what the words say? In English, you know, for boring boys like me who can't read foreign languages."

Leona rolled her eyes. "You're not boring. Not at all."

This remark made his eyes twinkle. She strained to look away.

Focusing her eyes on the German words, as if she hadn't already memorized them, she read, 'Behold, I send you out as sheep amid the wolves.' My father had a pendant with this saying on it. It was destroyed in the fire that killed my parents and grandparents."

"I'm so sorry, Leona. I used to pity myself because I have no memories of my parents, but perhaps remembering is more painful."

"No one's pain is insignificant," she replied. He offered her a sad smile of acknowledgement.

Leona tried not to obsess over her suspicions of Bradlee. If he were a Werewolf and didn't know it, their relationship would become very complicated, and his life would be turned upside-down. Suddenly Fitz's one-sided infatuation with Clementine seemed more palatable. Less complicated, at least.

"What are you thinking about now?" Bradlee asked.

Lifting her head, Leona's eyes widened, and she burst out in laughter.

"What?"

She licked her finger and wiped a huge pencil mark off Bradlee's nose. His face reddened, then his expression turned serious.

Their faces were inches apart. Bradlee leaned forward, shrinking the gap. His breath warmed her cheek. She closed her eyes, lost in the moment, blind to all her anxieties.

His soft lips brushed hers. But he didn't kiss her. He nuzzled his face against her cheek. It was as smooth as suede. The touching was gently intimate, and more passionate than Leona had ever dreamed a kiss would be. She cherished his sweet, featherlike caress.

"Where's my bwankie?" a little boy's voice demanded. The child, clothed in long underwear, stood inches away.

Leona and Bradlee parted. Bradlee took the boy's hand.

"Oliver, you aren't supposed to be out of bed. Let me take you back to your dorm and we'll look for your blankie there."

He winked at Leona over his shoulder as he escorted the little boy down the hallway.

Chapter Thirteen

Leona's heart pounded. Mr. Green finally returned late last night. She had to question him, but she feared the answer. If he could sense immature lycanthropes, that would be a relief. Maybe he could teach her how he did it.

But, if he didn't know, she would have to confront her uncle.

It was best to find out if her suspicions about Bradlee were correct now, before they got any closer. She feared it was already too late to avoid a broken heart.

Papa had insisted that Leona only marry another Warden, one he approved of. What would happen if a Warden married a Werewolf? No, it was a ridiculous idea. The two beings balanced each other's existence in the world. Marrying someone who held your life in their hands made for an unequal yoke.

Leona knocked on the office door.

"Come in!"

She inhaled deeply, gathering strength from the crisp fall air that filled her lungs. The windows were open, and the whole

The Good Shepherd

Home smelled like falling leaves and harvest apples.

"Are you here to check on my preparations for the upcoming cycle? I assure you, Leona, everything is set. I even replaced one of the locks on the chains. Mrs. Green and I leave for the sanctuary at five o'clock this afternoon, long before sunset."

"That's wonderful. My mind is at ease, Mr. Green. I trust you."

Mr. Green's eyebrow rose. "You don't look at ease, Miss Schaeffer." He gestured at Leona's feet. She had been tapping them unaware.

"I need to ask you a question. I should have asked before now. I'm not being a very good Shepherd."

"You are the fairest Warden I've ever encountered, I assure you, Miss Schaeffer. You're responsible, compassionate, and mature, especially for someone so young."

Leona's eyes fell to the floor and she inhaled a deep breath, full of regret and humility.

"I thank you for that compliment," she wanted to explain the reasons for her lack of confidence but pushed them aside. She had a more pressing matter to attend to. "There's an area of the job where I'm at a loss. And unless I'm fully equipped as a Warden, I fear I will fail and death will win. Please help me."

"Have a seat. How can I help?"

Leona grasped the back of a chair and sat down. Her full skirt pleated naturally over her lap. She met his blue eyes and continued, "There's something my father didn't teach me before he died. I—" Leona's throat constricted at the memory. She forcibly cleared her throat and added, "I lost my parents quite suddenly."

"No one ever expects death," he replied. His blue eyes washed gray with sadness.

At his comment, the memory of the stronghearted, compassionate Mrs. Wickersham filled her mind. She took a deep breath.

"Can you detect immature lycanthropes, Mr. Green?"

He smiled wryly. "Why do you think I became the director of an orphanage, Miss Schaeffer? Yes, I can."

Leona breathed a sigh of relief, then felt a rush of impatience. "How?"

"Well, that's easy. I can smell them."

She groaned. "But *I* can't smell them. I can smell *mature* Werewolves, even in their human form, but not those who've never transformed."

Mr. Green stroked his beard. "Now, it might just be a rumor, but I was told that Wardens have a special detector that alerts them when a lycanthrope, mature or immature, is near. I don't know what it is. That's a well-kept Warden secret. Your parents never mentioned this?"

"No, they didn't."

Her skin heated and she curled her hands into fists. Why hadn't they divulged this crucial piece of information to her? *Why didn't they trust me?*

Mr. Green sighed. "Parenting is a complicated job. Add Warden training to it—well—your parents had quite the challenge. I'm sure they had their reasons for not telling you about the device, Leona."

She frowned. "Thank you for filling me in." *I'll have to*

confront my uncle after all. Her frown deepened.

"Do you want to know about the immature lycanthropes here at the Home?"

She perked up. "Please."

"There are only three at present. Two are under thirteen years old. I haven't spoken to them yet, but I will when the time is right. I've had to explain the condition to ten children over the years in total. It's quite a shock for them. Since there's a risk they won't believe me, I wait until the night of their first transformation to tell them, whenever that may be."

Her eyes widened. "The night of their first transformation?"

"It's the safest way. I drug them and take them to the sanctuary. Jane sets up another cage in the cellar. The first transformation is the worst one. No one should be alone for that." One corner of his mouth dipped into a serious frown.

"You said there were three here right now. If two are under thirteen, how old is the third?"

"The third one is almost eighteen. It's a special case. I plan to speak to him very soon."

Her eyes met his. "What if he doesn't believe you?"

"He will. He trusts me more than any of the others did."

"Let me help," she insisted. "It's my job, Mr. Green. Can I join you this time?"

"I wanted to take care of this one myself. I've been preparing for this particular conversation for quite a while. It's a special case."

Leona breathed, "It's Bradlee, isn't it?"

Mr. Green raised an eyebrow. "I thought you couldn't detect

them."

"There were signs." Leona's heart sunk. "His ice-blue eyes, his reaction to silver—"

"Cats fear him, too."

Leona tilted her head. "I didn't know that was a sign." Again, this was also vague. Cats hated lots of people, even her.

Mr. Green gestured to the calendar on the wall. "The most obvious sign is his moon-date."

"His moon-date?"

Mr. Green pilfered through a pile of books on the desk and pulled one out. "This is the Farmer's Almanac from the year of Bradlee's birth, 1887. His birthday is October 31. Notice anything about that day?"

Leona perused the page Mr. Green had turned to. It was the moon cycle calendar.

"He was born on the night of the first full moon," she observed.

Mr. Green smirked. "All lycanthropes are. You didn't know?"

Leona shook her head. She felt angry. What right did she have to be a Shepherd if she didn't know such information? Papa should have taught her!

"That's my birthday, too."

"It is? Maybe we're all born during full moons. Werewolf or Warden, we are both slaves to the moon, forced to bow to its power."

Leona thought about that. It made sense. The power of the full moon was blamed for many things: odd behavior, headaches, labor pains...

"When are you going to tell Bradlee?"

"I thought it would be best to tell him on his birthday." In response to her frown, he added, "I know—what a terrible present, hmm?"

Leona grimaced. "Can I be there when you tell him?"

"Yes. But, fair warning—he's going to be angry."

That afternoon, all was quiet at the Home except for the pattering of rain on the roof. Leona and the girls played checkers and read after dinner. Leona tried to smile and ignore the pain stabbing her heart.

A spunky girl in pigtails named Catherine jumped over three of Leona's checkers and crowned her first king. Leona's mouth hung open in awe. Laughter burst from across the room. Bradlee had seen everything. He grinned at her from afar, his eyes lightened with laughter. She avoided meeting his eyes by staring at the checkerboard.

As she concentrated on her next move, a shadow fell over the board and her embarrassingly large quantity of red checkers.

"Miss Schaeffer, are you ill?" her opponent asked. "Your face is red. Do you have a fever?"

"You have a fever?" she heard Bradlee's voice say.

Leona glanced up. His eyebrows were furrowed.

"Oh, no. I'm fine. I never get sick," Leona replied, waving her hand dismissively.

"Me neither," said Bradlee. "I was wondering if I could steal

Miss Schaeffer away from you for a minute, Catherine?"

"Sure. I'm trouncing her anyway. She's terrible at checkers."

"I was letting you win," Leona said with a wink.

"Sure you were," Catherine replied, gathering checkers into a sack.

Bradlee led Leona out of the common room, opening the door for her like a gentleman.

"Where are we going?" she asked. "It's raining outside."

"I know. I brought umbrellas," he said, winking, and handed her one.

They opened their umbrellas under the porch. Bradlee paused, but then reached out boldly and took Leona's free hand. She tried to remain calm, but it was no use. A deaf person could surely hear the thumping in her chest.

They ventured out into the rain. Bradlee led her to a covered gazebo. They set down their dripping umbrellas by the entrance and sat on the bench in the middle, watching gallons of water pour off the roof.

"Not a very pretty sight, huh?" Leona commented.

"I think it's quite pretty," Bradlee said.

His smile stung her. She turned toward him. He wasn't looking at the sky. His ocean blue eyes were glued on her. The cool air made her shiver. He slid closer to her, his warmth radiated like the hearth of a fireplace. Leona longed to melt into him. She cursed the moon for being so cruel, though she knew the fault was her indulging her attraction to him.

She'd fallen for a man she could never have.

Lost in anguish, she didn't notice Bradlee's hand reaching for her. Before she could even consider pulling away, his fingers caressed her face.

Leona opened her mouth to protest. Bradlee leaned over and kissed her, silencing her voice and stunting her thoughts. She gave in to the passion of his kiss and returned it with equal fervor.

Embracing him, his warmth blanketed her. The muscles under his shirt tightened. Their kisses evolved, becoming more powerful and exciting. The encounter loosened her suppressed desire for him. It felt inevitable. Fated.

But it was wrong. Bradlee was not a Warden. He was a Werewolf.

Leona clutched his shirt in her fists and, with all the strength she could muster, pushed him back. She leaned her forehead onto his chin and sighed heavily.

"Stop," she said.

Bradlee's face turned red. He inched back. Absent of his warmth, Leona felt cold and alone. He avoided her eyes, shuffling his boots on the thin wooden planks of the gazebo.

"I'm sorry, Leona. I thought you felt the same way I do."

"No, I should be the one to apologize. We can be *friends*, Bradlee. But I-I'm... not interested in anything more. You're... uh," she paused, biting her lip as she tried to invent a plausible, human excuse. "You're just not the type of man I'm looking for."

He was a wonderful man, someone she knew she could love. But what else could she say? She couldn't tell him the truth, that she could only marry a Warden. Now she felt horrible, a liar and a tease.

He inhaled a deep breath. The hurt in his crystal blue eyes

broke her heart.

"I'm sorry to hear that. You're the kind of woman I've been looking for, Leona. You're beautiful, intelligent, fun, and good. I think I could love you forever. But if you don't feel the same way about me, I'll leave you alone."

A tortured expression marred his handsome face. He hurried out of the gazebo, into the rain without his umbrella, leaving her there alone.

The torrential rain slowed to a drizzle before she finished crying.

Chapter Fourteen

"Eugenics is a Greek word which simply means *well-born*. As I said in my last lecture, scientists have discovered that nature naturally selects good traits and eliminates the bad ones."

Mr. Hartman handed Clementine a copy of *On the Origin of Species*. He gestured for her to hold the book high in the air for everyone to see. They'd asked her to pack the book to bring to the professor's lecture. She held it tight, fearing she'd drop it on her head in front of the conservative-sized crowd.

"Francis Galton, Mr. Darwin's cousin and a brilliant scientist in his own right, has proffered that selective breeding will result in a better society. His studies indicate that talented individuals pass on their talent."

The professor paused to clear his throat.

"Raising the quality of our nation is a logical, achievable goal. My fellow Americans, wouldn't you agree that it is better to be healthy and strong rather than sick and weak?" The crowd murmured its unanimous agreement.

At his behest, Clementine lowered the book and handed it

back to Mr. Hartman. The turnout for the professor's lecture was sparse. Rain from the previous day had turned the roads to mud. Gray clouds threatened to cast down more precipitation. Strangely, the waiting moon shone brighter in the sky than the sun had at its peak.

Clementine sighed. She scanned the Common. Other organizations had also gathered there today. She recognized the Salvation Army symbol on a tent at the west end. The Boy Scouts were recruiting near a big oak.

From afar, familiar face blue eyes twinkled through the autumn shrubbery. *Bradlee?*

"Clementine, hold up the book again!" Mr. Hartman demanded.

She raised her arms mechanically, grasping the book loosely in her hands. Her eyes followed Bradlee's bobbing head. It stopped at the *Little Wanderers* wagon, the intricately painted sign half-obscured by framed art.

"They're here," she noted aloud.

"Shh!" Mr. Hartman scolded.

She cast him a look of apology. At the same time, her grip on the book faltered. The book slipped through her hands and fell squarely on her head.

"Damn it!" she exclaimed.

The crowd chuckled, clearly entertained and well distracted by Clementine's faux-pas. She panicked. *Will the professor fire me?* Turning her back to the crowd, she covered her face with her hands and sobbed.

"Don't cry, ma darlin'!"

The Good Shepherd

Fitz leaped onto the wooden platform. Clementine's embarrassment and fear turned to anger.

"Go away," she hissed.

The stupid boy didn't seem to hear her. He threw his arm around her shoulders.

"Leave me alone, you ugly leprechaun! You stink!" She thumped his chest.

"Now, now, darlin,' you can insult me all ya like, if it makes ya feel better. Go on!"

Clementine narrowed her eyes and spat, "You're short. And your clothes don't match!"

Fitz glanced down at the frayed hems of his mud-brown tweed pants. He shrugged. "Aye, what else?"

"Your hair is greasy. And your hat has moth holes!"

"True, lass. What else?"

"You smell like—like—pickles!"

The mesmerized crowd, gathered in front of the platform for a sociology lecture, suddenly burst into laughter.

Fitz's goofy face beamed at Clementine like a drunken madman.

She tittered. Then a small grin grew on her face. Soon she was rolling with laughter, along with the crowd.

"See, lass? I told ya I was good for ya."

Fitz took a bow. Clementine grimaced and tried to reign in her laughter, but it was as if she had gone insane or suffered from a giggling disease. It was uncontrollable.

She caught a glimpse of Mr. Hartman. The dour expression of disappointment on his round, bearded face should have fizzled her laughter, but Clementine thought it was the funniest thing yet. She pointed at him and howled. Fitz joined her.

"You look like ya ate a bad peach, Mister. Maybe you shoulda naturally selected something better. Perhaps you are ill-bred?"

This comment produced another roar of laughter from the audience, whose attention was now taken by Fitz. Mr. Hartman's face burned beet red.

Professor Taylor wagged his finger at them. "Young man, please leave the stage. Clementine, you can go with him. You're fired!"

The crowd booed as they proceeded to exit the platform. Fitz jumped off the edge first and held out his arms to catch Clementine. She shrugged and hopped. He grunted as he caught her, and the crowd cackled.

"You really do smell, Fitz. Yuck," she told him, coughing.

Fitz shrugged. He kept both his hands around her waist.

"I'm a working gent and proud of it. So what if I smell like vinegar? Small price to pay for a roof over me head."

Fitz turned to the crowd and removed his moth-eaten hat. He waved it in the air and the crowd cheered.

"If ya get tired of listening to this quack, come over and buy some artwork to raise money for *The Home for Little Wanderers*!"

"Lazy beggars!" someone yelled.

"Arrogant bastard!" Fitz shouted back. The man who had yelled had a neck like a bull. Clementine grabbed Fitz's arm and pulled him away.

The Good Shepherd

They ran and ran and ran. When Fitz stopped, so did Clementine. She hadn't realized it, but Fitz had clasped her hand sometime during their escape. Sweating from the exertion of their sprint, Clementine soon became conscious of her wet palms. She slipped her hand out of his and wiped it on her skirt.

She gasped. "What have I done? I just got fired. Father is going to be furious with me."

"Aye, ya did. It were quite romantic, ya know. Running off into the sunset with your lover." Fitz grinned wide.

Clementine punched his shoulder. "You are not my *lover*, you pockmarked pervert! And look at the sky, idiot—it's not even close to sunset. You're so... odd."

"Thanks, lass. I just wanted to hear ya insult me again. I think I love your angry face the most, darlin'. Not that ya aren't a stunningly beautiful sight to behold when ya aren't spittin' mad." Fitz winked at her.

"You think I'm *stunningly beautiful*?"

Clementine's heart melted a bit and she forgot how much she despised him again. He nodded, then sniffed and rubbed his snotty nose on his sleeve. She groaned and punched him again.

He smiled bigger.

A familiar voice behind her said, "Clementine, I didn't expect to see you here."

She turned and saw Leona. Behind her was Bradlee. *Of course, they're together.*

"Hello, cousin. I was just... um... I was assisting Professor Taylor. He's giving another lecture."

"Oh, really? Another speech on sociology?"

185

"Yes, he's quite popular. I've been working at Harvard, you know."

"Fitz told me. He had fun hunting you down."

Fitz's chest puffed out like a robin's. "Sure did! I went ta yer house on Joy Street first. Spoke to yer mum. She's grand, she is. She said you were at Harvard and I plum didn't believe her. Called her a liar!"

Clementine frowned. Mother had regaled the embarrassing tale to her. The headache it had caused her then was restarting.

"How's yer finger, darlin'?"

"My finger?"

"Ya burned it that day I spoke to ya at 'Arvard, don't ya remember?" Fitz remarked.

"Oh, it's better now. I guess I shouldn't go near a burning fireplace when I wear silver jewelry. It really heats up." Clementine adjusted the wolf pendant at her collar. "Wow, it's a little warm now, too."

Leona leaned closer and stared at it.

Good, she's jealous.

"That's the Schaeffer family crest."

Bradlee peered over Leona's shoulder. "It looks just like you described."

Leona inched away from Bradlee. *Interesting.*

"Father gave it to me. It's an heirloom," Clementine informed her, watching Leona's blue eyes closely for a hint of envy.

"My father had one, too. It was lost in the fire."

The sad expression on Leona's face pulled on Clementine's heartstrings. She recognized that distinct, bitter flavor of pain.

She'd lost her father, too.

"I'm sorry to hear that," Clementine offered, and meant it, mostly.

"Could I examine it?" Leona asked, gesturing at the silver pendant.

Clementine's empathy muted. She had something Leona wanted. Superiority proved a stronger substance than empathy. "I'm sorry. It would be improper to unpin my collar in public."

Leona's look of disappointment tugged on her. She reached for the pin.

"Clementine?" a shrill voice called out. "I searched for you at the lecture, but you weren't there. I was worried sick."

Mother approached at a rush, a stern expression on her round face. Her black skirt and petticoats jostled like a speeding buggy.

"Oh, Leona! Nice to see you. How are you doing, dear?"

Leona replied, "I'm well. How are you, Aunt Franny?"

The two continued chattering, like birds. Clementine frowned. Her mother clearly preferred Leona over her. She couldn't understand why. Trouble followed her cousin like a cloud. She'd been homeless and destitute, the police suspected her of something sinister, and Father detested her. But Mother's kindness toward the girl was unabashed.

An elbow prodded Clementine's side.

"Darlin', yer sad face makes my heart hurt," Fitz said. Clementine ignored his comment, her eyes stuck on Mother and Leona jabbering like best friends.

"Leona has agreed to come to supper!" her mother declared with a bright smile. Clementine forced a grin.

Bradlee pulled Leona aside. Clementine overheard him say,

"But we're leaving the Common at 4:00. Mr. Green already left for his trip. I'm taking his watch in the boys' dorms tonight. I can't retrieve you. How will you return to the Home?"

Leona's forehead crinkled. "That's right. Tonight is—"

"Allen can escort you back to the orphanage after supper, Leona. Your beau is sweet to be concerned for your welfare and safety," Mother said, winking like a fool.

"He's not my beau, Aunt Franny," Leona said. Her long eyelashes flickered over her troubled blue eyes. Bradlee stiffened. Clementine held back her glee.

"I have something important to discuss with my uncle, Bradlee. Please tell Mr. Green that I hope he has a safe trip," Leona said.

Bradlee's melancholy face matched Leona's in its degree of storminess. Interestingly, both reflected the cloudy, dark weather.

With Leona coming to dinner, there would be a distraction. Father and Mother might not ask Clementine about the lecture today. She feared Father's reaction when she inevitably confessed she would no longer be working at Harvard because she'd been fired.

Her hand clutched the pendant.

What if he takes back the heirloom and kicks me out on my derriere, like he did to Leona?

"Then it's settled!" Mother exclaimed, squealing like a schoolgirl.

As if on cue, the skies opened up and the gray clouds poured down rain. Leona, Bradlee, and Fitz ran to the *Little Wanderers* wagon. Meanwhile, Clementine and her mother raced to the closest covered area—the platform where the lecture was held. They stayed dry and watched the orphans racing around in the rain to move the wet artwork, placing it in the back of the old wagon and covering it up with a patched oilcloth the size of a bed sheet.

When the others finished at the wagon, they joined them. Drenched and cold, Fitz stood beside Clementine under the pavilion. He tried to grab her hand, but she slapped him away.

"'Fraid yer mum won't approve of yer orphan lover, eh, darlin'?" he whispered in her ear.

"I don't love you, you drowned rat!" she murmured under her breath.

"Aye, ya do."

"I do not!"

"Ya do."

"Aaagh!" Clementine grew tempted to run into the rain to escape the miserable boy, but figured he'd just chase after her.

"Is the artwork ruined?" Mother asked Leona.

"No, I think we saved most of it. Thankfully there were lots of oil paintings this month. Mr. Smith taught the children to paint landscapes."

"Boston is so lovely in the fall. What a brilliant idea," Mother replied.

"Then you should buy some paintings, Mother. It's for charity," Clementine said. Mother loved to impress her friends by outdoing them in her charity work.

"What a brilliant idea, Clementine. I will!" Her mother unfastened her purse and pulled out some money.

"Leona, take this money and pick out some artwork for me. You can bring it with you to the house."

Mother placed three silver dollars in Leona's cupped hands. Her cousin immediately handed the coins to Fitz. *That's odd. Bradlee kept the money box last time they sold art in the Common. Why doesn't she give it to him?*

"I will, Aunt Franny. I already have one in mind that I think you'll like."

"Regina's leaves?" Bradlee suggested. Leona nodded.

"Who's Regina?" Clementine asked.

"Oh, a sweet Russian girl from my dorm," Leona replied. "She does rubbings of leaves—oaks, maples, ashes. She's a collector."

"Russian, you say? Like your grandfather? The dead moron?"

Leona bit her lower lip, then frowned. "*Ded Moroz*." She then addressed Bradlee and Mother, "My grandfather, that is, my mother's father, looked like Santa Claus. *Ded Moroz* means Grandfather Frost in Russian."

Mother chuckled. "That's interesting. I didn't know your mother was Russian. But I guess with a name like Katarina, I should have guessed. I'm such a fuddy-duddy. Ezra never talked about his family. I wish I could have met them."

"They were good people," Leona replied. "Kind and generous, like you."

"Professor Taylor said he knew Father and his brother when they were children. He said they owned lots of cats. Can you believe that? Father despises Mr. Flufferbutter!"

Leona smiled. "My father loved cats, but they always hated me, so we never had any."

"Mr. Flufferbutter definitely doesn't like you," Clementine commented.

Fitz burst into a fit of laughter. "Ya named yer cat Mr. Flufferbutter? That's the stupidest name I've ever heard. Must be an ugly thing."

Nobody insults Mr. Flufferbutter.

"He's beautiful—and quite proud of his name, I'll have you know. He's normally well-behaved. Leona seems to bring out his mean side."

"I still can't believe that he attacked you so viciously, dear Leona," Mother said.

Leona shrugged. "Cats are territorial. It's okay."

"Cats hate me too," Bradlee commented.

"That's terrible," Clementine said. "I couldn't live without dear Mr. Flufferbutter. He's so soft and cuddly."

"*I'm* soft and cuddly, darlin'," Fitz murmured in her ear. She pinched his arm.

When the rain stopped, Mother insisted on getting home before Leona so they could prepare for their "special guest."

Leona said her goodbyes, promising to find the best painting left for Mother, while Bradlee hitched up the horses.

"I'll drive Leona over to your house. I wish we had room for all of you."

"Such a gentleman!" Mother declared and wished them well. "Walking is good for the heart, the newspaper says. We'll be fine. See you soon, Leona!" Mother waved.

The clouds had cried enough, it seemed. They disappeared, allowing the sun to shine finally.

Mother rushed Clementine along as they walked to the house on Joy Street, listing all the dishes she should ask Bridget to make. "No clam chowder!" she noted.

Clementine followed behind Mother, shuffling her feet cautiously along the wet streets, so she wouldn't slip. No one would catch her here. She had no desire to be saved from Bradlee again anyway. He wasn't right for her—or for Leona, it seemed.

Mother spoke over her shoulder at Clementine, "You still haven't told me why you weren't where you said you'd be. You owe me an explanation. We'll talk about it later, young lady. Let's enjoy Leona while we have her."

Clementine groaned.

Chapter Fifteen

Saturday, October 14
22 Joy Street, Boston

The aroma of freshly baked bread filled Leona's nose as she entered her uncle's home, making her nervous stomach growl. Her uncle would be angry she was here, but Aunt Franny seemed oblivious to his antagonism toward her.

She was dying to speak with Uncle Ezra alone and beg him to tell her how her father had detected immature lycanthropes. She sat on her hands to stop them from tapping on the chair.

How can I convince him to talk to me?

"Miss Leona! Tis good ta see yer face. Are you well?" Bridget said, placing a bowl of gravy beside a large roast on the dining table. She curtsied lightly. A loose auburn hair fell in her eyes and she puffed it away with her breath.

Leona returned Bridget's hearty smile. The maid's amiable presence distracted Leona from her anxiety. She felt a bond with the young woman, a fellow outsider in the Schaeffer household.

"I'm well, but I admit—I'm hungry. The food smells delicious."

Aunt Franny entered the room. Leona handed her the framed artwork from the orphanage. She'd brought her two pieces.

"Oh, this one is lovely!" she declared, admiring the colored wax leaf rubbing Regina contributed to the exhibit.

She opened the other picture. It was a charcoal drawing of a wolf howling at the moon—Bradlee's artwork. "This one is interesting. I'll display it prominently, dear."

Leona's mouth twitched. She relished the thought of reminding her uncle of his heritage, of the calling he'd so cowardly rejected.

Clementine entered the room, wearing a different outfit, a white dress with a full skirt and a satin blue ribbon adorning her waist. An ivory lace shawl lay wrapped around her shoulders, secured by the silver wolf pendant.

The Schaeffer crest, worn by someone void of Warden blood, mocked Leona. Clementine couldn't possibly comprehend the significance of the words or the symbolism of the heirloom. Her father's pin was lost to her forever. At least she still possessed one family heirloom, the silver hairpin that held back the mess of curls on her head.

Her hair was almost dry, but her thick, wool dress was still damp. She shivered.

"Oh, are you cold, Leona?" Aunt Franny asked. "Go stand by the fireplace until supper is ready. Bridget, how much longer will it be?"

Bridget lowered her eyes. "Supper will be ready in half an hour, miss." Aunt Franny peered at the grandfather clock. The hands showed it was fifteen minutes until five o'clock.

"Clementine, go with Leona."

"Yes, Mother," Clementine said. A tiny pout crept over her face.

On their way to the large living room, the cousins passed a dark hallway. A growl echoed from the hall. *Mr. Flufferbutter.* Leona quickened her steps.

The girls stood together near the fire. When the warmth on one side of her body grew too intense, Leona turned to warm another.

"That pendant looks beautiful with your shawl, Clementine."

Clementine raised an eyebrow. "Yes, isn't it lovely? Father gave his Schaeffer family crest pendant to me, though I'm not a Schaeffer by blood. Are you angry? Be honest with me, cousin."

"I'm not angry. I'm sad. My father's pendant was lost, and the Schaeffer family crest was very important to him. He wore it all the time. But I do have an heirloom from my grandmother that I cherish, though."

"What is it?"

Leona pulled out the silver hairpin, setting her curls free from its grasp. She held it out for Clementine to examine. She admired the two tapered, strong tines attached to the head of a wolf cast in pure silver. Leona didn't confess to Clementine that it was a weapon, used to kill dangerous lycanthropes. She would never believe her anyway.

"It's so much prettier than the Schaeffer pendant, Leona! Now I'm jealous. Shall we trade?" she asked, winking at Leona.

Leona stiffened.

"I'm joking," Clementine said, giggling. She fanned Leona's

drying skirt. "I think it's nearly done."

Leona relaxed. She wound her damp hair in a bun and pierced it with the pin.

Clementine's dimpled chin tilted as she reached out and touched Leona's chignon. "This is all you have left of your parents, then?"

"Yes."

"Would you like to hold the pendant, Leona?" Clementine asked, loosening her shawl from her shoulders. She touched the clasp. "Ouch!" she exclaimed, then thrust her fingers into her mouth. "Golly, the fire must have warmed it again! Sorry, Leona, it's too hot; I can't take it off—I can barely touch it."

Clementine's pale cheeks were flushed dark pink, so it was no wonder the metal broach was warm. But too hot to touch?

"That's okay," Leona replied. Her eyes stared at the pendant, like a compass fixed on the north star.

Papa had promised to pass on his heirloom pin to Leona on her eighteenth birthday. She sighed. *Now they're both gone forever.* She'd never even held the pendant in her own hands. Papa had never let her touch the important and irreplaceable object.

Clementine leaned over and tapped Leona's hairpin. "That's funny," she commented, jiggling Leona's hair. Her lips thinned as her eyebrows knitted.

"What's funny?" Leona asked. She turned a few degrees to warm another portion of her skirt.

"You've been baking by the fire but your pin is barely warm."

Leona grimaced. "That *is* odd. They're both made of silver."

196

The Good Shepherd

"Real—" Clementine began.

"Suppertime!" Aunt Franny bellowed.

The two girls made their way to the dining room. Leona's clothes were drier and warmer, the chill under her skin a memory.

Mr. Flufferbutter raced past them, bounding through the foyer. He knocked a book off a side table and ran away. Clementine turned around to scold him, but he was gone. As the book fell to the floor, a paper escaped its pages and floated down, landing at Leona's feet. She picked it up.

Under her thumb, the letters *L-E-O* peeked out from the folded parchment in her grasp. Curious, Leona unfolded the paper. Her name, one of a list, was circled. The other names, Schaeffer family members, were crossed out.

"Clementine, what's this?"

"Oh, it's nothing. Return it to me, please."

Leona held the paper tight.

"Is this your handwriting?"

"No, it's Professor Taylor's," Clementine said stiffly. "Now give it back!"

"Why would Professor Taylor write this? Why are these names crossed out?"

"Look, I'm not supposed to have it, so I can't very well ask him, can I? I accidentally found it on his desk. Maybe it's a Christmas card list."

"If you honestly believed it was a Christmas card list, you would've returned it. What do you think it really is?"

Clementine frowned.

"I don't know, and I don't care. They fired me, so I'll never find out now. Give it back!"

"Fired you?" Leona asked.

"Girls!" Aunt Franny called from the dining room.

Leona had a bad feeling about that list. Why was her name circled? What made her different from the rest of the Schaeffers?

She was a living, active Warden. Ezra Schaeffer was a Normalizer and her parents were dead. But Professor Taylor couldn't know about Werewolves and Wardens, could he?

The two cousins sat down. Franny faced them across the table. Leona could barely see Clementine through the brass candelabra, thankfully. She had so much swimming inside her head, preventing her from making polite conversation at that moment.

"Where's Father?" Clementine asked.

Aunt Franny sighed. "He refused to leave his office. He says he needs to finish reading a document. He's being quite rude, Leona. I scolded him, dear, but it's no use. Bridget, will you prepare a plate for Mr. Schaeffer and take it to him?"

"Yes, ma'am," Bridget replied.

Leona thought for a second and then said, "Bridget, allow me to take the plate to him whenever it's ready, please."

"You don't have to do that, Leona. That's what servants are for," Clementine said, loud and proud.

"I want to," Leona replied.

"Yes, miss," Bridget said, curtsying again.

The meal was much fancier than meals at the orphanage. There, they served corn on the cob. Here, fat kernels of corn swam in a buttery sauce garnished with chopped green herbs.

Aunt Franny rambled on about the news and the weather with

equal fervor. Then she set down her fork and narrowed her eyes at Clementine. "What happened at the Common today? Why weren't you with the Professor and Mr. Hartman?"

Clementine hesitated at first, but finally said, "I quit."

Aunt Franny's eyes grew wide.

"You did what?"

"If you must know, Mother, Mr. Hartman flirted with me too much. It made me quite uncomfortable. After all, he's old!"

"Well!" Aunt Franny declared. "I understand, dear, but your father will not. Men don't understand what it's like to be a woman at all. He would simply suggest that you ignore his advances. But I'm a woman. I understand men. You did the right thing, dear."

Clementine exhaled slowly. She'd told Leona she'd been fired. Had she lied to her mother about Mr. Hartman's attitude toward her? Flirtation was flattering to Clementine. She wasn't the type to be offended by such advances. Unless they were given by a pauper.

"Fitz was happy to see you today, cousin," Leona said in an attempt to save Clementine from further questioning about her job.

Clementine's face paled.

Aunt Franny grimaced, her lips landing in a pout. "Fitz? Is that the boy we met on our way to the Jane Addams lecture? The one who came looking for you at the house this week? The dirty, uncouth boy?"

"He's really a good boy. He's a bit rough around the edges, but he's a hard worker with a heart of gold," Leona said, coming to Fitz's defense.

"That may be true, but we can't very well have ruffians knocking on our door on Joy Street asking for Clementine. Rumors can ruin a girl, Clementine Elizabeth. I told him not to come back."

Clementine surprised both Leona and Aunt Franny by jumping to her feet.

"You're so mean, Mother!" She rushed out of the room.

Aunt Franny's mouth hung open. "Well, isn't she in a mood? She looked as if she'd eaten a pickle."

Leona raised an eyebrow. Was it possible Clementine felt something for Fitz? Why else would she have barked at her mother like that?

Her aunt sipped her wine. "Now, that Bradlee, he's a clean, upright-looking orphan. If he came to the door, I would be pleased to speak with such a humble, handsome lad."

Leona's heart ached. *I can't love Bradlee. I can't.*

Until she met him, she'd expected to marry a Warden. But the tortuous pain in her heart made her want to break her promise to Papa.

Bridget cleared the table. "I'll bring out Mr. Schaeffer's dinner plate for you soon, Miss Leona," Bridget said in a low voice, her light brogue lifting the l's and lengthening the oo's in her words.

"Thanks, Bridget."

"You're a good niece, Leona. I must apologize for my husband's unjustified rudeness. He refuses to tell me what you argued about, but it's probably not as awful as he made it seem.

You're too nice a girl. I hope you can forgive that grumpy old man for his callous nature. We all have our flaws."

"Yes, Aunt Franny."

Bridget entered, carrying a tray with a plate filled to the edges with food. A clear jar of golden-brown liquid sat at the side.

"Mr. Schaeffer sure likes his beer. Some Yankee he is. I can't seem to get the German out of him. The temperance ladies at our church would be appalled. Simply appalled!"

Leona nodded politely and carried the tray out. She knocked on the door, then entered with the tray.

"Thank you. You're dismissed," her uncle said without looking up from his papers.

Leona cleared her throat and straightened her back. "Uncle, I know about the detector. I don't know what it is, but I know that's how my father found immature lycanthropes. Did you know about this?"

"Yes," he said. "I had one also."

"You knew I was going to work at an orphanage. Didn't you think I should have this detector?"

"No. Then you would use it."

Leona's hands grasped her skirt to contain her frustration.

"Uncle! Please tell me what and where it is."

"It's too late. Eben didn't give his to you. Don't you wonder why? Maybe it's because he didn't think you were cut out for the job, Princess!"

Leona let go of her skirt. "What did you call me?" She glowered at his cowardly face, her blood hot.

Sweat formed on his pale skin. He turned his blue eyes to his food, picking up his knife and fork. He cut his meat and said, "Y-your mother almost named you Alexandra, you know, like the Grand Princess of Russia."

"I didn't know." Another thing they'd never shared with her.

Uncle Ezra continued, "Katarina thought the Romanovs walked on water. Guess we'll have to wait and see what becomes of them. Russia isn't a very happy place right now. Anyway, I'm relieved Eben named you after our mother instead."

"I'm not here to talk about my name. Tell me about the detector. Please!" she begged.

"No."

He sipped his beer and then added, "Go back to the orphanage, Leona."

Leona, defeated, rose to leave.

As she placed her hand on the doorknob, her uncle asked, "How did you find out about the detector anyway?"

She didn't respond.

"There's a rogue at the orphanage, isn't there?"

"Yes." There was no use in lying. But she'd never tell him it was Mr. Green.

"If the Hunters discover there's a rogue there, they'll come after him. And then they'll find you. If you're lucky, they'll give you time to choose."

"Choose what?"

Uncle Ezra grimaced. "To join them or to normalize. They don't abide Shepherds."

"I'll never join them. Or you."

Her uncle sighed. "You're just like Eben. Stubborn. You need to understand something—the Hunters aren't completely wrong. Werewolves *are* dangerous creatures—even you must admit that. After their first human kill, their lust for human blood becomes insatiable." He finished his beer and plunked the jar back on the tray.

"Yes, they're dangerous. That's why Wardens possess the ability to fight them. But the Hunters are wrong. Werewolves should have the chance to live their lives, not be slaughtered outright," Leona said.

Her uncle was silent. Before the silence became too unbearable, he spoke, though it was a small whisper.

"I was optimistic and naïve, just like you, once. Despite the Code's rules against it, I fell on love with a Werewolf."

Did I hear him correctly? She studied at her uncle's mouth, ready for it to break into guffaws. But the vacant, sad look in her uncle's eyes remained. He was telling the truth. "What happened?"

"She killed someone."

"And you exacted mercy?"

"Yes," he whispered, "*Mercy.*" A frown morphed his face.

"I'm sorry, Uncle."

A quick wave of anger flashed over his countenance. He stood. His cold blue eyes pierced Leona's. "I too have burdens to bear. I thought I could leave the past behind. Then you—"

His voice caught. Leona opened her mouth to reply but the words camped in her mind. *I came back and ruined everything.*

He sat down and picked up the fork on his tray. Without looking up, he said, "I regret that you've chosen to remain a

Warden. You're only embracing pain and heartache. I cannot abide your choice and put the rest of my family at risk. Leave this house, Leona. And don't ever come back again."

She backed away from the desk. Though curious about the story behind her uncle's pain and angry about his refusal to tell her more about the detector, this conversation was over.

Leona opened the door and left, leaving her uncle alone with his burdens.

Chapter Sixteen

Saturday, October 14
22 Joy Street, Boston

"Miss Leona, the horses are hitched and ready to go. Are you?" Allen asked. A polite grin decorated his dark wrinkled face.

Leona guessed the Schaeffer's servant was over fifty years old. His short hair was clouded gray above his ears. He wore a simple brown jacket over a corduroy vest, topped with a matching newsboy cap, an outfit normally worn by younger gentleman, children even.

To be honest, Boston wasn't what she'd imagined it would be. The heart of the city was deeply segregated. People lived in separate communities respective to their heritage, race, or religion: Irish, German, Negro, and Jew. She'd expected more cultural unity. Instead, the divisions were stark and precise.

Lycanthropes existed among every heritage and every social class. Bridget was just as likely as Clementine was to turn into a vicious monster three nights a month. Leona's attention was focused on the color of people's eyes, and not the tint of their skin.

Uncle Ezra refused to help her detect untransformed Werewolves. At least she had Mr. Green. He could sniff out those in the orphanage who would need her guidance.

She felt a sting of guilt for not being there tonight to wish him a safe transformation. Mr. Green was proof that the Hunters were misguided. Lycanthropes deserved a chance to live safely. Wardens existed to offer assistance and protect humanity. Why had these Hunters rejected what Wardens had believed for centuries?

"Miss?"

Leona shook her head. She'd been lost in her thoughts.

"Yes, Allen, I'm ready."

Bridget ran into the alley, out of breath.

"Miss Leona? Can I speak with you?" She turned to Allen. "In private?"

Allen walked to the wagon. "It's a cold night. I better lay down a blanket or two on this seat."

"Thanks, Allen. I'll meet you there soon." She smiled at the man.

Allen smiled back and left. Bridget grabbed Leona's arm and held on tight. She spoke in hushed tones.

"Miss Leona, I have to confess something to you. I feel horrible—just horrible—about it, but I-I stabbed you on the street that day—with this." She held up a small, silver letter opener.

"Why?" Leona demanded. She was shocked. She liked Bridget. *How could she do such a thing?*

Bridget's eyes fell, her face full of shame.

The Good Shepherd

"A man paid me to. He offered me real silver to do the evil deed. Miss Leona, I beg your forgiveness. My youngest brother is sick. We needed the money to pay for his hospital bills. I'm so sorry."

"Did this man tell you why he wanted you to do this?"

"Yes, but it was awful strange." Bridget dropped the letter opener in her apron pocket.

"Go on, tell me," Leona insisted.

Bridget cocked her head sideways. "He said it was a test, that you were a witch and it wouldn't really hurt you. And he was right—you recovered fast, miss. Are you a witch?"

Leona frowned. "No, I'm not a witch, Bridget." The maid's eyes narrowed. Leona supposed Bridget did not believe her. She tried to ignore the maid's suspicious glances, cleared her throat, and asked, "What did the man look like?"

"He was tall and well-dressed... and he had a mustache. That's all I can remember. I'm so sorry, Miss Leona. It hurt, didn't it? When I repaired the hole in the garment, I wept, I did. But I figured, if you're a witch, you're a good one." She shook her head to and fro. It made Leona quite dizzy to watch her.

Bridget stopped, rose her head, and grimaced. "I feel so ashamed for harming a nice young lady like you. Can you find it in your heart to forgive me?"

Leona took Bridget's hands in hers. "I forgive you."

The maid grinned, then bowed her head and repeated, "Thank you, thank you, thank you."

Leona was relieved that the maid was contented now, even if she believed Leona was adept at witchcraft. She still had questions for her.

"Do you remember the policeman who came to see me?"

Bridget paled. "Oh, please don't send me to jail. My family needs me!"

"No, that's not why I asked. I was just wondering if the man he found in the alley was the man who told you to stab me. His name was Goldberg."

"I don't know. He didn't tell me his name."

Leona's frown deepened. She'd never seen Warden Goldberg. Had he paid Bridget to test Leona, to see if she would heal from a wound quickly, like a Warden would? Did he doubt she was who she claimed to be?

"Promise me that you'll tell me right away if you see that man again, okay Bridget?"

"Yes, miss," the maid agreed.

As upsetting as it was to believe she'd been attacked by a fellow Warden, Leona hoped the culprit *had* been Warden Goldberg. After all, he couldn't harm her from the grave.

Saturday Evening, October 14
The Home for Little Wanderers

The night sky was dotted with stars. A streetlamp threw a yellow haze onto the city street. As Allen guided the carriage into the orphanage's driveway, Leona sighed.

"Everything all right, miss?" he asked.

The Good Shepherd

Leona wanted to reply, "Everything is all wrong." Instead she said, "Everything's fine, Allen. Thank you so much for the ride. Drive home safely."

"Yes, Miss Leona." He tugged the brim of his newsboy cap. "Good night." The carriage disappeared down the street.

What a terrible evening.

Leona had planned on escorting Mr. Green to the sanctuary tonight, but the opportunity to speak to Uncle Ezra took precedence. Too bad it had ended so horribly.

She decided to check in to see how Mrs. Green was coping with her husband's absence.

On her way, Leona mused over her uncle's disturbing revelation that he'd loved a Werewolf. Not only that, he'd had to exact mercy on her. If she had to, could she kill someone she cared for? If Bradlee or Mr. Green killed a human, the bloodlust would be uncontrollable. They'd kill again. It would have to be done.

Her uncle had done the right thing. But it had caused him to hate who he was, *what* he was.

What about Warden Goldberg? Had he been a Hunter? Did he pay Bridget to test her? She could forgive Bridget for doing the wrong thing for the right reasons. But the man who'd paid her to do the deed? That was another thing altogether.

Leona knocked on Mrs. Green's door. In a few moments, it opened, and Mrs. Green's humble face appeared. Understandably, her eyes held a dash of sadness. She ushered Leona in and offered her a seat.

A wicker basket rested on the floor by Mrs. Green's feet.

Fuzzy brown wool bubbled over the top. A thick, cabled scarf-in-progress lay on the chair, pierced through with two wooden sticks.

Leona attempted to push her own worries out of her mind and focus on her duty, both as a Warden and as a friend.

"Everything went smoothly. Teddy is secure," Mrs. Green assured her.

Leona smiled weakly. "It must be hard for you. Is there anything I can do to help you pass the time over the next few nights?"

"Do you knit?" she asked, gesturing to a large burlap bag in the corner. "A local mill donated that wool fleece, so I planned to keep busy either washing, carding, and spinning it into yarn or knitting items for the children. Winter will be here soon. Knitting and spinning help calm my nerves." Her hands manipulated the two needles like a marionette worked the strings of a puppet. They danced on her lap as the fabric grew. "You'd think after twenty years of marriage I'd be used to Teddy's condition, but I'm still just as fretful as ever. Even though I know he's secure, these nights are hard on him. And on me."

"Mrs. Green," Leona said, "You're not alone. I'm here to help."

The matron's chest rose and fell at a steady pace as her needles clicked along. "Thank you, Leona. I'm sorry, but I can't help being a bit nervous around you. Granted, they're just rumors, but over the years, I've heard terrible things about Wardens."

"You have? Like what?"

Mrs. Green's hands never slowed as she explained, "Years ago, stories spread about a Warden called The Collector, who trapped lycanthropes. He kept them in cages and sold them to traveling carnivals. Teddy always said he'd rather die than be caught by the Collector." She stopped knitting. "Forgive me, I'm not myself tonight. I must be strong for the children. But when I'm alone, it all rises to the surface."

Leona patted her hand. "It's okay. You can cry in front of me, Mrs. Green."

"It would help calm my nerves a good deal if you addressed me by my first name. I know it might seem odd, since I'm many years your senior and your employer, but under these circumstances, I think propriety is foolish, don't you?"

"Yes, Jane." Leona returned her smile as best she could. The weight of her feelings for Bradlee, her uncle's revelations, and Bridget's confession haunted her.

"How was your visit with your family?" Jane asked, resuming her needlework.

"Terrible. My uncle is as stubborn as ever. He refuses to change his opinion about Wardens. He hates the fact I chose to remain one."

"He's not a Warden then? I thought it was a hereditary position?"

"He's a Normalizer. They have the abilities of a Warden, like fast healing and fighting instincts, and they pass on these traits to their offspring, but they live like a normal human. It's a cowardly life, if you ask me."

"What's his reasoning?"

211

Leona was tactful despite her inner angst.

"He has different priorities. He's a Brahmin, first and foremost."

"I see," Jane said, her needles tapping like wooden shoes.

Leona continued, "But tonight he said something startling." She fidgeted in her seat. "He said he loved a wolf once. But she killed someone, and… well… he had to exact mercy."

Jane's needles slowed as she replied, "I suppose that experience might make one angry, wouldn't it? Imagine if you were forced to exact mercy on someone you loved, Leona."

Leona rubbed her palms together. She didn't want to think about that. She covered her face with her hands but couldn't halt her tears.

The tapping stopped. "Whatever is the matter?" Jane said, her hands relinquishing her project.

"Can I confess something to you?" Leona asked. Jane's chin dipped, encouraging her to continue, "I care deeply for Bradlee. But I can't. He's a Werewolf and I'm a Warden. My uncle said it's against the Code for us to be together. And I promised my papa I would only marry a Warden."

"I see." Jane replied. The knitting needles in her hands tapped at a steady rhythm.

"I can't love Bradlee," Leona asked. "How do I stop?"

"Dear, no one can control who they fall in love with. Trust me, I know a thing or two about loving the wrong person," Jane said. She patted Leona's hand.

Leona thought back to when she'd started her job at the orphanage, about their conversation concerning the beast inside everyone. "What if I don't feed these feelings? Will they die?"

Jane's eyes narrowed. "I wish it were that easy. But you must make a choice, Leona. If you believe that keeping the promise you made to your father is important, then somehow you'll find the strength to let go of Bradlee."

"I think I already love him, Jane." Saying the words aloud didn't ease her mind. They left her feeling exposed and pathetic.

"Oh, dear." Jane fiddled with the wedding ring on her left hand. "Love is stubborn, Leona. Maybe I should have tried to starve my love for Teddy when we first met, but I chose not to. Now I can't imagine living without him, even with the risks. Love is always a risk."

Leona wrung her hands together.

Jane picked up her knitting and added, "Why can't you love a Werewolf?"

"I don't know. Papa always said I could only marry a Warden. Uncle Ezra just said it was against the Code," Leona said, twisting the fabric of her skirt in her hands.

"Have you studied the Code?"

"No. Papa said I was too young to study and train as a Warden. When the fire killed my family, it also destroyed the Code book."

"Teddy says that Werewolves have a guidebook also. It says the same thing. Werewolves can only mate with other Werewolves. All other unions are 'cursed.'"

Leona tilted her head. "What does that mean?"

"I don't know. I don't feel cursed, though I was never blessed with children. Maybe that's what it means." Jane set down her knitting, her kind eyes examining Leona's face. "You need some rest. It's been a long day."

Leona protested, "I'm not tired."

"Maybe not your body, but I think your heart and mind could use some rest. Go to your dorm. The girls are waiting for you. They missed you. I heard the exhibit went well, despite the rain. Tell them all about it. Get your mind off heavier thoughts."

"That's wise. I will. But I'd like to accompany you to the sanctuary tomorrow to check on Mr. Green."

"That would be lovely. I'll meet you after church and we'll go then. Reverend Busch is giving a sermon on forgiveness tomorrow."

Leona exhaled sharply.

"I suppose I should apologize to him, hmm?"

One side of Mrs. Green's mouth rose. She picked stray brown fuzz off her skirt. "Oh, maybe. Sometimes I want to argue with Reverend Busch, too." She sighed. "The man is only following what he's been taught, I suppose. In my opinion, one can be so heavenly minded it hinders their earthly work."

"What would Reverend Busch think of Werewolves and Wardens, I wonder?"

They both chuckled. Jane commented, "I think the good Reverend would be very shocked. Very shocked indeed. There is no room in his mind for such a fantastical intrusion on reality. He would probably blame the Catholics." She turned sullen. "It's not easy for any of us, is it?"

"No, Jane. It's not."

The women embraced.

"Goodnight, Leona."

The Good Shepherd

As Leona turned to exit, a door to the back room of the Green's apartment opened. Fitz entered the main living area.

"All yer supplies are stocked, Mrs. Green."

"Thank you, Fitz. Would you mind escorting Miss Schaeffer to the girls' hall?"

"Aye, Mrs. Green," he said, his face unusually pale. His freckles were indistinguishable in the twilight.

Leona and Fitz walked out into the hall together. When they reached the intersection of the main hall and the girls' hall, Fitz turned to Leona, his face deadly serious. It was an unexpected and uncomfortable sight.

"Leona, is it true? Are Mr. Green and Bradlee Werewolves?"

Chapter Seventeen

"What are you talking about, Fitz? Don't be a fool. I'm not sure what you think you heard, but—"

Fitz narrowed his eyes.

"I'm not a fool. You're no regular lass, are ya?"

Leona tried to manufacture a reply, but Mrs. Green's observation about her exhaustion had been quite accurate. She didn't possess the mental strength to lie.

"No, I'm not a regular girl. I'm a Warden, a protector. I police the Werewolf community—and help the rogues, the orphans. But Fitz, you can't tell a soul. Even Bradlee. He doesn't know yet."

Fitz's mouth gaped. "Wait—yer serious? He don't know? Poor bloke. This is going to ruin his life, ya know. He 'ad big plans—college, touring Europe, and such. Now he's gonna be tied up, I s'pose, eh?" He tittered nervously, scratching his auburn head.

"Fitz, this isn't a joking matter. Bradlee will turn into a Werewolf for the first time next month, on the night of the first full moon."

"When's that?"

"November 12. I plan to explain everything to him tomorrow night. Can you keep it a secret for now?"

"Aye," he tipped his chin and placed one hand over his heart, "I promise not to say anything ta him." He rubbed his neck. The reddened skin absorbed his freckles. "How did it 'appen? Did someone bite Bradlee?"

Leona grimaced. The popular legends about Werewolves generated plenty of fear and fright. Keeping the truth a secret wasn't difficult. Fables and lore would always prevail.

But Leona trusted Fitz. He asked out of sincere concern for his best friend and his mentor, so she told him the truth, "No, lycanthropes are born, not made."

"Lyca—what?"

"Lycanthropes. Werewolves. It's a condition that runs in the family. Werewolves usually live in small communities, in packs. Lycanthropia is an inherited condition."

"Like webbed toes?"

Leona bit her lip at Fitz's comical example. "I suppose."

"But I thought Werewolves go around biting folks and turn them into monsters too. It's catching—*cortageous*, right?"

"*Contagious*? No, Fitz. That's a fantastical tale, a myth. The truth is more difficult to understand," she narrowed her eyes at him, "and must be kept a secret. For safety reasons, understand?"

"Yes. I s'pose that makes sense. But, what happens if a person does get bit by a lycratop?"

"Ly-can-thrope. That's a good question. I heard my papa say that if it's rare to survive a Werewolf attack. If a Werewolf bites you, you die a slow and painful death. There's poison in their saliva."

"That's terrible!" Fitz's shoulders shook.

"Yes. But my job is to make sure Werewolves without a pack live safely among humans. There's no reason Bradlee can't live a happy life, with some adjustments."

Fitz elbowed Leona. "Aye, 'adjustments'… he may not like them 'adjustments.' I heard everything, Leona. Bradlee's not gonna want ta starve his love for ya." Leona's face grew hot. Fitz continued, "But Bradlee would do whatever ya ask 'im. If ya asked him to run away with—"

Leona cleared her throat and avoided eye contact with the grinning boy. "Why would you suggest such an improper thing?"

He waved his finger in her face. "I heard what ya said to Mrs. Green, lass. Ya love him, but your love is forbidden. That's the most excitin' kind 'o love, Miss Leona! Like Clementine an' me."

"So… Clementine has confessed her love for you?" Leona crossed her arms and waited for his bubble to pop.

But Fitz only smiled bigger. "'Tis only a matter 'o time. We bonded real good today in the Common. She and I ran off into the sunset. Well, it was raining, but ya get my inference."

Leona remembered the note in Clementine's pocket. "Fitz, does Clementine like her job assisting the professor at Harvard?"

"Nay. She's been fired, she 'as."

"Why?"

"She defended me honor and they told her to git."

Though she was shocked at the idea of Clementine defending Fitz in public, she believed Fitz's story. Leona smirked, imagining the professor or Mr. Hartman telling Clementine to 'git.'

She cleared her face. "That's a shame."

"Why? Ma darlin' isn't meant for a life of books and learnin.'"

Fitz might be right about Clementine's aptitude regarding education, but his comment made Leona frown. As much as Clementine might portray a doll, she wasn't one. She had a brain and a heart, somewhere inside. Deep inside, maybe, but it was there.

"Forget Clementine. Tell me, Fitz, what do you want to do in the future, when you leave the orphanage?"

Fitz twisted his mouth, his boyish countenance turning introspective and serious.

"I don't ever want to leave the orphanage. I want to stay here forever."

"But don't you have any other dreams? Don't you want to become something more than a kitchen assistant?"

"Like what? The first Irish orphan to walk a tightrope at Barnum and Bailey's? Come ta think on it—that might be alright! All them gypsy acrobats better make room for me," he joked, chuckling so hard his thin body jiggled.

Leona rubbed her eyes and sighed. "Very funny, Fitz. But that's not what I meant. What are your interests—besides dreaming about Clementine?"

Fitz shrugged.

"I like cookin,' I s'pose. My sisters and I used ta dream about running a restaurant of our very own. We'd call it, '*Fitzgerald's Fixin's.*' But now I wish I could do what you do, Miss Leona. Your Warden job sounds mighty excitin'."

"Exciting?" Other words came to her mind: burdensome, necessary, and stressful.

"I see." He yawned, his eyes pinching tight. "Well, I was just gonna visit Bradlee. He's subbin' fer Mr. Green and it's gotta be mighty boring. Golly, I can hardly believe my best friend is a Werewolf. Golly, I say!"

Apprehension and doubt over Fitz's ability to keep a secret crept into Leona's gut. A chill ran down her back. She held herself up by grasping the heavy bookend on the shelf behind her. "Fitz, maybe you shouldn't visit Bradlee. You've just had a shock."

Fitz took a step toward the boys' dorm.

"A shock? Are you worried I can't keep a secret, Leo—"

She conked Fitz on the back of his head with the bookend, with just enough force to knock the poor boy out. His body went limp. She caught him under his arms and drug him to the couch in the hall, gently covering him up with an afghan.

Tucking it under his sides, she whispered in his ear, "Sorry, Fitz. I can't take the chance. I hope you can forgive me tomorrow."

Rain pounded on the windows, waking Leona early Sunday morning. One by one, she woke the girls. They took turns bathing in the tub by the fireplace in the girls' washroom, then donned their Sunday best.

Plaiting the girls' hair was Leona's favorite—and most

tiring—part of the Sunday morning routine. Once a week, she braided eighteen heads of damp hair. Strips of fabric from old dresses and blankets served as hair ribbons. Leona imagined Clementine's vanity dresser drawers, filled with dozens of beautiful ribbons: sky blue, light rose, and sage green.

"Thank you, Miss Leona," Regina said, as Leona tied her head kerchief at the back of her neck, under the fresh braid. She spoke in English often now, working extra hard to remove any trace of an accent. Leona missed speaking with her in Russian.

The girls formed a line and marched briskly to the dining hall. The two dorms had a friendly rivalry over promptness to meals. The girls beat the boys this morning, but everyone was forced to wait for the ten-year-old boys to arrive before they could eat breakfast. Bradlee led them into the room, looking a little frazzled. He ordered them to stand by their chairs and then led them in an apology.

The group of boys spoke in unison, "Sorry we're late for breakfast, Mrs. Green!"

Jane tipped her chin in acknowledgment of their collective apology. She smiled at Bradlee, who grimaced boyishly and smoothed the top of his unruly dark hair.

"After breakfast, dorm monitors will lead their groups to the chapel for Sunday service. Bow your heads. I'll say the blessing."

The children joined her in ending the mealtime prayer with a slow "A-men."

Fitz stumbled into the dining hall. His hair was beyond disheveled. It stuck out in every direction like straw in a trough. He apologized to the kitchen master for his appearance and his lateness. Mrs. Green approached, setting her hands on both his shoulders in an attempt to calm the boy.

"I don't know what 'appened, Mrs. Green. I just woke up on the common room sofa, I did. I have a mighty big headache."

Leona kept her head down and sighed lightly. He was fine. But soon he would remember everything they discussed last night and be tempted all over again to inform Bradlee about his condition before Mr. Green and Leona planned to face Bradlee and explain it to him together.

Fitz would have little chance to blab today. He spent every Sunday in the kitchen. Reverend Busch's long sermons brought out Fitz's industrious spirit.

How will *Bradlee react to the news that he's a Werewolf?* It would be Leona's first time revealing to a rogue their condition. She had left the job up to Luke's uncle last time, with horrible results. It couldn't have gone worse. Leona vowed that could never happen again. She couldn't change the past, so she focused on the future, on the next Werewolf, Bradlee Smith, the orphan found at Boston Harbor, a talented artist and gifted teacher, her friend.

"Miss Schaeffer, are you going to eat your toast?"

Leona shook her head and handed her dark toast to the girl beside her.

"Hurry, it's almost time for church."

"Aw, why do we have to go to church?"

"Now, now, be polite and listen. You may learn something valuable."

"Yeah, like how to sleep with your eyes open!" an ornery girl across from them replied. Leona furrowed her brows at her, but, honestly, she didn't always enjoy Reverend Bushes' sermons, either.

To the girls' surprise, the tall, thin pastor entered the cafeteria, sprinting across the floor, his stick frame a blur. He was sopping wet. Leona half expected the man to fall on his bottom as he crossed the wood floor in his wet boots.

"Mr. Green! Mr. Green!" he shouted.

Jane waved him over. "Mr. Green is away on a trip. Whatever is the matter, Reverend?" She handed him a towel.

"I have terrible news." He wiped his brow and cheeks, then blew his nose into the towel.

"Perhaps we should discuss it in my office." Jane gestured to the dining room doors and he stumbled toward them.

"Yes, yes, it's far too tragic. I—I came as quick as I could. Oh, it's terrible, just terrible." The man's hands trembled. He gripped the towel tight and inhaled slowly, before mouthing a prayer.

Jane followed the man out of the room. The cafeteria erupted with voices. Leona shushed the children. She left Rachel in charge as she slipped away to join Jane and the minister.

The reverend settled down in a chair, where he appeared a little less flummoxed, as Leona entered the office.

"A-an urgent telegraph arrived this morning," he began. "The train derailed near Kansas City."

Mrs. Green crumbled into a chair. "The orphan train?"

"Yes," Rev. Busch replied, twisting the towel in his hands.

"And our children?"

He lowered his head. "They all died, Mrs. Green. Every single soul."

Leona grasped the wall to hold her body up. *Mary and Grace are dead?*

Jane's eyes were fixed on the door. Leona had left it open.

"Oh no—Fitz," Jane gasped.

Leona turned and saw Fitz standing in the doorway, tears streaming down his face. Backing away from them, he ran, bursting through the front doors of the Home and into the storm.

"Miss Schaeffer," Jane addressed Leona, "Find Mr. Smith. Tell him the details quickly and send him after Fitz. I'll ask Calvin to escort the boys to the chapel."

Leona nodded, numb. Her feet moved willfully toward Jane. The heavy news did not lighten as they embraced. Jane squeezed Leona's shoulders. Her eyes were filled with an uncanny strength.

"You can do this," Jane insisted. "Right, Reverend?"

The reverend removed his brimmed hat, displaying the only remaining dry part of his body, his bald head, which he nodded weakly. The smell of moldy tobacco and wet wool emanated from him.

Jane's face remained surprisingly calm. "Reverend, we need to inform the children of this tragedy. Then I think some prayer is in order. Wouldn't you agree?"

"Yes, ma'am."

"I'll fetch some of Mr. Green's clothes for you to change into." Jane blinked at Leona. "Miss Schaeffer, why are you still standing here? Fitz is out there in this storm all alone and in pain.

The Good Shepherd

It's *dangerous*. Go tell Mr. Smith to search for him."

Leona woke, as if from a nightmare. Everything that happened in the last twenty-four hours seemed like a diaphanous dream. Jane's words hit Leona like a brick. Bradlee must find Fitz before sundown.

She sprinted off toward the cafeteria. She found Bradlee and pulled him aside. Her blue eyes met his.

"Bradlee, I need you."

Chapter Eighteen

Rain drops slid down the windowpane by Clementine's bed.

Should I beg for my job back? When she walked along the grand halls of the College, she felt important. Even when she dusted bookshelves and pushed Mr. Hartman in his wheelchair, it felt good—like she was special, needed. Though she didn't understand the men's discussions on sociology and their intellectual banter, she felt smarter just being in their presence. Mr. Hartman even lent her a book from his personal collection.

She'd lied to Mother. Mr. Hartman hadn't harassed her. The professors normally treated her well. And she didn't really blame them for being disappointed in her at the recent lecture in the Common. After all, she'd been a dolt, dropping the book and causing a scene.

Clementine glanced at the pilfered note she'd shoved into *The Wonderful Wizard of Oz.*

Now I'll never have another chance to find out what that list is for. Why do I care, anyway? My name isn't on it.

Picking up the borrowed book, Clementine smiled. She

enjoyed reading about Dorothy's outrageous trip via cyclone to a magical land where they treated her like a princess. *Why can't anything this fantastic ever happen to me? Real life is so drab.* Then she remembered Mr. Hartman saying the book was allegorical, which dulled the fun. She preferred to think of it as a fantasy. She often dreamed about the land called Oz, the great wizard, the Wicked Witch, Munchkins, and a brave girl wearing silver slippers traveling on a yellow brick road to the Emerald City accompanied by a scarecrow, a tin man, and a lion.

Outside, the gray rain pattered on her window. She read the book, letting a cyclone of imagination whirl her troubles away.

Sunday Evening
The Home for Little Wanderers

By dusk, the rain had slowed to a drizzle. Leona stared out the window, hoping to spot Bradlee and Fitz returning on the dappled mare he saddled to search for his friend.

The girls in the dorm were understandably disturbed. Each of them swore to never board a train. They didn't cry, though. Orphans were not unacquainted with grief. They had each done much weeping in their short lives. They already felt a decent portion of loss when Mary and Grace left the orphanage last week. In their world, they had already said goodbye and begun the mourning process, as they had done often in the past as friends left the orphanage.

It was different for Fitz. He was their brother. Mary and Grace's departure on the train had depressed him, but he held onto the hope they would see each other again someday. But now there was no possibility of their reunion. No more sibling arguments. No more forgiving hugs. No future *Fitzgerald's Fixin's*.

Leona never had a sibling to argue with, to love, or to miss. Certainly, it was different than losing a parent. She tried to imagine how it would feel if anything happened to her cousin. She barely knew Clementine. But her initial feelings of warmth toward her remained. Yes, Clementine was self-centered. But she had a charm all her own. If only her cousin could rid herself of her silly misconceptions about those she didn't understand, the girl's heart would be less burdened by shallow concerns like social status, wealth, and beauty. The world consisted of much, much more. Maybe Fitz's stubborn love for Clementine could temper her selfish attitude and broaden her worldview—unless his pain took away the strength needed to love Clementine. Was that possible?

Bradlee would find Fitz. Leona believed he wouldn't return until he did. In the meantime, she prayed for them both.

A knock sounded from the dormitory door. Leona answered it.

"Leona, may I speak to you alone, please?" Jane asked.

She stepped outside the dorm. "What's wrong? Is it Fitz?

What happened?"

Jane wrung her hands. "No, it's not Fitz. At least, Bradlee hasn't returned yet, so I don't know anything. It's Mr. Green. Usually I visit him in the afternoons, but I couldn't leave the Home. Reverend Busch is still here."

"I can go to the sanctuary and check on him if it would ease your mind."

"I appreciate the offer, but it's almost sunset. And you need to be with the girls at this stressful time. How are they coping with the news?"

"They're upset, but not traumatized, as Fitz must be."

"The children here are tough. Sometimes too tough, I think. But I'm relieved to hear they are coping well. I'll let you get back to the girls now."

"Let me know when Bradlee and Fitz return—even if it's late, Jane."

"I will."

What was taking Bradlee so long to find Fitz?

"Fitz, where are you?" Leona mumbled.

Late Sunday Evening
22 Joy Street

Clementine smoothed her hair, staring at her reflection in the mirror of her vanity case. After being stuck in braids for hours, her usually straight, golden hair was temporarily kinked. She admired the waves around her face and shoulders. No, her hair wasn't naturally curly, like Leona's, but it looked just as nice. Nicer even, Clementine noted, because her curls had taken time and effort.

"Bridget! Come brush my hair!" she bellowed.

Mr. Flufferbutter, sitting on her lap, meowed.

"Aw, who's a pretty kitty? C'mon, who's a pretty kitty?" she teased him, scratching his furry chin until he rumbled like a steam engine.

Then his ears perked. Seconds later, he arched his back.

"What's wrong, Mr. Flufferbutter?"

The rain had stopped only an hour ago. It was ten o'clock in the evening. Mother and Father had retired for the night and Clementine forced herself to stop reading and begin her evening toilette. Her washbasin needed emptying and her hair still needed brushing.

She heard footsteps on the stairs, nearing her door.

"Bridget?"

Her door opened. Without looking up, Clementine sensed it wasn't Bridget. A familiar odor of vinegar made the surprise visitor's identity clear. She raised her head and glared at her unwelcome visitor.

She had swung her arm up, ready for assault, but pulled back. Though she hadn't touched him, pain disfigured his boyish face.

"What are you doing here, Fitz?"

There was no response. Clementine lightened her grip on the

hairbrush in her hand and examined Fitz. He was a fine mess.

"Whatever is the matter? You're soaked!" she exclaimed, pulling him inside the room.

She rummaged through her closet and gathered some towels, resting them on his outstretched arms. He stood there holding the pile of towels, stiff as a mannequin in a Jordan Marsh department store window display. Clementine took a towel from his frigid arms and rubbed his wet mop of red curls.

"If my Mother finds you here, she'll call the police."

He said nothing. No jokes, no humming, no crude remarks.

She wrapped his stiff hands with the towel to warm them. His skin was goose-pimpled and ghostly white. Even his freckles had paled. Wary of walking away from him for too long, Clementine ran to the closet again, quickly returning with a dressing gown that was less frilly than the others. She hung it over his arms.

"Here, take this and change in the watercloset. It's next door. Wait—I think I hear Bridget coming."

She slipped outside and confronted Bridget, excusing the maid for the night.

"Yes, Miss Clementine," Bridget replied, returning down the stairs.

Clementine sighed. She shoved the statuesque boy out of her bedroom and pointed to the watercloset. He shuffled toward it. She opened the door and pushed him inside.

"Change quickly, before you catch pneumonia. Then you can explain why you've broken into my house and invaded my privacy!" She expected a rude, Fitz-like remark about how she was too ugly to invade or something, but he simply nodded.

After ten minutes, Clementine returned to the watercloset door and knocked. There was no response.

"I'm opening the door now," she whispered.

The door creaked as she pushed it open. Fitz stared at his feet. He wore the long, white gown. She would have laughed out loud but for the sorrowful expression on his usually impish face. Instead, she reached out and took his hand in hers. It was still freezing. She guided him back into the dark hallway and then into her room, guiding him to the sofa and setting his wet clothes by the fireplace to dry.

Covering him with a wool blanket, the warmth soon melted his rigidity. He stretched his neck and yawned.

"You're alive after all! I thought I'd lost you for good, you ugly leprechaun," she remarked.

At her comment, a tear trickled from his left eye.

Fitz was usually so talkative, offensive, and blunt. This melancholy version of him confused her. "What happened, Fitz?"

"Me sisters. They're dead."

Clementine's stomach sunk. "What? The ones that went to Iowa?"

"Nebraska. Their train crashed. Mary and Grace died. That damn preacher told us about it. This is all his fault! He picked them to go. I begged them to stay. I should've done more."

"Fitz, I'm so sorry." She pulled his blanket-wrapped body into an embrace. She didn't mind his vinegar stench that much, not really.

All the fight was gone from him. He was a shell of his former spirited self. Fighting with Fitz had always made her feel *something*. Strangely, it felt good. Clementine was surprised to discover that holding Fitz in her arms felt good too. They huddled by the fire together under the blanket and fell asleep, warm in each other's embrace.

Monday Morning, October 16
The Home for Little Wanderers

Leona sat at the dining table with the girls, unable to swallow her coffee. Her eyes darted to the door every time someone entered the room. Bradlee hadn't come to breakfast yet. Calvin tended to Bradlee's charges, cheerfully buttering the boys' toast and pouring their apple juice.

She scolded herself. She should have gone searching for Fitz instead of Bradlee. *That's what a good Warden would've done.*

Jane walked through the door, making a beeline for Leona. Her heart raced. Whispering, Leona asked her, "Did Bradlee find Fitz?"

Jane shook her head and sighed. "Bradlee returned on Myrtle. He's brushing her down now. I ordered him to rest in his room when he finishes. His classes are canceled for the day."

"Did he tell you where he searched?"

"Yes. He said he ventured down the main road and returned on the back roads. He found Fitz's hat in the bushes outside the front door."

"It's Bradlee's hat, really. Fitz borrows it without asking all the time," Leona commented. She had no idea why she mentioned this useless detail.

Jane touched her shoulder lightly. "Did you get any sleep last night, Leona?"

"Not much," she admitted.

Jane sighed. "Neither did I. But we need to think of the children now, Miss Schaeffer. They need us. We'll talk more after Mr. Green returns."

Mrs. Green departed, and the girls finished their porridge. Leona led them to the dorm where they cleaned and dressed. She escorted them to their morning classes, going through the motions, a Shepherd leading her lambs, distracted and heavy-hearted.

Chapter Nineteen

An odd sound woke Clementine. It was Fitz, snoring by her ear. She eased his heavy head onto a pillow without waking him. He slept hard, like a toddler, his chubby, freckled face adorably innocent, his red wavy mop flat on one side. *Poor boy.*

A bell rang from downstairs.

Time for breakfast.

Fitz stirred slightly and cuddled the pillow. A grin snuck onto Clementine's face at the sight of him curling up on the sofa.

What should I do? Let him sleep or wake him?

She stumbled to her wardrobe, remnants of sleep languishing in her eyes, and pulled out her warmest dressing gown, a purple velvet and silk lined frock with a fox fur collar. The Battenberg lace on her bell-sleeved cotton nightdress hung from her elbow.

Mr. Flufferbutter slept in a ball on the rug between the fireplace and the sofa where Fitz snored. Clementine's stomach growled. The irresistible smell of bacon and cinnamon wafted up the stairs. *Fitz will be fine.* She followed the delicious scents.

Bridget served all of Clementine's favorite things: bacon,

cinnamon rolls, apple butter, pancakes, and scrambled eggs. Mother sat at the table. Father's place was empty. He was at the office by now.

"Sleep well, dear?" Mother asked.

Clementine hid her nervousness by stuffing her mouth with a sweet roll. Thankfully, eating wasn't a suspicious activity at breakfast time. She didn't speak, so she couldn't lie about anything, like letting a strange boy sleep in her room. Besides, next to Bridget's delicious cinnamon rolls, there were few rivals, even a cute boy. She almost forgot about Fitz.

Wait—did I just consider Fitz cute? My mind is befuddled indeed.

As she swallowed, the warm, gooey, cinnamon filling sliding down her throat, she remembered his sleeping face. It was quite adorable, she admitted, for a vagabond. If only he weren't a good-for-nothing orphan. He had no ambitions, as far as she could decipher, other than rambling on and on about how Clementine needed him. In fact, it seemed clear that *she* was his only ambition.

How disappointing. Sure, I'm pretty and well-to-do, but a boy like him must realize I'm not within his grasp.

After she allowed him to spend the night in her room, he might start thinking he actually had a chance to win her hand. She simply felt sorry for him. After all, he lost his sisters, his only remaining family. If he assumed anything else, she would have to set him straight.

I could never be interested in a poor, listless immigrant boy whose sole area of expertise is vinegar.

She scoffed and lifted another roll from the pyramid of buns on the plate between her and Mother. She almost choked on her next bite. *What if he blackmails me? Threatens to tell the world he stole my virtue?*

No, she was certain enough about Fitz's character to know he'd never do any such thing. As desperate as he was, he wasn't a maligner. He wouldn't try to slander her. He worshipped her.

Clementine smiled without intending to. It felt nice to be worshipped. Her body tingled with delight. She came to her senses as she considered the vessel of this worship.

Ugh. If only the lie about Mr. Hartman were true—that he fancied her. A college professor's assistant would be a decent catch. And Mr. Hartman was tolerable, at least. Sometimes he smelled like dusty old books, but never like vinegar.

Sighing heavily, she lowered her fork.

Mother sipped her tea and cocked an eyebrow at Clementine. "Something wrong, dear?"

"Oh, no. I'm fine. Are you going to Mrs. Lowell's today?"

"Yes, yes. As I do every Monday morning. We're going to the dressmaker's. Penny needs a few of her bodices altered. Too many tea cakes as of late, I presume." Mother giggled and pushed her plate of half-eaten food away.

Mother exaggerated her thin waist by wearing her corset as tight as possible, like a Victorian heroine. Her thin frame was easily maintained, since she couldn't eat much more than a few bites or the corset would strangle her. Clementine never wore a corset at breakfast.

"I expect you to return to your usual studies tomorrow, young lady, now that you quit your job at the College. I must admit, Ezra and I are disappointed in your failure to keep your commitments. If you continue to throw away perfectly fine opportunities for social success, I might have to send you to the boarding school in New York that Ezra attended."

"Isn't that for boys?"

Mother's eye twitched.

"I'm referring to its sister campus, dear."

"I'd rather live at *The Home for Little Wanderers!* Mother, I promise to study hard here in Boston. Please don't send me away."

Mother frowned playfully. Her rouged pout held a surprising similarity to a clown's grin. She winked at Clementine.

"I could never be apart from my Clementine. Ezra insisted I try to scare you into compliance. He is none too happy about your termination."

Clementine bowed her head.

"I'm sorry, Mother. It was a landslide of unfortunate events that led me to terminate my commitment to Professor Taylor. Like I said, Mr. Hartman made me uncomfortable." She glanced at the newspaper on the table, its frontpage headline accompanied by a large photo of women holding signs at the courthouse. Clementine gestured at the paper. Mother's eyes followed. "With woman's suffrage in sight, don't you think it's my duty to womankind to defend our rights in the workplace. I'm a mature young woman and I will be successful! I swear it on my father's grave."

"Clementine!" Mother lifted her embroidered handkerchief

to her open mouth. "There is no need to bring your father, God rest his soul, into your vows. You sound like a superstitious heathen. Or a Catholic. And woman's suffrage isn't going to become a reality any time soon, I assure you. Men run this world. Always have, always will. I recommend that you remain mindful of that, especially if you find yourself uncomfortable in the workplace again. Men are men, after all."

Clementine nodded politely. No, it wasn't true that Mr. Hartman had been ungentlemanly toward her. But if he had been, should she have excused such behavior? Most women would have, like Mother. But she was old and Victorian. This was the age of the New Woman. That's what the advertisements proclaimed, anyway. Clementine wasn't surprised that Mother spouted such old-fashioned notions.

Which was right, a traditionalist view or a progressive stance? Surely a person of the weaker sex could still be valuable to society, if they possessed wealth and influence. Wasn't that what the sociologists, like Professor Taylor, believed?

If Dorothy had only sold her silver slippers, she wouldn't have needed to beg the great and powerful Oz for help. Thank goodness I'm not a poor girl like Leona. Or a male orphan like Fitz. Then what value would I have?

Professor Taylor once said, *Society holds no obligations to useless citizens.* He's smart, so it must be right. People should make themselves useful to society.

Satisfied with her conclusions, Clementine felt better. Her high social standing made her important, useful. In fact, her heritage alone guaranteed that she would succeed, not to mention her wealth.

She needed to get rid of the orphan in her room first. Associating with riffraff like Fitz, Bradlee, and Leona was a mistake. They weren't good enough to be her friends. Even if they were in mourning.

But she still possessed a heart. She wrapped a few slices of bacon in a napkin and grabbed an apple to feed the vagrant loitering in her room upstairs. Besides, this food would get thrown out anyway.

Bridget entered the dining room and curtsied. Mother and Clementine waited for her to speak, but the maid seemed unable to do so. Her eyes darted back and forth from the front door to the women.

"Th-there's a man at the door to see you, Miss Clementine," she said, twisting her apron in her hands and glancing back at the door.

Clementine's eyes narrowed as she examined the maid at the door. Bridget's hands shook as she smoothed the wrinkles she'd created in her frock.

Is it another policeman? Clementine grabbed the apple and linen napkin stuffed with bacon, then rose from her chair and accompanied Bridget.

To Clementine's surprise, Professor Taylor stood outside the door, wearing a duster jacket. His gloved hand fidgeted with his ascot. His breath formed clouds.

Bridget held the door ajar. The professor peeked his head inside and spotted Clementine.

"Ah, Miss Bell. May I come in? It's mighty cold and breezy

this morn."

"Certainly," Clementine replied.

Bridget stared at the professor like she'd never seen a man before. She pulled the door full open, her eyes dropping to stare at the floor as he entered.

Professor Taylor shivered. He kept his gloves and hat on. Clementine hadn't shivered like that since the time she went ice-skating on the frog pond in the Common with her mother years ago. *It's funny to see an old man shiver like a little boy.*

Ugh... little boy... Fitz is still upstairs...

Clementine prayed Fitz would remain sound asleep for a few minutes longer.

"Professor Taylor, please allow me to apologize for my behavior on Saturday in the Common. You see, I've had this awful headache lately."

"I didn't come to wrench an apology from you, but I'll accept it all the same. The thing is," he rubbed his right collarbone, "I injured myself on a hunting trip yesterday. As you are already familiar with our schedule and surroundings at the college, I don't suppose I can convince you to return? Mr. Hartman and I are both in quite a sorry state, Miss Bell. Will you please come back?"

She perceived the physical pain he was in from his thin-lipped expression as he rubbed the injury. Father hurt himself similarly once before in a bicycle accident. Allen had fetched dry ice from the cellar to numb the pain. Maybe agreeing to help them again would ease Professor Taylor's pain.

"Okay, I'll come back."

The professor smiled, his mustache curling up on the ends.

"Thank you! If you'd like, I can wait and escort you to the school this morning."

Bridget interrupted, "Miss Clementine, I think I hear your mother calling me." She curtsied to them. "Please excuse me."

"Okay," Clementine replied. Bridget scampered off, quick and fearful as a mouse.

Watching Bridget steal away, Clementine was again reminded of the vagrant hiding in her bedroom. Her heart skipped a beat. *I have to get rid of Fitz before Bridget finds him first.*

She turned to Professor Taylor. "Um—I confess—I'm a vain girl. I'd hate to make you wait for me to finish my toilette, sir. It might take some time for me to make myself presentable."

"Oh, my first class isn't until noon. I have time to wait for you. If I could bother you for a cup of coffee—"

Clementine was stuck. Looking down, she realized her hands were full. She still held the wrapped bacon and apples.

"I'll pass on your request for coffee to Bridget on my way upstairs, Professor." She tipped her chin in the direction of the dining room. "Please make yourself at home in our dining room. Mother is there. Oh, do try the warm cinnamon rolls. They're the most delicious thing in the world."

Clementine tripped over her feet as she backed away. She almost dropped the makeshift food parcel as she raced up the stairs. She reached her bedroom door in a jiffy. As soon as she opened it, Mr. Flufferbutter bolted from the room. She gasped as his fluffy body whipped past her ankles.

"You rascal!" she scolded.

"Darlin'?"

She slammed the door behind her. Fitz was right where she left him—on the sofa, his mop of red curls resting on a silk pillow and his bony body covered with a blanket in front of the dying fire.

"Fitz, look, I'm sorry for your loss, truly. But I need to get dressed and go to work now. It's time for you to leave."

"Work? You were fired. I was there."

Clementine's eyes blinked at her wardrobe. *Did Bridget iron my new suit set?*

"Yes, well, they changed their minds. It turns out I'm invaluable. The professor is downstairs. He begged me to come back."

Fitz cocked his head at her and yawned. "You wanna work for them arrogant bastards?"

Clementine set the food package down on a side table and skipped over to her vanity. She sat down on the cushioned chair and, seeing her reflection in the mirror, panicked at the state of her hair.

Over her shoulder, she replied, "You're so rude. Mr. Hartman and Professor Taylor are respected, well-to-do intellectuals. I'll not have you bad-mouthing them again. If you can't say anything nice—"

"Oh, I've got nothing nice to say 'bout them two, I guarantee ya that, lass. If ya think they're something special just because they got schooling and wear suits every day, you're mistaken. I already told you what's important, darlin'—the heart. Them professors don't have a lick of compassion for the downtrodden. They're blowing hot air for applause."

Clementine brushed her hair while he jabbered on. When he was done with his unusually verbose tirade, she focused her gaze on his chin, and, as stern as she could manage, said, "Fitz, you must leave. You can't come here again."

He ran his fingers through his auburn hair. It fell back on his forehead. He blew it out of his eyes and pleaded, "But darlin,' you're my only sunshine now."

Clementine stared at her reflection in the mirror. *He has to take care of himself. He's not my responsibility,* she reminded herself.

She replied, "I am *not* your sunshine, Fitz, or your darlin'. You need to stop trying to woo me. You're an orphan. I'm a Brahmin. We aren't the same. Face the facts, Fitz. I'm just not the right girl for you. Find a nice girl at the orphanage and forget about me."

Clementine could hear him behind her, sliding off the sofa. By the sound of his breathing, he was approaching. He walked slowly, coming closer and closer. She couldn't bring herself to turn around and face his sad eyes and crooked mouth, so she picked up the brush and attempted to straighten her wonky hair.

Breakfast had given her strength, and the professor's visit bolstered her confidence. This little urchin brought out the worst in her—pity and shame. Fitz made her weak and, according to Darwin, only the strong survived.

Before she succumbed to pity again, Clementine reminded herself of the facts: Fitz was useless. He could never provide her with the life she was accustomed to. They could never have a proper, socially approved future. The boy was delusional.

Instead of arguing, he whispered, "I understand, lass." It sounded like he was inches away from her left shoulder, just out of view in the mirror.

"Good," she replied, refusing to turn and face him. She continued brushing her hair, though her scalp hurt. "Bridget should be busy getting the professor some coffee. If you sneak out the back stairs quickly—I assume you came in that way last night—then you shouldn't be seen. But you need to go *now*."

He took the brush out of her hand and set it on her vanity, then turned her around to face him. She tried to look past his sad freckled face and stare at a painting on the wall instead.

He grasped her chin gently and she had to look at him. Dried tears had left salt crystals on his face. His freckles were faded. He didn't look like a boy. This Fitz standing before her was a young man. Pain marred his previously innocent face. His emerald eyes, like the magical city of Oz, challenged her dispassion. Her heart ached. He'd lost so much.

He whispered again. "I won't call you *darlin'* anymore, Clementine. And you can stop calling me Fitz. My name is Charles—Charles Fitzgerald," he said, his voice uncharacteristically serious.

"Charles," she whispered back, unable to break away from his eyes. She cleared her throat and blinked. "You're right. I should call you by your given name."

He leaned in. As the green pools came closer, she held her breath.

His freckled forehead touched hers and he lifted his hand, caressing her cheek and gently tucking her loose hair behind one ear.

Without asking permission, he kissed her forehead. The part of Clementine that wanted to scold him was silenced by the part of her that melted at the lovely touch. His lips on her skin, like a butterfly landing delicately on a flower petal, displayed a sincere tenderness that she'd never experienced before.

"Thanks for giving me sanctuary last night, Clementine."

He spun her back around. She faced her reflection in the mirror. Her hand jumped to the bodice of her dressing gown and pressed on her heart, hoping to stop the excruciating pitter patter underneath.

What's wrong with me?

Within seconds, the door clicked open and shut again.

Charles was gone.

Chapter Twenty

Leona couldn't eat. Bradlee's absence from the dining hall at supper worried her, suppressing her appetite. But he needed to rest. After searching all night for his best friend, he hadn't found him. Reverend Busch had volunteered to take over the search.

Where could Fitz be? He'd been gone for twenty-four hours. If Leona had known him better, then maybe she could help. Then she'd know where he went when he was upset. Most of the children here had a favorite spot. Fitz spent most of his time in the kitchen, but they'd already searched there, with no luck.

Fitz possessed not only a funny smell and a multitude of freckles, but a jovial, mischievous, and brazen spirit. Could losing his only family destroy his spirit? One thing was certain; the cold weather could destroy his body.

Fitz's love for his sisters was rivaled most by his affections for Clementine.

Maybe I should tell Clementine that Fitz disappeared?

The last time Leona saw her cousin, it seemed like she had

softened her harsh view of Fitz. Maybe she was assuming too much. A girl like Clementine acknowledged the lower class but expected them to remain in their station.

Divisions of class and race were vastly more distinct in Boston than Leona had expected. The Civil War was long over, but not much had changed. If Boston was any indication, America was growing more and more divided. Her uncle's social climbing and his step-daughter's vanity proved this unfortunate truth. Uncle Ezra refused to help Leona, his brother's only daughter, to protect his reputation. What would Clementine do to protect hers?

Clementine won't care that Fitz is missing. Her cousin was probably reclining comfortably in ignorance by the fire at the beautiful house on Joy Street, admiring her heirloom pendant and petting Mr. Flufferbutter's head.

A shadow fell over Leona's plate, interrupting her thoughts.

"Jane? What's the matter?"

"Teddy isn't back from his… trip." Jane sat down across from Leona, right beside Regina, who was nibbling a dry biscuit.

"When does he usually return?"

Jane hesitated. "By suppertime."

"Supper isn't over yet," Leona tried to reassure her. "He'll probably walk through that door any minute."

Jane wrinkled her brow. "I know. I have so much weighing on my heart at the moment, with the orphan train and Fitz and—." She choked back tears.

"I understand. But try not to worry yet. Let me worry for you. I'll look for him after supper."

Panic washed over Jane's face after Leona said this.

"Jane—don't fret. If he's in trouble, I'll come to you first. I'm sure he's just extra tired. He's probably sleeping. After three tumultuous days—" she glanced at Regina "—of pheasant hunting—it's understandable." Jane wrung her hands together.

Leona laid her hand over Jane's. "Mr. Green is fine. If it'll ease your mind, though, I'll head out right now." Leona turned to the girl at her side. "That is, if Rachel here can be trusted to be in charge and get the girls ready for bed tonight?"

The girl nodded, sitting up straight and making herself taller. Rachel was the most mature of the bunch, now that Mary Fitzgerald was gone. Sweet little Mary—gone forever. Leona's heart pumped painfully as she grieved once more. She rallied for Jane's sake, casting a comforting smile at the woman.

"Okay. Ease your mind, Mrs. Green. I'll return in a couple hours."

Leona rose and exited the dining hall. She ran by her dorm and retrieved a scarf, hat, and gloves, handknit by Jane. The sun was setting low in the autumn sky and the evening chill would soon return.

She bundled up in the thick woolens, exited the building, and went to the stable to ready Hugo. The handsome palomino whinnied as she entered the stables, shaking his golden mane. She returned his effervescent greeting with a smile and an offering of oats.

"Hello, my friend. Want to go for a walk?"

Patting the horse's shoulder, she threw the saddle over his back and tightened the understrap. She embarked for the cabin as the sun slowly disappeared under the horizon. A purple haze filled the sky.

Hugo relished the chance to get some exercise. He pranced along the dirt road with little guidance from Leona. They communicated without words. Leona spent her energy scanning both sides of the road for a shock of ruddy curls, in the hope Fitz was returning to the Home. But there was little foot traffic along the dusky street. Leona turned off the road and directed Hugo toward Mr. Green's sanctuary, the fortified cabin the couple had shown her. He pursued the darker trail through the forest with caution.

Hugo whinnied, notifying Leona that the dirt trail in the forest had ended. Leona dismounted and stroked the horse's handsome neck.

"I'll be back soon, my friend."

Leona tracked Mr. Green's smell to find the hidden cabin, using the light of a portable oil lamp to illuminate her path. Her foot slipped slightly on a loose rock. She grasped a low tree branch to steady herself. Long scratch marks marred the bark of its thick trunk.

Her senses heightened. Her ears heard two squirrels scampering in the tree above. She catalogued the smell of various animals traversing over the leafy carpet of the forest floor. The cold environment didn't affect Leona. The adrenaline underneath her wool garments warmed her from the inside. Soon sweat moistened her face.

The cabin loomed before her, dark and eerily quiet. Its windows revealed nothing of the contents inside—a basement prison, with cages and chains, and locks strong enough to hold a writhing werewolf. Leona pulled out the ring of keys Mrs. Green gave her to open the dual locks and approached the heavy wooden front door.

The locks weren't there. Raw splintered wood took their place on the door. Leona searched her surroundings, using the pale light of the lantern. The two metal padlocks lay in the grass beside the doorstep. She ripped off her woolen hat and pulled the silver hairpin out of her hair. Her long curls fell over her shoulders. Holding the lamp high, she eased the broken door open and entered the cabin, taking cautious steps.

Cold, biting air blew past her. The lantern's light reflected off something on the floor. Her boots crunched debris as she progressed further into the interior. Broken glass. She searched for its origin. The window across from the fireplace was shattered, the wooden crossbeams of its panes torn like paper. Pieces of glass trailed from the window all the way across the room.

She crept through the upstairs living area and reached the door to the cellar below, leading to the cages and shackles. The locks on this door were also busted. One hung by a single screw. Leona's blood pounded in her ears. Her tightening throat felt strangled by the overly warm scarf.

She'd fought Mr. Harris in the open forest, wearing a borrowed wool dress and a knitted shawl. If it came to it, could she fight Mr. Green in this dark, confined space wearing woolen garments his own wife had knitted? She prayed this imaginary scenario would remain imaginary. Jane's kind, gentle face flashed into Leona's mind. They were friends, despite knowing what Leona's responsibilities were, her duty to protect the world from the monster her dear husband became.

A raven screeched in the forest. The sudden noise caused Leona to skip a step on the stairs. There were no sounds of breathing in the cabin, animal or human. The complete silence screamed that the dark basement was deserted.

Leona lifted the lantern and found what she expected—the cage was empty. Though the knowledge didn't surprise her, it caused a ripple of anxiety to roll through her.

Broken metallic shackles glistened on the straw, the shiny metal twisted and abandoned. But Mr. Green's clothes were not on the chair outside the cage.

As a perfunctory gesture, Leona swung the lamp around, to cast light on every corner. The floor was littered with straw from hay bales inside the cage. She shuffled her feet across the floor, clearing away the debris. Dark spots dotted the stone.

Leona removed her glove and touched her finger to one of the spots. It was thick, sticky, and reddish-brown. *Blood.* She sniffed. *Human blood.*

"Mr. Green, what happened?"

Late Monday Evening
22 Joy Street

The Good Shepherd

What a strange day, Clementine mused, sitting alone on her sofa.

Thankfully, her confusion over last night and this morning was sidelined upon her arrival that afternoon at Harvard. Professor Taylor had accompanied her to the office with a smile, as if all was forgotten.

There were an extraordinary number of freshmen enrolled in Sociology 101. It wasn't even a required class. But it was one of the few sociology classes offered in America. Harvard was progressive, like President Roosevelt, an alumnus. Clementine's chest filled with pride.

Of course, she wasn't a student. She couldn't even imagine the endless hours of studying, reading, and writing required to procure a college degree. *Such tedium!* She reveled in awe of the studious men here. Maybe she would marry a Harvard graduate someday. Then her future spouse would be prestigious, highly educated, and wealthy. For men, the proper education was necessary for success. She only needed to catch the eye of the right one.

Bridget handed her a steaming cup of tea. Clementine waved her hand at her. "You may leave now. I want to be alone, Bridget."

"As you wish, Miss Clementine." Bridget closed the door behind her.

Mr. Flufferbutter got to his feet. "Meow!" He jumped onto the sofa beside her. He marched in a circle twice before nesting onto a silk pillow.

Clementine was reminded of Fitz—*Charles.*

She scratched the cat's white head. "How's that poor ragamuffin doing, do you think, Mr.Flufferbutter? I hope he went straight back to the orphanage."

She couldn't forget him. The kiss rattled Clementine. She'd never been kissed before.

"He stole my first kiss!" She exclaimed to Mr. Flufferbutter. He licked his paw. "Wait—it didn't count— it wasn't on the lips."

"Meow! Meow!"

"Don't worry. I still have my virtue." She scratched his velvety ears.

"Meow," he said.

"Oh, you're probably right, Mr. Flufferbutter. Leona and Bradlee can help Fitz. They understand him better than I. You know, I didn't even cry when my father died. You can't miss someone you didn't really know. For example, I barely miss Leona at all."

A low rumble emerged from Mr. Flufferbutter's throat. Clementine narrowed her eyes at the white poufy feline.

"You really don't like Leona, do you?"

"Ree-ow!"

"Golly. I'm glad you like *me*... Don't you, pretty kitty?" Clementine scratched his chin until the growl dulled to a contented purr.

She unwrapped her shawl from around her shoulders and set it on the sofa. The fireplace burned bright, warming her feet. The reflection of its sparks glittered on the wolf pendant fastened to her shawl. She reached to remove the brooch.

Suddenly, she pulled her hand back.

The Good Shepherd

"I shouldn't touch it now, Mr. Flufferbutter. See, I'm learning—I remembered how it heats up when it gets near the fire. I won't let it burn me again."

"Meow!"

She scratched behind his ears and he closed his eyes in pleasure. After a few minutes, he rose from the pillow and wandered over to her shawl. He was about to plop his body down when Clementine shouted.

"No, Mr. Flufferbutter! The pendant will burn you!"

She snatched the shawl away. The heavy pin spun around and hit her wrist.

It was cool to the touch. Clementine was confused. The pendant had burned her twice while she'd been near a fireplace: the day Fitz and Bradlee visited at Harvard, and when she stood by Leona to dry her dress.

Flames roared in the fireplace. Red sparks flickered behind the wrought iron screen, the shape of a large Japanese fan, as smoke rose into the flue. The intense heat had warmed her enough for her to remove her shawl. Why wasn't the pendant hot?

Clementine felt utterly idiotic. Science mystified her. She thought she knew why the pendant had burned her, but now she felt stupid. Was there some strange alloy in this metal that only heated up sometimes? There must be some explanation for it that was beyond her comprehension.

"It's time for bed, Mr. Flufferbutter." She placed the pendant in her large jewelry box, her only other treasured item. "Father bought me this. It's from an exotic island in the Pacific. Not the

Atlantic, the ocean near Boston—but the Pacific. It's far, far away, near *Japan*. See, I'm not stupid," she informed the cat, who was preening.

"I bet Leona has never even heard of Japan. I'm surprised a poor country girl like her can even read." Clementine picked up the Farmer's Almanac from her dresser and flipped to the astronomy charts.

"The moon is waning tonight. So, there'll be no more strange phenomena, like unwelcome visitors in the middle of the night. You know, the full moons were exceptionally bright this weekend. That explains everything, doesn't it?"

Pulling her pink chenille curtains back to watch the waning moon shimmer against its black, star-studded backdrop, Clementine sighed. She frowned at Mr. Flufferbutter, and he frowned back, as usual. He couldn't help it. Persians had permanently grumpy faces. Clementine chose to interpret his dour expression as one of empathy.

Pulling thick covers over her shoulders and laying her head down on her embroidered silk pillowcase, Clementine whispered a silent prayer for Charles, since he needed help and she couldn't provide it for him. *But that kiss.* She shook the thought from her head and thanked God in advance for her future husband and fantasized about his wealth, intelligence and popularity, drowning out the disturbing memory of Charles's kiss.

The Good Shepherd

"Jane? It's Leona."

The door ripped open and an anxious Mrs. Green appeared, her eyes red and tired.

Leona didn't speak. The look on her face must have hinted her bad news. She stepped inside the Green's apartment and they both sat down.

"Mr. Green is missing. The cabin locks were destroyed. The upstairs window was broken from the outside."

Jane inhaled deeply. "If he broke his shackles and escaped, he'd have left his clothes behind. Did you search for his change of clothes?"

"His clothes weren't there."

Jane exhaled sharply. "That's a relief." Then her brow furrowed. "Actually, now I feel more worried. What if he was in his human form when the cabin was broken into—in his more vulnerable state?"

"There's one more thing I need to tell you. I found blood. Human blood."

Jane broke into sobs. Leona put her arm around the woman's petite frame. She couldn't explain what had occurred in the cabin. Her investigation was indeterminate.

"I'll go back in the morning. Maybe in the daylight, more

evidence will appear and help solve this mystery." She rose and went to the door. Jane opened it for her but grabbed her arm before she could leave.

"Oh, Leona, what if those rumors about the Collector are true. What if—"

"Stop. You're becoming hysterical. Don't lose hope."

Jane's hands shook. Her face contorted. "Help him, Leona. You're his Shepherd!"

"His what?" asked a familiar voice behind them.

She turned. Bradlee's ice blue eyes were wide with curiosity.

Jane met Leona's eyes. They held a question. Leona answered with a simple nod.

The petite woman stepped out of the apartment and faced Bradlee. "Mr. Smith, I think it's time we told you something very important. Will you come inside so we can talk?"

Bradlee's eyebrows knitted together. He hesitated but agreed, stepping inside.

"What's going on?"

Chapter Twenty-One

Bradlee, Leona, and Jane sat around a small oval table in the Green's apartment.

"I wish I could offer you some warm cider, but the fire is too fierce to hang the kettle," Jane said, gesturing to the roaring fire in the hearth.

"I'm not here for refreshments, am I? So," he furrowed his brow at them, "have you been keeping secrets from me?"

Leona's fingers tapped the table, in rhythmic competition with the crackling fire. Jane patted her hand. The gesture forced her fingers to stop tapping, but her heart still drummed out a militant beat. She took a deep breath.

Unlike Leona and Jane, Bradlee had lived a relatively normal life, one without fantastical beasts and a strict Warden Code. He lived without the burdens that accompanied the knowledge of Werewolves.

Bradlee cared for Mr. Green like a father. The break-in and disappearance, while disturbing, was a human problem. Leona wanted to withhold supernatural revelations until the end. Those revelations would remove his ignorance of the paranormal without and within.

Leona wrangled her nerves and began, "Bradlee, Mr. Green hasn't returned from his trip and we're very concerned."

His eyes widened. "First Fitz goes missing and now Mr. Green?" He turned to Jane. "Where did he go on his trip? Should I search for him?" Bradlee blinked. Dark circles shadowed his eyes.

Jane grimaced and replied, "No, dear boy, you're still tired from your search for Fitz."

Leona twisted and untwisted a handful of her skirt, the thick fabric remaining wrinkled after its release.

Bradlee rubbed his eyes, then focused them on a painting on the wall—Jane and Teddy accompanied on a sofa by a young Bradlee. He blinked hard and said, "What was that about needing Leona's help? If Mr. Green's missing, I think what we really need are the police."

Jane shook her head vehemently.

Leona gestured at Jane to let her explain. "Bradlee, Mr. Green wasn't exactly on a regular kind of trip. He went to a little cabin he built in the woods. He goes there for three days and nights each month. It's his *sanctuary*. He locks himself up in the basement for those nights because—" she paused. "Bradlee, Mr. Green is a Werewolf."

He tilted his head, as if he'd heard her incorrectly. "A what?"

"A Werewolf," Leona repeated.

Jane grasped his hand. "It's true, Bradlee," she said.

260

The Good Shepherd

Bradlee's eyes widened at the two women. Then he laughed. "Very funny, ladies. Is Mr. Green going to pop out in a furry costume and scare me now? You do know it's not Halloween yet? Quit joking with me."

"This isn't a joke, Bradlee," Leona said. She laid her hand on her chest. "My parents were Wardens. I inherited the responsibility to help Werewolves live safely and the ability to, well—to fight them. Werewolves also inherit their condition."

"So, there're baby Werewolves running around? You better go catch them, Leona!" he said, scoffing.

"Werewolves don't transform until after they turn eighteen. Then, every month, for the rest of their lives, at night, while the moon is full, they become a fearsome creature."

Leona didn't meet his eyes as she spoke. She worried that if she stopped talking, he'd get up, leave, and never speak to her again, so she blurted out everything she could while he sat there with them, listening, his mouth gaping open.

"Usually, Werewolves live in communities together, but for various reasons, some are on their own, like Mr. Green. Rogues, according to the Warden Code, must secure a facility for their transformation, a sanctuary. Mr. Green was supposed to return from his sanctuary today. I went to check on him. It's obvious he was there, but now—he's missing."

After her speech, she looked up and studied him. He perched on the edge of his chair, as if ready to bolt out of the room at any second. Then he slid back, shaking his head in disbelief.

"Bradlee, I know this is difficult to accept, but you must," Jane added, reaching out to touch his hand.

"Accept this—this—nonsense? Why? Why must I sit here and listen to this? Have you both gone mad?" He rose, marching toward the fire and staring into it. Orange flames reflected in his light eyes.

Leona rose and stood behind him. Gently, she said, "There's more. Please listen."

Jane interrupted. "Mr. Green wanted to be here for this conversation, Bradlee, but it can't wait. If he doesn't return—"

Leona stopped her. "I *will* find him, Jane."

Bradlee stared at the women as if they were insane.

"Finish what you were saying, Leona. Please," Jane urged. Bradlee grimaced, then gestured for her to continue.

Leona continued, "Lycanthropes live completely human lives until after their eighteenth birthday. On October 31, we both turn eighteen. The next full moon is November 12."

"So?" he asked curtly.

Leona thought of her papa and his gentle confidence. She tried her best to emulate him now.

"Bradlee, You're a Werewolf, like Mr. Green. He and I planned on having this conversation with you on our birthday, but I thought you should know. I need help to find Mr. Green and it wouldn't be fair to ask you to help without telling you the truth. I want to help you accept your condition and make preparations. Your life is going to change drastically. It will be difficult—"

Bradlee burst into laughter. The flames from the fire cast a yellow hue over his twisted grin.

"Difficult? Everything you've said thus far sounds like a

Grimm fairy tale. I'm a human being, Leona! I'm not some mythical creature from a bedtime story. But, please, tell me more—this is entertaining, indeed."

Leona, with her eyes, beseeched Jane's assistance.

Jane pursed her lips together in thought. "There are signs, proof, that Bradlee is a... you know. Right, Leona?"

Leona lit up. She nodded. "Yes, for instance, Bradlee, your allergy to silver. Also, cats hate Werewolves. Do you find cats are belligerent toward you?"

He laughed again. "Cats hate most people. That's a stupid way to prove someone is a Werewolf. There must be dozens in this school then."

Leona grimaced. "Arguably, that is the weakest proof. But, there's other signs—all Werewolves have pale blue eyes."

Bradlee raised an eyebrow. His thin, long finger, smudged with charcoal at the knuckles, uncurled in Leona's face. "Like yours?"

"Well, Wardens also have blue eyes." She sighed. "Of course, not *everyone* with pale blue eyes is affected." She paused to think, then exclaimed, "Oh—your birth date! Lycanthropes are born on the first full moon. Mr. Green showed me the Almanac from the year 1878. October 31st was the day of first full moon."

Bradlee grimaced at Jane. "I was four years old when you found me, Mrs. Green. Maybe I remembered my birthday wrong."

Jane contested, "Halloween is a memorable day to celebrate a birthday, dear."

"I had my doubts, too." Leona interjected. "But I spoke to

Mr. Green about it and he confessed that you *are* a Werewolf. He's known from the moment he met you."

"How?" Bradlee spat.

"Mr. Green knew because—well—he can smell you."

"This is truly incredible. Such details! You've gone to a lot of trouble to think up all this," Bradlee replied. Panic rose in Leona's throat as he scowled at them. "I *smell* like a Werewolf?" His frown deepened. "Is that why you said I wasn't the kind of man you're looking for? Because I *stink*?"

His bitter tone, along with his inference, stung. Leona recalled their intimate embrace. And her rejection of him. But she understood his reaction. He was in denial, lashing out in disbelief. Leona kept her voice calm and stared at the fire.

"Unfortunately, my parents died before they taught me how to detect underage Werewolves. Apparently, they used a device. Whatever it was, it must've been destroyed in the fire that killed them," she replied, averting her gaze from the bright flames of the fireplace, and resting on Bradlee.

His hard expression softened.

"I'm sorry about your parents, Leona. But I'm worried your trauma has made you delusional. Maybe you can't cope with the loss—or maybe you needed to invent an excuse to explain your lack of feelings for me. I'm curious, in this fantasy world of yours, can we be together? Can a wolf and a Warden court?"

She frowned at him. "No. As a Warden, I'm only permitted to be your friend."

"How convenient."

Leona insides squirmed as Bradlee's narrow eyes assessed

her. His lips bent in disgust, like she had devised a penny dreadful tale. Everything they told him was true, but, to his ears, it sounded like a ridiculous, horrible, cruel fable.

She'd failed again. She let herself care deeply for Bradlee. If she hadn't rejected him as a beau, he might be able to accept his condition. That pain blinded him to the truth.

Bradlee has to accept the truth before November 12th. When he transforms, it'll be too late.

Clenching his jaw tight, he marched toward the door, but Jane ran after him and grabbed his arm.

"When Mr. Green returns," she said, "he'll tell you we're not liars. We love you like a son, Bradlee. I would never lie to you."

He jerked his arm out of her grasp and replied, "And yet, you have."

Tuesday Morning, October 17
Harvard College

Clementine handed Mr. Hartman the manila envelope he'd requested. He didn't smile at her. In fact, his expression had soured more and more by the minute. *He hates me.* But Professor Taylor treated her well, as though her rudeness at the lecture on Saturday had been erased from his mind. Mr. Hartman was holding a grudge. *How long will he be upset?*

She was pleased to be working at the school again, but Mr. Hartman's frown caused her discomfort, like conversing with their servant, Allen. She attempted to remedy this.

Sporting her imagined, best expression of humility, she puffed out her lower lip and said, "I'm truly sorry for my rash words on Saturday, Mr. Hartman."

He raised an eyebrow and narrowed his green eyes at her. "Who was that vile boy? How do you know such a raggedy, disgusting child?"

Clementine waved her hand in the air. "Oh, that was just Charles, I mean, *Fitz*. He's from *The Home for Little Wanderers*. He's been following me around since I helped my cousin get a job there."

Mr. Hartman grimaced, seemingly satisfied with her apology and explanation. He stuffed a pencil into his cast and scratched his leg. Professor Taylor broke off a long branch from the potted plant in the corner and handed it to Hartman. He winced from his injury as he leaned forward.

"Your cousin, Leona?" the professor asked.

"Yes. Leona's an orphan, you know. I guess that's why she fits in at the Home so well. She's one of them."

The warmth from the fire caused Clementine to feel faint. She inched a fair distance away, enough to feel warm, but not sweat profusely. She was a lady, after all.

Pointing, she asked the professor, "Why are you still wearing your gloves?"

"I have cold blood, dear. Tell me more about Leona," the professor said as Mr. Hartman thrust the broken stick into his cast and continued scratching.

Clementine bit her lip. "Well, she had incredibly kinky hair and such pale blue eyes, she looks ill. And she enjoys running! She can speak Russian, because her mother was a poor immigrant. It's very charitable of you to ask about my simple country cousin, Professor. Honestly, she's a bit backwards and boring. Mr. Flufferbutter hates her."

"Who's Mr. Flufferbutter?" he asked.

"Oh, he's a Persian."

"A foreigner?"

Clementine giggled. "No, Mr. Flufferbutter's from Boston, Professor. I got him for my birthday last year. Did I ever tell you my birthday is on New Year's Day? Anyway, Mr. Flufferbutter is wonderful. He's the prettiest cat in the entire world.

The professor chuckled. But Mr. Hartman frowned. "So, your cat's from Boston, but your cousin is not? Well, I'm not from the city either. Do you think I'm backwards also?"

Clementine blushed in embarrassment. "No, sir. You're a scholar! You teach at Harvard, not a flea-ridden orphanage."

Before Mr. Hartman replied, the professor interjected, "I'm curious about something. But it might seem like I'm prying if I ask about it, so I'll keep my curiosity to myself."

Clementine's interest piqued. "Ask me anything!"

"When is Leona's birthday?"

Clementine cocked her head to the side and thought. "It's on Halloween—a peculiar birthday for a peculiar girl."

"And she's almost eighteen?"

Why does he care so much about Leona? Clementine pouted.

D. Marie Prokop

"Yes. But *I* was born on New Year's Day! Fourteen years ago, *my* birth was announced in the newspaper. New Year's Day babies are special, you know."

"How nice," Professor Taylor replied, gently removing a thick volume from his bookshelf. He winced, then dropped the book. Clementine retrieved it and handed it to him.

"How did you injure yourself, Professor?" she asked.

He sighed. "Hunting is indeed a dangerous hobby—your father warned me as much. I made a stupid error, honestly. I simply didn't account for the additional power inside my new rifle. Now my collarbone won't let me forget my stupidity."

Clementine offered him a sympathetic grin, though she was completely unfamiliar with hunting or rifles or any of the outdoor pastimes men like him enjoyed.

Mr. Hartman responded to Professor Taylor's explanation with undeniable empathy, "You'll get the hang of it, sir. The Winchester repeating rifle is excellent. Now you can display that old antique of yours over the fireplace."

"Indeed. My father's old rifle is worthy of display. When I'm fully healed, I plan to use it often. I do appreciate the gift, George. You have fine taste in weapons. Maybe I should have taken you hunting with me, despite your condition. You can still ride a horse, correct?"

Mr. Hartman nodded. "It's the mounting and dismounting that gives me trouble," he replied, thumping the stick against the cast.

The professor chortled and reached in his coat pocket. Grimacing, he said. "Miss Clementine, it appears I left my favorite pen on the podium in room 502. Would you fetch it for me?"

"Yes, sir."

Clementine ran out the door immediately, escaping the small warm room and the dull masculine conversation.

The campus buzzed with students. On her way to classroom 502, Clementine passed dozens of young men, all well-dressed. They walked straight, their faces more serious than the average man's. They were somebodies. *Like me.*

The hall was as packed as a jar of pickles. Unable to avoid it, Clementine bumped into some of the students on her journey to retrieve the pen for Professor Taylor.

"Watch where you're going," a man wearing a dapper gray bowler hat growled at her.

"Sorry, sir," she replied.

"What's that Bridget doing here?" another student asked.

"I'm Professor Taylor's intern," Clementine said, raising her chin and making herself taller.

"A female intern?" The gentleman raised an eyebrow. "Do they pay you to do scholarly things like dusting books and running errands? Admit it—you're a *maid*, darling."

The crowd in the hall burst into laughter. Angry, she pushed through the students and opened the classroom door. She couldn't believe they'd mistaken her for a maid. She looked down at her suit dress. *I'll just have to beg Mother for a new dress—one that makes me look older and smarter.*

After retrieving the pen from the podium, she scanned the hall before exiting. Thankfully, the cavernous hall was empty of ridiculous young men.

She sidled out of the room and marched down the hall, her footsteps echoing. When she exited outside, she was stopped by a mob gathered along the campus sidewalk.

"Someone fetch a policeman!"

"Get a doctor!"

Clementine jumped high to catch a glimpse past the mob.

"Out of my way!" she cried.

A thin gentleman stepped aside. "You know her?"

"Yes, she's our servant. What happened?"

She knelt beside Bridget, who lay motionless, face down on the ground. There was a streak of blood above her left eye.

"Nobody knows. We heard a bloodcurdling scream, ran out, and found her here. Maybe she fell. Here's a basket. I think it's hers."

The basket was half-full of food—in jars and tied cheesecloth bags. Clementine gathered the strewn food items, stepping around the broken glass.

It was hard to look at Bridget's expressionless face. Bridget *always* smiled. It bothered Clementine to see her this way. It was as if the whole world had gone topsy-turvy.

"Bridget, Bridget. Please wake up!"

Clementine jostled her shoulder, but a man with spectacles scolded her. "Don't touch her. You might make it worse." Clementine didn't argue. What did she know about these things?

A motorized carriage arrived to transport Bridget to the hospital. Clementine ran back to the professor's office. Out of breath, she attempted to explain.

The Good Shepherd

"I need to be dismissed. M-my Bridget. Sh-she's here. And she's hurt—must inform Mother."

She rode the trolley back to Joy Street and told her mother about finding Bridget on the ground at Harvard.

"I don't understand," she replied. "I didn't send Bridget to visit you."

"Then why was she there, Mother?"

Chapter Twenty-Two

Tuesday Afternoon, October 17
The Home for Little Wanderers

"Mr. Green is missing? Then we should notify the police," one of the teachers suggested after Jane told the staff as much as she could about his disappearance. Bradlee was absent from the meeting, to Leona's dismay.

"The police? Oh, I don't know. Miss Schaeffer, what do you think?" Jane asked, ripping Leona from her gray cloud.

"Well—"

Suddenly, the door burst open and Bradlee marched in, his dark hair mussed and his collar askew. "Mrs. Green, I found something. May I speak with you—and Miss Schaeffer—in private?"

Jane and Leona left the staff and followed Bradlee down the hall. When they turned the corner, Jane gasped.

"Fitz! We were worried sick about you!" she scolded, then threw her arms around the boy, squeezing him tight.

Leona exhaled a sigh of relief. Reverend Busch stood in the hall, watching Fitz and Jane's reunion. Recalling Fitz's anger at the man, she was surprised to see them together.

"Where have you been?" Jane asked Fitz, her face stern, with the exception of her red-rimmed, tired eyes.

He sniffed, pulled out a handkerchief, and sneezed into the white cloth. His eyes matched Janes, pink and swollen. "I needed ta see ma darlin,' Clementine."

"You went to Clementine's house?" Leona asked. She'd suspected he might go there but had dismissed the thought. Now she felt like a fool.

He wiped his nose again, after another sniffle, then jammed the cloth into his pocket. "She sent me away. Said she was sorry about ma sisters, but we weren't suited to be anythin' more than acquaintances. She's a proper lady and I'm a poor orphan."

The pained expression on his face was hard to bear. Grasping his freckled hands, Leona said, "Oh, silly Clementine. Someday, Fitz, you'll find someone kinder, with a bigger heart. You need to forget her."

Fitz shook his head, pulled his hands out of her grasp, and rubbed his eyes like a young child before naptime.

"Oh, you're exhausted!" Jane exclaimed, wrapping an arm around his shoulders. "You better get some rest before you fall ill."

"You're right, Mrs. Green—I'm dang tired. But Leona—you're wrong about ma darlin."

Bradlee pointed to the reverend, still lingering in the hall. "What's he doing with you, Fitz?" he whispered.

Fitz yawned, then explained, "If it wasn't for Reverend Busch, I wouldn't have made it this far. He even paid for my trolley ride." Fitz turned to the man, removed his hat, and bowed his red head. "I thank you, sir."

"It's the least I can do, young man," Reverend Busch replied.

"Yes, thank you, Reverend," Jane added. She embraced Fitz again. "Come with me, dear. Let's get you settled in your room. I'll have Calvin bring you a huge meal. You're too skinny."

A glimmer of relief flicked in Bradlee's aquamarine eyes. He exhaled slowly, closing them. Reopening them, a cold, oddly stalwart expression replaced the spark of relief. He'd just been reunited with his best friend, but Leona sensed his continuing anger at her and Jane.

Leona directed her gaze upward to Reverend Busch. "How did you find him?"

"It was providence. I went on a prayer walk, and there he was, sitting on a bench by the frog pond in the Common," the reverend said.

"Well, thank God," Leona said. Bradlee's mouth twitched. He leaned over and whispered in her ear, "I still need to talk with you. Alone."

His voice boomed unnaturally loud and authoritative as he extended his hand to the reverend, "Thank you for bringing Fitz back. You must have other business to attend to. We won't keep you."

Reverend Busch's eyes fluttered back and forth between Leona and Bradlee.

"Yes, well, I wish there were more I could do."

"Wait! There *is* something else you could do. Mr. Green has been delayed and we are concerned for his safe return," Leona said.

He lowered his chin, the age lines on his face appearing deeper since his last visit. "I will petition the Lord, the Good Shepherd, to deliver Mr. Green safely home."

"Thank you," Leona said with a strained smile.

The reverend tipped his hat and exited the room. She turned to Bradlee. His hands were closed into fists, his knuckles turning white. *He still thinks we lied to him.*

"While I was searching the woods, I found something," he said, his voice low. He opened his fist. A brass tube lay in his palm.

"A shell casing?"

He rolled the yellow-colored metal in his fingers and nodded. "I ran back as fast as I could after I found it. It was nowhere near the cabin you told me about—and yes, I found that too. It's been ransacked."

"I know," Leona replied, lowering her eyes. The memory of the scene still mystified her.

She touched Bradlee's arm. "Did you see the cellar?"

His blue eyes turned dark and sullen. "Yes. I saw the cages and the chains. I guess you weren't telling me lies after all. I'm sorry for—"

"No, Bradlee. Don't apologize. It's a difficult thing to believe," she replied. She offered him an empathetic half-smile. "So, does this mean you've accepted your condition?"

He grimaced back at her. "I don't really have a choice, do I? I must believe in the impossible." He smoothed back his dark hair and frowned out the window at a partial view of the forest.

"Now that Fitz has returned, the most important thing is finding Mr. Green. With the state of that cabin, I'm afraid something horrible happened to him. What if he's wounded and needs a doctor?"

Leona barely heard him. She was examining the casing. She held the shell up to her nose and frowned.

"What's wrong?"

"There's a lot of blood on this shell, but it's not Mr. Green's," she replied.

"Are you sure?"

"Yes. Wardens can smell the difference between human and lycanthrope blood. Look, the staff is insisting on getting the police involved."

Bradlee's brow spiked. "Do you think that's a good idea?"

Leona returned his concerned look and asked, "I do. Do you trust me now, Bradlee?"

His expression softened. He nodded. "You're my Shepherd, right?"

Leona grinned. "And Mr. Green's. You can trust me, okay?"

"Okay."

Later Tuesday Afternoon
The Home for Little Wanderers

Mrs. Green thanked the group of policemen gathered outside the stables.

"We're so thankful for your help. Officer Buchanan, thank you for responding so quickly."

"Your staff made an impassioned plea. And the sooner we begin, the fresher the trail will be. Don't worry, ma'am, I brought my best deputies."

"I wish I could go with you, but I must attend to the children," Jane said.

The officer tipped his hat, then dabbed his firm mustache with a handkerchief. "Ma'am, it's my job. Now, Mr. Smith, can you show us whereabouts you found this?" He held up the shell casing.

"Yes, sir." Bradlee mounted Leona's favorite horse, Hugo, and offered a hand to Leona. She took it. He pulled her up and she sat behind him on the saddle.

Officer Buchanan blew his whistle and the rest of the policemen mounted their steeds. Bradlee guided them into the forest along the dirt path.

"Don't take them too close to the cabin, Bradlee," Leona whispered in his ear. He smelled of pine, no doubt he had been cutting wood earlier, making charcoal for drawing.

She tried not to feed her feelings for him, but it was difficult. Bradlee was such a good person—resourceful, intelligent, kind, loyal, talented.

And a Werewolf.

As his Shepherd, Leona must also be a good person. This required a more disciplined mind. She couldn't dwell on how much she enjoyed being this close to Bradlee. Thoughts like that were useless. They would only cause more pain. She focused on the task of finding Mr. Green.

She inhaled deeply. Faint indications of a lycanthrope lingered in the air, coming and going with the breeze.

Bradlee pulled the reins to the right and Hugo headed west, off the dirt path and into a grove of evergreens. It reminded Leona of Christmas. Images of her grandfather handing out humbly wrapped presents from under the tree made her heart ache for her departed family.

Leona missed them desperately. Nothing could fill the hole left in her heart by her parents' deaths. The last two Christmases without them felt empty, even with Mrs. Wickersham's company. She cringed thinking of Bradlee spending this Christmas without Mr. Green, whom he loved like a father.

Suddenly, Hugo whinnied. He bucked slightly, backing up a few paces. Leona gripped Bradlee's waist tight. His arm muscles flexed as he tightened his grip on the reins. "Whoa, boy. It's okay."

Hugo settled down but refused to move forward.

"We'll have to go on foot from here," Bradlee yelled to the policemen who'd accompanied them into the grove. They hitched their agitated horses, calming them with treats, and gathered around.

Bradlee pointed, announcing, "I found the shell casing over that way, about 100 yards or so."

"Spread out, men," Officer Buchanan instructed. "Let's cover as much ground as possible."

Leona sniffed the air again. The strong aroma of pine overwhelmed her, making it difficult to discern other smells. She inhaled slowly once more and concentrated.

Horses. Sweat. Sulfur.

Gun powder.

"This way, Bradlee. Come with me," Leona sprinted past the officers, gracefully bounding across the slippery pine needle floor of the woods. Bradlee kept up easily, staying close to her side.

"Stop!" she cried.

Through a hole in the canopy of trees above her, a golden light shone on the beautiful foliage at her feet. Lying there among the leaves, a smattering of shells glittered.

Officer Buchanan caught up to them. Panting, he picked up a brassy gold and faded yellow cylinder. He held it close to his eyeball. One brow, as thick as his mustache, jutted skyward as he remarked, "These are from an 1896 Winchester repeater. I use one for hunting. These shells can be used in revolvers too, but with this amount of spent ammo, I'm certain it was a rifle."

Leona scanned the trees around her. She spied a mark on an old thick pine and examined the trunk. A bullet was lodged there, marring the tree's bark. She stared at the dot. It was silver. Her heart pounded.

"Bradlee, come here."

He ran to her side.

"Touch this," she commanded, indicating the bullet in the trunk.

His blue eyes narrowed. "Why?"

"Hopefully it's nothing. But I need to be sure. Trust me."

He stuck his pointer finger into the divot. He grimaced at

Leona as she grabbed his hand and examined it. The skin on his fingertip was red and blotchy. His grimace transformed into a full frown.

She whispered so the officers wouldn't overhear. "This bullet is made of silver."

"What does that mean?" Bradlee whispered back.

"It means that someone was hunting Werewolves."

Tuesday Evening
Massachusetts General Hospital near Harvard College

"Has she woken up yet?" Mother asked the physician.

"No, her body needs to rest. She suffered a definitive blow to the head. Right now, we're monitoring her and watching for swelling of the brain."

Mother gasped. "Swelling of the brain? That sounds dreadful. Will she die?"

"No, I believe she'll come 'round in a few days. Does she have family?"

Mother stuttered, "I-I don't know. Wait—yes! I remember now. Her family's quite large. She has four—no—five siblings. Her father and brothers work at a rope factory by the harbor, I think. Clementine, can you stay here with Bridget? I need to send Allen to inform her family of her condition."

"Yes, Mother."

She left the hospital room in a flutter. The doctor unveiled a contraption displaying a dial, like a clock face, at the top. He wrapped a rubber tube around Bridget's upper arm and squeezed a small balloon. Clementine asked him, "What were you doing?"

"This is a new invention, the sphygmomanometer. It measures blood pressure."

"Isn't that clever?" Clementine watched the silver liquid in the gauge rise. "So, you're taking her pulse?"

He chuckled. "No, that's something different. You don't need a special device for that. You see, there's an artery in the wrist that pumps blood. If one applies light pressure with these two fingers," he signaled his pointer and middle fingers, "you can count how many times the heart beats in a minute. That's called a pulse. Thankfully, Miss Collins' blood pressure and pulse rate are normal."

"Who's Miss Collins?"

"That's what her chart says." The doctor glanced at Bridget. "Siobhan Collins."

Clementine never heard Bridget's full name before. She had no idea the woman had a family either. She was simply Bridget, the maid who baked the yummiest cinnamon rolls in the world and brushed her hair without pulling it too hard, unlike the last Bridget.

The doctor exited the room and Clementine leaned over Bridget's disturbingly immobile form.

"Oh Bridget, please wake up! What happened to you? Why were you at Harvard?"

A knock caused Clementine to turn around. She opened the door and was surprised to see Professor Taylor there with Mr. Hartman, yawning in his wheelchair.

"How's your friend?" the professor asked.

"Oh, she's not my friend. She's my servant," Clementine explained. "They said she had a contusion."

"I think you mean a *concussion*," the professor said, peering over her shoulder at Bridget's still body. "How dreadful. Are you holding up well, Clementine?"

She shrugged. The hospital smelled awful, the nurses frowned a lot, and Mother left her in charge of the maid. It was a wonder she was as well as she was.

"I'm fine. Thank you for asking. I only wish I knew what happened." She attempted a look of deep concern over the maid's still body, focusing her gaze on Bridget's rising and falling chest.

"Me, too," Professor Taylor replied. "It's terrible that someone got hurt visiting our campus. Isn't it, Hartman?"

Hartman scratched his leg and frowned, unable to reach much beyond the edge of his cast. "Bad things happen everywhere. Once in my hometown in New York, there was a whole family found dead, all lying in their beds without a mark on them. To this day, no one knows what happened."

"Don't scare the child with such horrors, Hartman." The professor scowled.

Mr. Hartman gave up trying to reach his itch and looked up at her. "I'm sorry, Clementine. Did I frighten you?"

"No, I'm not a child. I don't scare easily," Clementine lied.

Two days ago, she almost fainted when she opened the door and found an intruder.

Is Charles okay? She shook her head. *Surely, he is. Orphans are tough.*

Is Bridget tough? Though Bridget spent all week taking care of the Schaeffer family, Clementine realized that she didn't know her very well.

She remembered the day she discovered Bridget was Catholic. Bridget mentioned to Leona that she'd left her rosary behind in the confession booth. Clementine asked Bridget what she needed to confess. Bridget's expression had turned so dour, Clementine feared the maid had committed murder. To her relief, Bridget's face lightened, offering a jovial wink, saying that that was between her and her confessor.

I'm glad that Christ Church doesn't make us confess our sins.

As she ruminated on her lack of sinfulness, Clementine caressed her wolf pendant and ignored the visitors in the room.

A cough, loud as a dog's bark, came from Professor Taylor. She jumped at the sound, her hand dropping from the silver heirloom. He covered his mouth to cough again and she noticed he was still wearing his gloves. She wanted to ask him why, but he spoke first, "Forgive me, Clementine, but we must depart now. I have a lecture this afternoon."

She tipped her chin.

He continued, "If you need to stay, I understand. But I'm obligated to inform you that, if you do, we'll have to find someone else to take your place. I hope you understand. As we are both handicapped at the moment, we simply can't function without an assistant."

Clementine pursed her lips and stared at Bridget lying on the bed, her eyes closed and her breathing steady.

"I don't see how I can be much of help here. That's what doctors and nurses are for, right?"

She grabbed the wooden handles of Mr. Hartman's wheelchair. "Allow me," Clementine offered and pushed Mr. Hartman to the door. The professor held it open and they proceeded down the hallway together, stopping at the front doors to let some nurses in crisp white uniform dresses enter.

The professor flashed Clementine a comforting smile.

"I'm sure Miss Collins will be fine after some rest, dear. Besides, this hospital is one of the best hospitals in all of Massachusetts. Look at all the nurses! She'll be well cared for."

"How did you know our maid's full name, Professor? I only learned it myself today."

The professor replied, "I overheard a nurse discussing her case on the way in."

Clementine fluttered her lashes. "I'm a terrible girl. I never knew it. She has brothers and sisters too. What else don't I know about her?" She pushed the wheelchair over a threshold. "Golly, I hope Bridget doesn't die."

Clementine remembered Fitz's sorrow over the death of his sisters. She clutched her heart and stopped walking.

"Dear girl," Mr. Hartman started. "We're all going to die someday. It's best we accept our mortality. Perhaps I should have lent you Darwin's book, not Frank L. Baum's."

The professor clicked his tongue, "Hartman. Don't be so

harsh. Strong, virulent young folks hold the irrepressible hope that they'll live forever. It's a natural response."

Clementine didn't like it when people spoke about her as if she wasn't there. Father, Mother—and now Professor Taylor and Mr. Hartman. But she didn't express her annoyance. Professor Taylor had already threatened to replace her, and Mr. Hartman would accuse her of making a scene, like she did that day in the Common under Fitz's bad influence.

Worrying about other people was exhausting. Clementine glanced at her reflection in a window. Her hair was a downright mess. Thin tendrils had escaped from the chignon bundled under her hat. She was no more a glamorous Gibson Girl than the ragamuffin on the street begging for spare change was.

I'll ask Bridget to fix—oh—I'll have to do it myself! It's okay. I'm not a child—I can brush my own hair.

An image of Charles—Fitz— taking the brush out of her hand and setting it on her armoire filled her thoughts. The memory of his gentle kiss made her cheeks warm.

She shook the image from her mind. That raggedy boy had spent enough time there, contaminating her with his poverty, tempting her to pity him. Instead, she used her imagination to fantasize about her future husband. Brahmin. Harvard-educated. Blue-eyed. Respectable. Wealthy.

Someday Mr. Flufferbutter would venture with her to another Boston brownstone, with another Bridget, another Allen, and no Fitz.

Chapter Twenty-Three

Tuesday Evening, October 17
22 Joy Street

"No, I didn't send Bridget to Harvard. Why would I, Franny? I was at work all day," Father said.

"I don't understand it. Why was she there? And what happened to her?" Mother asked.

"Maybe she tripped on the cobblestone path and hit her head," Clementine suggested, then took a bite of pickled ham. The combination of tartness and saltiness made her reach for her water glass, but it was missing. Allen scrambled to place a glass in front of her and filled it to the brim. She glared at him, impatient. *I miss Bridget.*

"Well, it was nice of Professor Taylor and his assistant to stop by," Mother said with a pearlescent grin. Clementine gulped another mouthful of water, then nodded.

Father's eyebrows rose but he didn't comment.

"I'll speak with the doctor first thing in the morning. Allen delivered a message to her brother, so I expect her family will care for her now," Mother said. Allen poured more beer into Father's stein. Mother rolled her eyes.

Clementine watched Allen, who was barely able to keep pace with the domestic demands upon him, but she didn't realize she was staring until he spoke to her.

"Miss, is there something you need?"

Thinking fast, she asked, "Allen, what's your surname?"

He hesitated before answering, like a fearful child. "I... uh... Patrick. My full name is Allen Laurdine Patrick."

Clementine repeated it aloud, *"Allen Laurdine Patrick.* That's an odd name for a servant. It sounds prestigious, like a politician. Wouldn't you agree, Mother?"

Mother nodded absently, as if her head were pulled by invisible strings.

"Allen, I'll finish my meal in the study," Father announced, rising out of his chair.

"Yes, sir," Allen replied. He bolted toward the kitchen to fetch a tray to transport Father's meal. Father wiped his mouth with a linen napkin and took another sip from his stein.

"You're leaving?" Mother asked, holding her knife tightly in one hand and laying her fork on the edge of her plate.

"I have urgent paperwork to finish." He scuttled out of the dining room.

When the heavy study door closed, Mother's knife squeaked across her plate.

Tuesday Evening
22 Joy Street

Clementine couldn't sleep. After gazing out her window at the North Star and waning moon for a full hour, she decided to venture to the kitchen for some food. Bread with a thick layer of jam sounded mighty nice, just the thing to fill her tummy and help her sleep. She whispered a farewell to Mr. Flufferbutter, who snored lightly at the foot of her bed, as usual.

Rounding the corner of the dining room, a strange noise stopped her cold. *Clitter-bang.* Grasping the dining table, Clementine froze, still as a statue.

Bang. Clitter-clatter.

The noises came from the kitchen. Light spilled through the crack of the open dining room door. *A thief wouldn't light the kitchen lantern—unless they were exceptionally stupid.*

"Fitz?"

Clementine crept on her tip-toes, in her stockings, toward the kitchen. The door burst open and a towering figure emerged, blocking the light.

"Father!"

"Clementine, what are you doing out of bed at this hour?"

He scowled at her. She pressed two fingers over her wrist and felt the blood pulse through her artery. Waiting for her pulse to slow, she took deep breaths.

"I-I was hungry," she finally answered.

"Clementine, no respectable man is going to want to marry a chubby, greedy, immature young lady like you. You're not a child anymore, remember? You need to be disciplined in every manner of life. Do you eat like a greedy oaf at work, too? Taylor probably finds your strangeness interesting. He's an odd bird. Always has been."

"No, sir," she replied. She hung her head, embarrassed. Ever since Leona came to Boston, Father had been perpetually angry. If he'd caught Fitz in her room the other night, what would he have done? Walloped her? Harmed Fitz?

I shouldn't care a fig about what would've happen to him, but I do—a little. Disciplining her heart and her stomach was no small feat. But she would do it.

"What are you doing up?" she asked, hoping to distract him.

Father answered gruffly, "I have paperwork to do."

"But you're not in your study."

"Look, young lady—this is *my* house. I can go to any room I want, any time I want. Stop interrogating me and go back to bed!"

Clementine pouted. Golly, she only wanted some bread and jam. Before she turned to go back to her room, she noticed the cellar door was wide open. This made her even hungrier for jam.

She sulked as she backed out of the kitchen. She journeyed through the dark dining room. At the stairs, she dunked down and sat on the bottom step, well hidden in the shadows. She waited in silence. Father returned to his study with a large bottle of brown liquid and closed the heavy door with a thud.

"Meow?"

Mr. Flufferbutter rubbed his soft body along Clementine's back. She scooped the cat into her arms.

"Hello, kitty. Do you like adventures? I'm off to see the Land of Bread and Jam. If you come with me, maybe the wizard there will give you some butter."

She hurried across the dining room and ducked into the kitchen.

"The jam is in the cellar, Mr. Flufferbutter. You're not a

cowardly lion, are you? Never fear—I know the way," she whispered, scratching him under the chin. He purred his approval.

She lit a lantern and carried it in front of them, holding Mr. Flufferbutter's body tight. The stairs groaned and creaked as she descended. Her stocking feet eventually landed on the dirt floor, and she raised her lantern, searching for jars of elderberry jam, her favorite.

A reflected flicker of light beside the shelves caught her attention instead. "That's strange. The lid on Father's dumpy old chest is open. I better close it."

Mr. Flufferbutter wriggled out of her grasp and jumped to the floor. He eclipsed the stairs in three pounces, leaving Clementine all alone in the damp cellar.

"Coward," she whispered.

She put one hand on the open lid of the chest. Light from the lantern revealed its contents.

Clementine gasped.

The chest was filled with various weaponry: silver blades, pistols, rifles, and ammunition boxes. Clementine lifted a sheath the length of a quart jar. A symbol was burned onto the flap of the light-toned leather—a wolf. German words circled the beast. *The Schaeffer family crest.* Inside, there was a gleaming silver knife.

If Bridget had had a knife like this, she could've fought her attacker. Clementine closed the flap and stuffed the knife into her dressing gown pocket. Forgetting all about the jam, she closed the lid, clicked the padlock shut, and ran back to her room.

The Good Shepherd

Late Tuesday Evening
The Home for Little Wanderers

"Thanks for helping us search for Mr. Green," Bradlee said, shaking Officer Buchanan's hand. The sky was dark except for the swathe of timid stars twinkling above them.

"I'm sorry we didn't find him. I can send a couple of my men back at sunrise to resume the search."

"I appreciate your help, but we'll take over the search, Officer Buchanan. Thanks, anyway," Bradlee replied.

The policeman's head bowed. "If you change your mind, telegraph the station." He turned to Leona, "Miss Schaeffer, I'm sorry we keep meeting under such ominous circumstances."

Leona frowned. "Me, too."

"Have you remembered anything about that Mr. Goldberg fellow that could help us?"

"You haven't found his killer yet?"

"No, ma'am. The streets are so crowded at that time, yet no one witnessed the incident. It's likely to be filed as unsolved. Unsolved crimes ruffle my feathers, miss."

"Did you say *Goldberg*?" Bradlee asked.

"Yes," Leona and Officer Buchanan replied together.

Leona listened with surprise as Bradlee explained, "A Mr. Goldberg visited the Home the day before you came to live here, Leona. I forgot all about it. Fitz was supposed to tell you."

"What? He did?"

Aunt Franny didn't seem familiar with the name when Officer Buchanan came to the house that Saturday morning. Maybe Warden Goldberg visited the house at Joy Street while she was away. Uncle Ezra must have sent him here...

"Yes. We should go ask Fitz about it. He left a message and made Fitz promise to give it directly to you. Sorry, I was supposed to remind him."

Officer Buchanan tipped his tall black policeman's hat. "If there's anything in that message that'll help our investigation—times, places, plans, or dates—let us know. I abhor unsolved crimes. They wake me up at night."

"Yes, sir."

Leona understood. Many of her nights were spent tossing and turning. But she feared involving the officer any deeper in Warden business. It was dangerous—for him and for her.

The policemen departed, leaving Leona and Bradlee alone at the stables. She brushed Hugo's dusty coat while Bradlee fed and watered the tired steed before returning to the main building.

They stood in the dimly lit foyer. Maybe it was the large room, or their failure to find Mr. Green, or both, that made Leona feel small and powerless.

Bradlee unbuttoned his coat. She stared absently at his tired face. He blinked, his long lashes brushing his creamy skin. Blinking took milliseconds, but to Leona, the motion lasted an eternity. He turned to her. She looked away quickly and began unbuttoning her coat as well. He cleared his throat.

"Wait here. I'll find Fitz. If he's not sleeping, I'll ask him to come here so you can talk to him. Then, I think we should have a talk of our own."

Her stomach twisted. She feared he wanted to discuss their relationship, not ask her questions about his condition. Though he'd accepted the truth of what he was, she feared he would never accept that they could never be anything more than co-workers or good friends. She didn't want to hurt him again.

"I'm so relieved Fitz is okay," Leona said to Bradlee, instead of the million other thoughts flittering in her mind.

The gravity of their present problem would surely remind Bradlee that there were more important things in life than courting or romance. He must prepare for his first transformation, possibly without Mr. Green's guidance. On top of that, the discovery of the silver bullet made Leona angry. Werewolves were being hunted.

Bradlee winked. "Yeah, Fitz seems okay, but Mr. Green—"

"I know. But we haven't given up, though. We just need to rest. Then we'll search again."

"Agreed."

He left her in the lounge area and ran to fetch Fitz. A few minutes later, footsteps echoed from the boys' dorm hallway.

Leona hurried toward them. She hugged Fitz, feeling the thin boy's ribcage through his shirt. His eyes were slightly less red though.

"I'm so glad you're back. Are you all right, Fitz?"

"Of course not," he replied. "I'll never be all right. There's pain in ma heart." He pointed at his chest. "Right here, where Mary and Grace are."

Leona's eyes filled with tears. She hated seeing him in such pain.

"I know. It's awful. There's nothing I can say to make it better. But we're here with you, Fitz."

"Yeah, we're best friends, you know," Bradlee remarked sternly. "Don't run off like that ever again, you hear me?" He jabbed his fist into Fitz's shoulder while a tear meandered down one side of his strong face. Then he pulled his friend into his arms.

"I won't. I won't," Fitz promised. "I'm sorry." Soon they both had tears creeping down their cheeks.

Leona dabbed her eyes as she waited for them to part before questioning Fitz about Warden Goldberg's visit.

"Mr. Goldberg? Oh, I remember! It was before I knew who ya were, Leona. I plum forgot. All I did was hand him some paper and a pen. He wrote his message and folded it up tight. He made me promise to put it into your hands only, so I stuck it in a safe place."

"Where is it?"

Fitz stroked his chin. "I put it in my pocket. Let's see… it were… ma brown tweeds!"

"Surely those pants have been washed by now, uh, haven't they, Fitz?" Bradlee asked.

Fitz shook his head vigorously.

"Nope. I wore those the day I met ma darlin' Clementine. I

can't wash 'em! They're my good luck charm."

"Fitz—go fetch them," Bradlee insisted. Fitz ran back down the hall.

When he returned, he handed Leona a lump of paper.

"I'm sorry, Leona. Mrs. Green must have gathered my clothes for the laundry while I was away. I shoulda never taken those pants off."

The message was now one thick block of paper. Leona tried to pry it apart, but it cracked instead. White lint flew into the air.

"Mr. Goldberg was a… friend of my parents," she said. "He was supposed to meet me at my uncle's house on Joy Street. Did he mention why he come here instead?"

"Oh, I can answer that! He said your Uncle Ebenezer sent him here to find you."

"You mean Uncle Ezra?"

"Sorry, right! Yer uncle's maid told him you were here. Mr. Goldberg seemed angry about that."

"I see," she said, remembering how many times she'd disobeyed Warden Goldberg's instructions not to tell people her name and knew he was probably angry at *her*, not her uncle, or poor Bridget.

"I didn't really know him, but Mr. Goldberg helped me. He sent me money so that I could travel to Boston and visit my uncle. He died before I ever had the chance to thank him."

Fitz yawned. His mouth gaped open for a good long time. "I'm sorry about your Mr. Goldberg and the messed-up note. But friends, I'm awful tired. I don't think I'll ever sleep as well as I did in Clementine's arms, but I gotta try."

"What?!?" Leona and Bradlee exclaimed in unison.

"Another time," Fitz replied and yawned again. He disappeared down the hall.

"Fitz is prone to exaggeration," Bradlee said. Leona shook her head in agreement. *He must be tired or delusional or something.*

Bradlee gestured to the long sofa in the lounge. She sat down. Bradlee collapsed on the couch beside her, smelling of sweat, pine, oats, and lye. He was close, but not too close. He took Goldberg's note from her hand and turned the paper cube around and around in his fingers.

"It's too late. I'll never know what it says," Leona said, frowning.

"I have an idea," Bradlee said. "Can I borrow it? I'll conduct some experiments and let you know if any are successful."

"Go ahead. What do I have to lose? Look, Bradlee, we need to discuss your first transformation. Preparations need to be made. I'd hoped Mr. Green would be here to help, but—"

"He'll be here. We'll find him. Anyway, let's get some rest and talk about it in the morning."

Leona suppressed a yawn. "Good idea. After supper, we can search the woods again. Mrs. Green will watch the girls."

"I don't have any classes after 3:00. I can go by myself, you know."

"No. You shouldn't search the forest alone. Someone was out there shooting silver bullets. If they go out again and shoot you—"

A look of dread washed over Bradlee's face. "What if they

shot Mr. Green?"

Leona shook her head vehemently. "There's been no sign of that. The blood I found wasn't his. Let's not assume the worst."

"Then, where is he? Why isn't he here with us now?"

Leona placed a hand on his whiskered cheek. His skin was sweaty and hot.

She didn't believe Mr. Green was dead, but his absence stupefied her. She wanted to ease Bradlee's concern.

Without thinking, Leona guided his face closer to hers and kissed his soft, salty lips. He returned her kiss with unbridled passion.

Stopping for breath, he whispered in her ear before continuing, kissing the side of her face in short, light steps. "Leona, please let me love you," he begged.

She winced. The words cut her heart. She jumped to her feet.

"I'm sorry," she replied, stepping away. "I can't."

Chapter Twenty-Four

Monday Evening, October 30
22 Joy Street

Clementine sat in her room alone. Even Mr. Flufferbutter was gone. Father and Mother were at a dinner with his law partners celebrating a victory of some sort.

She pulled open the curtains and tied them back. The sky stared back at her, black as ink. There was a new moon in the sky, with no light reflecting off its invisible face. A few stars twinkled lightly, as if shy to announce their presence. Clementine stared at their frailty, missing the unabashed brightness of the full moon.

She ignored the pathetic celestial party outside and opened her book, traveling to the Emerald City with Dorothy and her companions: the scarecrow, the tin man, and the cowardly lion. The Wicked Witch was dead. She was about to turn the page and start the chapter entitled, The Secret of Oz, when something fell out of her dressing gown pocket and clattered onto the hardwood floor.

Clementine had stored the knife she pilfered from Father's chest two weeks ago in her gown pocket, stuffing it under her bed when she wasn't at home, since Bridget had healed and returned to her duties last week.

Bridget explained, when questioned, that she'd come to Harvard to surprise Clementine and her employers with a batch of cinnamon rolls. Someone must have made off with them before Clementine arrived on the scene because she didn't notice them. She couldn't blame the thief; Bridget's cinnamon rolls were irresistible.

Unfortunately, the maid couldn't recall what happened to her after she arrived on campus. The doctors assured them her memory would return in time. Mother made Clementine check if Bridget's family had been to the hospital.

Fortunately, for Mother's conscience, two of Bridget's brothers were already there when Clementine arrived. She stopped her approach and viewed them from a distance. One was short and beefy, with arms thicker than Clementine's leg, and the other was lanky and dull-faced. Since Bridget was obviously being cared for, Clementine backed away and went home in a rush without greeting her.

Everyone else was healing as well. Professor Taylor didn't wince anymore now that his collarbone hurt less, and Mr. Hartman would have his cast removed next week.

Charles must be healing too.

No. I won't worry about that ruffian. He has friends. And I'm not one of them.

Sending Charles Fitzgerald away was for the best. The Wizard of Oz did not reside in Boston. There was no one here that could make him rich, intelligent, and Brahmin. Magic wasn't real. It was fiction, fodder for books and songs.

Clementine placed a piece of paper in the book to mark her place and set it down. She retrieved the safely encased knife from the floor. She'd already compared the symbol with the wolf on her broach. She had no doubt it was the Schaeffer family crest, but something was different about the leather-burned symbol. The German words surrounding the wolf face weren't the same. The phrase on the leather contained three words, whereas the silver pendant had a full verse on the back, hidden behind the fearful-looking beast.

She had copied the words on the sheath down, knowing the professor would be able to translate them for her. To her, they looked like gibberish—*Verschonung ist erforderlich.* But the translation confused her more—*Mercy is required.*

Professor Taylor had bombarded her with questions. Where did she see these words? Why did she want them translated? Clementine lied, hoping he'd stop asking soon. Eventually, she declared it was extremely personal and if he asked her any more questions, she'd cry. Men fear weeping women. It worked.

Father never mentioned the missing item or the open chest. Maybe he didn't want to waste time and energy searching for an old letter opener. He didn't rummage the house or accuse anyone of theft.

The unlocked chest was now locked, thanks to Clementine. But maybe he'd been drunk and assumed he had closed it. Inebriation would also explain his extra sour mood when Clementine ran into him in the kitchen late that night. He'd been crueler than usual. Father had never insulted her like that before, calling her chubby, undisciplined, and greedy.

Why did Mother marry Ezra Schaeffer? She knew the answer—money. Mother was in debt because of her deceased father's gambling. Ezra Schaeffer, the wealthy law man, offered to rescue them from a life of misery. Clementine winced. Like her mother, she couldn't think of anything worse than being poor, not even Father's foul moods.

Again, Charles' freckled face entered her mind. If he were rich, he could kiss her forehead without risking her reputation. They could get engaged. Then he could even kiss her hand in public. Alas, he was poor, an undesirable and crude orphan boy.

Clementine slipped the knife out of its sheath. She touched her plump finger to the end of the thin silver blade. The sharp tip pierced her flesh, leaving a small mark that blossomed bright red. She didn't cry out, in case Bridget or Mother was in the hall, but it hurt.

She wrapped her wound with two silk hair ribbons and wiped the blood off the thin blade. She returned the knife to its leather case and stuffed it back into her gown's pocket.

That fancy letter opener is dangerous.

Clementine peered at the night sky one more time before slipping under her covers. An arc of twinkly light traveled across the inky backdrop—a shooting star. It was magical.

Bradlee handed Leona a sheet of wrinkled paper the size of her hand.

"My experiment didn't go as well as I hoped," he said with a grimace.

Leona scanned the smeared ink on the paper in her hands. She made out the words "danger" and "father."

"Well, you're not a magician. But thanks for trying. What did you do?" she asked.

"Lots of things, but what worked best was steam. It loosened the folds so I could open it, but most of the ink was washed away. I'm sorry."

She stuffed the wrinkled paper into her pocket and smiled courageously. It had been a long two weeks since Fitz gave her Warden Goldberg's note.

Mrs. Green approached the breakfast table they were sitting at with the students.

"Happy birthday, you two! I hope you're ready for the party tonight. Fitz is working on the cake right now."

"We can't have a party, Mrs. Green. Not while Mr. Green is still missing. It's just not right," Bradlee said. His dark hair needed trimmed. It brushed his nose as he shook his head in defiance.

Leona agreed.

"But you're both turning eighteen. It's an important milestone. Celebrating will keep me busy," Jane replied. Her eyes were bloodshot.

"You're already too busy running the orphanage. Please don't worry about us. We can celebrate when we're all together again," Leona said. She tried to smile, but her mouth refused to cooperate.

Leona was tired, too. She spent all her extra time searching the woods around the Home for signs and clues or repairing the sanctuary with Bradlee. The cabin needed to be secure by November 12.

Mr. Green had been missing for over two weeks. Everyone had begun to lose hope.

"Miss Schaeffer, we made you a present," Rachel said. She handed Leona a box wrapped in tissue paper. The rest of the twelve-year-old girls stood in a muddle around Regina. After the orphan train crash, the girls stopped teasing the lonely girl with the Russian accent. They even welcomed the new girl, Laura, and never teased her about her gimpy leg. The girl suffered from rickets, which had affected her growth. The girls babied Laura, feeding her all day long. After a few days, Laura's gaunt face had brightened and plumped.

Leona was proud of her lambs. Love had grown stronger in each of them. Despite the heavy spirits of the staff and teachers over Mr. Green's mysterious absence, the children rallied. Their strength inspired Leona.

"*Spasibo*," she said as she took the present out of Regina's hands. "Thank you, girls." Leona carefully unwrapped the paper and opened the box. She reached in and grasped a squishy woolen object.

Rachel cleared her throat and explained, "Mrs. Green taught us how to knit. We took turns knitting until it was long enough for a hat. Mrs. Green bound off the stitches for us because she didn't teach us that yet. I sewed the seams together."

"Do you like it?" Regina asked, in perfect English. Nineteen pairs of eyes focused on Leona at once. She pulled the misshaped hat over her curly hair.

"I love it!"

"That warm brown looks good on you," Bradlee commented, with a shy smile.

Leona blushed. She shooed the girls away to wash up before classes began.

"Are we still meeting at 3:00?" she asked Bradlee before he left to prep for his first art class of the morning.

"Yes, I'll meet you at the stables. Hugo's tired from all the exercise he's been getting. Calvin thinks we should take Myrtle."

Myrtle was the oldest horse in the stables. She was an orphan, too. The farmer who owned her had died and the family donated the old mare to *Little Wanderers*.

"Do you think she's up to the challenge?"

Bradlee nodded and offered her his usual sheepish smile. Leona stifled her heart's reaction.

They had agreed not to discuss matters of a personal nature until after Bradlee's first transformation. Leona had convinced him that basic lycanthrope education took priority. Besides, they also needed to strengthen the sanctuary. They finished securing new chains to the cabin floor. But they couldn't afford new windows, so those were boarded up and the broken glass swept. A new door was on order and the replacement padlocks had arrived from the blacksmith's yesterday.

"Myrtle's slow, so she's the best choice for pulling a wagon of glass windows."

"You bought windows? How did you manage that?"

"Mr. Green used to manage the glass factory in town. I told them he sent me and needed a favor. They let me have two thick glass windows at no cost."

"That's... wonderful. Maybe we should go the extra mile and add bars to the new windows, too. Just in case."

"Smart thinking. You're a good Warden. I mean, a good *Shepherd.*"

She had explained the recent division to him, at least, as much as she could. He absorbed the information well, but it was a lot to comprehend. Leona tried to handle this situation like her father and mother would. She imagined how they would teach a rogue like Bradlee. The task was daunting.

Bradlee screwed up his mouth and said, "I guess that's why we can't be together. You're *too* good. But, maybe the Werewolf Guidebook is wrong. It doesn't explain what the curse *is.*"

Jane and Leona had taught him about the stance on Warden and Werewolf relationships, about their inherited responsibilities, about delivering mercy without second chances, and about the curse, as much as they knew, anyway.

"So, you have to marry another Warden?"

Leona's eyes fell to her cracked leather boots.

"Look, that's not important right now. We agreed, remember. First, we get you safely through your first transformation."

He stepped closer. "Then we'll discuss matters of the heart?"

Leona couldn't speak. She gave him a noncommittal head bob, hoping it would be enough for now.

Her lambs brought her comfort. She thanked God for them. At first, they fought and grumbled. Their hard pasts stained them like oil paint. Many of the girls needed healing with large doses of love, sometimes in the form of sharp discipline, a linseed oil to cleanse their messy hearts. Some days Leona thought they'd never change, that the hate inside them had grown too strong. But love proved stronger than hate, as Jane had claimed the day Leona confessed that she loved Bradlee.

She watched his figure disappear down the hall and tugged the knitted hat off her head, examining it. The rows of stitches were uneven, some loose, some tight. But the girls had created it just for her, and they accomplished it by taking turns. She held the imperfect, well-meaning accessory over her face, inhaling its wooly aroma and allowing it to absorb her tears.

Chapter Twenty-Five

Tuesday Evening, October 31
The Home for Little Wanderers

"It's time for cake! Where's Bradlee?" Fitz asked.

He set down a lop-sided tower of white-frosted cake on the center table, in front of a semi-circle of glowing jack-o-lanterns. The kids had carved the pumpkins. They milled around the cafeteria, enjoying the combined birthday and Halloween festivities. A line for the apple-bobbing barrel weaved through the room and everyone wore a homemade mask or a costume. Leona couldn't help smiling.

Jane rushed over to Leona. She wore a feathered owl mask. "Fitz, the cake looks wonderful. But where's Bradlee? Have you seen him, Leona?"

Leona shook her head, though the movement was hindered by the large box above her shoulders. She removed the lion head she'd crafted from a used apple crate, newspaper, torn rags, yarn, and loads of paint.

"He's here somewhere. I have no idea what he's dressed up like."

307

"It was a secret," Fitz added. "Wait 'til you see him!"

At that moment, a barnyard animal cry broke through the party chatter. Leona, Jane, and Fitz turned toward the odd sound. Fitz snapped his orange bowtie and roared in laughter. He, Jane, and Leona found Bradlee's sheep costume hilarious and adorable. They weren't the only ones. The youngest girls giggled and begged to pet his woolen head.

"Baa-baa!" Bradlee called out. Leona was reminded of Gunshot, Farmer Thompson's runaway sheep.

"Mr. Smith, you're so cute!" the kids teased.

He smiled a wide grin that warmed Leona's whole body. The girls giggled and worked his jaw, pretending to chew on the decorative straw. He finally wandered over to the cake table.

"Did Mrs. Green give you the fleece for this?" Leona asked, patting his soft head. "It's impressive."

"Why, thank you," he replied with a wink.

"I-it, well, it's very well done, Bradlee," Jane remarked. "You're such a creative artist." Her eyes filled with tears. "I'm sorry. I just wish Teddy were here. He loves parties."

Bradlee took her hands in his. "We *will* find Mr. Green. I promise."

She brightened a little.

"I want cake!" one of the boys demanded. Soon, all the children were in line.

Leona fished an eggshell out of her mouth. Bradlee chuckled. "He's pretty proud of that cake."

Leona winked. "Don't worry, I won't tell him. Hey—who's that?"

The Good Shepherd

She pointed across the room to a large frame with a red velvet curtain hung across all four sides. Black boots peeked out from the bottom.

"*What's* that, you mean?" Bradlee said, squinting.

As they made their way towards the curtained frame with feet, Leona recognized Bridget standing beside the red velvet curtains. Leona walked faster.

"Hello, Bridget! I'm pleased to see you again."

Bridget lowered her eyes and held out a box with a huge bow on top. "This is for you. Happy birthday, Miss Leona."

A muffled, yet familiar voice emanated from behind the curtain. "Happy birthday, cousin!"

"Clementine? What kind of costume is this?"

"Shh! I don't want Fitz to know I'm here, so keep your voice down. I'm the Wizard of Oz, silly. Don't you read?" She turned to face Jane. "Mrs. Green, thanks for inviting us. Mother insisted I come and deliver Leona's present. Luckily Bridget has recovered from her accident and agreed to accompany me. Allen is waiting with the wagon outside. If you don't mind, I'll just have a slice of cake—ahem, *Bridget*—and be on my way."

Bridget rushed over to the cake, which was disappearing fast. Fitz handed her a small plate without looking up.

"Thank ye," she said with a light brogue.

Fitz's eyes rose. He blinked hard at the maid before asking, "Don't you work for the Schaeffer's? For…for… Clementine?"

Bridget nodded and rushed back. Fitz followed at her heels. Leona stood aside as he flung the curtain open, revealing a red-faced Clementine.

"Ah… it *is* you. Did you just come for the cake? Or did you come to your senses?"

Clementine scoffed, but Leona had seen a tiny spark in her eyes when Fitz appeared before her. A smile had grown in them that vanished as quickly as it came. She was happy to see him.

"Charles, I have no senses to come to. I mean—uh—where's my cake, Bridget?"

Bridget handed her the slice of white frosted cake. Clementine shed her costume and hurried away with her gluttonous treasure. Fitz shook his head but turned to follow her. Bridget's eyes darted from Clementine's disappearing back to the wieldy costume lying on the floor.

"Bridget, how are you? What was that Clementine said about an accident?" Leona asked her before she decided to run off after her mistress.

"Oh, miss. It was nothing. I went to Harvard to surprise Miss Clementine with her favorite treat and, in my hurry, I tripped, like a fool. I bumped my head, is all. I spent a week in hospital, but I'm fine now. I better take this," she said, rustling up the cumbersome Wizard of Oz costume. "Miss Clementine!"

"Don't go yet. Can I ask you a question? Did a man named Goldberg ever visit my uncle?"

Bridget's mouth twitched. "I don't remember 'is name, but right before you left us to work here, a funny-looking gentleman came to call on Mr. Schaeffer. No one else was home at the time. Mr. Schaeffer and the man argued."

"What about?"

"I only heard pieces. Something about your uncle not being a very good father. Mr. Schaeffer threatened him."

"Threatened him how?" Leona was intrigued.

"Threatened his life! Now, I must go find Clementine. Bye!"

Bridget left Leona, Jane, and Bradlee staring after her.

"Who the hell *was* this Goldberg guy?" Bradlee asked.

"Was he a Hunter, Leona?" Jane asked, fear cinching her brow.

Leona shook her head. "I don't know. But my uncle threatened his life. And now he's dead. But Uncle Ezra's a Normalizer. He would never—"

Bradlee interrupted, "People do crazy things when they're scared."

"True. Maybe it wasn't planned. Maybe—"

"Happy birthday, Leona and Bradlee," Reverend Busch exclaimed. He'd approached so stealthily that Leona jumped at the sound of his voice. She wasn't used to being startled. In fact, she'd never been surprised like that. Her mental exhaustion must have weakened her supernatural senses.

"Oh, I didn't mean to startle you, dear!"

"I'm fine, Reverend. Thank you for coming."

"Oh, I wouldn't miss it. Though I wish you wouldn't encourage these pagan practices, Mrs. Green. Jack-o-lanterns? Spooky costumes? It's blasphemous."

"I'm sorry if you're offended, Reverend. But look at the children," Jane replied, pointing at the apple barrel surrounded with kids giggling and munching on wet, red apples.

At first, the reverend's expression remained sour. Then it turned sad. Leona didn't understand the man. She understood the importance of obedience, probably more than many outside the ministry, but his devotion seemed detached from reality. Rules were his god.

He gave a quick nod and excused himself. His tall, thin figure approached the front door. He held it open for Bridget and Clementine as they struggled to pull her massive costume through the exit.

Fitz rushed past the minister and exited without speaking to the man. Fitz's anger at the reverend was understandable. The orphan train selections had been made by Reverend Busch. No one could have predicted the train would crash, killing Fitz's sisters, but the disastrous event had formed a wall between them. Leona felt sad for both parties. It was a miracle Reverend Busch had convinced Fitz to return to the orphanage.

They could use some more miracles.

"Leona, you haven't finished your cake," Jane said. "Are you okay?"

"None of us is okay. Thanks for throwing us a birthday party, Jane. But Bradlee and I want to go search the woods one more time."

Jane reached out and grasped one of Bradlee's hands and one of Leona's, forming a little circle.

"Friends, you can go out one more time. But if you don't find anything tonight, I think we have to conclude that Teddy isn't in those woods anymore."

"No!" Bradlee raised his voice. Some of the people around them stopped talking and stared. He lowered his voice to a whisper. "I can't give up on him."

"I didn't say you should. I pray for his return every chance I get. But you need to stop looking for him in the forest. It's less and less likely he's still out there. The search is harming you both, physically and emotionally. You can't keep on like this. The sanctuary still needs to be readied and secured."

"I know it seems like we're tired, but we're okay," Bradlee assured her. Leona nodded her agreement.

"No. You possess important roles here. I can't keep taking your place at night with your girls, Leona. They're *your* sheep, remember. Bradlee. the children depend on you to be alert and at your best. It's time to let God take over. He'll return Teddy to us if it's His will."

Bradlee growled. "It's hard for me to trust in something I can't see, Mrs. Green. I need to *do* something."

"I understand your reluctance. So—do something—prepare for your first transformation. Mr. Green would want you to be ready and stay safe. If anything bad happened, he'd be devastated."

Leona didn't want to think about the worst, but Bradlee voiced her greatest fear.

"The last thing I want is to harm anyone. That bloodlust thing sounds horrible. I'll do whatever is necessary to avoid becoming a homicidal maniac. Besides, I don't have a death wish," he replied, casting a nervous glance at Leona.

"I don't want to exact mercy on you," Leona said.

Bradlee avoided her eyes.

"But you've done it before?"

Leona's eyes dropped. "Yes, and it was preventable. It was

my fault, really. I should have known the man wouldn't take my advice. He wasn't trustworthy and decent, like you."

Leona and Bradlee looked at each other, silent. The moments felt like days.

Eventually, Bradlee broke the spell. "If we're going to search the woods, we ought to leave now," he said.

"Promise this is the last time." Jane stood before them looking strong, but Leona sensed she was still fraught with concern. Her heartbeat was quicker than usual. Leona yearned to return Mr. Green to Jane. It was her job. She was his Shepherd, after all.

Bradlee took Mrs. Green's hands in his. "We promise, just one more time—then we'll focus on the kids and the sanctuary."

"Thank you, my dears."

Chapter Twenty-Six

"Clementine!"

She stopped, not because Charles yelled her name, but because her costume fell out of Bridget's hands and blocked her path. Bridget scrambled to collect it. Allen climbed out of the wagon to lend his assistance.

Clementine thrust her cold hands into her pockets. One pocket was already full. *Fiddlesticks! I forgot to show Leona the knife.*

Allen and Bridget loaded the broken costume into the wagon. Clementine turned around and addressed Charles.

"I wasn't here to see *you*, Charles. Mother made me come."

She barely glanced at him but couldn't help chuckling. He had a thick smudge of ivory frosting on his chin.

"Go on, laugh at me! I know I'm a fool. A willing fool, mind you, but a fool. Though I do love hearing you say my name." Her heart skipped as his mouth curled up adorably on one side. She had to admit, Charles was a little endearing. A little.

No! He's a useless orphan. Useless.

"Whatever. I'm laughing because, well—you have food on your face."

His eyes widened. His fingers searched his freckled skin for the mess. "Where?"

Clementine stepped forward and wiped the frosting off his chin with the corner of her shawl. Before she stepped back, his hand clasped her wrist. His deep emerald eyes froze her in place. Lifting her hand gently, he kissed the top of it. His warm lips, like the touch of feathers, tickled her cold flesh.

"Thanks, darlin'."

Her frozen body melted, then wavered. Charles caught her sinking frame in his arms and held on tight. He didn't smell like vinegar tonight; he smelled delicious—like vanilla, butter, and sugar.

"Clementine, I wish I were rich. But I ain't. I'm not handsome or brave or—"

The sound of a horse galloping by interrupted him. Clementine raised her head. He was staring at the horse so intently. She followed suit.

"Is that Bradlee and Leona?" she asked, straightening to her feet.

Charles nodded. "Where are they taking Hugo? It's their birthday party and they're chucking it to go for a ride?"

"I have a crazy idea," Clementine said. "Charles Fitzgerald, do you like adventures?"

A huge grin swallowed his face. "Yes. Yes I do, darlin'."

"We should head north," Leona suggested. "Wait—I hear something."

"So do I," Bradlee replied. Behind them, a horse whinnied. "That sounds like Myrtle."

As they waited, the old mare emerged through the bushes, lit up by the autumn sunset. Clementine sat sideways on her back, swaddled in her shawl. Fitz waltzed along beside them, holding the lead.

"What are you guys doing here?" Bradlee asked with a deep frown.

"We're following the yellow brick road," Clementine said, grinning childishly. Leona and Bradlee glanced at each other. Leona had no explanation for Clementine's weird response.

"What? It's allegorical. This path is like the yellow brick road in *The Wonderful Wizard of Oz*." Clementine repeated.

Leona and Bradlee stared at her.

Clementine continued explaining, "It's a very popular book—and a play. Mr. Hartman told me so." She rolled her eyes at them. "Fine. Forget it. It's a silly joke. Anyway, we thought it was a nice night for a ride. Didn't we, Charles?"

The giddy expression that grew on Fitz's face was contagious. Still, if Leona hadn't been so tired and confused, she wouldn't have returned it. She shook her head to remove her senseless smile.

"*Charles?*" Bradlee asked, bursting into laughter.

Fitz's broad smile remained intact. "You heard the little lady. My name *is* Charles, you know. But only my darlin' calls me by my true name."

Clementine breathed a sigh of exasperation and then shivered. Her teeth rattled. She rubbed her palms together rapidly. Bradlee removed his wool mittens and held them out. Fitz took them and passed them on to Clementine.

Fitz winked. "Consider this a gift from me."

"They're from Bradlee, you idiot," Clementine said flatly.

"True, but I took them first. I decided to be a gentleman and give them to my darlin' instead of keeping them for myself. You're welcome."

Before Clementine could form a rebuttal, Leona interrupted. "You two need to turn around and go back. See that Clementine gets home to Joy Street safely, Fitz."

"Oh, Allen and Bridget are waiting for me in the wagon back at the stables," Clementine said, pulling on the woolen mittens. "I don't need Charles."

"Aye, but ya do, lass," he teased, his Irish accent excessively thick.

The scent of other people in the woods filled Leona's nose. They couldn't waste any more time being nice. "Go back," she demanded.

"What're ya doin' out here, anyway?" Fitz asked, tugging on Bradlee's coat.

Bradlee replied, "We're looking for Mr. Green. It's almost dark. You need to go back. Myrtle is almost blind as it is, Fitz."

"That's why I'm holding the lead," he replied, holding up the straw rope.

Suddenly, something whizzed past Fitz's head and struck the tree beside Bradlee.

"Get down! Someone's shooting," Leona insisted. Clementine leapt off Myrtle. The aging horse shook her head violently. Fitz lost his grip on the rope attached to the snaffle. Myrtle bolted away, galloping back toward the stables.

Clementine and Fitz crouched low. Leona and Bradlee scanned the periphery before joining them. The shooter remained well hidden. Leona crawled toward Clementine, but another shot rang out and she flattened to the ground.

"They must be far. I don't smell them," Leona told Bradlee. He nodded in silence.

Clementine's eyebrow rose. "Smell them? What are—"

"Shh!"

The group waited. Leona closed her eyes and concentrated. *Leaves rustling. Crickets chirping. No birds singing. Footsteps faint and approaching.* Another gunshot rang out, closer than the first two. An ominous thud sounded in Leona's ears. Her stomach felt queasy.

Myrtle. They shot Myrtle!

Soon, two strange voices called out, less than ten yards away.

"The horse came from that direction. They must be here somewhere."

"Stop shooting. We need them alive."

Clementine's face was white as a sheet as she crawled along the forest floor. Her fear-filled sobs grew louder. Leona bit her tongue, stifling the urge to scold Clementine to stop moving and hush her crying. Her cousin's petite body wriggled along the ground, cracking twigs and shuffling through the crunchy dead leaves. Then Clementine hiccupped. The loud gulping sound echoed into the gray forest.

"Ah-ha!" a voice exclaimed.

A man in a fisherman's cap, with a rifle flung over his shoulder, lifted Clementine up by the back of her coat and perched her on her feet. Her knees buckled as she fainted. The man's companion caught her in his arms.

"Come out, come out, wherever you are! We have your little friend. If you don't want anything to happen to her pretty little face, you better do what we say. And quick!"

Leona and Fitz joined Bradlee. Together they marched over to the scruffy-looking pair. One was round and short. The other was tall and wiry. Their knit caps resembled the ones that dock workers at the Harbor wore. They both carried rifles.

Leona suspected their weapons contained silver bullets.

"Who are you?" Bradlee asked.

The tall man slapped him across the face. Bradlee snarled, but his companion grabbed Clementine by the throat and squeezed. Her face turned pink.

"Bastard!" Fitz yelled.

The man loosened his grip. He squinted at Bradlee. "If you try anything, the doll suffers. Got it? Now, leave your horse and follow us."

His partner whined, "Paddy, it's a long way. I can't carry this gal all the way there."

"Fine," he replied. He bent down and slapped Clementine's face in a crude attempt to wake her. It was Fitz's turn to growl. His hands squeezed into fists.

Clementine's eyes fluttered. When her eyes fully opened, the sight of the two men made her scream. They gagged her with a cloth quickly, then proceeded to tie and gag the rest of them.

What had God given Wardens an instinctual ability to fight off a Werewolf, but not a vicious human being? She considered attacking them anyway, since she healed quickly, no matter who injured her. Bridget's attack with the knife proved that.

Bradlee tugged on his restraints. The one called Paddy smirked at him.

"Stop wiggling. You're about to be reunited with an old friend. But if you cause a fuss, maybe we'll have to cancel the festivities. That would be an awful shame, wouldn't it, boy-o?"

Bradlee and Leona exchanged looks. A reunion with an old friend? Leona considered Paddy's strange comment as she followed Bradlee's back through the forest.

I hope they're taking us to Mr. Green.

When the sun sunk in the sky, their captors lit torches to illuminate the dirt path.

An hour or so later, they emerged from the forest. They walked along a road that paralleled the woods until they reached a pub, the rowdy patrons inside oblivious to their plight. Soon their captors forced the group into the back of a wagon, commanding them to lie down.

They jostled around on its splintery floor. Someone's boots accidentally kicked Leona's. Clementine made choked, sobbing sounds of protest through her gag all the way to their unknown destination, accompanied by Fitz's muffles of comforting. Clementine's futile whining burned into Leona's conscience. Whoever kidnapped them surely wanted her and Bradlee, not

Clementine or Fitz. Uncle Ezra was right; Leona's choice to embrace her gifts as a Warden had put his family in danger.

The wagon lurched to a stop. Leona pulled herself into a sitting position. Darkness, combined with dizziness, blinded her for a moment. Clementine scrambled around beside her, twisting her petite frame off the uncomfortable floor and sitting up.

Where are we being taken?

Clementine's eyes narrowed as she peered into the shadowy night. Then they turned to saucers.

One of the men opened the gate. They forced burlap sacks over their heads and pulled them to their feet. Leona was lifted down roughly. Her boots stumbled on their grassy foundation. When she regained her balance, she relied on her other senses to find clues to their location. *Birdsong, crickets, fresh-cut lumber, masculine voices.*

Shoes thudded on the ground behind her. Bradlee and Fitz reeked of sweat, wood, and sugar. Clementine smelled like wood smoke. She must have been standing by a fireplace today. Her breaths were staggered, panicked, and muffled.

Leona mumbled through her gag, "I won't let them hurt you, cousin."

Clementine's reply was a shuddering, high-pitched whimper.

Leona meant to keep her promise. She'd failed enough in her short career as a Shepherd. Losing another sheep was unacceptable. Though not her blood relation, Clementine was still family.

Finding Mr. Green was the only thing that lent a spark of hope to the dire situation.

The Good Shepherd

The men attached lead ropes to the knots around their bound hands and jerked them forward. Leona sensed they walked west, then north. Their captors seemed to be in quite a hurry. They tripped on the uneven surface of the path as they were pulled along.

"Stop!"

They obeyed, standing still as statues, apprehensive of the future and fearful that they'd done something to Mr. Green. Would they be reunited with him soon?

She focused on her senses again. Their captors were sweating. Their heartbeats raced. *They're afraid too.* These men were goons, not ringleaders.

A door opened. "Watch your step," said one goon, chuckling at his inane joke. "There's ten steps. We're going down now."

They descended the steps one at a time, blinded by the sacks over their heads. When they reached the bottom of the stairs, the men removed the sacks and pulled down their gags. Shadows obscured their surroundings.

Leona felt a cup being placed to her lips.

"Drink up," the goon said, chuckling again. Leona sipped the water. It tasted chalky. The men continued to tip the cup into their mouths until they drained the cup. Their hands remained bound in front of them.

Leona didn't fight her captors. Wardens fought Werewolves, not *men*. She didn't even know how to punch someone. And until she knew if their inference to Mr. Green was real or a ploy, her hands were tied, literally and figuratively.

She did possess a weapon. The silver hairpin. And there was

a fiercer weapon among them than that—Bradlee. During the next full moon cycle, he would transform and become violent, murderous, uncontrollable. Tonight, he remained frustratingly human, like Leona. Surely his concern for Mr. Green subdued him as well.

Leona yawned. She felt unusually lethargic.

The water. It contained… a draught. So… tired.

Chapter Twenty-Seven

Clementine stretched her arms high above her head. Her previously bound appendages reveled in the ability to move. After rubbing sleep from her eyes, she examined her surroundings. She was in a cage. The enclosure was approximately half the size of the water closet in the house on Joy Street. The iron bars were as thick as her thumb.

She sympathized with Dorothy. Clementine had been whisked away from her home violently, not by a twister, but by thugs. Regretting that she hadn't finished *The Wonderful Wizard of Oz* yet; now she feared she never would. She rose to her knees and prayed for a miracle, begging for a good witch to float down from the sky and save her.

"Hello, is anyone else awake?" she whispered.

Charles replied first. "Clementine? Are you okay?"

"No, I'm not okay! I'm in a cage. My stomach feels funny, too."

Leona spoke next. Her words slurred together. "I'll g-get us out of here. I just need to think of a plan. Ummm, Bradlee, are you awake?"

"He's still asleep," Charles replied. "That scruffy bastard made him drink two cups of that nasty water."

A lamp hanging on the wall burned steadily. It flicked scant light over the dingy room.

"Fitz? Leona? Is that you?" a parched speaker asked from across the shadowy room. The male voice was low-pitched and hoarse, like some spooky specter from Clementine's worst nightmares.

"Mr. Green?" Charles asked.

Clementine sighed in relief—it wasn't a ghost.

Leona exclaimed, "Mr. Green! We've been looking for you for weeks. It's good to hear your voice again."

Charles added, "Yeah, Mr. Green. We were worried 'bout ya. Hey, where are we?"

Mr. Green attempted to speak but broke into a coughing fit.

Clementine yearned for the chance to explain to their captors that she had nothing to do with the orphanage. She wasn't associated with the others. Then they would realize their mistake and let her go home.

"I don't know where we are," Mr. Green said. He coughed again dryly. "I was shot. It happened after my last night at the cabin, early the next morning, as I was walking through the woods on my way back to *Little Wanderers*. A bullet struck me in the leg."

He barked out a long series of coughs before continuing. "It's still lodged there. I've felt miserable ever since. You know, I've never been sick before—never in my entire life."

The Good Shepherd

"The bullet is made of silver," Leona said. "You have to get it out. It's poisoning you."

"I can't," Mr. Green said, his voice barely reaching a whisper. "It's too late for me. But you must escape, Leona. Promise me that you'll tell Jane I love her. Tell her I want her to be happy and that I—that I'm sorry."

"You can tell her when we get you home," Leona said. She grasped the bars and shook them, much fiercer than Clementine expected.

"Don't make them angry," she scolded Leona. They wouldn't listen to her pleas if Leona vexed them.

Leona grimaced. "You don't understand."

"What don't I understand?"

Charles began, "Look, Clementine—"

Leona interrupted, "Fitz. Don't. I'll explain it all to her later."

"Explain what?" She raised an eyebrow at her cousin, but Leona only rubbed her eyes and yawned. Clementine glared at Charles. He offered an apologetic grin, then twisted around to face Mr. Green. The man looked near death.

"Fine. Keep your little secrets. All I want to know is how we're going to get out of here. I want to go home!"

A groan erupted from the person in the cage next to Mr. Green's.

"Bradlee, how are you feeling?" Leona asked.

He raised his rumpled body off the floor and leaned against the bars. Even in his weakened condition, Clementine couldn't ignore his natural beauty. He combed back his unkempt ebony bangs with his fingers. Mr. Green coughed uncontrollably.

Bradlee's foggy blue eyes turned to him.

"Mr. Green, I promise to get you out of here. We'll… think… of something," he promised the older man.

Bradlee's cage was located beside Mr. Green's. Across from them, Clementine was trapped between Charles and Leona's cages.

She examined Bradlee and Mr. Green.

At this moment, Bradlee didn't look capable of walking, much less dragging someone else around. His shoulders were slumped, his breath uneven. The ghostly weak pallor of his face was extenuated by the dark clumps of matted hair falling over his forehead. And Mr. Green's skin was the color of his name. His eyes had swelled in their sockets and flies buzzed around him. Leona kept rubbing her eyes and yawning, fighting to stay awake.

Mr. Flufferbutter would be a better ally than these losers.

"Leona, I don't mean to be rude, but you need to do something. Quick." She placed two fingers over her right wrist, like one of the nurses had done to take Bridget's pulse. "My heartbeat is terribly fast. I think I might faint."

Leona's mouth bent down at the corners. "I'm sorry, cousin, but can you be quiet? I need to think."

Clementine hmphed. She hated waiting.

After allowing Leona a few minutes of contemplation, Clementine couldn't hold back. "Well? What are we going to do?"

A strange smirk appeared on Leona's face. "We overcome. Be patient, my friends. And follow my lead. If I tell you to run, do it. If I tell you to play dead, do it."

Charles and Mr. Green nodded without hesitation, as if Leona's ridiculous pronouncement made sense to them. Trying to think of a snappy retort to this odd response, Clementine's hand found the heirloom pendant pinned to her collar.

"Ouch!"

"Clementine—are you hurt?" Charles asked. His freckled forehead crinkled.

She examined her hand. The tips of her fingers were bright red.

"This stupid pendant burned me again! What the dickens is wrong with this thing?"

"That *is* odd," Leona commented.

Not as odd as you, Clementine wanted to retort. Instead, she replied, "There're more important things to worry about now. For instance, why did they bring us to Harvard?"

"Harvard?" Leona asked. "We're at *Harvard?*"

"Yes! Before they put that sack over my head, I saw that watchtower they're building by the dormitories. They've been constructing it for weeks. The noise was obnoxious."

"Do you know which building we're in?"

"No, but I've heard rumors about deserted dungeons in the medical school, where they cut open dead bodies." In a frightened whisper, she added, "I always imagined they looked like this."

"Calm yourself, darlin,'" Charles said, though he shivered. His eyes darted to and fro.

Clementine tried to shake the horrific image of butchered

bodies from her mind. "It doesn't matter where we are." She rattled the bars, shaking the padlock holding the cage door closed. "We're trapped! And I'm starving."

Leona was staring at Mr. Green, not even listening to her. Maybe—hopefully—she would think of a plan. Leona was the only one alert enough to lead them. *Unless I think of a plan first...*

Charles' stomach rumbled. "Ah, why'd ya have to say you're hungry? Now all I can think about is food."

Another stomach growled. "It doesn't help... that... you smell... like... cake," Bradlee remarked weakly.

A loud scraping sound came from above. Light traveled down the middle of the room from an opened door at the top of the staircase. The door scraped again. Before the light from the closing door vanished, Clementine caught sight of a thick figure descending the stairs. The scrumptious smell of cinnamon bread affronted her nostrils. Her stomach groaned.

A tenor voice with a light, distinctively non-Yankee accent said, "Good mornin'. I brought you something ta eat. We can't have you all starvin' ta death. Besides, that special brew you drank has some side effects. One of them's a mighty appetite." His accent was familiar. *Like Bridget's.*

"Who are you?" Leona demanded.

"That's not important right now, Leona Schaeffer. You'll find out when the time is right."

"How do you know my name?"

"You've been sharing it with everyone, despite your mentor's sound advice. You should've listened to him—not that it would've saved you. You Shepherds are all a bunch of mamsy-pamsy idealists. Your righteous arrogance leaves its own trail."

"I assume you're a Hunter?" Leona asked.

What are they talking about—Shepherds and Hunters?

The man laughed. The cinnamon-sugar aroma made Clementine's knees buckle. She held her aching belly and prayed their stupid banter would end so she could eat.

"You really think you can hold us here? The police must have been notified by now. You won't get away with this," Leona threatened.

"Oh, I think ye'll be unpleasantly surprised at what we can get away with," the man replied.

"Shut up!" Clementine yelled. "Stop teasing us and start feeding us."

"Cousin, hush," Leona scolded.

The man bowled over in laughter.

"This girl—I'm glad Sissy told us to get you, too. Ain't you a laugh? And worth a pretty penny, to boot. Here's your breakfast, ya glutton."

He squeezed a sticky cinnamon roll through the bars and Clementine snatched it out of his hand. Cinnamon-sugar goo oozed down her chin after she bit the warm, sweet bread. It was every bit as delicious as Bridget's, which was hard to believe.

Oh no! Did they kidnap Bridget, too?

Everyone ate their cinnamon buns, except Bradlee. He bounced in and out of consciousness, while his roll sat languishing on the floor of his cage, crying to be devoured. Clementine couldn't take her eyes off it. Licking her lips and fingers, she stared at the unappreciated pastry, salivating like a dog.

"Look at you. You're mighty hungry, ain't ya?" the crass Irishman teased.

Clementine nodded her head rapidly. The stocky man pulled another cinnamon bun from the pan he held and tossed it into her cage. It hit the bars above her head and bounced off her shoulder. When she scrambled on the floor for it, the man burst into dry heaves, his laughter fierce.

"You're like a pup! If I didn't know better, I'd think you were a lycanthrope, too."

Clementine didn't understand what he meant, and she didn't care. She gobbled the bread, hoping this additional bun would appease her raging appetite.

"Clementine, they already drugged us once. Slow down," Leona scolded her.

Ha! She ate her roll as quickly as I did.

She was tired of the amazing Leona and her bossiness. She wasn't doing anything to get them out of this mess, unless spouting nonsensical instructions counted. The least Leona could do is let her eat without criticism. Maybe the amazing Leona could live without food, but Clementine couldn't.

"I feel fine. They're delicious, just like my Bridget's."

The man snickered. "You're dumb as a doornail, ain't ya? I can't wait to milk your pa for all he's worth. Though I'm not sure he'd want a pretty piggy like you back under his roof."

"What are you talking about?" she asked, forcibly swallowing the last bite of the second bun.

"Your ransom will fund their incarceration." He gestured toward Mr. Green and Bradlee.

"How long do you plan to keep us here?" Leona asked.

"Well, Miss Schaeffer, we was hoping you'd all grace us with your presence for two weeks, minimum. At that point, some of you will leave us. And some of you won't." The man snarled at Bradlee and Mr. Green, then his belligerent gaze landed on Leona. Her cousin didn't acknowledge his ugly glare. Her eyes were stuck on the beautiful, weakened Bradlee.

The man addressed her cousin. "I hope you're not as stubborn and foolish as yer parents, Miss."

Seeing pain mar Leona's perfect face would normally have given Clementine a silent thrill, but this time, it hurt to witness misery wash over Leona.

Nothing about this ordeal was thrilling.

The uncouth man threw the last cinnamon bun into Mr. Green's cage and trudged up the steep staircase. His heavy steps echoed in the small dungeon-like room, reverberating through Clementine's body like the bass drum from a funeral march.

"We gotta get out of here," Charles said.

Bradlee made a feeble noise. Clementine could only guess he'd seconded the sentiment.

His eyelids fluttered as he brought the dirty cinnamon roll toward his lips and attempted to bite down. But the circle of sticky sweet bread wasn't close enough. The scene would've been comical under any other circumstance, but in this moment, Clementine couldn't have laughed if she'd tried.

She shoved her cold hands into her deep coat pockets and

pulled out the mittens. Something fell from her pocket onto the floor. "Oh! I forgot—I have a knife!"

Chapter Twenty-Eight

Leona examined the knife's leather sheath. "It's a wolf," she stated.

After licking sugar from the corner of her mouth, Clementine replied, "Yes, it's the Schaeffer family crest, silly. Don't you recognize it?"

"Yes, of course. Where did you get it?"

Leona waited for her to answer. Clementine's mouth was still speckled with cinnamon sugar on one side. But not for long. After savoring the sweetness, she cleared her throat and finally explained, "I, um, found it in the cellar. Father has a trunk full of weapons down there!"

"I wish there were a trunk full of weapons down here," Fitz grumbled. "I'd—well, I'd show that piece of shite a thing or two. Leona, give me that knife."

"No! It's mine," Clementine protested. She thrust her hand through the bars and grabbed it from Leona. The weapon fell out of its sheath, landing on the straw floor of her cage. The blade glittered in the shadowy lamplight.

"You could hurt yourself with that thing, darlin.' It looks mighty sharp," Fitz said with a stern look.

Clementine balled her fist around the handle. "I found it. It's mine. Now I can fight. When that dunderhead returns, I'll kill him."

Leona frowned. "Clementine, taking a life is not that easy. And it will haunt you forever."

"How would you know?"

Leona's blue eyes went to the floor. "It's a long story."

Clementine's eyes widened. "You've killed someone? Is that why the policeman came to see you? Did you kill that man in the alley?"

"No, Clementine. I didn't. Something happened, yes, but it was before I came to Boston. I... I failed."

"You did what you had to do, Leona. You followed the Code," Mr. Green assured her.

"True, but it shouldn't have happened. My father wouldn't have failed like that."

"You did the best you could. I think your father would've been proud of you," he replied, though his troubled gaze was set on Bradlee. He tipped his chin toward Leona now. "Fathers aren't perfect either, Leona. Sometimes, no matter how hard they try, they let down the people who depend on them most."

Bradlee smiled sadly. "You've never let me down, Mr. Green," he whispered. "I know you wanted to tell me yourself, but Mrs. Green told me about our shared condition."

"I wish I could be there to help you prepare, son."

Leona sighed, her heart heavy. Nothing was how it was supposed to be.

What did their captors want with two Werewolves, two

humans, and a Warden?

Clementine slid the knife in and out of the sheath, faster each time. Leona addressed her, "Cousin, trust me. You don't want to live with the memory of killing someone."

Clementine hugged the knife to her breast. "Then I'll just maim him. I could live with *that*," she replied, her jaw set. A vengeful look marred her young hazel eyes.

Leona feared her bravado. It was fueled by half-hearted passion that would fizzle in the heat of battle. The situation could easily turn against her.

"We must find out more about their plan," Bradlee said. "They want Mr. Green and I to stay for another two weeks. Why?"

Clementine piped up, "The next full moon is in two weeks."

"Oh no," Mr. Green murmured. His skin was tinted blue. He was dying slowly, poison coursing through his veins, weakening him. Leona feared, at the next full moon, the inevitable transformation might kill him.

Leona groaned in frustration. "Ergh! What do they want?"

"Money. They're going to ask Father for ransom money, right?" Clementine asked.

"Right! 'To fund their incarceration,'" Fitz quoted, pointing to Mr. Green and Bradlee.

"Maybe Father will refuse to give them any money. I mean, he's pretty stingy," Clementine frowned.

"Shh, Clementine, I'm trying to think," Leona said. Nothing made sense. Hunters wanted to kill rogues. Kidnapping and extortion were unnecessary and tedious.

"He'll pay the ransom," Fitz assured Clementine.

Leona's instincts told her that money wasn't their kidnapper's prime motivation.

"I don't understand any of this!" Clementine pouted.

Leona considered some possibilities. Maybe these goons were working for the mysterious 'Collector' Jane had mentioned once, the one who displayed Werewolves in traveling circuses. Or they could be setting up a fighting match, pitting wolf against wolf, for profit and sport. Maybe they planned to attack an enemy using Mr. Green and Bradlee as their weapons of choice. Leona shuddered at the thought of each of these scenarios and kept silent.

Mr. Green lifted his injured leg with his hands and repositioned himself on the flattened straw on the hard floor of his cage. Leona worried he wouldn't live another two weeks. She'd found Jane's beloved husband, only to witness his slow, painful death, helpless to save him.

No! I must return him to her. Think, think...

Loud noises, like crashing pots and pans, sounded from above, accented by thundering footsteps and shouting voices. Soon, the door scraped open again. Two figures descended the steep staircase.

"Reverend Busch?" Fitz said.

The reverend's mouth was gagged with a dingy gray cloth and his hands were fastened behind him. The stocky man who'd brought them breakfast pushed him forward.

"We caught this weasel sneaking in a window upstairs. We've run out of room in this hotel, mister preacher. But we could use some help making preparations for an upcoming special event. If you don't want any harm to come to your little flock here, you'll obey and not make a fuss. Do you understand?"

The reverend nodded his compliance. A tear trickled down his thin face.

Special event? Leona's heart raced.

Bradlee scowled at their captor. "You'd hurt a man of the cloth? What's wrong with you? What do you want from us?"

The man tittered in private glee. "You'll find out in good time. Now, the nice reverend will escort the men to the facilities." He freed the reverend's hands and handed him the bundle of rope. "Tie their wrists together and lead them upstairs one at a time." He placed a burlap sack in his hands. "Put this over their heads. And no talking to the prisoners."

The reverend bowed his head. After an audible *Amen*, the goon grumbled and opened Mr. Green's cage. Leona watched helplessly as the minister placed the sack over Mr. Green's head and tied his wrists.

Their captor oversaw the reverend escort the limping Mr. Green upstairs to the bathroom and waited for their return. Then Fitz took his turn.

Finally, Bradlee descended the stairs. The bars of his cage rattled as the door slammed shut.

"Now for the ladies. Sissy!"

The door scraped at the top of the stairs again and a female figure appeared. They stared in shock as the feminine form became clear.

Clementine gasped. "Bridget? They got you, too!"

The previously kind maid's eyes burned at them with disdain. Leona sighed, realizing the truth. Bridget wasn't a prisoner.

Unlocking Clementine's cage, the maid tied her former mistress' wrists and covered her head with a sack. Clementine walked up the stairs mechanically, clumsily lifting her skirt above her boots with her fettered hands. Leona feared her poor cousin would trip and fall. But she made it to the top and disappeared through the door.

When Clementine returned, Leona studied her cousin's demeanor. She seemed perplexed—possibly shocked—just as Leona was.

Bridget's involvement was something nobody had expected.

It was Leona's turn to use the bathroom. As they reached the top of the staircase, she couldn't hold her questions back any longer.

All she could manage to say was, "Why?"

Bridget sighed. "It's simple, Leona. I'm a Hunter. My brothers agreed to assist me with this important mission." She smirked. Her twinkling eyes mocked Leona. "I considered eliminating you soon after you arrived at the Schaeffer's house, but I bided my time. First, I had to make sure you were really a Warden. One stab convinced me you were."

"Why didn't you finish me off then?"

Bridget shrugged. "I liked you. So I decided to try bringing you to *our* side. I knew it would take a lot of convincing. Dear, dear Leona, I've planned all this… for you."

Her patronizing tone caused Leona to grind her teeth.

"All this just to convince me to become a Hunter? You guys

must be desperate, bored, or stupid. I'm a Shepherd. I've sworn to fight your rebellion, like my parents did. I'll never join you!"

"We shall see. Your compassion for the Werewolves weakens you." Bridget's mouth twisted in obvious joy over what she was about to reveal. "You think the Werewolves are worth saving? What if I told you they killed your parents?"

Leona distrusted anything the woman said, but she was jarred by this accusation.

"Prove it."

"I will. Or rather, Warden Goldberg will." Bridget slipped a paper into Leona's hands and removed the sack from her head.

She stared down at a handwritten letter.

Dear Leona,

I wanted to tell you this in person, but time is running out. Forgive this crude delivery. I need to tell you what really happened to Eben and Katarina Schaeffer.

They were targeted by Werewolves, for reasons I must discuss with you in person. They set your cabin on fire in the middle of the night.

Both the Werewolves and the Wardens thought you were dead, Leona. When reports came in about the funeral of a young man with a registered lycanthrope family name, the Warden Council investigated and found you alive and well in Framingham.

I sent you to Boston for your own safety. I hope you've obeyed my command not to give out your name. If the Werewolves that killed your parents discover you survived, they will hunt you down.

You're in danger, Leona. I'll meet you as soon as I can and take you to safety. Until then, be cautious and stay alert. Don't trust anyone.

-Warden Goldberg

"How did you get this?" Leona asked Bridget.

"I found it in his pocket after I stabbed him in the alley. The policeman delivered the empty envelope to you, if you recall."

"I thought you were my friend," Leona said.

Bridget gave her a sideways grin. "We can be friends. But first, you must come to your senses and join the right side."

"I'll never join you!"

Bridget laughed. The awful sound echoed in Leona's ears.

"Aren't you angry?" Bridget asked. "Don't you want vengeance? Werewolves are dangerous, evil. They killed your parents!"

Leona felt like she was being strangled. Her precious family—her sweet grandparents, Mama, and Papa. They were all gone. Stolen from her. Yes, she was angry. But nothing she did could bring them back. She straightened, inhaling a deep breath and finding strength in the memory of her loving family.

"I still believe Wardens must protect and serve, not exterminate Werewolves. Only the guilty should be punished. We're still their caretakers, their Shepherds."

"You're a fool. They're killers! All of them!"

"Bridget—"

"Stop calling me that! My name is Siobhan Collins."

342

The Good Shepherd

Leona's blood pumped hard through her veins. She couldn't believe this woman was behind their kidnapping—and whatever other sinister deeds they had planned. It boggled her mind.

"What do you plan to do with Mr. Green and Bradlee?" she asked Siobhan.

"They're here to convince you the Hunters are right. With the tremendous growth in America's population, there are fewer and fewer open spaces for Werewolves to hide. Rogues are entering the cities, risking the safety of humanity. Exacting mercy on the whole lot of them is the only way to truly protect everyone. Hunters want peace."

"Murder doesn't bring peace."

Siobhan scoffed. "So high and mighty. Tell me, Shepherd, has anyone died because you failed to protect them from Werewolves?"

Leona hung her head. "I admit, I've failed. But I won't give up. Eliminating Code-abiding Werewolves is detestable and cowardly. Does my uncle know you're a Warden?"

"No. Ezra Schaeffer only sees what he wants to see, like a good Brahmin. Luckily, he's chosen a life of non-interference. As long as he remains a Normalizer, we have no issue with him."

"Why are you keeping us here until the next full moon?"

Siobhan set one hand on her hip and grimaced. "Did Paddy spill the beans? He's such a mouthy brat. I suggest you contemplate the past for a few days, and then I'll fill you in on your future. For now: eat, sleep, and behave. In two weeks, the fun begins. I'm bringing in some outside assistance for that."

"So, the Schaeffers—Uncle Ezra and Franny—are

unharmed? Aren't they worried sick about Clementine?"

"Allen returned to Joy Street in the wagon this morning with a note pinned to his jacket, after waking up alone outside the *Little Wanderers'* stables with a nasty bump on his head. I hated to hurt the old man, but it had to be done. The Schaeffers were instructed not to report her missing to the police. Clementine is a spoiled, annoying little brat, but I don't really want her to die. It all depends on you, Leona. If you change your mind, I'll send her home right now."

Leona imagined poor Aunt Franny overcome with concern. She even felt sorry for Mr. Flufferbutter.

Leona grimaced. "I don't believe you."

"Believe what you like," Siobhan winked.

"Why take Mr. Green? He's married and runs an orphanage. He's a good man."

"I'm keeping them all safe! He's dangerous. Mrs. Green is the ultimate fool—a human in love with a monster."

Leona's heart twinged like it had been jabbed with a sharp stick.

"The silver bullet is poisoning him. Please, take it out," she begged Siobhan.

"Oh, it's not pure silver. There's just enough to weaken him. It's all part of the plan. You'll see soon enough."

She pushed Leona into the watercloset and slammed the door.

Chapter Twenty-Nine

Clementine glanced at each of her companions in their cages. She sighed loud and long. No one noted her ominous despair. *Can't they hear me?* Her next sigh echoed through the room, dripping with despondence. Still, nothing.

"I miss Mr. Flufferbutter."

Charles offered her a small, understanding look, then cleared his throat and addressed the group.

"Tonight's the first full moon."

Leona's eyes stared at the floor. She remained silent.

Clementine pleaded with her, "Tell them you changed your mind. Please! I want to go home."

She'd begged Leona every day for the last two weeks, but now it was November 12. Their time was up. Something bad was going to happen tonight and no one would tell her what. All she knew was that their fate was in Leona's hands. They wanted Leona to agree to some deal. If she agreed, they promised to let the rest of them go. But Leona kept refusing.

"Do you really think they'd let you go if I change my mind?" Leona replied. "You've seen their faces. You know who they are. They'll kill you." She frowned. "We already discussed this."

Clementine wouldn't stop trying, even if everyone else had accepted Leona's stupid decision.

"If you say so. At least I have a knife. I know you don't approve, but I'm glad I'm armed.

Leona frowned at her. Clementine ignored her haughty, know-it-all face and clutched the knife stashed in her pocket.

On her other side, Charles piped up, "I'm scared, I am. I can't pretend otherwise." Addressing Bradlee, he added, "Sorry, mate." *Why was he apologizing to him?*

"I understand, Fitz. I'm scared too," said Bradlee. *Well, I don't understand...*

Across from Clementine, Leona, and Charles, the sickly Mr. Green whispered to Bradlee. Clementine couldn't make out what they were saying, but after he spoke, Mr. Green wiped tears from his eyes.

"Mr. Green looks terrible, Leona," Clementine commented.

Her cousin's dark head fell, her stringy curls barely moving. Her apparent exhaustion and hopelessness was shared by everyone but Clementine.

Leona had acted more and more depressed as the big day neared, and now—her eyes looked up at Clementine from a bottomless pit. "I know," she said finally.

"You could save him. All you have to do—" Clementine started.

"Cousin, I won't do it. I can't! You don't know all the details."

The Good Shepherd

"Why won't you tell me? I can handle it," she said.

Leona shook her head. "It's not your burden to bear, cousin. I'm sorry, but I've let my parents—and others—down enough. I can't divulge the reason, Clementine. Unfortunately, there are horrible, evil things that happen to people who don't deserve it. But there's still hope." She blinked her ice blue eyes and looked mournfully at Mr. Green. "I promised Jane I'd find you and bring you home to her. I intend to keep my promise."

"If it comes to it, Leona, know that you have my permission and my forgiveness to do whatever needs to be done to protect the others. Give me mercy, if you must," Mr. Green said.

"What's he talking about, Leona?" Clementine asked. When Leona didn't respond, she turned to Charles. "What's that supposed to mean? Give him mercy?" Clementine demanded. He just shook his head and shrugged. "Why won't you tell me what's going on? I know you know!"

Leona's pained face turned to Clementine.

"I promise to protect you and Fitz, cousin. You must trust me."

Clementine pouted. She caressed the wolf symbol on the sheath of the thin knife in her pocket.

Bradlee's blue eyes stared her down. He'd been calcitrant and gloomy-faced these last two weeks. Suddenly, his blue eyes blazed. He looked quite impassioned. It was scary.

Speaking to her for the first time in days, he growled, "You've spent every day mourning Mr. Flufferbutter and whining about your empty belly. You're an immature, pampered, ignorant rich girl who wants everything to conform to your privileged Brahmin world. You only care about your own welfare. Shut. Up."

Clementine wanted to refute him, but sentences wouldn't form in her mind. She was too hungry. And tired. Again.

He continued, "Leona would give her life to protect you, to protect *us*. But you? You don't know the meaning of the word sacrifice."

His words stung. She slid to the floor and used her shawl to blanket her face.

"Bradlee, I—" she heard Leona say.

"Stop," Bradlee retorted. "Don't make any promises you can't keep. I think I finally understand you, your sacrifices. I understand why we can't be together. The differences between us are too great of a barrier. How can you love someone you fear?" Their blue eyes met.

"I don't fear you," she said.

"You should," he replied.

Clementine choked back her tears. Not only had she been viciously insulted, she had to witness this incomprehensible conversation between Bradlee and Leona.

Charles reached through their bars and grasped Clementine's hand.

"I want you to know, darlin' that I would give my life for you." He squeezed tight.

"Charles, um… well… I want you to know that I think you're…" she paused.

He perked up and leaned closer, his bright eyes glimmering at her. "Yes? I'm what?

She closed her eyes tight, then said, "You're an awful, ugly leprechaun. And—and I like you."

He squeezed her hand and hummed a familiar folk tune. It calmed Clementine as much as she could be calmed. Charles was her only ally. Him and the knife.

The door creaked open and the reverend descended the stairs. He carried a tray covered with a white cloth. Clementine was confused. They'd just been served breakfast, though none of them ate much.

Reverend Busch cleared his throat and set the tray on a table in the middle of the cellar. He lit a few candles and then pulled off the cloth, revealing a large brass goblet and a loaf of bread.

"I insisted on offering you communion."

Clementine had only taken communion once or twice in her whole life. What good would it do her now? She didn't want to make peace with God, she wanted to go home.

"If I need the last rites, well, could ya do that for me, Reverend?"

The reverend swallowed hard. A tear streamed down his sallow cheek. "I could try. Whatever you need."

Charles wrung his hands together. "Thanks, Reverend. I know you aren't fond of, well, Catholics."

Reverend Busch addressed Charles. "I must ask for your forgiveness. I was prideful. God has shown me in these dark days that we are all children in desperate need of salvation. Will you forgive me for my consternation?"

"Well, Reverend, I s'pose I have a bit too much pride meself. I forgive you."

The reverend sighed and grasped the cloth, lining the corners perfectly as he unfolded it.

"We're all sons of Adam, inheritors of a sinful nature. Our only recourse is to trust in God's sacrifice to reconcile us to Himself."

"Well said, Reverend," Mr. Green remarked.

Bradlee nodded reluctantly. "I hope you're right."

Reverend Busch tipped his head to Charles and proceeded to serve communion. First, he passed the loaf of bread, followed by the cup. Charles lingered a bit longer with the wine than the rest.

Clementine could barely swallow her chunk of bread. Thankfully, the bitter wine dissolved the lump of dough lodged in her throat.

Mr. Green winced as he adjusted his hurt leg. "Reverend, I'm sorry you got messed up in this."

The thin pastor bowed his head. His hands shook as he lifted the tray. "May God give you strength. I will continue to plead with your captors to release you."

The color had returned to Leona's pale, despondent face after taking communion. Maybe she'd been calmed by the sacrament. Clementine didn't feel any different after eating the bread and wine. But maybe her participation would show God that she was doing her part, so he should do his.

"I pray we all survive this," Charles remarked. The knife in Clementine's hand felt warm and comforting. Bradlee had it all wrong. She didn't need to sacrifice, she needed to fight.

Leona's expression stiffened. "I'll add my prayers to yours, Fitz."

The Good Shepherd

"As will I," Reverend Busch said and exited the dungeon.

Chapter Thirty

Lack of daylight in the cellar prison resulted in a blanket of ambiguity as to the exact hour.

When their captors finally made their appearance, Clementine felt a strange sense of relief. At least it would be over soon.

Bridget and Paddy marched down the stairs. In her left hand, Bridget grasped a cast iron circle with the keys to their cages.

Clementine found it hard to believe Bridget had instigated this. But the woman was no longer a demure servant in a maid's uniform. Her tone of voice had become uncharacteristically smug.

"It's almost sunset, Leona. Have you come to your senses and decided to join us? Or are you still selfishly clinging to your ridiculous Code? Are you willing to condemn your friends along with you?" She sneered at Leona. "This is your last chance. Are you a Hunter or a Shepherd?"

Leona didn't hesitate. "I'm a Shepherd."

Clementine closed her eyes and pleaded with heaven. *Save us. Save us. Save us.*

Bridget snarled, "Paddy, bring down our guest."

While the oaf did her bidding, Bridget paced the floor. The

stairwell door squealed open and two men descended. Charles gripped Clementine's hand.

"Professor!" Clementine cried. She released Charles' hand. *It's a miracle. Thank you, God!*

Professor Taylor scanned the faces of the group in their cages, not pausing to acknowledge Clementine.

"Professor, you've come to take me home, haven't you?"

He didn't answer her. His eyes were glued on her cousin.

"You've stayed true to your name, Leona Schaeffer. A stubborn lioness to the end, hmm? And a Shepherd, too. What an interesting conclusion."

"What's going on, Professor? Why are you here?" Clementine was confused. *Why won't he look at me?*

"As you know, I'm a social scientist. I observe and study society's influences and evolution. This situation is more extraordinary than even Charles Darwin could have imagined. It's a rare opportunity to examine a hidden society's mores and practices. Does survival of the fittest apply to them as well?" He gestured to Mr. Green and Bradlee. "I paid Ms. Collins handsomely to allow me to conduct an experiment on the subject. My money came in handy, didn't it, Ms. Collins?"

A sneer appeared on Bridget's face as her chin dipped.

"But—but—how did you even know about us?" Leona asked. *What are they talking about?*

"Do you remember our first conversation, Leona?"

She nodded.

"My father, a hunter, was killed in the woods. A wild animal, the police said. But I knew it was no animal." He glanced at

Clementine. "As I've mentioned, I grew up with the Schaeffer brothers. I suspected they were different than regular boys, so I spied on them. I learned many of their secrets. They had no idea, of course. Their arrogance kept them from believing it was possible that any mere human would discover and understand their unnatural world without slipping into lunacy. But I did it. I've been recording the genealogies of Warden and Werewolf families for years. It's been a little obsession of mine. Your lineage is quite fascinating, Leona."

Werewolves?

"But why did you get involved with the Hunters now?" Leona asked.

The professor stroked his beard and grinned slyly. After a quick look at Bridget, he replied, "I think I'll keep some secrets to myself for a little longer. Tonight is a special night indeed. I do hope I'll see you in the morning, Leona. Alive."

Everyone stared at Leona, who appeared as perplexed and confused as Clementine.

I can't believe it. Professor Taylor barely looked at me. He certainly wasn't her miracle. God had let her down. She wallowed in disappointment.

Bridget waited, tapping her foot impatiently and shifting the ring of keys in her hands.

A sliding sound made Clementine look up. Curtains parted, revealing a window on the upper east wall. Behind the glass stood the professor, with a bird's eye view of the room below.

"I told you he was a bastard," Charles growled.

Bridget reached through the bars and slapped Charles across

the face.

Clementine rose to her feet and yelled at Bridget until her throat was sore.

"Leave him alone! Unlock these cages! Let me out of here so I can scratch your eyes out, you ugly, wicked old witch!"

Bridget laughed. "I'm going to enjoy watching them rip you apart, princess."

Clementine's hand went to the knife in her pocket. "Say that to my face," she seethed.

Bridget sauntered closer, donning a haughty smirk. Clementine's fingers grasped the handle of the tiny saber inside her pocket. When Bridget was close enough for Clementine to feel the warmth of her breath, she pulled the knife out and stabbed at her through the bars.

Bridget yelled out a few choice profanities and placed a hand over her stomach. She bent at the waist and fell to her knees.

Charles whooped his approval, but Leona frowned. Clementine didn't care what Leona thought. She'd *done* something—fought against her captors. She felt powerful. Maybe she could save them all.

The keys had fallen out of Bridget's grasp during the attack. Clementine pointed her chin at them and Charles acted. He removed his belt and swung it like a lasso, attempting to snag the keyring and drag it toward them.

Bridget pulled her hand away from her abdomen and stared at the bright red blood creeping down her wrist. She clenched her jaw and snarled at Charles. Her bloody fingers reached for the keys. Charles whipped his belt through the bars again and slapped her arm. She spat at him.

He hurled the leather strap at the keys once more. To everyone's shock, Bridget's hand moved unnaturally fast toward the belt. She grabbed it, yanking it hard. The belt slipped out of Charles's grasp and he fell on his rear.

Bridget stood up easily. Her face contorted, phasing from one of pain to one of frivolity. She threw the belt across the floor, far away from the cages. Clementine stared at the hole in Bridget's blouse. The skin underneath was smeared with blood, but looked healthy and smooth.

"You fool. I'm a Warden. I heal quickly. Your pitiful plan was all for naught."

Clementine wanted to slash her again and again, to rip that awful smile off her face.

Suddenly, Bradlee and Mr. Green groaned and collapsed to the floor.

Bridget, the wicked witch, retrieved the ring of keys and proceeded to unlock the cages, casting the heavy padlocks on the floor. Before escaping up the stairs, she smiled over her shoulder menacingly.

"You made the wrong choice, Leona. Farewell, Clementine."

Bridget disappeared into the darkness. The door screeched before thudding shut, followed by the echo of a lock bolt.

Charles exclaimed, "I'm so sorry, darlin.' You were quite brave."

"But, how did she heal so fast? What's a Warden?"

"It's a long story. You did well, Clementine," Leona said.

She was stunned. She'd expected an 'I told you so,' not a

compliment. "Um… thanks, Leona."

Collapsed on the floor, Bradlee groaned in pain. He clutched his stomach and turned his face away from them. Mr. Green began whimpering like a puppy. Clementine swore she saw his bearded face morph, his nose becoming longer and wider, like a dog's.

"It's happening. How long does it take?" Charles asked.

What's happening?

Leona replied, "About ten minutes."

Searching the straw on the floor of the dungeon, Leona found a padlock and locked Bradlee's cage door shut. Then she ran across the room and picked up the discarded belt. Racing over to Charles, she pulled him out of his cage and pushed him into Clementine's. Leona wrapped the belt around the bars and fastened it, tying them in.

Bradlee writhed on the straw bottom of his cage, like a child with a stomachache. Leona continued searching the floor of the dungeon, scrambling desperately.

"What's happening to him?" Clementine asked, clutching Charles' shirt in her fist.

"Leona, it's too late. Get in here!" Charles cried. He loosened the belt and flung the door open.

Mr. Green's cage was ajar. Clementine doubted her eyes, but it looked like he was transforming into some kind of animal!

Clementine's heart felt like it was in her throat. She couldn't tear her eyes away from Mr. Green. The skin on his face was now completely covered with fur. His incisors had lengthened. He snarled at Leona, who was desperately searching the room for another padlock. Clementine flinched at the menacing sounds coming from the altered Mr. Green.

"Get in here with us!" she called to Leona.

With a look of resignation, Leona slipped inside. Charles fastened the belt again, securing the cage door.

Leona wagged her finger at them and warned, "Whatever happens, don't open the door until they change back."

"I promise," Charles said, his face pale.

Change back? What were they changing into?

Clementine watched the two men across from them. At least Bradlee was locked up. But the cage she was in with her cousin and Charles was tied with a leather strap.

Whatever was happening to Mr. Green and Bradlee, Charles and Leona knew, but hadn't trusted her enough to explain it to her.

Confused, irritated, and distracted by the oddities around her, Clementine barely heard Leona remark, "I don't feel so good."

But Leona's voice echoed in Clementine's ears, as if the words had spun into the sky and bounced off a mountain. She fought against her rising fear and turned around.

Leona was curled in a ball on the floor at Clementine's feet, convulsing.

The Good Shepherd

Leona's stomach wrenched. *Did they poison me again?* She inhaled and exhaled slow, deep breaths, like a woman in labor, attempting to ease the cramps in her abdomen. But they continued, coming in increasingly harsher waves.

Fitz and Clementine's mouths moved, but their voices were muted. All she could hear was the blood pounding in her head. Shadows overtook the remaining light in the dungeon. Soon, Leona became mute and blind. And the pain—the pain—dear God.

They must have slipped something into the wine. Whatever it was, it was powerful. She'd never experienced such mystifying turmoil. Her heart beat erratically. Sweat soaked her clothes.

Am I dying?

The pain proved too intense. Leona collapsed on the floor. Everything faded into oblivion.

Leona woke with a start. Renewed energy flowed through her body. Her head tingled. The pain was gone.

She felt like she'd been re-born. A full symphony of sounds filled her ears—four distinct heartbeats, a steady dripping, inhales and exhales, snarls and growls.

Was anyone else affected by the poison? She examined her friends. Clementine and Fitz stood close, locked in a tight embrace beside her in the cage, awake and not in visible pain. *Thank God.* She asked them if they were okay.

Clementine burst into tears. Fear must have overcome her. Leona understood. This was the first time her pampered cousin had ever seen such terrifying things. Maybe they should have explained it to her first, but Leona doubted Clementine would have believed them.

She smelled Werewolves.

Did Bradlee and Mr. Green complete their transformation? Yes, Bradlee was now a magnificent ebony-haired wolf with piercing blue eyes. He prowled inside his cage, throwing his weight against the locked door and snarling in frustration.

Mr. Green also paced inside his cage. The door lay slightly ajar, but Mr. Green didn't seem to have noticed yet. He was snarling and dragging his back leg behind him and whimpering loudly. His thick fur was light brown with gray tips, lying over his back like a field of autumn wheat.

Leona had tried to protect her sheep, but she hadn't been able to find the padlocks for all the cages in time. She readied herself to fight. About to reach for her hairpin, she stopped when she saw it lying on the floor under Fitz's shoe.

That's when she realized she was also lying on the floor. The pain must have caused her to faint. The floor of the iron cage was black as night, littered with bits of blonde straw. Leona was surprised it didn't feel cold.

She rose to a sitting position.

Clementine yelped and embraced Charles tighter. *What had frightened her?* Clementine and Fitz bundled together, just inches away from her in the cage. Fitz caressed Clementine's straight blonde hair, which hung loose and wild around her shoulders. Wrapped in her shawl, Clementine shivered.

But Leona felt warm, almost hot.

"Don't be afraid, darlin.' I'll protect you," Fitz whispered in Clementine's ear.

Fitz's love for Clementine was indomitable. She *must* save these two innocents from harm. They were undeserving participants this terrible experiment. Siobhan Collins must pay for her crimes, along with that insane Professor Taylor. Leona determined to save her friends and survive this.

Then she would find the culprits responsible for the fire that killed her family and bring them to justice.

Professor Taylor's face pressed close to the glass in the window above. His eyes were wide, like a child at the circus seeing an elephant for the first time. Leona snarled at him. How could he stand there and watch this? It went against both human law and the supernatural code of conduct. Not to mention, the moral law.

Bradlee and Mr. Green nipped at each other's tails between the bars. But their animal play would not last forever.

Bradlee's icy eyes met Leona's. He snarled, showing off his canine incisors. His furry snout wrinkled as he sniffed the air. His piercing eyes wandered to the amorphous mound of Clementine and Fitz bundled together as one beside her in the cage.

A low rumble emerged from Bradlee's throat. Mr. Green joined in. Their menacing duet forced Leona to react in turn. She growled back at them, like a wolf.

"Leona, w-what's going on?" Fitz asked, his eyes wide.

"I need my hairpin," she explained, pointing her nose at his boot. "It's under your shoe."

Before he could answer, Mr. Green clawed at the loose door of his cage and unintentionally opened it. He balked at the high-pitched ring of the turning metal hinge. Timid, he breached the cage and howled. Bradlee accompanied him. The hair on the back of Leona's neck rose.

Leona yearned to howl with them. What would their spectator, Professor Taylor, think of that? A Warden that howls?

Mr. Green had stumbled out of his cage by accident. Would Bradlee try to escape? Could he break the padlock open?

Dragging his left hind leg behind, Mr. Green wandered around the cellar. The cold blue of his eyes reflected his battle against the poison weakening his body. Leona was relieved he'd survived the transformation, but now feared that he was the one most likely to attack. Hurt animals lash out easily, even at those trying to help them.

Bradlee's howl turned into a sweet, low whimper. He begged to be free, like his companion. Mr. Green sat down on the middle of the cellar floor and stared at the threesome in the cage tied shut by a belt. Leona stared at his sapphire, pain-filled eyes.

"Mr. Green? Bradlee? Are you still in there?" Fitz asked.

Leona replied, "I already explained this. Bradlee's a wolf now. He doesn't care that you're his friend. Now, get behind me. And give me my hairpin!" She didn't mean to shout, but she was bursting with nervous energy. Blood ran hot through her veins.

Clementine whimpered again. All the color left Fitz's freckled face. She must have spoken more harshly than she meant to.

"Sorry. Please hand me my hairpin," she added, in a softer tone.

Fitz gulped. He stared at her in confusion, as if she'd spoken to him in Russian. "Leona?"

"My hairpin is under your shoe. I need it!"

Leona reached toward his shoe but kept one eye on the Werewolves.

Suddenly, Clementine screamed, fierce and high. Bradlee barked and snarled, baring his huge fangs. Her cousin quieted.

"L-leona? Please don't bite us," Fitz whispered. "We're your friends."

"Bite you? What are you—"

Leona glanced down at her feet. Something was wrong. They were hairy.

Chapter Thirty-One

Bradlee, Mr. Green, and Leona had all turned into huge dogs!

Clementine held onto Charles as the beast in the cage, er, Leona, snapped its jaws at them again.

She couldn't believe her awful luck. Leona, her cousin, the one who promised to protect her, was trapped inside the cage with them and had transformed into a frightful dog-wolf-creature.

Leona kept snapping her menacing jaws at them. Charles took a deep breath and spoke to her, "Shh… it's okay, pretty… doggy."

Clementine pointed at the fearsome beast at their side.

"What is she? Did you know this was going to happen?"

Charles scratched his head. "Uh, I knew about Bradlee and Mr. Green being Werewolves, but Leona's supposed to be something else, a Warden—the good kind—a Shepherd, they call 'em. I'm j-just as surprised as you, darlin.'"

Werewolves? How in the world is this possible?

They both stared at the transformed Leona. Her barking ceased. The glossy haired dog—*Werewolf*—whimpered at them like a puppy, her head bowed.

Charles lifted an eyebrow. "Maybe Leona's not like other

Werewolves. Maybe..." He leaned over, inching closer to the beast in the cage.

"Uh, Leona, are ya still there?"

The Werewolf's dark head dipped down and back up.

Charles reached his hand out. Clementine bit her lip and curled her body as far away from them as she could manage in the small cage.

He petted her head, and nothing happened. Leona didn't attack him. She didn't even growl. Clementine timidly joined him and brushed Leona's head lightly with her fingertips. The fur was thick and luxurious, like Mother's cherished mink stole. She dug her fingers in and combed the wavy hair behind Leona's pointed ears.

Gorgeous girl, gorgeous wolf. But concern over her cousin's unbelievable condition overrode her recurring jealousy.

Loud growls came from outside the cage. The blue eyes of the Werewolves across from them were cold and calculating. The beasts snarled at them and each other.

"Golly, I almost forgot they were there," Clementine said, her voice higher than usual. "Bradlee, please stay in your cage. Please, please, please," she begged.

Charles' eyes wavered between the two male beasts. Mr. Green curled up on the floor, but Bradlee continued snarling, pacing the borders of his confines, appearing growing more and more restless.

Clementine realized she was still petting Leona, who panted like a contented dog enjoying its master's touch. It was strange, to say the least. She half expected a yellow brick road to appear in front of her now.

Charles pointed at the window above. "Look at that—that bastard." Professor Taylor stared down at them, his expression unreadable. Clementine glanced up and frowned. Charles yelled, "Get us out of here, you nutter!"

Mr. Green raised his huge head and bellowed. Bradlee snarled at him, bearing his fangs.

Leona barked a long train of something through the bars at Bradlee and Mr. Green. The two Werewolves barked back, then simpered and quieted down. But Bradlee soon resumed pacing in his cage, throwing his body against the bars.

"We want to ask you some questions, Leona," Charles said. "Bark once for yes and twice for no. Got it?"

Leona barked once.

Charles asked, "Did you know that you would turn into a wolf?"

Leona barked twice.

"You must be confused."

"Bark!"

Stuck in his cage, Bradlee sat back on his haunches and whimpered again. The beautiful creature mesmerized Clementine, just like he had when they first met. She forgot he was a vicious predator for a second.

Mr. Green limped toward Bradlee's cage, dragging one hind leg.

Leona leaned into the bars of their shared cage and nudged Charles back, forcing him and Clementine behind her. With Leona, the Werewolf, protecting them, Clementine felt safe—

for the moment at least. She still hid her face in Charles' back.

A loud rattle sounded from Bradlee's cage. Then a massive *bang*. The metallic clang was followed by eerie silence.

Leona's upper lip furled, displaying ivory fangs, and a fierce growl rumbled through her body. Clementine felt it and dared to look.

Bradlee had broken out of his cage, and was now snarling aggressively at Mr. Green, his tail upright. Mr. Green's gray-brown tail was tucked between his legs. He backed away from Bradlee, tripping over his injured limb.

"Leona, I gotta open the cage. You have to stop this." Charles pleaded.

Leona barked twice. She growled, barking and pawing at the bars. Then she backed away and lowered her head, appearing shamed. Or tired. Clementine couldn't tell. She didn't understand dogs, much less wolves. She was indubitably a cat person. She stroked Leona's soft fur, more to calm her own nerves than anything else.

"Don't you remember, Charles? She made us promise not to open the cage until they changed back."

Charles' face contorted. "I know, I know. It's too dangerous, huh, Leona?"

Leona barked once, lowering her head again, a distressed rumble rising from her throat.

Bradlee circled Mr. Green, who was now seated with his head bowed submissively, waiting in passive stillness for Bradlee's next move. He steadied his ice blue eyes on the floor, not once daring to meet the eyes of the coal black Werewolf circling him, snarling.

Saliva dripped from Bradlee's gaping mouth. All of a sudden, he lunged at Mr. Green's throat.

Clementine gasped. The dark Werewolf's jaw clamped down and squeezed tight. Mr. Green moaned, his body twitching, unable to fight off the surprise attack. Bradlee's jaws released, leaving crimson gashes in Mr. Green's fur. Blood trickled from the holes. The gray-brown wolf collapsed in a heap.

"Mr. Green!!" Charles screamed. The gray Werewolf lay immobile on the floor, his hairy chest struggling to fill with air as he wheezed slowly. Bradlee continued pacing him, preparing for another attack.

Leona howled long and low. Clementine reached around her cousin's neck and held on tight, hiding her face in the thick fur.

Tears fell down Charles' face. Bradlee was no longer his best friend or Mr. Green's ally. He was wild, a monster, and had proven his dominance in less than a minute. The fittest had taken down the weakest.

Was Professor Taylor pleased? Clementine's eyes went to the window. The man's jaw gaped, then he scribbled frantically in a notebook.

Leona grabbed the belt holding the bars closed in her mouth and tugged.

"Now you want me to untie it?" Charles asked, wiping tears from his cheeks.

Leona barked out, "No." She laid her right leg over her snout and whined.

The fire burning in one of the torches along the wall fizzled.

The Good Shepherd

The light in the cellar diminished, allowing more shadows to play games on the ceiling. Clementine's hopes of a miracle diminished as well.

Charles chewed his lip. He tapped Leona's back and hunched down beside her, whispering in her perked ears. She responded to him with a rumble in her throat at first. Then her dark head nodded. He whispered in her ears again. She barked twice.

He stood and, stroking her head, spoke louder, "You can do it, Leona." Then he proceeded to unbuckle the belt holding their cage door in place.

"What are you doing? Are you insane? You promised not to open it," Clementine scolded. "Bradlee will kill us!" She tugged on his arm.

"Trust me," he said. "We have a plan. Okay, Leona—go!"

The ebony beast flew out of their cage and rammed her head into Bradlee's side, knocking him away from Mr. Green. Then she leapt into the air and knocked the torch out of its holder.

Flames exploded from the oil spilling out of the lamp and traveled along the floor. Straw and fabric were eaten up in seconds. Leona backed away from the flames. Bradlee's icy blue eyes searched for a path out of the room.

Smoke polluted the air in the dungeon. Clementine coughed. Charles pushed her to the floor, where it was easier to breathe. She placed her shawl over her mouth.

Crackling fire, barking, and whimpering filled her ears. Leona's desperate bark was higher pitched than Bradlee's and Mr. Green's low bark was silent now. *Is he dead? Poor Mr. Green!*

She opened her eyes and caught a glimpse of two dark Werewolves wrestling on the floor. Fur, straw, and spit all flew through the smoky atmosphere. But the smoke stung her eyes, so she pinched her eyes shut tight. Wiping away the tears that leaked out, she reached out for Charles' hand. His thin fingers wrapped around hers.

"Stay low. It's all up to Leona now."

Clementine bunched up the rest of her shawl and curled into a ball on the floor, laying her head on the makeshift pillow and covering her nose and mouth with one corner of the wooly fabric. But the smoke wheedled its way in. She coughed until her chest ached.

The room darkened, except for an orange glow on the far side of the room. Tears rained from her throbbing eyes. She couldn't breathe anymore. Her lungs hurt. Everything hurt.

Leona struggled to hang on to Bradlee's leg with her teeth. The fire strained her nerves, taunting her: *You're going to die just like your parents.*

But she couldn't give up. She'd agreed with Charles. The professor was too eager to prove his theories to let all his subjects die in the initial experiment. Starting a fire was the only way to force his hand.

The Good Shepherd

She'd been out of ideas, had practically given up, too shocked by her unexpected transformation to think straight.

What am I? I can think like a human, but I'm also a Werewolf?

After a few minutes, both Bradlee and Leona were too overcome by the smoke to fight. They collapsed on the floor, barely able to breathe. The air entering her throat burned like poisonous gas.

The cellar door squeaked open. Faint footsteps grew louder, closer. Smoke whooshed up the stairs and exited through the door. The fire doubled its strength, whooshing into a great wall of orange flames around them. Leona breathed shallow breaths, barely able to tolerate the burning sensation in her lungs and throat. Her healing powers struggled to keep up.

"Are they dead?" a voice asked, coughing. Water splashed on the floor, again and again.

"Drag them back to their cages, Paddy. Hurry!"

Leona opened one eye. Her vision as a Werewolf was amazing. Even in the smoke, she clearly saw Clementine and Charles crumpled together on the floor of their cage. Their backs rose and fell in a slow, yet steady rhythm. *Good, they're alive.*

The stench of blood was strong, as was the acrid smoke. Bradlee's large form lay beside her. His staggered breaths, like an overworked horse, pained her. He survived, fighting like a tenacious predator, even against the smoke and flames.

Paddy's face came into view and Leona forced her eyelids to flutter and close. He grunted and leaned over, grabbing Bradlee's front legs. Sharp smells of beer, cigars, and urine combined with the stench of burnt straw and hair.

"I thought this would be fun. I put money on that there darkie 'thrope. He was chipper and virile. I thought for certain he would kill them all. Now we gotta wait another day. Bollocks."

Rage boiled inside Leona. But the energy to act on it eluded her.

Siobhan replied, "But now we know this one's secret," she nudged Leona's side with her boot. "She's a wolf in Shepherd's clothes."

Paddy guffawed. "Can you believe it? A Warden that's also a 'thrope! The Council will have a hissy fit. Somebody's mama danced with the enemy."

"Those dumb Shepherds have probably bred dozens of mongrel children. That's why we need to eliminate the Werewolves, before it gets worse. Even the Council will agree with the Hunters about that."

Bradlee's limp body slid out of Leona's vision. She fluttered her eyes. If the thugs noticed, they didn't say anything. A new voice joined the conversation.

"I am *amazed*, Miss Collins. Simply amazed. Please be careful with this one," he said, tapping Leona's back with his shoe. "I want to interview her when she returns to human form. I obviously have her genealogy all wrong. She's a lion *and* a lamb."

"I doubt she'll be able to enlighten you. I wonder if Eben and Katarina even knew what she was. She wasn't their daughter, that's for certain. Whoever her real parents are, they must be exposed and punished, to set an example to the others," Siobhan seethed.

Professor Taylor protested. "No! If you ever find out who her parents are, bring them to me. At least let me take their blood samples and interview them. Then you can do whatever you like to them. I'll pay you handsomely. Oh, what a fascinating discovery!"

Siobhan groaned as she pulled Leona along the floor. "It's sickening, not fascinating. Laying with a 'thrope—how disgusting!"

Her brother made a gagging sound.

They'd made the mistake of rambling on, allowing Leona to rest and gather her strength. She wrenched out of Siobhan's grasp and lunged at the woman, taking her by surprise and knocking her to the floor.

The back of Siobhan's head hit an iron padlock on the floor, rendering her unconscious or dead, Leona didn't know which.

She lunged at the professor next. He fell on his back. She drooled on his fine suit jacket as she growled in his face. He fainted like an old woman with the vapors.

Leona jumped off Professor Taylor's chest and snarled at Paddy. The chunky man's eyes jerked from her to his unconscious sister, then to the professor. He dropped Bradlee's legs and raced to the stairs.

She let him leave. *One less body to drag around.*

Most of the smoke had dissipated up the stairs. The fire had been extinguished and the air was humid from the steam. After pulling Professor Taylor and Siobhan into a cage, Leona approached Clementine and Charles. She licked Charles's freckled face until he roused. He sat up and hugged her, encircling his arms around her middle.

He shook Clementine's shoulder and woke her. She frowned. "Miracles are supposed to be lovely, not full of dirt, smoke, and furry beasts."

Leona spoke, or rather, barked. Realizing they couldn't comprehend her words, she gestured with her snout toward their captors lying in the cage.

Charles helped Clementine to her feet. They unfastened the belt on their cage and followed Leona to the one holding Siobhan and Professor Taylor.

The sound of canine moaning made everyone turn.

"Mr. Green!" yelled Charles and ran to the injured wolf's side. Leona growled a warning. He was still a Werewolf. But he ignored her.

"How is he?" Clementine asked, tiptoeing backwards.

Charles lifted his hand from Mr. Green's neck. It was wet and bright crimson. Suddenly, the Werewolf panted, taking in quick bursts of air. As quickly as he'd begun, he stopped.

Tears streamed down Charles' face.

"He's dead." He sank his mournful face into Mr. Green's fur.

Chapter Thirty-Two

22 Joy Street

"Clementine! Leona! You're alive!" Aunt Franny screamed as they entered the door at 22 Joy Street. She engulfed them in her petite embrace, her side curls tickling Leona's face. Franny was surprisingly strong. Leona found it hard to breathe in her grasp.

"It's good to see you, too."

Loosening her grip, Aunt Franny fawned over her daughter next. Leona smiled at the two blonde relatives, so alike in their features. So pretty. So human.

Allen brought them mugs of steamy tea as they convalesced by the fireplace in the living room. Clementine kept insisting on a bath, squirming uncomfortably in her smudged dress, picking straw and wiping soot from her shawl and skirt.

Reverend Busch had escorted them home this morning.

"That minister rescued you?" Franny asked, her eyes wide as saucers. Her curls bounced against her cheeks as she shook her head. "I can't believe it. We must attend church every Sunday, Clementine."

The whites of Clementine's eyes were rimmed in red. So were Aunt Franny's.

"What a nightmare," Franny commented. "I was so worried. At first, I insisted that Ezra notify Officer Buchanan about the matter. But he refused. He said the kidnappers would retaliate if they found out he told the authorities."

Siobhan Collins understood the Schaeffers well. She'd created a story they would believe without giving away her true identity. She sent the Schaeffers a note that said the two girls were kidnapped by a group who despised the Brahmin, awful foreign revolutionaries who hated the upper classes, a lie Franny believed without question.

Aunt Franny rose, holding her hand discretely over her nostrils. "I'll tell Allen to fill the bathtub so you can wash, girls. I will need to find us a new Bridget. The old one disappeared after the note arrived from the kidnappers. I suppose she was scared." Leona met Clementine's eyes. "I still can't believe they held you prisoner for two weeks. How could there be such evil in the world? What has the upper class ever done to deserve such vitriol? I have no idea. No idea."

Aunt Franny left the room shaking her head, her curls swinging madly.

Alone in the room together, Clementine pinched Leona's shoulder. It hurt.

"I think you owe me an explanation, cousin!"

Leona wished she could just disappear. But Clementine's fierce stare had her trapped. She sighed. "Apparently, I don't know everything. But I'll tell you what I do know, now that

The Good Shepherd

you've seen more than enough to prove I'm not talking crazy."

Clementine interrupted, "Oh, this is all *crazy*! But, you're right, if I hadn't seen it with my own eyes, I'd never have believed it."

Leona lowered her voice, in case Aunt Franny or Allen returned. "For hundreds of years, the Schaeffers have been Wardens. We're born with a supernatural responsibility to serve and protect the world from Werewolves. The Wardens have divided into two camps, Hunters and Shepherds. I'm a Shepherd. I want to help Werewolves live by the Code. Hunters, like Siobhan, have rebelled against the Code."

"But you turned into a Werewolf! How do you do that? With sorcery?" Clementine's eyes bulged. "Are you a witch, too?"

Leona frowned. She didn't know exactly *what* she was. "I'm not a witch. Both Wardens and Werewolves inherit their conditions from their parents."

Clementine tilted her head. "So, one of your parents was a Warden, and one was—"

"—a Werewolf."

Leona's heart ached as she voiced the thing that hurt her most, "The people I thought were my parents weren't my parents."

"Are we still cousins?"

"Yes. I'll always think of you as family."

Clementine brightened. "Good." She hesitated before continuing, "So, Father is also a Warden?"

"Yes, but he refuses to use his gift. He's what we call a Normalizer."

"Oh." Clementine rubbed her face with her dingy gray shawl.

Leona's heart ached at the sight of the silver wolf pin holding Clementine's shawl together, the pin identical to the one Papa never let her near. *Because it detects unturned lycanthropes. Like me.*

All these years, she'd believed her parents were good. But they'd lied. *Everyone lies.*

Leona wagged her finger at Clementine. "Now that you know about Werewolves and Wardens, you must promise to keep them a secret. People like Siobhan would hurt you if you told anyone."

Clementine scoffed. "No one would believe me if I told them anyway!" A tender expression washed over her dirty face. She removed the silver pin, wrapped it up in her shawl, then handed it to Leona. "Cousin, this is yours."

Leona pushed it away. "Thank you, but I want you to keep it." Now she possessed a Werewolf's sense of smell and didn't need a device to detect immature lycanthropes.

"So, do you remember anything that happened while you were a... a... Werewolf?" Clementine asked, rubbing her red eyes with her sleeve.

"I remember everything." Leona swallowed hard. "Clementine, I need to apologize. I'm sorry I let you get mixed up in all this. I put you in danger."

Clementine frowned. "It *was* quite frightening. But, I'm fine." Allen entered the room and waited to be acknowledged. Clementine patted Leona's hand. "You can bathe first."

Leona's eyebrow rose. "Are you sure?"

"Yes. Not to be rude, cousin, but you smell like a dog."

The Good Shepherd

Clementine stared at the orphanage. While Leona was bathing, she'd snuck out of the house and boarded the late trolley. She'd fell asleep in her seat, almost missing the stop.

Before Clementine and Leona had arrived at Joy Street, the reverend, Bradlee, and Charles returned Mr. Green's body to the Home. Leona had refused to go inside with Bradlee and Charles. Clementine stayed with her as they waited for the reverend to escort them to Joy Street. It was quite uncomfortable. Leona cried a lot, claiming she had failed again, and made Clementine swear to never tell Bradlee he'd attacked and killed Mr. Green. She asked her to say that *Leona* had been forced to do it. Clementine had agreed to lie.

She was pleased that Leona still wanted to be her cousin. Bradlee had said such cruel things to her while they'd been held captive. After their horrific ordeal, his words haunted her.

"I can sacrifice," she whispered in reply to his accusation.

Her quiet voice echoed in the foyer. The Home was quiet and somber. They were in mourning.

"Mrs. Green?" she called out multiple times before a lone figure approached.

"Clementine? What are you doing here?" The familiar woman's face appeared.

Mrs. Green looked horrible. Her mousey brown hair hung

loose around her shoulders, unkempt. Her blouse was untucked, veined with wrinkles. She pulled a handkerchief from her pocket and wiped her reddened nose.

Clementine took a deep breath. "I have a confession to make."

After her bath, Leona felt more human. But, she wasn't human. She was more. Much more.

What exactly am I? And who are my real parents?

She had gone in search of Clementine but now found herself lurking outside Uncle Ezra's study.

Aunt Franny might have believed the story about their abduction, but her uncle must have guessed that the kidnapping had nothing to do with foreign revolutionaries.

She knocked on the thick oak door. There was no response. She knocked louder and longer.

The door flew open and Uncle Ezra pulled her inside.

"Say whatever you need to say, and say it quickly. I want you out of my home as soon as possible! Don't you have a job and a residence to return to?"

"No, I don't. Mr. Green is dead. I can't go back there. Everything that happened—it—it's all my fault. Besides, I have some questions for you. Did you know Bridget was a Hunter?"

His jaw dropped. "Bridget? No! But, I warned you, Leona.

The Good Shepherd

You should've Normalized. You're dangerous."

She scowled at him. "Yes, I am. And I'm not leaving this room until you answer all my questions."

He backed away from her, a deep frown creasing his pathetic face. He reclined in his leather cushioned chair and gestured for her to sit in the wooden chair across from him.

She placed her sore back against the harsh wood, stretching her arms above her head, allowing her joints to crack and groan as her uncle tapped his fingers on the desk, waiting for her to begin her interrogation.

His blue eyes resembled Eben Schaeffer, the man she'd always believed was her father. She tried not to show her anguish over her unknown parentage. Her heart throbbed inside her chest, threatening to jump out.

Finally, she leaned forward, thrust her chin up, and asked, "Who are my birth parents?"

Her uncle's skin waned. His blue eyes never looked paler.

"It doesn't matter," he replied. His eyelids fluttered, and he turned his gaze away from hers.

She stood, towering slightly above him, slouched in his fine chair.

"You know, though, don't you? I'm part Werewolf and part Warden. I'm cursed. If the Council finds out, will they eliminate me? And my parents? I have the right to know who they are before I'm hunted down and killed. Tell me!"

His face fell into his hands. Suddenly, his shoulders convulsed.

"What are you laughing about?"

When he raised his face, Leona saw he was not laughing. His blue eyes were shaded crimson. A tortured look had taken over his usual apathetic demeanor.

He reached for a picture on his desk and handed it to Leona.

Confused, she looked at the picture in her hand. It was a pencil sketch of a beautiful young lady with dark, curly tendrils. The woman's strong jaw line resembled her own.

"Who is this?"

Her uncle spoke into his hands. "I told you I loved a Werewolf once.

"This was her?"

"Yes." He raised his head slightly. "She killed a human, so I—exacted mercy on her. I killed her. I killed your *mother*."

Leona caressed the glass of the portrait. She supposed she should be shocked, but the relief of finally knowing the truth comforted her, as if she'd somehow known all along.

"What was her name?"

"Lorraine. Lorraine Boudreaux. She was the most beautiful girl I'd ever seen. And stubborn. Much like you."

Leona sat down in the cold chair. Her hands shook.

"I was a foolish young man in love. We lived together in secret on our own for five years, alone in the Catskill mountains, happy and free. We raised you for two years before—"

He took a deep breath before continuing, "One day, we went for a walk in the woods while Lorraine's sister watched you at the cabin."

He winced, glancing down, then away, to somewhere deep in his memories. "We lost track of time. The sun was setting as we ran toward the woods to her sanctuary. But it was too late. She transformed and ran off. There was a young man on his way home from a hunting trip. He never saw her coming. She ripped his throat out in one motion. Then she turned on me." He paused, closing his eyes, as if he could stop the memory and change history. "I slit her throat with a silver knife my father gave me."

"What happened then?"

His tortured look deepened.

"Eben and Katarina agreed to raise you and promised to keep your parentage a secret—for your safety and theirs. The Warden Council would have executed you, as a warning for others."

"What would they do to you?"

He squirmed uncomfortably.

She continued, "That's the real reason you became a Normalizer, isn't it? To stay out of the Council's sight." He nodded. She leaned in, "What about the curse?"

"The curse? It's an urban myth. There're no details in the Code. It's just a scare tactic to keep Wardens and Werewolves apart. To separate natural enemies."

"No, the curse is real. I'm both a Warden *and* a Werewolf. I transformed for the first time last night."

His eyes widened. "But—but—how could that happen?"

"I don't know how, but I wasn't like other Werewolves. I could still reason and feel emotions. Why didn't anyone tell me about my heritage?"

"Eben promised to tell you when he felt the time was right. Unfortunately—"

"He died first."

"Yes."

"Eben and Katarina promised to keep you safe. And out of the Council's attention."

Leona had considered him a coward before this confession. She would never have guessed the real reasons for him becoming a Normalizer. Shame, fear, and cowardice.

"You left me behind."

His mouth twisted. "You have a strong character, Leona. You learned that from Eben, not me. I'm weak. I always have been. I disobeyed the Code because I loved Lorraine. When she died, I was broken—distraught—completely unfit to raise a child, so I entrusted you to my honorable brother, and left New York for Boston."

Leona absorbed this information. She showed no sign of sympathy, though, as angry as she was, a part of her desired to reach out and comfort him.

She continued her questioning. "Bridget told me that Werewolves set fire to our cabin. Do you know anything about that?"

He inhaled sharply.

"I don't believe that. Why would Werewolves want to kill Eben and Katarina? They were good Shepherds. I'm sure it was the Hunters."

"Warden Goldberg left a note for me that supported her story. But why would a Werewolf hurt them? They were kind and compassionate, helping rogues for years."

Ezra added, "And they must know the Council would execute them." He paused, deep in thought. "The day before you left for the orphanage, Goldberg visited me. It seems my brother confided in Goldberg sometime before they died. I sent him to the orphanage, but he was murdered in an alley soon after that." He met Leona's narrowed eyes. "I didn't do it."

"I know. Bridget killed him because he was a Shepherd. Ugh. Why would anyone want to hurt my par—Eben and Katarina Schaeffer?"

Ezra tapped his fingers on the desk and skewed his mouth. Then his eyebrows rose. He smacked the desk with his palm.

"Julia!"

Leona didn't understand. "Who?"

"Lorraine's sister."

Leona thought hard. She asked, "Did Julia know Lorraine broke the Code? If she thought you killed her for any other reason—"

He interrupted. "She'd hate me. Julia adored Lorraine. She'd want vengeance."

"Did Julia know you were a Warden?"

"Yes, but she only knew my last name. She always called me Mr. Schaeffer. The girl was only twelve at the time."

Leona wiped a thick tear from her eye. "She found a Warden named Schaeffer." She frowned. "But it was the wrong one."

Ezra leaned his head back onto his leather chair and pressed his fingers on his eyes.

"Dear God. I'm so sorry, Leona."

All she'd wanted was to be a good Shepherd, like her parents. Her parents.

She handed the picture of Lorraine back to Ezra.

He waved his hand. "Keep it."

As she walked toward the door, she held the picture to her chest. Before turning the knob, she paused.

"Goodbye, Father," she said, and left the room.

Epilogue

Spring, 1906

Leona slept curled under canopy of evergreens, nestled in a blanket and cushioned by a mattress of pine needles.

The sun woke her, ending her fitful slumber yards outside of Bradlee's sanctuary cabin. Her transformation back to human form, she shivered and dressed quickly under the blanket.

Keeping as quiet as possible, she waited in the trees for the click of the door. At the anticipated sound, her heart raced, as if the noise were a starting pistol.

A dark-haired young man stepped into the crisp morning sunshine. His blue eyes twinkled.

I made the right decision. Didn't I?

Leona departed from Boston the day after they returned to Joy Street. She escaped to the place she'd felt most welcomed after her homelessness—Mrs. Wickersham's.

Bradlee had no memory of the night he'd killed Mr. Green. He would be devastated to know the truth. Before leaving town, Leona had made Fitz swear to tell him it had been her who'd killed Mr. Green.

387

Fortunately, Clementine had also agreed to keep her secret. In a surprisingly sentimental gesture for her cousin, she'd assured Leona she would do whatever was necessary to protect Bradlee.

Leona couldn't stay in Boston. Her presence put them all at risk, including her birth father, Ezra. Unfortunately, Siobhan Collins, Paddy, and Professor Taylor had escaped. Leona feared they would never stop hunting for her, each for their own nefarious reason.

She observed Bradlee from a distance. He stretched, then trudged through the snowy woods until he reached his horse. Before mounting the dappled palomino, Bradlee sniffed the air. "Hello, Leona."

Her boots crunched through the snow as she approached. "Hugo's looking well. How are you?"

He glared at her, his frown casting an unsavory shadow over his handsome face.

He must hate me. He thinks I killed Mr. Green, after all. She swallowed her sorrow over losing his friendship—and his love—forever. She'd accepted this sacrifice as part of being a Shepherd.

Expecting to find anger, she met his eyes. But instead of belligerence, concern flashed through the blue.

"Leona, where have you been? No one's heard from you for months. Jane said you didn't even tell her you were leaving. I thought we—well, I thought you'd at least have the decency to say goodbye to me. I thought we were friends."

"I couldn't. I mean, after Mr. Green—"

"I know it's hard. But it's not your fault."

"What?" Leona was confused. He should think it *was* her fault. Leona had fought and killed his beloved Mr. Green—that's how the story went, anyway.

"Fitz told me everything." Leona's heart jumped to her throat. "I know the truth."

"Y-you do?"

"Clementine confessed to Jane. Mr. Green attacked her, and she had no choice. She stabbed him with the knife. She feels horrible about it."

Leona grasped a tree branch nearby.

He continued, "It was an unfortunate tragedy. It was brave of Clementine to tell Mrs. Green. She was afraid she would hate her. But it's not really her fault. Siobhan Collins and Professor Taylor are responsible. If they ever come near me, I'll—"

Leona interrupted, "I understand." But she didn't. Self-centered Clementine had taken the blame for Mr. Green's death? Leona was stunned. Somehow, she feigned normalcy and added, "That night was quite traumatic for Clementine. She's braver than I expected."

"Yes, she is. I underestimated her."

They both fell silent for a moment. Then Bradlee's eyes softened and he asked, "Where have you been, Leona?"

"I went to visit Mrs. Wickersham."

He examined her closely, as if he suspected she were lying. But she hadn't lied about where she'd spent the winter convalescing. And planning.

His brows knit together under his brown wool cap. Seeing

him here, not hating her—it was almost too much to fathom.

"Jane misses you."

Leona's heart clenched. She missed Jane also. But she suspected he didn't only mean Jane. She cleared the knot in her throat.

"I miss her too. I miss everyone. How's Regina?"

"She's sad without you." He pointed to the full rucksack on her back. "Are you here to stay?"

Leona couldn't bear to look at his gentle, handsome face. She fixed her gaze on a waxy evergreen tree behind him. "No, I'm just visiting. I'm traveling to New York soon, on Warden business."

"So, you're here to check on me?" He stepped closer. "As a Warden or as a friend?"

"Both." He took another step. His warm breath permeated the coldness between them. He smelled like pine.

Her body felt like iron, incapable of movement. But finally, she overcame her paralysis and stepped back, putting space between them.

For months, Bradlee's ice blue eyes had haunted her dreams, replacing those from her previous nightmares, teasing her with hope. But he didn't know what she was. *She* didn't really know what she was, only that, as Mrs. Wickersham had indicated last year, she was *more*.

No one else could discover that she was both a Warden and a Werewolf. Too many people knew already.

Bradlee's beautiful, hope-filled eyes reflected his heart, a heart she must break. He assumed they couldn't be together because of the Code. She would let him believe that.

She stared at a tall evergreen, avoiding his gaze.

I need to find Julia. And I have to do it alone.

She'd been staring into the forest. As she pulled her eyes away from its comforting greenery, she gasped.

In the time she'd spent staring at the trees in contemplation, Bradlee had inched closer. He nuzzled his cheek against hers and embraced her. The warmth of his touch beckoned her to stay in his arms.

Grasping his collar, she kissed his cool lips long and hard. Then she bolted into the woods.

About the Author

D. Marie Prokop enjoys writing and reading stories with riveting adventures, spiritual insights, and thought-provoking cultural or social critiques. Her favorite authors include Madeline L'Engle, Pearl S. Buck, John Green, Agatha Christie, and C. S. Lewis.

The National Novel Writing Month challenge helped D. Marie discover her love for writing fiction. A member of WriteSpace Houston and the Houston Writer's Guild, D. Marie gains both education and comradery from her local writing community. She writes YA, science fiction, adventure, fantasy, horror, poetry, and middle-grade fiction.

D. Marie Prokop has been published in various anthologies by Inklings Publishing, in Texas's Emerging Writers: An Anthology of Fiction, and Texas's Emerging Writers: An Anthology of Nonfiction by Z Publishing House, and also in the collection, Hair Raising Tales of Horror.

D. Marie is also a singer-songwriter and avid fiber artist/knitter. Born and raised in Pennsylvania, the former Yankee now resides in Houston, Texas, along with her loving family, their feisty cats, her beloved ukulele, and much, much yarn.

Want to be notified when volume two of the Werewolf Warden Series is released?
Keep in touch!

Follow D. Marie Prokop on Instagram, Facebook, Twitter, Goodreads, and on dmarieprokop.com.

You can sign up for her newsletter here.

Please leave an honest review on Amazon, Goodreads, etcetera, etcetera... Thanks!
It is all for the bright,
D. Marie